PRAISE FOR ELIZABETH PETERS AND

THE SNAKE, THE CROCODILE AND THE DOG

"Clever...plenty of interesting Egyptian and archeological lore, lots of danger."
—*New York Times Book Review*

"High adventure, narrated in Amelia's witty, inimitably resplendent style. Peabody fans will rejoice."
—*Library Journal*

"It's a tongue-in-cheek tightrope walk between parody and homage, brought off flawlessly....Amelia is rather like Indiana Jones, Sherlock Holmes, and Miss Marple all rolled into one....A juicy new extract...to curl with."
—*Washington Post Book World*

"Amelia's back, and she has laid in a new supply of attack parasols. Seems as if there's no rest for Elizabeth Peters' feisty, turn-of-the-century Egyptologist detective, who has a propensity for peril and a prediction for pantaloons....High spirits and lucid repartee."
—*Christian Science Monitor*

"Surefire entertainment."
—*Publishers Weekly*

"Enemies old and new abound...but there's still fun to be had for Amelia's fans and lovers of Egyptology."
—*Kirkus Reviews*

THE SNAKE,
THE CROCODILE
AND THE DOG

ELIZABETH
PETERS

GRAND CENTRAL
PUBLISHING

NEW YORK   BOSTON

Copyright © 1992 by Elizabeth Peters
All rights reserved. In accordance with the U.S. Copyright Act of 1976, the scanning, uploading, and electronic sharing of any part of this book without the permission of the publisher is unlawful piracy and theft of the author's intellectual property. If you would like to use material from the book (other than for review purposes), prior written permission must be obtained by contacting the publisher at permissions@hbgusa.com. Thank you for your support of the author's rights.

Grand Central Publishing
Hachette Book Group
1290 Avenue of the Americas
New York, NY 10104
www.HachetteBookGroup.com

Grand Central Publishing is a division of Hachette Book Group, Inc. The Grand Central Publishing name and logo is a trademark of Hachette Book Group, Inc.

The Hachette Speakers Bureau provides a wide range of authors for speaking events. To find out more, go to www.hachettespeakersbureau.com or call (866) 376-6591.

The publisher is not responsible for websites (or their content) that are not owned by the publisher.

Printed in the United States of America

Originally published in trade paperback by Hachette Book Group

First mass market edition: February 1994
First oversize mass market edition: July 2013

10 9 8 7 6 5 4
OPM

For Olivia Grace Brown Mertz
January 18, 1992
with love from Ammie

EDITOR'S NOTE

A brief explanation of Arabic and ancient Egyptian terms may be in order for the benefit of readers unfamiliar with those languages. Like certain other Semitic scripts, Arabic and hieroglyphic Egyptian do not write the vowels. It is for this reason that English spellings of such words may legitimately vary. For example: the hieroglyphic writing of the name of the little servant figurines consists of five signs: sh, wa, b, t, and i or y. (Some of these may look like vowels, but they aren't. Take the editor's word for it, will you please? You really don't want to hear about semi-vowels and weak consonants.) This word may be transcribed into English as "ushebti," "shawabti," or "shabti." NOTE: A glossary of Arabic words and phrases can be found on page 499.

Arabic personal and place names are subject to similar variations when written in English script. Fashions in these things change; the spellings common in Mrs. Emerson's early days in Egypt have sometimes been replaced by other, more modern versions. (Dahshoor with Dashur, Meidum with Medum, and so on.) Like most of us, Mrs. Emerson tends to cling doggedly to the habits of her youth. In some cases she has modernized her spellings; in other cases she has not. Since this does not bother her, the editor sees no reason why it should bother the reader and feels that a sterile consistency in these matters might mar to some extent the dashing spontaneity of Mrs. Emerson's prose.

(The editor also wishes to remark that she is not the individual referred to in Chapter One. She has absolutely nothing against poetry.)

The quotations at the head of each chapter are from *The Collected Works of Amelia Peabody Emerson*, Oxford University Press, 8th ed., 1990.

EGYPT AND THE SUDAN ▲ 1898

Mediterranean Sea

ALEXANDRIA

Suez Canal

PORT SA'ID

GIZA · CAIRO · SUEZ

MEIDUM (Rikka) · MEMPHIS

AMARNA

WESTERN DESERT

EASTERN DESERT

Gulf of Suez

EGYPT

THEBES (Valley of the Kings) · LUXOR

ASSUAN

Red Sea

ABU SIMBEL

WADI HALFA

NUBIAN DESERT

NAPATA

SANAM ABU DOM · GEBEL BARKAL

SUDAN (NUBIA)

MEROË

OMDURMAN · KHARTOUM

N
W · E
S

CHAPTER 1

"Some concessions to temperament are necessary if the marital state is to flourish."

I believe I may truthfully claim that I have never been daunted by danger or drudgery. Of the two I much prefer the former. As the only unmarried offspring of my widowed and extremely absentminded father, I was held responsible for the management of the household—which, as every woman knows, is the most difficult, unappreciated, and lowest paid (i.e., not paid) of all occupations. Thanks to the above-mentioned absentmindedness of my paternal parent I managed to avoid boredom by pursuing such unwomanly studies as history and languages, for Papa never minded what I did so long as his meals were on time, his clothing was clean and pressed, and he was not disturbed by anyone for any reason whatever.

At least I thought I was not bored. The truth is, I had nothing with which to compare that life, and no hope of a better one. In those declining years of the nineteenth century, marriage was not an alternative that appealed to me; it would have been to exchange comfortable serfdom for absolute slavery—or so I believed. (And I am still of that opinion as regards the majority of women.) My case was to be the exception that proves the rule, and had I but known what unimagined and unimaginable delights awaited me, the bonds that chafed me would have been unendurable. Those bonds were not broken until the death of my poor papa left me the possessor of a modest fortune and I set out to see the ancient sites I knew only from books and photographs. In the antique land of Egypt I learned at last what I had been missing—adventure, excitement, danger, a life's work that employed all my considerable intellectual powers, and the companionship of that remarkable man who was destined for me as I was for him. What mad pursuits! What struggles to escape! What wild ecstasy!

I am informed, by a certain person of the publishing persuasion, that I have not set about this in the right way. She maintains that if an author wishes to capture the attention of her readers she must begin with a scene of violence and/or passion.

"I mentioned—er—'wild ecstasy,' " I said.

The person gave me a kindly smile. "Poetry, I believe? We do not allow poetry, Mrs. Emerson. It slows the narrative and confuses the Average Reader." (This apocryphal individual is always referred to by persons of the publishing persuasion with a blend of condescension and superstitious awe; hence my capital letters.)

"What we want is blood," she continued, with mounting enthusiasm. "And a lot of it! That should be easy for you, Mrs. Emerson. I believe you have encountered a good many murderers."

This was not the first time I had considered editing my journals for eventual publication, but never before had I gone so far as to confer with an editor, as these individuals are called. I was forced to explain that if her views were characteristic of the publishing industry today, that industry would have to muddle along without Amelia P. Emerson. How I scorn the shoddy tricks of sensationalism which characterize modern literary productions! To what a state has the noble art of literature fallen in recent years! No longer is a reasoned, leisurely exposition admired; instead the reader is to be bludgeoned into attention by devices that appeal to the lowest and most degraded of human instincts.

The publishing person went away shaking her head and mumbling about murder. I was sorry to disappoint her, for she was a pleasant enough individual— for an American. I trust that remark will not leave me open to an accusation of chauvinism; Americans have many admirable characteristics, but literary taste is rare among them. If I consider this procedure again, I will consult a *British* publisher.

I suppose I might have pointed out to the naive publishing person that there are worse things than murder. Dead bodies I have learned to take in my stride, so to speak; but some of the worst moments of my life occurred last winter when I crawled on all fours through indescribable refuse toward the place where I hoped, and feared, to find the individual dearer to me than life itself. He had been missing for almost a week.

I could not believe any prison could hold a man of his intelligence and strength so long unless... The hideous possibilities were too painful to contemplate; mental anguish overwhelmed the physical pain of bruised knees and scratched palms, and rendered inconsequential the fear of enemies on every hand. Already the swollen orb of day hung low in the west. The shadows of the coarse weeds stretched gray across the grass, touching the walls of the structure that was our goal. It was a small low building of stained mud-brick that seemed to squat sullenly in its patch of refuse-strewn dirt. The two walls visible to me had neither windows nor doors. A sadistic owner might keep a dog in such a kennel...

Swallowing hard, I turned to my faithful reis Abdullah, who was close at my heels. He shook his head warningly and placed a finger on his lips. A gesture conveyed his message: the roof was our goal. He gave me a hand up and then followed.

A crumbling parapet shielded us from sight, and Abdullah let out his breath in a gasp. He was an old man; the strain of suspense and effort had taken their toll. I had no sympathy to give him then, nor would he have wanted it. Scarcely pausing, he crawled toward the middle of the roof, where there was an opening little more than a foot square. A grille of rusted metal covered it, resting on a ledge or lip just below the surface of the roof. The bars were thick and close together.

Were the long days of suspense at an end? Was he within? Those final seconds before I reached the aperture seemed to stretch on interminably. But they were not the worst. That was yet to come.

The only other light in the foul den below came from a slit over the door. In the gloom of the opposite corner I saw a motionless form. I knew that form; I would have recognized it in darkest night, though I could not make out his features. My senses swam. Then a shaft of dying sunlight struck through the narrow opening and fell upon him. It was he! My prayers had been answered! But—oh, Heaven—had we come too late? Stiff and unmoving, he lay stretched out upon the filthy cot. The features might have been those of a waxed death mask, yellow and rigid. My straining eyes sought some sign of life, of breath...and found none.

But that was not the worst. It was yet to come.

Yes, indeed, if I were to resort to contemptible devices of the sort the young person suggested, I could a tale unfold...I refuse to insult the intelligence of my (as yet) hypothetical reader by doing so, however. I now resume my ordered narrative.

As I was saying: "What mad pursuits! What struggles to escape! What wild ecstasy!" Keats was speaking in quite another context, of course. However, I have been often pursued (sometimes madly) and struggled (successfully) to escape on more than one occasion. The last phrase is also appropriate, though I would not have put it quite that way myself.

Pursuits, struggles and the other sentiment referred to began in Egypt, where I encountered for the first time the ancient civilization that was to inspire my life's work, and the remarkable man who was to share it. Egyptology and Radcliffe Emerson! The two are inseparable, not only in my heart but in the estimation of the scholarly world. It may be said—in fact, I have often said it—that Emerson IS Egyptology, the finest scholar of this or any other era. At the time of which I write we stood on the threshold of a new century, and I did not doubt that Emerson would dominate the twentieth as he had the nineteenth. When I add that Emerson's physical attributes include sapphire-blue eyes, thick raven locks, and a form that is the epitome of manly strength and grace, I believe the sensitive reader will understand why our union had proved so thoroughly satisfactory.

Emerson dislikes his first name, for reasons which I have never entirely understood. I have never inquired into them because I myself prefer to address him by the appellation that indicates comradeship and equality, and that recalls fond memories of the days of our earliest acquaintance. Emerson also dislikes titles; his reasons for this prejudice stem from his radical social views, for he judges a man (and a woman, I hardly need add) by ability rather than worldly position. Unlike most archaeologists he refuses to respond to the fawning titles used by the fellahin toward foreigners; his admiring Egyptian workmen had honored him with the appellation of "Father of Curses," and I must say no man deserved it more.

My union with this admirable individual had resulted in a life particularly suited to my tastes. Emerson accepted me as a full partner professionally as well as matrimonially, and we spent the winter seasons excavating at various sites in Egypt. I may add that I was the only woman engaged in that activity—a sad commentary on the restricted condition of females in the late-nineteenth century of our era—and that I could never have done it without the wholehearted cooperation of my remarkable spouse. Emerson did not so much insist upon my participation as take it for granted. (I took it for granted too, which may have contributed to Emerson's attitude.)

For some reason I have never been able to explain, our excavations were often interrupted by activities of a criminous nature. Murderers, animated mummies, and Master Criminals had interfered with us; we seemed to attract tomb-robbers and homicidally inclined individuals. All in all it had been a delightful existence, marred by only one minor flaw. That flaw was our son, Walter Peabody Emerson, known to friends and foes alike by his sobriquet of "Ramses."

All young boys are savages; this is an admitted fact. Ramses, whose nickname derived from a pharaoh as single-minded and arrogant as himself, had all the failings of his gender and age: an incredible attraction to dirt and dead, smelly objects, a superb disregard for his own survival, and utter contempt for the rules of civilized behavior. Certain characteristics unique to Ramses made him even more difficult to deal with. His intelligence was (not surprisingly) of a high order, but it exhibited itself in rather disconcerting ways. His Arabic was of appalling fluency (how he kept coming up with words like those I cannot imagine; he certainly never heard them from me); his knowledge of hieroglyphic Egyptian was as great as that of many adult scholars; and he had an almost uncanny ability to communicate with animals of all species (except the human). He...

But to describe the eccentricities of Ramses would tax even my literary skill.

In the year preceding the present narrative, Ramses had shown signs of improvement. He no longer rushed headlong into danger, and his atrocious loquacity had diminished somewhat. A certain resemblance to his handsome sire was beginning to emerge, though his coloring more resembled that of an ancient Egyptian than a young English lad. (I cannot account for this any more than I can account for our constant encounters with the criminal element. Some things are beyond the comprehension of our limited senses, and probably that is just as well.)

A recent development had had a profound though as yet undetermined effect on my son. Our latest and perhaps most remarkable adventure had occurred the previous winter, when an appeal for help from an old friend of Emerson's had led us into the western deserts of Nubia to a remote oasis where the dying remnants of the ancient Meroitic civilization yet lingered.* We encountered the usual catastrophes—near death by thirst after the demise of our last camel, attempted kidnapping and violent assaults—nothing out of the ordinary; and when we reached our destination we found that those whom we had come to save were no more. The unfortunate couple had left a child, however—a young girl whom, with the aid of her chivalrous and princely foster brother, we were able to save from the hideous fate that threatened her. Her deceased father had called her "Nefret," most appropriately, for the

* *The Last Camel Died at Noon*

ancient Egyptian word means "beautiful." The first sight of her struck Ramses dumb—a condition I never expected to see—and he had remained in that condition ever since.

I could only regard this with the direst of forebodings. Ramses was ten years old, Nefret was thirteen; but the difference in their ages would be inconsequential when they reached adulthood, and I knew my son too well to dismiss his sentiments as juvenile romanticism. His emotions were intense, his character (to put it mildly) determined. Once he got an idea into his head, it was fixed in cement. He had been raised among Egyptians, who mature earlier, physically and emotionally, than the cold English; some of his friends had fathered children by the time they reached their teens. Add to this the dramatic circumstances under which he first set eyes on the girl...

We had not even known such an individual existed until we entered the barren, lamplit chamber where she awaited us. To see her there in all her radiant youth, with her red-gold hair streaming down over her filmy white robes; to behold the brave smile that defied the dangers that surrounded her...Well. Even I had been deeply affected.

We had brought the girl back to England with us and taken her into our home. This was Emerson's idea. I must admit we had very little choice; her grandfather, her only surviving relative, was a man so steeped in vice as to be an unfit guardian for a cat, much less an innocent young girl. How Emerson persuaded Lord Blacktower to relinquish her I did not inquire. I doubt that "persuaded" is an appropriate word. Blacktower was dying (indeed, he completed the process a few months later), or even Emerson's considerable powers of eloquence might not have prevailed. Nefret clung to us—figuratively speaking, for she was not a demonstrative child—as the only familiar objects in a world as alien to her as Martian society (assuming such exists) would be to me. All she knew of the modern world she had learned from us and from her father's books, and in that world she was not High Priestess of Isis, the incarnation of the goddess, but something less—not even a woman, which Heaven knows was low enough, but a girl-child, a little higher than a pet and considerably lower than a male of any age. As Emerson did not need to point out (though he did so in wearying detail), we were peculiarly equipped to deal with a young person raised in such extraordinary circumstances.

Emerson is a remarkable man, but he IS a man. I need say no more, I believe. Having made his decision and persuaded me to accept it, he admitted to no forebodings. Emerson never admits to having forebodings, and he becomes incensed when I mention mine. In this case I had a good number of them.

One subject of considerable concern was how we were to explain where Nefret had been for the past thirteen years. At least it concerned me. Emerson tried to dismiss the subject as he does other difficulties. "Why should we explain anything? If anyone has the impertinence to ask, tell them to go to the devil."

Fortunately Emerson is more sensible than he often sounds, and even before we left Egypt he was forced to admit that we had to concoct a story of some kind. Our reappearance out of the desert with a young girl of obviously English parentage would have attracted the curiosity of the dullest; her real identity had to be admitted if she was to claim her rightful position as heiress to her grandfather's fortune. The story contained all the features journalists dote on—youthful beauty, mystery, aristocracy, and great amounts of money—and, as I pointed out to Emerson, our own activities had not infrequently attracted the attentions of the jackals of the press, as he was pleased to call them.

I prefer to tell the truth whenever possible. Not only is honesty enjoined upon us by the superior moral code of our society, but it is much easier to stick to the facts than remain consistent in falsehood. In this case the truth was not possible. Upon leaving the Lost Oasis (or the City of the Holy Mountain, as its citizens called it), we had sworn to keep not only its location but its very existence a secret. The people of that dying civilization were few in number and unacquainted with firearms; they would have been easy prey for adventurers and treasure hunters, not to mention unscrupulous archaeologists. There was also the less imperative but nonetheless important question of Nefret's reputation to be considered. If it were known that she had been reared among so-called primitive peoples, where she had been the high priestess of a pagan goddess, the rude speculation and unseemly jests such ideas inspire in the ignorant would have made her life unbearable. No; the true facts could not be made public. It was necessary to invent a convincing lie, and when forced to depart from my usual standards of candor, I can invent as good a lie as anyone.

Luckily the historical events then ensuing provided

us with a reasonable rationale. The Mahdist rebellion in the Sudan, which began in 1881 and had kept that unhappy country in a state of turmoil for over a decade, was ending. Egyptian troops (led, of course, by British officers) had reconquered most of the lost territory, and some persons who had been given up for lost had miraculously reappeared. The escape of Slatin Pasha, formerly Slatin Bey, was perhaps the most astonishing example of well-nigh miraculous survival, but there were others, including that of Father Ohrwalder and two of the nuns of his mission, who had endured seven years of slavery and torture before making good their escape.

It was this last case that gave me the idea of inventing a family of kindly missionaries as foster parents for Nefret, both of whose real parents (I explained) had perished of disease and hardship shortly after their arrival. Protected by their loyal converts, the kindly religious persons had escaped the ravages of the dervishes but had not dared leave the security of their remote and humble village while the country was so disturbed.

Emerson remarked that in his experience loyal converts were usually the first to pop their spiritual leaders into the cook pot, but I thought it a most convincing fabrication and so, to judge by the results, did the press. I had stuck to the truth whenever I could—a paramount rule when one concocts a fictional fabrication—and there was no need to falsify the details of the desert journey itself. Stranded in the empty waste, abandoned by our servants, our camels dead or dying…It was a dramatic story, and, I believe, distracted the press to such an extent that they did not question other more important details. I threw in a sandstorm and an attack by wandering Bedouin for good measure.

The one journalist I feared most we managed to elude. Kevin O'Connell, the brash young star reporter of the *Daily Yell*, was on his way to the Sudan even as we left it, for the campaign was proceeding apace and the recapture of Khartoum was expected at any time. I was fond of Kevin (Emerson was not), but when his journalistic instincts were in the ascendancy I would not have trusted him any farther than I could have thrown him.

So that was all right. The biggest difficulty was Nefret herself.

I would be the first to admit that I am not a maternal woman. I venture to remark, however, that the Divine Mother herself might have found her maternal instincts weakened by prolonged exposure to my son. Ten years of Ramses had convinced me that my inability to have more children was not, as I had first viewed it, a sad disappointment, but rather a kindly disposition of all-knowing Providence. One Ramses was enough. Two or more would have finished me.

(I understand that there has been a certain amount of impertinent speculation regarding the fact that Ramses is an only child. I will only say that his birth resulted in certain complications which I will not describe in detail, since they are no one's business but my own.)

Now I found myself with another child on my hands, not a malleable infant but a girl on the threshold of womanhood, and one whose background was even more unusual than that of my catastrophically precocious son.

What on earth was I to do with her? How could I teach her the social graces, and complete the enormous gaps in her education that would be necessary if she was to find happiness in her new life?

Most women, I daresay, would have sent her off to school. But I hope I know my duty when it is forced upon me. It would have been cruelty of the most exquisite variety to consign Nefret to the narrow female world of a boarding school. I was better equipped to deal with her than any teacher, because I understood the world from which she had come and because I shared her contempt for the absurd standards the so-called civilized world imposes on the female sex. And... I rather liked the girl.

If I were not an honest woman, I would say I loved her. No doubt that is how I ought to have felt. She had qualities any woman would wish in a daughter— sweetness of character, intelligence, honesty, and, of course, extraordinary beauty. This quality, which many in society would rank first, does not count so high with me, but I appreciated it. Hers was the style of looks I had always envied. It is so unlike my own. My hair is black and coarse. Hers flowed like a river of gold. Her skin was creamy fair, her eyes cornflower-blue. Mine... are not. Her slim little figure would probably never develop the protuberances that mark my own. Emerson had always insisted these characteristics of mine pleased him, but I noted how appreciatively his eyes followed Nefret's dainty form.

We had returned to England in April and settled down at Amarna House, our home in Kent, as usual. Not quite as usual, though; normally we would have set to work immediately on our annual excavation reports, for Emerson prided himself on publishing them as soon as possible. This year we would have less to write about than usual, for our expedition into the desert had occupied most of the winter season. However, after our return to Nubia we had put in several productive weeks in the pyramid fields of Napata. (In which activity, I must add, Nefret had been a great help. She showed a considerable aptitude for archaeology.)

I was unable to assist Emerson as I usually did. I am sure I need not explain why I was distracted. This placed a considerable burden on Emerson, but for once he did not complain, waving aside my apologies with (ominous) good nature. "It is quite all right, Peabody; the child's needs come first. Let me know if there is anything I can do to help."

This uncharacteristic affability, and the use of my maiden name—which Emerson employs when he is feeling particularly affectionate or when he wishes to persuade me into some course of action to which I am opposed—aroused the direst of suspicions.

"There is nothing you can do," I retorted. "What do men know of women's affairs?"

"Hmmm," said Emerson, retreating in haste to the library.

I confess that I enjoyed fitting the girl out with a proper wardrobe. When we arrived in London she had hardly a stitch of clothing to her name, except for the brightly colored robes worn by Nubian women, and a few cheap ready-made garments I had purchased for her in Cairo. An interest in fashion, I believe, is not incompatible with intellectual ability equaling or exceeding that of any man; so I wallowed (the word, I hardly need say, is Emerson's) in tucked nightgowns and lace-trimmed petticoats, frilly unmentionables and ruffled blouses; in gloves and hats and pocket handkerchiefs, bathing costumes and cycling bloomers, wrappers and buttoned boots, and a rainbow assortment of satin sashes with matching ribbons.

I indulged in a few purchases for myself, since a winter in Egypt always has a deplorable effect on my wardrobe. The styles in vogue that year were less ridiculous than in the past; bustles were gone, the balloon sleeves of the past had shrunk to a reasonable size, and skirts were soft and trailing instead of bunched up over layers of petticoats. They were particularly suited to persons who did not require "artificial additions" to assist in delineating certain areas of the body.

At least I thought the styles were less ridiculous until I heard Nefret's comments on them. The very idea of a bathing costume struck her as hilarious. "What is the point of putting on clothes that will get soaking wet?" she inquired (with some reason, I had to admit). "Do women here wear washing costumes when they take a bath?" As for her remarks on the subject of underdrawers... Fortunately she did not address them to the clerk, or to Emerson and Ramses. (At least I hope she did not. Emerson is easily embarrassed by such matters—and Ramses is never embarrassed by anything.)

She fit into our household better than I had expected, for all our servants have become more or less accustomed to eccentric visitors. (Either they become accustomed or they leave our service, usually at their own request.) Gargery, our butler, succumbed at once to her charm; he followed her as devotedly as did Ramses, and never tired of hearing the (revised) story of how we had found her. Gargery is, I am sorry to say, a romantic person. (Romanticism is not a quality I despise, but it is inconvenient in a butler.) His fists would clench and his eyes would flash as he declared (forgetting diction in his enthusiasm), " 'Ow I wish I could 'ave been with you, madam! I'd 'ave thrashed those treacherous servants and fought those beastly Bedouins! I'd 'ave—"

"I am sure you would have been a great help, Gargery," I replied. "Another time, perhaps."

(Little did I know when that careless comment passed my lips that it was in the nature of prophecy!)

The only member of the household who did not fall victim to Nefret was dear Rose, our devoted housemaid. In Rose's case it was jealousy, pure and simple. She had helped raise Ramses and had a wholly unaccountable affection for him—an affection that was, or had been, reciprocated. Now Ramses's offerings of flowers and interesting scientific specimens (weeds, bones, and mummified mice) were bestowed upon another. Rose felt it, I could see she did. I found Rose a great comfort whenever the combined adulation of the male members of the household got too much for me.

The cat Bastet was no comfort, though she was female. She had been somewhat slow to discover the attractions of the opposite sex, but she had made up for her delay with such enthusiasm that the place was overrun with her progeny. Her latest litter had been born in April, just before our arrival, and Nefret spent some of her happiest hours playing with the kittens. One of her responsibilities as High Priestess of Isis had been the care of the sacred cats; perhaps this explained not only her fondness for felines but her almost uncanny powers of communication with them. The way to get on with a cat is to treat it as an equal—or even better, as the superior it knows itself to be.

The only persons who knew Nefret's true story were Emerson's younger brother Walter and his wife, my dear friend Evelyn. It would have been impossible to conceal the truth from them even if we had not had complete confidence in their discretion, and indeed I counted on Evelyn to advise me in the proper care and rearing of a young female. She had had considerable experience, being the mother of six children, three of them girls, and she had the kindest heart in the world.

I well remember one beautiful day in June, when we four adults sat on the terrace at Amarna House, watching the children at play upon the lawn. The great Constable might have captured the idyllic beauty of the landscape—blue skies and fleecy white clouds, emerald grass and stately trees—but the talents of quite another sort of painter would have been necessary to limn the laughing children who adorned the scene like living flowers. Sunlight turned their tossing curls to bright gold and lay caressingly on limbs pink and plump with health. My namesake, little Amelia, followed the toddling steps of her year-old sister with motherly care; Raddie, the eldest of Evelyn's brood, whose features were a youthful version of his father's gentle countenance, attempted to restrain the exuberance of the twins, who were tossing a ball back and forth. The image of innocent youth blessed with health, fortune, and tender love was one I will long cherish.

Yet I fancy mine were the only eyes fixed upon the charming figures of my nieces and nephews. Even their mother, whose youngest child lay sleeping on her breast, looked elsewhere.

Nefret sat apart, under one of the great oaks. Her legs were crossed and her bare feet peeped out from under the hem of her dress—one of the native Nubian garments in which I had clothed her, for want of anything better, while we worked at Napata. The background color was a strident parrot-green, with great splashes of color—scarlet, mustard-yellow, turquoise-blue. A braid of red-gold hair hung over one shoulder, and she was teasing the kitten in her lap with the end of it. Ramses, her inevitable shadow, squatted nearby. From time to time Nefret looked up, smiling as she watched the children's play, but Ramses's steady dark eyes never left her face.

Walter put his cup down and reached for the notebook he had refused to relinquish even upon this social occasion. Thumbing through it, he remarked, "I believe I see now how the function of the infinitival form has developed. I would like to ask Nefret—"

"Leave the child alone." It was Evelyn who interrupted her husband, her tone so sharp I turned to look at her in amazement. Evelyn never spoke sharply to anyone, much less to her husband, on whom she doted with (in my opinion) uncritical adoration.

Walter glanced at her in hurt surprise. "My dear, I only want—"

"We know what you want," Emerson said with a laugh. "To be known and honored as the man who deciphered ancient Meroitic. Encountering a living speaker of that supposedly dead language is enough to turn the brain of any scholar."

"She is a human Rosetta Stone," Walter murmured. "Certainly the language has changed almost beyond recognition over a thousand years, but to a trained scholar the clues she can offer—"

"She is not a stone," Evelyn said. "She is a young girl."

A second interruption! It was unheard of. Emerson stared at Evelyn in surprise and some admiration; he had always considered her deplorably mild-tempered. Walter gulped, and then said meekly, "You are quite right, my dear Evelyn. Not for the world would I ever do anything to—"

"Then go away," said his wife. "Go to the library, both of you, and immerse yourselves in dead languages and dusty books. That is all you care about, you men!"

"Come along, Walter." Emerson rose. "We are in disgrace and may as well spare ourselves the trouble of self-defense. A woman convinced against her will—"

I threw a muffin at him. He caught it neatly in midair, grinned, and walked off, trailed unwillingly by Walter.

"I do beg your pardon, Amelia," Evelyn said. "If I have put Radcliffe in a bad humor..."

"Nonsense, your criticism was much milder than the sort he is accustomed to receive from me. As for being in a bad humor, have you ever seen him more pleased with himself, more cursedly complacent, more infuriatingly good-natured?"

"Most women would not find that a source of complaint," Evelyn said, smiling.

"It is not the Emerson I know. Why, Evelyn, he has

not used bad language—not a single, solitary 'damnation!'—since we returned from Egypt." Evelyn laughed; I went on in mounting indignation, "The truth is, he simply refuses to admit that we have a serious problem on our hands."

"Or rather, under the oak tree." Evelyn's smile faded as she contemplated the girl's graceful figure. The kitten had wandered off and Nefret sat perfectly still, her hands in her lap, looking out across the lawn. Sunlight sifting through the leaves struck sparks from her hair, and the diffusion of light made her look as if she were enclosed in a golden shadow.

"She is as remote and beautiful as a young goddess," Evelyn said softly, echoing my own thought. "What is to become of such a girl?"

"She is willing and intelligent; she will adjust," I said firmly. "And she seems happy enough. She has not complained."

"She has learned fortitude in a hard school, I fancy. But then, my dear Amelia, she has little to complain of so far. You have—quite rightly, in my opinion—kept her relatively sheltered from the outside world. All of us accept her and love her as she is. Sooner or later, however, she must take her rightful place in the world that is hers by birth, and that world is pitilessly intolerant of anything different."

"Do you suppose I am unaware of that?" I said, adding with a laugh, "There are some individuals who actually consider ME eccentric. I pay no attention to them, of course, but...well, I admit I have wondered if I am the best possible mentor for Nefret."

"She could not do better than emulate you," Evelyn

said warmly. "And you know you can count on me to help in any way I can."

"We shall get on all right, I expect," I said, my natural optimism reasserting itself. "After all, I survived ten years of Ramses. With your help, and that of Walter... You were perhaps a little hard on him, dearest Evelyn. The decipherment of ancient unknown languages is not only his profession but his most passionate interest. Next to you, of course—and the children..."

"I wonder." Evelyn looked like a Raphael Madonna, golden-haired and sweet-faced, with the babe cradled in her arms, but her voice held a note I had never heard in it before. "How strangely the years change us, Amelia... I dreamed last night of Amarna."

It was the last thing I ever expected to hear her say, and it had the oddest effect on me. An image flashed across my eyes, so vivid that it replaced reality: a scene of baking desert sands and frowning cliffs, as empty of life as a lunar landscape. I could almost feel the hot dry air against my skin; I seemed to hear again the ghastly moaning cries of the apparition that had threatened our lives and sanity.... *

With an effort I shook off this seductive image. Unaware of my distraction, Evelyn had gone on speaking. "Do you remember how he looked that day, Amelia—the day he first declared his love? Pale and handsome as a young god, holding my hands in his as he called me the loveliest and most courageous of women? No crumbling papyrus or Rosetta Stone would have replaced me in his heart then. Danger,

Crocodile on the Sandbank

doubt, and discomfort notwithstanding, those were wonderful days! I even find myself thinking fondly of that wretched man and his absurd mummy costume."

I sighed deeply. Evelyn looked at me in surprise. "You too, Amelia? What can you possibly regret? You have gained everything and lost nothing. I can hardly pick up a newspaper without finding an account of some new escapade—pardon me, adventure—of yours."

"Oh, adventures." I gestured dismissively. "It is only natural they should occur. Emerson attracts them."

"Emerson?" Evelyn smiled.

"Only consider, Evelyn. It was to Emerson Lord Blacktower appealed for assistance in locating his missing son; Emerson who unmasked the criminal in the case of the British Museum mummy. To whom else would Lady Baskerville come when seeking a man to continue her husband's excavations, but to Emerson, the most preeminent scholar of his time?"

"I never thought of it that way," Evelyn admitted. "You have a point, Amelia. But you have only strengthened my argument. Your life is so full of the excitement and adventure mine lacks—"

"True. But it is not the same, Evelyn. Dare I confess it? I believe I do. Like you, I often dream of those long-gone days, when I was all-in-all to Emerson, the only, the supreme object of his devotion."

"My dear Amelia—"

I sighed again. "He hardly ever calls me Amelia, Evelyn. How well, how tenderly, I remember his snarl when he addressed me by that name. It is always Peabody now—my dear Peabody, my darling Peabody..."

"He called you Peabody at Amarna," Evelyn said.

"Yes, but in such a different tone! What began as a challenge has now become a term of complacent, lazy affection. He was so masterful then, so romantic—"

"Romantic?" Evelyn repeated doubtfully.

"You have your fond memories, Evelyn; I have mine. How well I remember the curl of his handsome lips when he said to me, 'You are no fool, Peabody, if you are a woman'; how his blue eyes blazed on that never to be forgotten morning after I had nursed him through the crisis of his fever, and he growled, 'Consider yourself thanked for saving my life. Now go away.'" I fumbled for a handkerchief. "Oh, dear. Forgive me, Evelyn. I had not meant to succumb to emotion."

In sympathetic silence she patted one hand, while I applied the handkerchief to my eyes with the other. The mood was passing; a shriek from Willie and an answering shriek from his twin brother betokened one of the rough-and-tumble encounters that characterized their affectionate relationship. Raddie rushed to break up the fight and staggered back, holding a hand to his nose. Simultaneously Evelyn and I sighed.

"Never believe that I repine," she said gently. "I would not exchange one curl on Willie's head for a return to that life. I love my children dearly. Only— only, dear Amelia—there are so many of them!"

"Yes," I said forlornly. "There are."

Ramses had moved closer to Nefret. The image was irresistible and unnerving: the goddess and her high priest.

And they would be with me, day and night, summer and winter, in Egypt and in England, for years to come.

CHAPTER 2

"One may be determined to embrace martyrdom gracefully, but a day of reprieve is not to be sneezed at."

I believe in the efficacy of prayer. As a Christian woman I am obliged to do so. As a rationalist as well as a Christian (the two are not necessarily incompatible, whatever Emerson may say), I do not believe that the Almighty takes a direct interest in my personal affairs. He has too many other people to worry about, most of them in far greater need of assistance than I.

Yet almost could I believe, on a certain afternoon a few months after the conversation I have described, that a benevolent Being had intervened to answer the prayer I had not dared frame even in my most secret thoughts.

I stood, as I had done so many times before, at the rail of the steamer, straining my eyes for the first glimpse of the Egyptian coast. Once again Emerson was at my side, as eager as I to begin another season of excavation. But for the first time in oh! so many years, we were alone.

Alone! I do not count the crew or the other passengers. We were ALONE. Ramses was not with us. Not risking life and limb trying to climb onto the rail; not with the crew, inciting them to mutiny; not in his cabin concocting dynamite. He was not on the boat; he was in England, and we ... were not. I had never dreamed it would come to pass. I had not ventured to hope, much less pray, for such bliss.

The workings of Providence are truly mysterious, for Nefret, whom I had expected to be an additional source of distraction, was the one responsible for this happy event.

For some days after the younger Emersons left us, I watched Nefret closely and concluded that the forebodings I had felt that pleasant June afternoon were no more than melancholy fancies. Evelyn had been in a strange mood that day; her pessimism had infected me. Nefret seemed to be getting on quite well. She had learned to manipulate a knife and fork, a buttonhook and a toothbrush. She had even learned that one is not supposed to carry on conversations with the servants at the dinner table. (That put her one step ahead of Emerson, who could not, or would not, conform to this rule of accepted social behavior.) In her buttoned boots and dainty white frocks, with her hair tied back with ribbons, she looked like any pretty English schoolgirl. She hated the boots, but she wore them, and at my request she folded away her bright Nubian robes. She never breathed a word of complaint or disagreed with any of my suggestions. I therefore concluded it was time to take the next step. It was time to introduce

Nefret into society. Of course the introduction must be gradual and gentle. What better, gentler companions, I reasoned, could there be than girls of her own age?

In retrospect, I would be the first to admit that this reasoning was laughably in error. In my own defense, let me state that I had had very little to do with girls of that age. I therefore consulted my friend Miss Helen McIntosh, the headmistress of a nearby girls' school.

Helen was a Scotswoman, bluff, bustling and brown, from her grizzled hair to her practical tweeds. When she accepted my invitation to tea she made no secret of her curiosity about our new ward.

I took pains to ensure that Nefret would make a good impression, warning her to avoid inadvertent slips of the tongue that might raise doubts as to the history we had told. Perhaps I overdid it. Nefret sat like a statue of propriety the whole time, eyes lowered, hands folded, speaking only when she was spoken to. The dress I had asked her to wear was eminently suitable to her age—white lawn, with ruffled cuffs and a wide sash. I had pinned up her braids and fastened them with big white bows.

After I had excused her, Helen turned to me, eyebrows soaring. "My dear Amelia," she said. "What have you done?"

"Only what Christian charity and common decency demanded," I said, bristling. "What fault could you possibly find with her? She is intelligent and anxious to please—"

"My dear, the bows and the ruffles don't do the job. You could dress her in rags and she would still be as exotic as a bird of paradise."

I could not deny it. I sat in—I confess—resentful silence while Helen sipped her tea. Gradually the lines on her forehead smoothed out, and finally she said thoughtfully, "At least there can be no question as to the purity of her blood."

"Helen!" I exclaimed.

"Well, but such questions do arise with the offspring of men stationed in remote areas of the empire. Mothers conveniently deceased, children with liquid black eyes and sun-kissed cheeks... Now don't glower at me, Amelia, I am not expressing my prejudices but those of society, and as I said, there can be no question of Nefret's... You must find another name for her, you know. What about Natalie? It is uncommon, but unquestionably English."

Helen's remarks induced certain feelings of uneasiness, but once her interest was engaged she entered into the matter with such enthusiasm that it was hard to differ with her. I am not a humble woman, but in this case I felt somewhat insecure. Helen was the expert on young females; having asked her opinion I did not feel in a position to question her advice.

It should have been a lesson to me never to doubt my own judgment. Since that time I have done so only once—and that, as you will see, almost ended in a worse catastrophe.

Nefret's first few meetings with Helen's carefully selected "young ladies" seemed to go well. I thought them a remarkably silly lot, and after the first encounter, when one of them responded to Emerson's polite greeting with a fit of the giggles and another told him he was much handsomer than any of her teachers, Emerson barricaded himself in the library and refused to come out when they were there. He agreed, however, that it was probably a good thing for Nefret to mingle with her contemporaries. The girl seemed not to mind them. I had not expected she would actively enjoy herself at first. Society takes a great deal of getting used to.

At last Helen decided the time had come for Nefret to return the visits, and issued a formal invitation for the girl to take tea with her and the selected young "ladies" at the school. She did not invite me. In fact, she flatly refused to allow me to come, adding, in her bluff fashion, that she wanted Nefret to feel at ease and behave naturally. The implication that my presence prevented Nefret from feeling at ease was of course ridiculous; but I did not—then!—venture to differ with such a well-known authority on young ladies. I felt all the qualms of any anxious mama when I watched Nefret set off; however, I assured myself that her appearance left nothing to be desired, from the crown of her pretty rose-trimmed hat to the soles of her little slippers. William the coachman was another of her admirers; he had groomed the horses till their coats shone and the buttons of his coat positively blazed in the sunlight.

Nefret returned earlier than I had expected. I was in the library, trying to catch up on a massive accumulation of correspondence, when Ramses entered.

"Well, what is it, Ramses?" I asked irritably. "Can't you see I am busy?"

"Nefret has come back," said Ramses.

"So soon?" I put down my pen and turned to look at him. Hands behind his back, feet apart, he met my gaze with a steady stare. His sable curls were disheveled (they always were); his shirt was stained with dirt and chemicals (it always was). His features, particularly his nose and chin, were still too large for his thin face, but if he continued to fill out as he was doing, those features might in time appear not displeasing—especially his chin, which displayed an embryonic dimple or cleft like the one I found so charming in the corresponding member of his father.

"I hope she had a good time," I went on.

"No," said Ramses. "She did not."

The stare was not steady. It was accusing. "Did she say so?"

"SHE would not say so," said my son, who had not entirely overcome his habit of referring to Nefret in capital letters. "SHE would consider complaint a form of cowardice, as well as an expression of disloyalty to you, for whom she feels, quite properly in my opinion—"

"Ramses, I have often requested you to refrain from using that phrase."

"I beg your pardon, Mama. I will endeavor to comply with your request in future. Nefret is in her room, with the door closed. I believe, though I am not in a position to be certain, since she hurried past me with her face averted, that she was crying."

I started to push my chair back from the desk, and then stopped. "Should I go to her, do you think?"

The question astonished me as much as it did Ramses. I had not meant to ask his advice. I never had before. His eyes, of so dark a brown they looked black, opened very wide. "Are you asking me, Mama?"

"So it seems," I replied. "Though I cannot imagine why."

"Were not the situation one of some urgency," said Ramses, "I would express at length my appreciation of your confidence in me. It pleases and touches me more than I can say."

"I hope so, Ramses. Well? Be succinct, I beg."

Being succinct cost Ramses quite a struggle. It was a token of his concern for Nefret that on this occasion he was able to succeed. "I believe you should go, Mama. At once."

So I did.

I found myself strangely ill at ease when I stood before Nefret's door. Weeping young ladies I had encountered before, and had dealt with them efficiently. Somehow I doubted the methods I had employed in those other cases would work so well here. I stood, one might say, in loco parentis, and that role was not congenial to me. What if she flung herself sobbing onto my lap?

Squaring my shoulders, I knocked at her door. (Children, I feel, are as much entitled to privacy as human beings.) When she replied I was relieved to hear that her voice was perfectly normal and when I entered, to find her sitting quietly with a book on her lap, I saw no trace of tears on her smooth cheeks. Then I realized that the book was upside down, and I saw the crumpled ruin on the floor near the bed. It had once been her best hat, a confection of fine straw and satin ribbons, its wide brim heaped with pink silk flowers. No accident could have reduced it to such a state. She must have stamped on it.

She had forgotten about the hat. When I looked back at her, her lips had tightened and her frame had stiffened, as if in expectation of a reprimand or a blow.

"Pink is not your color," I said. "I should never have persuaded you to wear that absurd object."

I thought for a moment she would break down. Her lips trembled; then they curved in a smile.

"I jumped on it," she said.

"I thought you must have."

"I am sorry. I know it cost a great deal of money."

"You have a great deal of money. You can stamp on as many hats as you like." I seated myself at the foot of the chaise longue. "However, there are probably more effective ways of dealing with the matter that troubles you. What happened? Was someone rude to you?"

"Rude?" She considered the question with an unnervingly adult detachment. "I don't know what that means. Is it rude to say things that make another person feel small and ugly and stupid?"

"Very rude," I said. "But how could you possibly believe such taunts? You have the use of a mirror; you must know you outshine those plain, malicious little creatures as the moon dims the stars. Dear me, I believe I was on the verge of losing my temper. How unusual. What did they say?"

She studied me seriously. "Will you promise you will not hurry to the school and beat them with your parasol?"

It took me a moment to realize that the light in her blue eyes was that of laughter. She hardly ever made jokes, at least not with me.

"Oh, very well," I replied, smiling. "They were jealous, Nefret—the nasty little toads."

"Perhaps." Her delicate lips curled. "There was a young man there, Aunt Amelia."

"Oh, good heavens!" I exclaimed. "Had I but known—"

"Miss McIntosh did not know he was coming either. He was looking for a school for his sister, for whom he is guardian, and expressed a wish to meet some of the other young ladies in order to see if they would be suitable associates for her. He must be very rich, because Miss McIntosh was extremely polite to him. He was also very handsome. One of the girls, Winifred, desired him." She saw my expression and her smile faded. "I have said something wrong."

"Er—not wrong. That is not quite the way Winifred would put it..."

"You see?" She spread her hands wide in a gesture as graceful as it was somehow alien. "I cannot speak without making such mistakes. I have not read the books they have read or heard the music. I cannot play on the piano or sing as they sing or speak languages—"

"Nor can they," I said with a snort. "A few words of French and German—"

"Enough to say things I do not understand, and then look at one another and laugh. They have always acted so, but today, when Sir Henry sat beside me and looked at me instead of looking at Winifred, every word was a veiled insult. They talked only of things of which I am ignorant, and asked me questions—oh, so sweetly!—to which I did not know the answers. Winifred asked me to sing. I had already told her I could not."

"What did you do?"

Nefret's expression was particularly demure. "I sang. I sang the Invocation to Isis."

"The..." I paused to swallow. "The chant you sang

in the temple of the Holy Mountain? Did you...dance, as you did then?"

"Oh, yes, it is part of the ritual. Sir Henry said I was enchanting. But I do not think Miss McIntosh will ask me to come to tea again."

I could not help it. I laughed till the tears flowed from my eyes. "Well, never mind," I said, wiping them away. "You will not have to go there again. I will have a word to say to Helen! Why I ever listened to her—"

"But I will go back," Nefret said quietly. "Not soon; but after I have learned what I must know; when I have read the books and learned their silly languages, and how to stick myself with a needle." She leaned toward me and put her hand on mine—a rare and meaningful gesture from so undemonstrative a girl. "I have been thinking, Aunt Amelia. This is my world and I must learn to live in it. The task will not be so painful; there are many things I desire to learn. I must go to school. Oh, not to a place like that, it cannot teach me quickly enough, and I am not—quite—brave enough to face girls like those every day. You say I have a great deal of money. Will it pay for teachers who will come to me?"

"Yes, of course. I was about to suggest something of the sort, but I thought you needed time to rest and accustom yourself to—"

"I did, and I have had it. These weeks with you, and the professor, and my brother Ramses, and my friends Gargery and the cat Bastet have been like the Christian Heaven my father told me about. But I cannot hide in my secret garden forever. You had thought, I believe, to take me with you to Egypt this winter."

"Had thought..." For a moment I could not speak.

I conquered the unworthy, contemptible emotion that swelled my throat, and forced the words out. "We had, yes. You seem interested in archaeology—"

"I am; and one day, perhaps, I will pursue that study. But first it is necessary to learn many other things. Would Mrs. Evelyn and Mr. Walter Emerson let me stay with them this winter, do you think? If I have so much money, I can pay them."

Tactfully, as is my wont, I explained that friends do not accept or offer payment for acts of kindness; but in every other way the plan was exactly what I would have suggested myself, if I had dared to propose it. I could have hired tutors and teachers who would have stuffed Nefret with information like a goose being fed for foie gras, but she could not learn from them what she really needed—the graciousness and deportment of a well-bred lady. There could be no better model than Evelyn, nor a more sympathetic guide. Walter could feed the girl's lust for learning while satisfying his own. In short, the solution was ideal. I had not proposed it because I did not wish to be accused, even by my own conscience, of neglecting my duty. Besides, I had not imagined for a moment that it would be considered acceptable by any of the parties concerned.

Now Nefret herself had proposed the scheme, and she stuck to her decision with a quiet determination that was impossible to combat. Emerson did his best to persuade her to change her mind, especially after Ramses, to the astonishment of everyone but myself, concluded that he would also remain in England that winter.

"I don't know why you persist in arguing with him,"

I said to Emerson, who was storming up and down the library as is his habit when perturbed. "You know that when Ramses makes up his mind, he never changes it. Besides, the scheme has a number of things to recommend it."

Emerson stopped pacing and glared at me. "I see none."

"We have often discussed the one-sidedness of Ramses's education. In some ways he is as ignorant as Nefret. Oh, I grant you, no one mummifies mice or mixes explosives better than Ramses, but those skills have limited utility. As for the social graces—"

Emerson let out a growling noise. Any mention of the social graces has that effect on him. "I told you," I went on, "about how the girls taunted Nefret."

My husband's handsome countenance reddened. Thwarted choler was responsible; he had been unable, in this case, to apply his favorite redress for injustice. One cannot punch young ladies on the jaw or thrash a respectable middle-aged headmistress. He looked rather forlorn as he stood there, his fists clenched and his shoulders squared, like a great bull tormented by the pricks and stabs of the picadors. Forlorn, yet majestic; for, as I have had occasion to remark, Emerson's impressive muscular development and noble features can never appear less than magnificent. Rising, I went to him and put my hand on his arm.

"Would it be so terrible, Emerson? Just the two of us, alone, as we used to be? Is my companionship so displeasing to you?"

The muscles of his arm relaxed. "Don't talk nonsense, Peabody," he muttered, and, as I had hoped he would, he took me into his embrace.

So it was arranged. Needless to say, Evelyn and Walter entered into the scheme with delight. I hastened to make the necessary arrangements for our departure before Emerson could change his mind.

He moped a bit, before and after we left, and I must confess I felt an unexpected sensation of loss when the steamer pulled away from the dock and I waved farewell to those who stood below. I had not realized Ramses had grown so much. He looked sturdy and dependable as he stood there—next to Nefret, of course. Evelyn was on Nefret's other side, her arm around the girl; Walter held his wife's arm and flapped his handkerchief vigorously. They made a pretty family group.

Since we had been able to get off early in the season, we had determined to take the boat from London to Port Sa'id instead of following the quicker but less convenient route by train to Marseille or Brindisi before boarding a steamer. I hoped the sea voyage would reconcile Emerson and put him in a proper frame of mind. The moon obliged me, spreading ripples of silvery light across the water as we strolled the deck hand in hand, gliding through the porthole of our cabin to inspire the tenderest demonstrations of connubial affection. And I must say it was a pleasant change to indulge in those demonstrations without wondering whether we had forgotten to lock Ramses in *his* cabin.

Emerson did not respond as quickly as I had hoped, being given to occasional fits of frowning abstraction, but I felt certain his gloomy mood would lift as soon as we set foot on the soil of Egypt. That moment was now only hours away; already I fancied I could see the dim outline of the coast, and I moved my hand closer to the strong brown hand that lay near it on the rail.

"We are almost there," I said brightly.

"Hmph," said Emerson, frowning.

He did not take my hand. "What the devil is the matter with you?" I inquired. "Are you still sulking about Ramses?"

"I never sulk," Emerson grumbled. "What a word! Tact is not one of your strong points, Peabody, but I must confess I had expected you to demonstrate the empathy of understanding you claim to feel for me and my thoughts. The truth is, I have a strange foreboding—"

"Oh, Emerson, how splendid!" I cried, unable to contain my delight. "I knew that one day you, too—"

"The word was ill-chosen," Emerson said, glowering. "Your forebodings, Amelia, are solely the products of your rampageous imagination. My—er—uneasiness stems from rational causes."

"As do all such hints of approaching disaster, including mine. I hope you do not suppose I am superstitious! I? No; premonitions and forebodings are the result of clues unnoticed by the waking mind, but recorded and interpreted by that unsleeping portion of the brain which—"

"Amelia." I was thrilled to observe that Emerson's blue eyes had taken on the sapphirine glitter indicative of rising temper. The dimple (which he prefers to call a "cleft") in his well-shaped chin quivered ominously. "Amelia, are you interested in hearing my views or expressing your own?"

Ordinarily I would have enjoyed one of those animated discussions that so often enliven the course of our marital relationship, but I wanted nothing to mar the bliss of this moment.

"I beg your pardon, my dear Emerson. Pray express your forebodings without reserve."

"Hmph," said Emerson. For a moment he was silent—testing my promise, or gathering his thoughts—and I occupied myself in gazing upon him with the admiration that sight always induces. The wind blew his dark locks away from his intellectual brow (for he had declined, as usual, to wear a hat) and molded the linen of his shirt to his broad breast (for he had refused to put on his coat until we were ready to disembark). His profile (for he had turned from me, to gaze out across the blue waters) might have served as the model for Praxiteles or Michelangelo—the boldly sculptured arch of the nose, the firm chin and jaw, the strong yet sensitive curve of the lips. The lips parted. (Finally!) He spoke.

"We stopped at Gibraltar and Malta."

"Yes, Emerson, we did." By biting down on my lip I managed to say no more.

"We found letters and newspapers from home awaiting us at both places."

"I know that, Emerson. They came overland by train, more quickly than we..." A premonition of my own made my voice falter. "Pray continue."

Emerson turned slowly, resting one arm on the rail. "Did you read the newspapers, Peabody?"

"Some of them."

"The *Daily Yell?*"

I do not lie unless it is absolutely necessary. "Was the *Yell* among the newspapers, Emerson?"

"It is an interesting question, Peabody." Emerson's voice had dropped to the growling purr that presages an explosion. "I thought you might know the answer, for I did not until this morning, when I happened to observe one of the other passengers reading that contemptible rag. When I inquired where he had got it— for the date was that of the seventeenth, three days after we left London—he informed me that several copies had been taken aboard at Malta."

"Indeed?"

"You missed one, Peabody. What did you do with the rest, toss them overboard?"

The corners of his lips quivered, not with fury but with amusement. I was somewhat disappointed—for Emerson's outbursts of rage are always inspiring—but I could not help responding in kind.

"Certainly not. That would have constituted a wanton destruction of the property of others. They are under our mattress."

"Ah. I might have noticed the crackle of paper had I not been distracted by other things."

"I did my best to distract you."

Emerson burst out laughing. "You succeeded, my dear. You always do. I don't know why you were so determined to prevent me from seeing the story; I cannot accuse you this time of babbling to that fiend of a journalist. He only returned to England ten days before we left, and as soon as I learned of his imminent arrival I made certain you had no opportunity to see him."

"Oh, you did, did you?"

"Kevin O'Connell"—Emerson's tone, as he pronounced the name, turned it into an expletive—"Kevin O'Connell is an unscrupulous wretch, for whom you have an unaccountable affection. He worms information out of you, Amelia. You know he does. How often in the past has he caused us trouble?"

"As often as he has come nobly to our assistance," I replied. "He would never do anything deliberately to harm us, Emerson."

"Well...I admit the story was not as damaging as I might have expected."

It would have been a good deal more damaging if I had not warned Kevin off. Emerson does not believe in telephones. He refuses to have them installed at Amarna House. However, we were in London for two days before we left, and I managed to put through a trunk call from the hotel. I too had seen the notice of Kevin's impending return, and my premonitions are as well-founded as Emerson's.

"I suppose he picked up his information while he was in the Sudan," Emerson mused. "He was the only one to use it; there was nothing in the *Times* or the *Mirror*."

"Their correspondents were concerned only with the military situation, I suppose. Kevin, however—"

"Takes a proprietary interest in our affairs," Emerson finished. "Curse it! I suppose it was unreasonable to hope O'Connell would not question the officers at Sanam Abu Dom about us, but one would have thought military persons would not spread gossip and idle rumors."

"They knew we had gone out into the desert after

Reggie Forthright, whose expedition was ostensibly designed to locate his missing uncle and aunt," I reminded him. "We could hardly conceal that fact, even if Reginald himself had not expressed his intentions to every officer at the camp. And when we returned, Nefret was bound to inspire curiosity and speculation. But the story we concocted was far more believable than the truth. Everyone who knew of poor Mr. Forth's quest for the Lost Oasis considered him a madman or a dreamer."

"O'Connell didn't mention it," Emerson admitted grudgingly.

He had not mentioned it because I had threatened him with a number of unpleasant things if he did. "Nefret's was not the only name to appear in Kevin's story," I said. "As I suggested...as I expected of a journalist of his ability, Kevin took for his theme the miracle of survival. Nefret's story was only one of many; no one reading the article could possibly suspect that she was reared, not by kindly American missionaries, but by the pagan survivors of a lost civilization. Even if the Lost Oasis was not mentioned, the suggestion that she had been reared among naked savages—for that is how our enlightened fellow countrymen regard the members of all cultures except their own—would subject her to ridicule and rude speculation by society."

"That's what concerns you, is it? Nefret's acceptance into society?"

"She has had trouble enough with narrow-minded fools as it is."

The clouds on Emerson's noble brow cleared. "Your kindly concern for the child does you credit, my dear. I think it is all a lot of nonsense, but no doubt the impertinent opinions of the vulgar affect a young girl more than they would ME. In any case we can't explain her origins without giving away the secret we have sworn to keep. All in all, I find I am glad the children are safe at home in England."

"So am I," I said truthfully.

The first person I saw as the steamer nosed into the dock at Port Sa'id was our faithful foreman Abdullah, his snowy-white turban rising a good six inches over the heads of the crowd that surrounded him.

"Curse it," I exclaimed involuntarily. I had hoped for a few more hours of Emerson's undivided attention. Fortunately he did not hear me; raising his hands to his mouth, he let out a ululating call that made the nearby passengers jump, and brought a broad grin to Abdullah's face. He had been our reis for years and was far too old and dignified to express his excitement in violent physical demonstrations, but his younger relatives were not; their turbans bobbed as they jumped up and down and shouted their welcome.

"How splendid of Abdullah to come all this way," Emerson said, beaming.

"And Selim," I said, spotting other familiar faces. "And Ali, and Daoud, and Feisal and—"

"They will be of great help getting our gear to the train," Emerson said. "I can't think why I didn't suggest they meet us here. But it is like Abdullah to anticipate our slightest desire."

The train from Port Sa'id to Cairo takes less than six hours. There was plenty of room in our compartment for Abdullah and his eldest son Feisal, since the other European passengers refused to share it with a "bunch of dirty natives," as one pompous idiot put it. I heard him expostulating with the conductor. He got nowhere. The conductor knew Emerson.

So we settled down and had a refreshing gossip. Abdullah was distressed to learn that Ramses was not with us. At least he put on a good show of distress, but I thought I detected a certain gleam in his black eyes. His feelings were clear to me—did I not share them? His devotion to Emerson combined the reverence of an acolyte with the strong friendship of a man and a brother. He had not been with us the year before; now he could look forward to an entire season of his idol's undivided attention. He would have disposed of ME as well had that been possible, I thought, without resentment. I felt the same about him. Not to mention Ali, Daoud, and Feisal.

We parted in Cairo, but only temporarily; before long we would visit the men at their village of Aziyeh, to recruit our crew for the winter's excavations. Emerson was in such a good humor that he submitted gracefully to being embraced by all the men in turn; for some time he was virtually invisible in a cloud of waving sleeves and flapping robes. The other European travelers stared impertinently.

We had booked rooms at Shepheard's, of course. Our old friend Mr. Baehler was now the owner, so we had no difficulty on that score, though Shepheard's is becoming so popular that rooms are hard to obtain. That year everyone was celebrating the victory in the Sudan. On September 2, Kitchener's troops had occupied Omdurman and Khartoum, ending the rebellion and cleansing the British flag of the stain of dishonor that had blemished it since the gallant Gordon fell to the hordes of the mad Mahdi. (If my reader is not familiar with this event, I refer him or her to any standard history.)

Emerson's amiable mood disintegrated as soon as we entered the hotel. Shepheard's is always crowded during the winter season and this year the crush was greater than usual. Sun-bronzed young officers, newly arrived from the battle zone, flaunted their bandages and gold braid before the admiring eyes of the ladies who fluttered around them. One face, adorned with a particularly impressive set of military mustaches, looked familiar, but before I could approach the officer—who was surrounded by a crowd of civilians, questioning him about Khartoum—Emerson took me by the arm and dragged me away. Not until we had reached our rooms—the ones we always had, overlooking Ezbekieh Gardens—did he speak.

"The place is more confoundedly overcrowded and fashionable every year," he grumbled, tossing his hat onto the floor and sending his coat to follow it. "This is the last time, Amelia. I mean it. Next year we will accept the invitation of Sheikh Mohammed to stay with him."

"Certainly, my dear," I replied, as I did every year. "Shall we go down for tea, or shall I tell the safragi to bring it to us here?"

"I don't want any confounded tea," said Emerson.

We had our tea on the little balcony overlooking the gardens. Greatly as I yearned to join the crowd below, which, I did not doubt, contained many friends and acquaintances, and catch up on the news, I did not deem it wise to persuade Emerson back into his coat and hat. I had had a hard enough time getting the latter object of apparel onto his head long enough to enter the hotel.

The white-robed servant glided in and out, noiseless on bare feet, and we took our places at the table. Below us the gardens were bright with roses and hibiscus; carriages and foot passengers passed to and fro along the broad avenue in the never-ending panorama of Egyptian life, as I once termed it. A hansom carriage drew up before the steps of the hotel; from it descended a stately figure in full dress uniform.

Emerson leaned over the edge of the balcony. "Hi, there," he shouted. *"Essalâmu 'aleikum, habib!"*

"Emerson," I exclaimed. "That is General Kitchener!"

"Is it? I was not addressing him." He gestured vigorously; to my chagrin his wave was answered by a picturesque but extremely ragged individual carrying a tray of cheap souvenirs. Several other equally picturesque persons in the crowd of would-be sellers of flowers, fruit, trinkets and souvenirs, attracted by the gesture, looked up and joined in the general shout of welcome. "He has returned, the Father of Curses! *Allah yimessikum bil-kheir, effendi! Marhaba, O Sitt Hakim!"*

"Hmph," I said, somewhat flattered at being included in this accolade—for Sitt Hakim, "Lady Doctor," is my own affectionate nickname among Egyptians. "Do sit down, Emerson, and stop shouting. People are staring."

"It was my intention that they should," Emerson declared. "I want to talk with old Ahmet later; he always knows what is going on."

He was persuaded to resume his seat. As the sun sank lower, the horizon was suffused by the exquisite glow of the dying day, and Emerson's countenance became pensive. "Do you remember, Peabody, the first time Ramses stood on this very balcony with us? We watched the sunset over Cairo together..."

"As we shall no doubt do again," I said rather sharply. "Now, Emerson, don't think of Ramses. Tell me the news I have been dying to hear. I know your engaging habit of keeping our future plans a secret from me until the last possible moment; you enjoy your little surprises. But the time has come, I think. Where shall we excavate this winter?"

"The decision is not so easy to make," Emerson replied, holding out his cup to be refilled. "I was tempted by Sakkara; so little has been done there, and I am of the opinion that there is a great Eighteenth Dynasty cemetery somewhere in the vicinity of Memphis."

"That is a logical deduction," I agreed. "Especially in view of the fact that Lepsius mentions seeing such tombs in 1843."

"Peabody, if you don't refrain from anticipating my brilliant deductions I shall divorce you," Emerson said amiably. "Those tombs of Lepsius's are now lost; it would be quite a coup to find them again, and perhaps others. However, Thebes also has its attraction. Most of the royal mummies of the Empire have now been found, but...By the by, did I tell you I knew of that second cache of mummies, in the tomb of Amenhotep the Second, fifteen years ago?"

"Yes, my dear, you have mentioned it approximately

ten times since we heard of Loret's discovery of the tomb last March. Why you didn't open the tomb yourself and get the credit—"

"Credit be damned. You know my views, Peabody; once a tomb or a site is uncovered, the scavengers descend. Like most archaeologists, that incompetent idiot Loret doesn't supervise his men adequately. They made off with valuable objects from that tomb under his very nose; some have already appeared on the market. Until the Antiquities Department is properly organized—"

"Yes, my dear, I know your views," I said soothingly, for Emerson was capable of lecturing on that subject for hours. "So you are considering the Valley of the Kings? If the royal mummies have all been found—"

"But the original tombs have not. We are still missing those of Hatshepsut, Ahmose, Amenhotep the First and Thutmose the Third, to mention only a few. And I have never been certain that the tomb we found was really that of Tutankhamon."

"It could have belonged to no one else," I said. "However, I agree with you that there are royal tombs yet to be found. Our old friend Cyrus Vandergelt will be there again this season, will he not? He has often asked you to work with him."

"Not with, but for him," Emerson answered with a scowl. "I have nothing against Americans, even rich Americans—even rich American dilettantes—but I work for no man. You have too many cursed old friends, Peabody."

My famous intuition failed on this occasion. No tremor of premonitory horror ran through me. "I hope you don't harbor any doubts as to Mr. Vandergelt's intentions, Emerson."

"You mean, am I jealous? My dear, I abjured that unworthy emotion long ago. You convinced me, as I hope I convinced you, that there could never be the slightest cause. Old married people like ourselves, Peabody, have passed through the cataracts of youthful passion into the serene pool of matrimonial affection."

"Hmmm," I said.

"In fact," Emerson went on, "I have been thinking for some time that we need to examine our plans, not for this year, but for the future. Archaeology is changing, Peabody. Petrie is still bouncing around like a rubber ball, tackling a different site each year—"

"We have done the same."

"Yes, but in my opinion this has become increasingly ineffective. Look at Petrie's excavation reports. They are..." Emerson almost choked on the admission that his chief rival had any good qualities, but managed to get it out. "They are—er—not bad. Not bad at all. But in a single season's work he cannot do more than scratch at the site, and once the monuments are uncovered they are as good as gone."

"I agree, Emerson. What do you propose?"

"Do you mind if I smoke?" Without waiting for an answer he took out his pipe and tobacco pouch. "What I propose is that we focus on a single site, not for one season, but until we have found everything that is to be found and recorded everything in painstaking detail. We will need a larger staff, of course—experts in the increasingly complex techniques of excavation. Photographers, artists, an epigrapher to copy and collate texts, an anatomist to study bones, students who can supervise the workers and learn excavation procedures. We might even consider building a permanent house to which we can return every year." He let out a great puff of smoke and added, "Then we wouldn't have to stay at this cursed hotel."

For a moment I could think of nothing to say. The proposal was so unexpected, the ramifications so complex, I struggled to take them in. "Well," I said, on a long breath. "The proposal is so unexpected I can think of nothing to say."

I fully anticipated Emerson would make some sarcastic remark about my loquacity, but he did not rise to the bait. "Unexpected, perhaps, but I hope not unwelcome. You never complain, my dear, but the tasks you have faced each year would daunt a lesser woman. It is time you had help—companionship—assistance."

"Of the female variety, I suppose you mean? A secretary would certainly be useful—"

"Come, Peabody, I had not expected you to be so narrow-minded. We could certainly use someone to keep the records straight, but why need that individual be female? And why not women students, excavators and scholars?"

"Why not indeed?" He had touched a tender chord; the advancement of my underrated sex has always been of deep importance to me. After all, I reflected, I had never counted on more than one year of solitary happiness. I had not even counted on that. Let me enjoy it now and not think of the depressing future. "Emerson, I have said it before and I will continue to say it: you are the most remarkable of men."

"As you have also said, you would have accepted nothing less." Emerson grinned at me.

"Do you have anyone in mind?"

"Nefret and Ramses, of course."

"Of course."

"The girl has demonstrated both interest and aptitude," Emerson went on. "I am also in hopes of inducing Evelyn and Walter to come out with us, once we have established a permanent base. There is a young woman named Murray at University College, a student of Griffith, who shows great promise...That is one of the things I hope to do this season, Peabody, interview potential staff members."

"Then," I said, rising, "I suggest we begin by dining downstairs."

"Why the devil should we? Ali's, in the bazaar, has better food—"

"But some of our colleagues are certain to be dining at Shepheard's. We can consult them about their more promising students."

Emerson studied me suspiciously. "You always have some excuse for forcing me into activities I detest. How do you know there will be any Egyptologists here tonight? You invited them, didn't you? Curse it, Peabody—"

"I found messages from friends awaiting us, as is always the case. Come along now. It is getting late and you will want to bathe and change."

"I won't want to, but I suppose I must," Emerson grumbled.

He began undressing as he stamped across the room, tossing collar, shirt and cravat in the general direction of the sofa. They fell on the floor. I was about to expostulate when Emerson came to a sudden stop and gestured emphatically at me to do the same. Head tilted, ears almost visibly pricked, he listened for a moment, and then, with the catlike quickness he could summon when he felt it expedient, he lunged at the door and flung it open. The corridor was dark, but I made out a huddled form crouched or collapsed on the floor. Emerson seized it in a bruising grip and dragged it into the room.

CHAPTER 3

"A woman's instinct, I always feel, supersedes logic."

For heaven's sake, Emerson," I exclaimed. "It is Mr. Neville. Drop him at once!"

Emerson inspected his captive, whom he held by the collar. "So it is," he said in mild surprise. "What the devil were you doing down on the floor, Neville?"

The unfortunate young man inserted a finger between his cravat and his neck, loosening the former from the latter, before he spoke. "Er...the gaslight in the corridor must have expired; it was extremely dark, and I could not be certain I had found the correct room. When I tried to look more closely at the number, my spectacles fell off."

Here a fit of coughing overcame him. "Say no more," I said. "Emerson, go and look for Mr. Neville's eyeglasses. I only hope you didn't step on them."

As it turned out, he had. Neville studied the ruined objects ruefully. "Fortunately I have another pair. I did not bring them with me, however, so perhaps you will be good enough to guide my steps tonight, Mrs. Emerson."

"Certainly. And of course we will replace your spectacles. Really, Emerson, you must get over the habit of leaping on people like that."

Neville was one of the younger generation of archaeologists, who had already demonstrated a remarkable talent for philology. In appearance he was one of the least memorable individuals of my acquaintance, for his beard and hair were of the same buff color as his skin, and his eyes were an indeterminate shade of gray-brown. His character was mild and accommodating, however, and he had a pleasant smile. "It was my fault, Mrs. Emerson. From the stories I have heard, you and the professor have good reason to be suspicious of people lurking at your door."

"That is true," Emerson declared. "In this case, however, I owe you an apology. No harm done, I hope?"

He began brushing Neville off with such vigorous goodwill that the young man's head rocked back and forth.

"Stop that, Emerson, and go change," I ordered. "You will have to excuse us, Mr. Neville; we are later than I had expected. There is a manuscript on the table that may interest you; it was in the hope of consulting you about certain passages that I asked you to do me the favor of coming early."

By the time I had closed the bedroom door Emerson was already in the bathroom, splashing loudly. I concluded he wanted to avoid a lecture—or inconvenient questions. Emerson is inclined to act hastily, but he seldom acts without cause (however inadequate that cause may seem to persons of duller intellect). Had he cause for apprehension that he had not seen fit to confide to me?

He gave me no opportunity to pursue the matter at that time, dressing with uncharacteristic speed and lack of fuss while I was performing my ablutions. I had to call him back from the sitting room, where he had gone to entertain our visitor, in order to request his assistance in buttoning my frock. The distractions that often occur during this process did not occur on this occasion.

I was wearing a gown of bright crimson, Emerson's favorite color. It was the latest fashion and I had had to badger my dressmaker to finish it in time. Emerson gave me a cursory glance and remarked, "You look very nice, my dear. I have always liked that dress."

When we returned to the sitting room, Mr. Neville was peering nearsightedly at the manuscript to which I had directed his attention. "Fascinating," he exclaimed. "Is this Mr. Walter Emerson's transliteration of 'The Tale of the Doomed Prince'? It seems much more accurate than Maspero's."

"To compare Maspero's knowledge of hieratic to that of my brother is an insult in itself," said Emerson rudely. "That is a trivial piece of work for Walter; he only transcribed it into hieroglyphs as a favor to Mrs. Emerson. She had a fancy to translate it, and her hieratic—"

"Comparisons are unnecessary as well as invidious, Emerson," I said. "I have never claimed to be an expert at hieratic."

(For the benefit of the ignorant, I ought to explain that hieratic is the cursive, abbreviated form of hieroglyphic writing—so abbreviated, in many cases, that the resemblance to the original form is almost impossible to make out. Walter was one of the leading authorities on this, as on other forms of ancient Egyptian. I was not. Neither was Emerson.)

"It is a fascinating tale," Neville agreed. "What passage in particular—"

"No time for that now," said Emerson. "If we must do this, let's get it over with. Lean on me, Neville, I won't let you fall. Take my other arm, Amelia; the cursed safragi has let the light go out, I can hardly see where we are going."

The lights at the other end of the corridor burned bright, and we proceeded with greater speed. A thrill of pride ran through me as we descended the staircase, for all eyes, especially those of the ladies, focused on the form of my husband. Unconscious of their regard, for he is in such matters a modest man, he led the way to the dining salon, where we found our friends waiting.

Such a gathering on the first evening of our return to Egypt had become a pleasant little tradition. As I took my place I was saddened to see that some of the familiar friendly faces were missing—gone forever, alas, until that glorious day when we shall meet again in a better world. I knew the Reverend Mr. Sayce would sadly miss his friend Mr. Wilbour, who had passed on the year before. Their dahabeeyahs, the *Istar* and the *Seven Hathors*, had been a familiar sight up and down the Nile. Now the *Istar* would sail alone, until it passed beyond the sunset and joined the *Seven Hathors* where it glided on the broad river of eternity.

Mr. Sayce's pinched face showed his appreciation

when I expressed this poetic sentiment. (Poetry again! Let the Average Reader beware!) "However, Mrs. Emerson, we are consoled for our loss not only by the knowledge that our friends have simply gone on before us, but by the appearance of new workers in the fields of knowledge."

There were certainly several unfamiliar faces—a young man named Davies, whom Mr. Newberry, the botanist who had worked with Petrie at Hawara, introduced as a promising painter of Egyptian scenes; a square-jawed, clean-shaven American named Reisner, who was serving as a member of the International Catalogue Commission of the Cairo Museum; and a Herr Bursch, a former student of Ebers at Berlin. Emerson studied them with a predatory gleam in his eye; he was considering them as prospective members of our staff.

Another stranger was older and of striking appearance, with golden locks and dark-fringed brilliant gray eyes any woman might have envied. His features were entirely masculine, however; indeed, the shape of his jaw was almost too rigidly rectangular. Though a stranger to me, he was not unknown to Emerson, who greeted him with a curt, "So you're back. This is my wife."

I am accustomed to Emerson's bad manners; I gave the gentleman my hand, which he took in a firm but gentle grasp. "This is a pleasure to which I have long looked forward, Mrs. Emerson. Your husband neglected to mention my name; it is Vincey—Leopold Vincey, at your service."

"You could have had the pleasure earlier if you had chosen to," Emerson grunted, waving me into the chair a waiter was holding. "Where have you been since that scandalous business in Anatolia? Hiding out?"

Our other friends are also accustomed to Emerson's bad manners, but this reference—which meant nothing to me—evidently passed even his normal bounds of tactlessness. A shocked gasp ran around the table. Mr. Vincey only smiled, but there was a look of sadness in his gray eyes.

Mr. Neville hastened to change the subject. "I have just been privileged to see Mr. Walter Emerson's latest transcription from the hieratic. He has turned 'The Doomed Prince' into hieroglyphs for Mrs. Emerson."

"So that is to be your next translation of an Egyptian fairy tale?" Newberry asked. "You are becoming something of an authority on that subject, Mrs. Emerson; the—er—poetic liberties you take with the original text are quite—er—quite..."

"In that manner I make them more accessible to the general public," I replied. "And there is certainly much of interest in such stories. The parallels to European myth and legend are quite remarkable. You know the story, of course, Mr. Vincey?"

My attempt to compensate for Emerson's bad manners was understood and appreciated. Mr. Vincey gave me a grateful look and replied, "I confess I have forgotten the details, Mrs. Emerson. It would be a pleasure to be reminded of them by you."

"I will be Scheherazade then, and amuse you all," I said playfully. "There was once a king who had no son—"

"We all know the story," Emerson interrupted. "I would rather ask Mr. Reisner about his studies at Harvard."

"Later, Emerson. So the king prayed to the gods and they granted his—"

It would be senseless to repeat Emerson's interruptions, which broke the smooth narrative I had intended to produce. I will therefore produce it here; for as the reader will discover, it had an unexpected and well-nigh uncanny influence on ensuing events.

"When the young prince was born, the Seven Hathors came to decree his fate. They said: 'He shall die by the crocodile, the snake, or the dog.'

"Naturally the king was very sad at hearing this. He ordered a stone house to be built and shut the prince up in it, along with every thing he could possibly want. But when the prince was older, he went up on the roof one day and saw a man walking along the road with a dog beside him; and he asked that a dog be procured for him. His father, who yearned to please the poor lad, caused a puppy to be given him.

"After the prince was grown he demanded his release, saying, 'If it is my doom it will come to me, whatever I do.' Sadly his father agreed; and the boy set forth, accompanied by his dog. At last he came to the kingdom of Naharin. The king had only one child, a daughter; and he had placed her in a tower whose window was seventy cubits from the ground, and told all the princes who wanted to marry her that she would be given to the one who first reached her window.

"Disguised as a chariot driver, the Prince of Egypt joined the young men who spent all their days jumping up at the window of the princess; and the princess saw him. When finally he reached the window she kissed and embraced him. But when the King of

Naharin heard that a common chariot driver had won his daughter, he tried first to send the boy away and then to kill him. But the princess clasped the young man in her arms and said, 'I will not stay alive an hour longer than he!'

"So the lovers were wed; and after some time had elapsed, the prince told his wife about the three fates. 'Have the dog that follows you killed!' she exclaimed; but he replied, 'I will not allow my dog, which I raised from a puppy, to be killed.' So she guarded him day and night. And one night while he slept, she set out jars of beer and wine, and she waited; and the snake came out of its hole to bite the prince. But it drank the wine and became drunk, and rolled over on its back; and the princess took her ax and chopped it to pieces."

"And that is where it ends," said Emerson loudly. "Now, Mr. Reisner, I believe you began in Semitic—"

"That is not the ending," I said, even more loudly. "There is a confused passage which seems to suggest that the faithful dog turned on his master, and that in fleeing the dog, he fell into the clutches of the crocodile. The manuscript breaks off at that point, though."

"It is the mystery of the ending that intrigues you, I suppose," said Mr. Newberry. "Was it the crocodile or the dog that brought the prince to his death?"

"I believe he escaped those fates as he did the first," I said. "The ancient Egyptians liked happy endings, and the brave princess must have played a part in the solution."

"That is the true explanation for your interest, Mrs. Emerson," said Howard Carter, who had come all the way from Luxor to join the party. "The princess is the heroine!"

"And why not?" I said, returning his smile. "The ancient Egyptians were among the few peoples, ancient or modern, who gave women their due. Not as often as they deserved, of course..."

At this point Emerson demanded the floor and, having had my say, I yielded it. He explained the plans we had discussed earlier.

"It will take a great deal of money and produce few results," said the Reverend Sayce. "The public wants monumental statues and jewels; they are not interested in pottery scraps."

"But that should not be our concern," declared Howard. He was one of the youngest of the group and he had not lost his boyish enthusiasm. "It is a splendid idea, Professor. Exactly what is needed. I don't mean to criticize M. Loret, but you know how he went about locating the tomb last year, don't you? Sondages! Pits, dug at random—"

"I know what the word means," Emerson growled, pushing away his plate of soup. "It is a disastrous technique. The whole area of the Valley needs to be methodically cleared down to bedrock." He reared back as a waiter snatched the empty bowl and deposited the fish course in front of him. "There is small hope of that, though, so long as the Antiquities Department keeps control over the Valley and gives concessions only to its favorites."

"What about Meidum?" the Reverend Sayce suggested. "The pyramid has never been completely cleared, and there are certainly more mastabas in the cemeteries around it."

"Or Amarna," said Mr. Newberry. "You worked there some years ago, I believe."

A thrill of emotion ran through me. Pyramids are my passion, as Emerson quaintly puts it, but the name of Amarna will always hold a special place in my heart, for it was there Emerson and I came to know and appreciate one another. I glanced meaningfully at my husband. He was looking meaningfully at Mr. Newberry, and I knew, from the glint in his eye, that he was about to say something provocative.

"Yes, we did, and I am giving the site serious consideration. It is of great importance, for it offers clues to one of the most confusing periods in Egyptian history. The archaeological remains have gone to rack and ruin since we left; no one has done a cursed thing—"

"Now, Emerson, you exaggerate," I said quickly. "Mr. Newberry was there, and Mr. Petrie was there—"

"For one year. Typical of Petrie." Emerson abandoned his fish. Leaning back in his chair, he prepared to enjoy himself by goading his friends. "I believe you also dropped in for a brief visit, Sayce."

The Reverend Sayce was, I am sorry to say, one of Emerson's favorite victims. A pinched, meager little man, he was regarded by many as an excellent scholar, though he had no formal training and never published anything. This failure would have been enough to inspire Emerson's contempt, and the reverend's religious convictions, of which Emerson had none, irritated him equally as much.

"I was with M. Daressy in '91," Sayce replied guardedly.

"When he found the remains of Akhenaton?" Emerson's lips stretched into the expression one may see on the face of a dog just before it sinks its teeth into one's hand. "I read about that incredible discovery and was surprised that it was not given greater prominence. Did you actually see the mummy? Daressy mentions only scraps of mummy wrappings."

"There was a body, or the remains of one," Sayce said warily. He had seen that smile on Emerson's face before.

"You examined it, of course."

Sayce flushed. "It was in wretched condition. Burned, torn to bits—"

"Very distasteful," Emerson agreed gravely. "What became of it?"

"It is in the museum, I suppose."

"No, it is not. I have examined the *Journal d' Entrée*. There is no mention of it."

"I hope, Professor, you are not implying that my eyesight or my memory are deficient. I saw that mummy!"

"I am sure you did. I saw it myself, seven years earlier." Emerson looked at me. He was enjoying himself so much I had not the heart to reproach him. I decided a little friendly teasing would not do the reverend any harm. "We didn't bother looking for the cursed thing, did we, Peabody, after it was stolen from us? The villagers must have dumped it near the royal tomb after taking it apart looking for amulets. No loss; it was only another tedious late mummy, that of some poor commoner."

Newberry was trying to hide his smile. We had not included the extraneous mummy in our publication report, since it had nothing to do with the history of the site, but many of our friends knew of our strange encounter with it. Carter, less tactful, exclaimed,

"Good heavens! I had forgotten about your peripatetic mummy, Professor. Do you think it was the one Daressy found?"

"I am certain of it," Emerson replied calmly. "None of the fools who examined it—excuse me, Sayce, I do not include you, of course—had the sense to see that it was of the wrong period. No doubt someone pointed this out to Daressy later, and he simply disposed of the embarrassing evidence and kept quiet."

"I am still of the opinion—" Sayce began angrily.

"Well, well." Emerson waved his opinion away. "Amarna does offer temptations. The Royal Tomb has never been properly investigated, and there are certainly other tombs in that remote wadi."

He took a bite of fish. Mr. Vincey, who had been listening in modest silence, now spoke. "I too have heard rumors of other tombs, but such rumors are common in Egypt. Have you any evidence?"

His voice was mild and the question was certainly reasonable; I could not understand why Emerson shot him such a hard look. "I don't deal in rumors, Vincey, as you should know. I knew of the Royal Tomb at least a decade before its 'official' discovery."

It was a testimonial to Emerson's reputation that no one expressed doubt of this statement, but Newberry exclaimed, with unusual heat, "You might have had the courtesy to inform your friends, Emerson. Petrie and I spent hours looking for the confounded place in the winter of '91, and I got myself in hot water when I wrote that letter to *The Academy* accusing Grebaut of falsely claiming credit for discovering the tomb."

"What's a little hot water, when the cause is just?"

demanded Emerson, who might be said to have spent most of his life up to his neck in boiling liquid. "Grebaut is the most incompetent, stupid, tactless nincompoop who ever called himself an archaeologist. Except for Wallis Budge, of course. I do not announce discoveries until I am in a position to deal with them myself. The depredations of the natives are hard enough on the antiquities; the depredations of archaeologists are even worse. Heaven only knows what meaningful objects were kicked aside by Daressy and Sayce when they—"

Sayce began to sputter, and Mr. Reisner said quickly, "Then you won't be returning to the Sudan? That region fascinates me. There is so much to be done there."

"It tempts me," Emerson admitted. "But Meroitic culture is not my field. Curse it, I can't be everywhere!"

I had hoped to avoid mentioning the Sudan, for I knew what would follow. Archaeologists are no more immune to idle curiosity than the next man. A general stiffening of attention ran round the table, but before anyone could frame a question we were distracted by the arrival of a short, stout individual who swept up to our table with the regal manner of a viceroy—which, in a professional sense, he was.

"M. Maspero!" I exclaimed. "How delightful! I did not know you were in Cairo."

"Only passing through, dear lady. I cannot stay; but upon hearing of your arrival I could not deny myself the pleasure of welcoming you back to the scene of your many triumphs." Ogling me in his amiable Gallic fashion, he continued, "You have the secret of eternal youth, chère madame; indeed you are younger and lovelier than you were that day of our first meeting in the halls of the museum. Little did I know what a momentous day it was! You may not think, gentlemen, that I resemble the little god of love, but I had the honor that day to play Cupid, for it was I who introduced madame to the gentleman who was to win her heart and hand."

With a grandiloquent flourish of *his* hand he indicated Emerson, who responded to the amused smiles of the others with a stony stare. He had been extremely critical of Maspero when the latter was Director of the Department of Antiquities, but he had detested the latter's successors even more. Now he said grudgingly, "You had better come back to the job, Maspero. The cursed Department has fallen apart since you left. Grebaut was a disaster, and de Morgan—"

"Ah, well, we will talk of that another time," said Maspero, who had learned from painful experience that it was necessary to cut Emerson short when he began talking about the failings of the Department of Antiquities. "I am in haste; I must go on to another appointment. So you must tell me at once, madame, what all Cairo aches to know. How fares the interesting young lady who owes you so much? Of all your triumphant adventures, this was surely the most magnificent!"

"She is in excellent health and spirits," I said. "How kind of you to inquire, monsieur."

"No, no, you cannot stop there, with conventional courtesy. You are too modest, madame; I will not allow it. We must hear the whole story. How you learned of her plight, what brilliant deductive methods you applied in order to locate her, the perils you faced on the dangerous journey."

Emerson's expression had petrified to such an extent his face might have been carved of granite. The others leaned forward, lips parted and eyes aglow. They would be able to "dine out" on this story for the rest of the season, since no one had heard it firsthand.

I had not looked forward to telling the tale to our professional colleagues. Unlike the general public, they had the expert knowledge to find the flaws in our little fiction. However, I had known the moment must come and I had prepared for it with my usual thoroughness.

"You do me too much credit, monsieur. I had no idea such a person as Miss Forth existed. As you must have heard, we went in search of her cousin, who had become lost in the desert after he set out to look for his uncle and aunt. Like many other rash travelers, they had vanished when the Mahdi overran the Sudan." I paused to take a sip of wine and select my words carefully. Then I resumed, "Since the region has been pacified, there have been rumors that some of these people in fact survived."

"It was some such idle rumor that sent Mr. Forthright into the desert?" Maspero shook his head. "Rash and foolish."

"It was Divine Guidance that inspired him," Sayce said reverently. "And led you to the rescue of this innocent child."

I could have kicked the kindly old man. A remark like this was bound to break through Emerson's silence, for he particularly dislikes giving God the credit for his own achievements. Unfortunately I could not kick Emerson, since he was seated across the table from me.

"Divine Guidance inspired him to lose himself in

the desert," said my husband. "Having better sense, we did not rely on—"

Since I could not administer a warning kick on the shin, I had to find another way of stopping him. I knocked over my wineglass. The heavy damask table-cloth absorbed most of the liquid, but a few drops spattered my brand-new frock.

"What did you rely on?" Carter asked eagerly.

"If it was not Divine Guidance, it was pure luck," I said, frowning at Emerson. "We had the usual adventures. You know the sort of thing, gentlemen—sandstorms, thirst, Bedouin attack. Nothing to speak of. From displaced persons we met along the way we heard of the missionaries—they belong to some strange Protestant sect, like the Brothers of the New Jerusa-lem*—you remember them, Reverend—and finally reached the remote village where they had miraculously survived fourteen years of war and misery. Mr. and Mrs. Forth had passed on, but their child lived. We were fortunate enough to be able to restore her to her heritage."

The waiter had supplied a fresh glass of wine. I took a hearty swig, feeling I deserved it.

"So you found no trace of poor Mr. Forthright?" Newberry shook his head sadly. "A pity. I fear his bones are whitening in some remote spot."

I certainly hoped they were. The young villain had done his best to murder us.

"But did I not hear some story of a map?" Mr. Vincey asked.

* The Mummy Case

My wineglass almost went over again. I managed to get hold of it. It was Maspero who came to the rescue. Laughing heartily, he said, "Willie Forth's famous maps! We have all heard of them, have we not?"

"Even I," Carter said, smiling. "And I did not know the gentleman. He is something of a legend in Egypt, though."

"One of the lunatic fringe always to be found in archaeology," Newberry said disapprovingly. "So his fantasies led him, not to the city of gold he hoped for, but to a village of miserable mud huts and an early death."

Maspero took his leave. For the rest of the evening the discussion focused on purely archaeological matters.

After we had returned to our rooms Emerson wrenched off his stiff collar. "Thank heaven that is over. I won't do it again, Amelia. This suit is as archaic as armor and almost as uncomfortable."

The wine had left visible spots on my skirt. I replied gently, "You won't have to wear evening kit to a fancy dress ball, my dear. I was thinking of something along Elizabethan lines. Those close-fitting hose would set off the handsome shape of your lower limbs."

Emerson had removed his coat. For a moment I thought he would throw it at me. Eyes blazing, he said in a muted roar, "We are not going to a fancy dress ball, Amelia. I would as soon attend my own hanging."

"It is in four days' time. We can find something in the bazaar, I daresay. Please help me with my buttons, Emerson. These spots may come out if I sponge them at once."

However, I was unable to tackle the spots that evening. By the time the buttons were undone I had other things on my mind.

Some time later, as a pleasant drowsiness wrapped around my weary frame, I reflected with pardonable complacency upon the events of the evening. Over the course of the succeeding months, as the story passed from speaker to listener, it would be altered and embroidered beyond recognition, but at least the original fiction had been accepted by those whose opinions counted most. How ironic, I thought, that it was Willoughby Forth's reputation for eccentricity that was primarily responsible for saving his daughter from vulgar gossip and the Lost Oasis from discovery and exploitation.

I was about to remark on this to Emerson when his regular breathing assured me he had fallen into slumber. Turning on my side, I rested my head against his shoulder and emulated his example.

I have a methodical mind. Emerson does not. It required prolonged discussion to convince him we ought to sit down with a map of Egypt and make a neat list of prospective sites, instead of rushing around at random. The more I thought about it, the more his plan appealed to me. Although I had enjoyed our vagabond existence, never knowing from one year to the next where we would be the following season, and although no one accepts with greater equanimity the difficulties of setting up a new camp in a new location yearly, often in places where water and shelter were inadequate, insects and disease proliferated, and the chance of snatching a few moments alone with Emerson

was slight, especially with Ramses always underfoot...
Well, perhaps I had not enjoyed it as much as I thought
I had! Certainly the idea of a permanent habitation had
considerable attraction. I found myself picturing how it
would be: spacious, comfortable living quarters, a pho-
tographic studio, an office for the keeping of records...
perhaps even a writing machine and a person to operate
it. I had mentally selected the pattern of the draperies
for the sitting room by the time Emerson, brooding
over the map, spoke for the first time.

"I don't believe we want to go south of Luxor, do
we? Unless there is some site between there and Assuan
that you yearn for."

"None that comes to mind. The Theban area offers
a number of interesting possibilities, however."

We had decided to breakfast in our room, for the
sake of greater privacy and also because Emerson did
not want to get dressed to go downstairs. His shirt was
open at the throat and his sleeves had been pushed up
to the elbows; the sight of him lounging at ease, long
legs stretched out, a pipe in one hand and a pen in the
other, almost distracted me from the matter at hand.
Unaware of my affectionate regard, he shoved the
map at me. "Have a look, Peabody. I have marked my
choices; add or subtract as you like."

"I think I had better subtract," I said, looking at the
emphatic crosses that marked the map. "We must narrow the possibilities down to half a dozen or less. Beni
Hassan, for instance, would not be my first choice."

Emerson groaned feelingly. "The tombs have deteriorated badly since I first saw them. They need to be
copied."

"That can be said of almost every site you have marked."

So the discussion proceeded; after a refreshing hour or so we had reduced the list to three—Meidum, Amarna and western Thebes—and I had agreed to Emerson's suggestion that we inspect the sites before making a final decision.

"It is still early in the season," he reminded me. "And we have not had the leisure to play tourist for several years. I would like to have a look at the tomb Loret found last year. He has left some of the mummies there, bloody fool that he is."

"Language, Emerson," I said automatically. "It would be nice to see the dear old Valley of the Kings again. What do you say we start with Meidum, since we are in the neighborhood?"

"Hardly in the neighborhood. Admit it, Peabody; you favor Meidum because there is a pyramid."

"We must start somewhere. After Meidum we could—"

A knock at the door interrupted me. The safragi entered, carrying a bouquet of flowers. I had already received several floral offerings from our guests of the previous evening; M. Maspero's was the largest and most extravagant. All the vases were in use, so I sent the servant out to find another while I admired the pretty arrangement of roses and mimosa.

"No red roses?" Emerson inquired with a smile. "I don't allow you to accept red roses from gentlemen, Peabody."

In the language of flowers, red roses signify passionate love. It was reassuring to hear him speak jestingly of a subject that had once driven him into a jealous rage. So I told myself, at any rate.

"They are white," I replied rather shortly. "I wonder who...Ah, here is a card. Mr. Vincey! A gentlemanly gesture, upon my word. I hardly had a chance to speak to him. By the by, Emerson, I have been meaning to ask you—what was the disgraceful business you referred to?"

"The Nimrud treasure. You must have read of it."

"I do remember seeing newspaper accounts, but that was some years ago, before I took a personal interest in archaeology. The cache was a rich one—gold and silver vessels, jewelry and the like; it was sold, as I recall, to the Metropolitan Museum."

"Correct. What the newspapers did not report, because they are well aware of the laws of libel, was that Vincey was suspected of being the agent through whom the museum acquired the collection. He was excavating at Nimrud for Schamburg, the German millionaire."

"You mean he found the gold and did not report the discovery to his patron or the local authorities? How shocking!"

"Shocking indeed, but not necessarily illegal. The laws regarding the disposition of antiquities and the ownership of buried treasure were even more undefined then than they are today. In any case, nothing could be proved. If Vincey did peddle the loot to the Metropolitan, he did it through an intermediary, and the museum was no more anxious than he to explain the transaction."

I could see that Emerson was beginning to get restless. He tapped out his pipe, shuffled his feet, and reached again for the map. Nevertheless I persisted.

"Then that is why I am not familiar with Mr. Vincey's archaeological career. The mere suspicion of such dishonesty—"

"Ended that career," Emerson finished. "No one would employ him again. It was a promising career, too. He began in Egyptology—did good work at Kom Ombo and Denderah. There was some talk...But why are we sitting here gossiping like a pair of old ladies? Get dressed and let us go out."

He rose, stretching. The movement displayed his form to best advantage: the breadth of his chest and shoulders, the lean, sinewy shape of the lower portion of his frame. I suspected he had done it to distract me, for Emerson is well aware of my appreciation of the aesthetic qualities of his person. I persisted, however, inquiring, "Were you, by any chance, the one who brought his malfeasance to light?"

"I? Certainly not. In fact, I came to his defense, pointing out that other excavators, including certain officials of the British Museum, were equally unscrupulous in their methods of obtaining antiquities."

"Why, Emerson, what a specious argument! I am surprised at you."

"The treasure was better off at the Metropolitan than in some private collection."

"An even less tenable argument."

Emerson started for the bedroom. It was his little way of indicating he did not care to discuss the subject further. I had, however, one more question.

"Why did you bring up the subject in that rude way? The others were willing to let the past be forgotten—"

Emerson whirled, his manly countenance aglow

with honest indignation. "I, rude? You know nothing about the traditions of masculine conversation, Peabody. That was just a friendly jest."

The succeeding days were very pleasant. It had been a long time since we had had the leisure to wander around Cairo renewing old acquaintances, to linger in the coffee shops fahddling with grave scholars from the university, and to explore the bookshops in the bazaar. We spent an evening with our old friend Sheikh Mohammed Bahsoor, and ate far too much. Not to have stuffed ourselves would have been a grievous breach of good manners, even though I knew I would have to put up with Emerson's snoring all night as a result. He always snores when he has taken too much to eat. The sheikh was disappointed to learn that Ramses was not with us and shook his head disapprovingly when I explained that the boy had remained in England to pursue his education. "What useful matters can he learn there? You should let him come to me, Sitt Hakim; I will teach him to ride and shoot and govern the hearts of men."

M. Loret, the Director of the Department of Antiquities, was in Luxor, so we were unable to call on him as was proper, but we spent time with other colleagues, bringing ourselves up-to-date on the current state of archaeological excavation and the availability of trained personnel. One day we lunched with the Reverend Sayce on his dahabeeyah in order to meet a student of whom he had great hopes. The *Istar* was not nearly so fine a boat as the *Philae*, my own beloved dahabeeyah, but it recalled poignant memories of that never-to-be forgotten voyage.

I could not restrain a sigh when we took our leave, and Emerson glanced questioningly at me.

"Why so pensive, Peabody? Were you not impressed with Mr. Jackson's qualifications?"

"He seems intelligent and well-trained. I was thinking of the past, my dear Emerson. Do you remember—"

"Oh, your dahabeeyah. They are picturesque but impractical. We can reach Luxor by rail in sixteen and a half hours. Shall we go to Meidum tomorrow? The nearest station is Rikka; we can hire donkeys there."

He went on chatting, seemingly unaware of my failure to respond.

As we went along the corridor toward our rooms I began to hear the sounds of what resembled a miniature war—shouts, crashes, thuds. The door to our sitting room stood open. It was from this chamber that the noises came and my astonished gaze fell upon a scene of utter confusion. Striped galabeeyahs billowed like sails in a storm as their wearers darted to and fro; cries and fulsome Arabic curses reverberated.

An even more fulsomely profane shout from Emerson, whose powers along those lines exceed any I have ever heard, rose over the uproar and stilled it. The men stood still, panting. I recognized our safragi, who had evidently recruited several friends to assist him in whatever endeavor he was pursuing. As their robes fell into place I saw the object of that endeavor.

It had alighted on the back of the sofa, where it stood at bay, fur bristling and tail lashing. For a moment a sensation of superstitious terror came over me, as if I beheld a supernatural emissary announcing disaster to one I loved. If the demonic Black Dog appeared to herald the death of a member of some noble families, what more appropriate Bane of the Emersons could there be than a large, brindled Egyptian cat?

"Bastet!" I cried. "Oh, Emerson—"

"Don't be absurd, Peabody." Emerson, wise in the ways of cats, cautiously circled around the animal. Its head swiveled to follow his movements and I saw its eyes; they were not golden, like those of our cat Bastet, but a clear pale green, the color of peridots. "For one thing," Emerson went on, "Bastet is at Chalfont with Ramses. For another... Nice kitty then, good kitty..." He bent down and squinted at the posterior of the feline. "It is a male cat. Very definitely male."

It was also bigger and darker in color. Nor did its countenance exhibit the benevolence of Bastet's. I have seldom seen a more calculating look in the eyes of any mammal, human or otherwise.

"Where did it come from?" I asked, and then repeated the question in Arabic.

The safragi held out his hands in appeal. They were bleeding from several deep scratches. The cat must have come in through the window; he had found it there when he entered to deliver a parcel and had tried in vain to evict it.

"So you enlisted an army of heavy-footed friends to help you," I said caustically, looking from the smashed vases and scattered flowers to the shredded curtains. "Go away, all of you. You are only frightening the poor creature."

The wounded safragi returned the animal's stare with one almost as malignant. I must say it did not look frightened. I was about to advance upon it—Emerson,

I noticed, had prudently retreated—when the safragi glanced at the open door and exclaimed, "We have found him, Effendi. He is here."

"So I see," said Mr. Vincey. He shook his head. "Bad cat! Naughty Anubis!"

I turned. "Good afternoon, Mr. Vincey. This is your cat?"

His face, so melancholy in repose, brightened in a smile. He wore a well-cut afternoon suit which became his trim form very well, but I noticed that though neatly brushed and pressed, the once expensive fabric was sadly worn. "My friend, my companion," he said gently. "But—oh, dear!—I see he has been very naughty indeed. Is he responsible for this chaos?"

"It was not his fault," I replied, approaching the animal. "Any creature, when pursued—"

Mr. Vincey's cry of warning came too late. I withdrew my hand, which was now marked by a row of bleeding scratches.

"Forgive me, my dear Mrs. Emerson," Vincey exclaimed. He passed me and scooped the creature into his arms. It settled down and began to purr in a deep baritone. "Anubis is what one might call a one-person cat. I do hope he didn't hurt you?"

"What an asinine question," commented Emerson. "Here, Peabody, take my handkerchief. Wait a moment—it was here, in my pocket—"

It was not in his pocket. It hardly ever was. I took the one Mr. Vincey offered me and wrapped it around my hand. "It is not the first time I have been scratched," I said with a smile. "No hard feelings, Mr. Vincey. And Anubis."

"Let me introduce you." Vincey proceeded to do so, addressing the cat as seriously as he would have done a human being. "This is Mrs. Emerson, Anubis. She is my friend and she must be yours. Let him sniff your fingers, Mrs. Emerson . . . There. Now you may stroke his head."

Somewhat amused at the absurdity of the business, I did as he asked, and was rewarded by a renewal of the deep purr. It sounded so much like Emerson's softer tones I could not help glancing in his direction.

He was not amused. "Now that that is settled, you will please excuse us, Vincey. We have just got back and want to change."

Another example of masculine repartee, I assumed. I would have called it rudeness.

"I am very sorry," Mr. Vincey exclaimed. "I came in the hope that you would take tea with me. I was waiting for you on the terrace when Anubis slipped his lead and I had to go in search of him. That is how it all came about. But if you have another engagement—"

"I would be delighted to join you for tea," I said.

Mr. Vincey's sad gray eyes lit up. They were most expressive optics.

"Please yourself," Emerson grunted. "I have other things to do. Good day, Vincey."

He opened the bedroom door and let out a profane exclamation. The exclamation—though not the profanity—was echoed by Mr. Vincey. "Oh, dear! Was Anubis in that room as well?"

"It appears he was," I replied, studying the crumpled linens and scattered papers with some chagrin. "Never mind, Mr. Vincey; the safragi and his friends did more damage than Anubis, I expect. They will—"

"Curse it!" shouted Emerson. He slammed the door.

I gathered up my handbag and my parasol, and after directing the safragi to tidy the rooms, I preceded Mr. Vincey into the hall.

"I need not apologize for my husband, I believe," I said. "You know his brusque manner conceals a heart of gold."

"Oh, I know Emerson very well," was the laughing reply. "To be honest, Mrs. Emerson, I am pleased to have you to myself. I have . . . I have a favor to ask."

I had a premonition of what that favor might be; but like the gentleman he was, Mr. Vincey waited to propose it until after we had found a table on the famous terrace and the waiter had taken our order.

We sat in silence for a time, enjoying the balmy afternoon air and watching the picturesque procession of Egyptian life passing along the street. Carriages let off passengers and picked up others; water carriers and vendors crowded around the steps. The tables were almost filled with ladies in light summer gowns and big hats, gentlemen in afternoon garb, and the usual sprinkling of officers. From his pocket Vincey had produced a lead and collar and fastened it on the cat. It submitted to this indignity more gracefully than its conduct had led me to expect, and squatted at its master's feet like a dog.

I found Mr. Vincey a pleasant companion. Our mutual affection for the feline species provided a useful introductory topic of conversation. I told him of the cat Bastet, and he replied with accounts of Anubis's intelligence, loyalty and courage. "For a good many years he has been not only my friend but my best friend, Mrs. Emerson. People talk of the selfishness of cats, but I have not found human friends so loyal."

I recognized this statement for what it was intended to be—a tentative reference to his unhappy history—but naturally I was too well-bred to indicate I knew of that history. I replied with a sympathetic murmur and a look that invited further confidences.

A flush mantled his cheekbones. "You must have guessed what I am about to ask, Mrs. Emerson. Your kindness and sympathy are well known. I had hoped—I am in need...I beg your pardon. It is difficult for me to sue for favors. I have not lost all my pride."

"Pray feel no self-consciousness, Mr. Vincey," I replied warmly. "Misfortune may come even to the worthy. There is no cause for shame in seeking honest employment."

"How eloquently and with what exquisite tact you express yourself!" Vincey exclaimed. I thought I saw a glimmer as of tears in his eyes. I looked away until he could conquer his emotion.

It was as I had supposed. Hearing of our plans for an enlarged, permanent staff, he was seeking employment. Once the difficulty of this admission was over, he proceeded to recite his qualifications. They were impressive: ten years of excavation, fluent Arabic, familiarity with the hieroglyphs, a good sound classical education.

"There is only one difficulty," he concluded, with a smile that showed even white teeth. "Whither I go, Anubis goes. I could not abandon him."

"I would think less of you if you did," I assured him. "That is not a difficulty, Mr. Vincey. You understand I cannot promise anything yet; our plans are still in the process of being formulated. However, I will speak to Emerson and—without wishing in any way to hold out false hopes—I have every reason to believe he will be favorably inclined to your offer."

"I cannot thank you enough." His voice broke. "That is the truth, Mrs. Emerson; you have no idea—"

"Enough said, Mr. Vincey." Touched by his sincerity, respecting his dignity, I pretended to glance at my watch. "Dear me, it is getting late. I must hurry and change. Are you coming to the ball?"

"I had not intended to, but if you will be there—"

"Yes, indeed. I look forward to it."

"What costume are you wearing?"

"Ah, that is a secret," I replied gaily. "We are all to be masked and in disguise. Half the fun will be trying to recognize one's friends."

"I can't believe you have persuaded Emerson to attend," Vincey said. "He used to roar like a chained bear at the very prospect of a social engagement. How you have civilized him!"

"He roared a bit," I admitted, laughing. "But I have found the perfect costume for him, one he cannot object to assuming."

"An ancient pharaoh?" Relieved of his embarrassment, Vincey was ready to enter into the spirit of the thing. "He would be a perfect Thutmose the Third, the great warrior king."

"Now, really, Mr. Vincey, can you picture Emerson appearing in public attired only in a short kilt and a beaded collar? He is a modest man. Anyhow, Thutmose was only a few inches over five feet in height."

"He would look magnificent in armor."

"Suits of armor are not so easily come by in the bazaar. You won't trap me so easily, Mr. Vincey! I must be off now."

"And I, if I am to find some fancy dress of my own." He took the hand I had offered him; with a rueful look at the makeshift bandage around it, he raised it, bandage and all, to his lips.

Emerson claimed he had forgotten about the fancy dress ball. Then he claimed he had never agreed to attend. After being driven back from both these positions, he retreated to a third line of defense, objecting to my ensemble. It began, "If you think I am going to allow my wife to appear in such a costume..." and ended, "I wash my hands of the whole affair. Do as you like, you always do."

In fact, I was rather pleased with my choice. I had dismissed the idea of some version of ancient Egyptian dress; there would be dozens of inappropriate variations of that, by ladies who hoped to conjure up the seductive image of Cleopatra, the only queen known to the idle tourist. I had considered Boadicea or some other prominent defender of women's rights, but it was not so easy to put together a costume in the limited time at my disposal. What I wore was not fancy dress. It would appear as such to the conventional travelers at Shepheard's, however, for I had determined to take the last, bold stride in my campaign of suitable working attire for archaeologically disposed ladies.

My first experiences in Egypt, pursuing mummies and climbing up and down cliffs, had convinced me that trailing skirts and tight corsets were a confounded nuisance in that ambience. For many years my working costume had consisted of pith helmet and shirtwaist, boots, and Turkish trousers, or bloomers. They had caused consternation enough when I first appeared in them, but eventually ladies adopted divided skirts and full trousers for sporting activities. They were a good deal more convenient than skirts, but they had certain disadvantages; on one memorable occasion I had been unable to defend myself from attack because I could not locate my pocket (and the revolver in it) among the voluminous folds of fabric.*

I had always envied gentlemen the abundance and accessibility of their pockets. My belt of tools—knife, waterproof container for matches and candles, canteen, notebook and pencil, among other useful objects— substituted for pockets to some extent, but the noise they made clashing together made it difficult for me to creep up on suspects unnoticed, and the sharp edges on a number of them impeded the impetuous embraces to which Emerson is prone. I did not intend to abandon my chatelaine, as I jestingly called it, but pockets, large pockets and many of them, would allow me to carry even more essentials with me.

The costume my dressmaker had produced, under my direction, was almost identical with the shooting suits gentlemen had been wearing for some years. There were pockets everywhere—inside the jacket and on its upper portion, and all over the skirts or tails of the said jacket. This object of apparel covered the torso

* *Lion in the Valley*

and the adjoining area of the lower limbs. Beneath it were knickerbockers cut like a man's (except for being somewhat fuller in the upper part) of a matching fabric. They were tucked into stout laced boots, and when I had clapped a pith helmet on my head and put my hair up under it, I felt I was the very picture of a young gentleman explorer.

Arms folded and head on one side, Emerson watched me assume this garb with an expression that left me in some doubt as to his reaction. The occasional quiver of his lips might have been amusement or repressed outrage. Pirouetting in front of the mirror, I addressed him over my shoulder.

"Well? What do you think?"

Emerson's lips parted. "You need a mustache."

"I have one." I produced it from the lower left-hand pocket of the jacket and pressed it into place. It was a red mustache. I had been unable to find a black one.

After Emerson had got himself under control I asked him to study the effect again and give me his serious opinion. At his request I removed the mustache; he claimed that appendage rendered serious consideration impossible. After circling me two or three times he nodded. "You don't make a very convincing young gentleman, Peabody. However, the outfit rather becomes you. You might consider wearing it on the dig, it would be much more convenient than those cursed bloomers. They have so many yards of cloth in them, it takes me forever to—"

"There is no time for that, Emerson," I said, gliding away from the hand he had extended in order to make his point. "Your costume is hanging in the wardrobe."

With a dramatic flourish I flung the wardrobe door open.

A number of establishments in the sûk sold various versions of native Egyptian robes, for they were popular with tourists. I had to search for some time before I found an ensemble that was not only completely authentic, but particularly suitable to Emerson's tall frame and individualistic character. Though he denies it, he has a secret penchant for disguises and a certain taste for the theatrical. I fancied this costume would appeal to him, for the embroidered jubba and woven kaftan, the gold-trimmed hezaam and loose trousers might have been worn by a prince of the Touareg—those extremely virile and violent desert raiders who are known to their despairing victims as "The Forgotten of God." They are also called "The Veiled Ones," because of the blue veils that provide protection against heat and blowing sand. It was this feature that had determined me to select the costume, for it would serve in lieu of a mask, which I felt sure Emerson would not consent to wear. The headdress, called a khafiya, was a square of cloth bound in place by a rope. It framed the face becomingly and, with the veil, would leave only his eyes exposed.

Emerson studied it in silence. "We will go well together," I said cheerfully. "My trousers and your skirts."

The ballroom was decorated in the style of Louis XVI and featured a superb chandelier whose thousands of crystals reflected the lights in a dazzling shimmer. The brilliant and fantastical garb of the guests filled the room with color. There were plenty of ancient Egyptians present, but some of the guests had been more inventive; I saw a Japanese samurai and a bishop of the Eastern Church, complete with miter. My own dress provoked considerable comment, however. I had no lack of partners; and as I circled the floor in the respectful grasp of one gentleman or another, I was delighted at how neatly I could perform the vigorous steps of polkas and schottisches.

Emerson does not dance. From time to time I would catch a glimpse of him wandering around the perimeter of the room, or talking to someone who shared his disinterest in terpsichorean exercise. Then I saw him no more and concluded he had got bored and gone off in search of more congenial company.

I was sitting in one of the little alcoves screened by potted plants, recuperating from my exertions and chatting with Lady Norton, when he appeared again. "Ah, my dear, there you are," I said, glancing over my shoulder at the tall veiled form. "Permit me to present you to—"

I was permitted to say no more. Arms like steel snatched me up out of my chair; stifled, breathless, enveloped in folds of billowing cloth, I was carried rapidly away. I heard a shriek from Lady Norton, and exclamations of surprise and amusement from the other guests—for my abductor's path led him straight across the ballroom toward the door.

I was not amused. Emerson was not the man to play such a silly trick, and I had known, the moment the person touched me, that the grasp was not that of my spouse. He felt me stiffen, heard the sharp intake of my breath; without slackening his pace he shifted his hold in such a fashion that my face was crushed against his breast and my cry was muffled by folds of fabric.

Astonishment and incredulity weakened my limbs; I could not believe what was happening. Could a person be abducted out of Shepheard's Hotel, under the very noses of hundreds of watchers?

The attempt might have succeeded by its very audacity. What else could the audience assume but that my notoriously eccentric spouse had entered into the spirit of the masque and was playing the role his costume had inspired? I heard one idiotic woman shriek, "How romantic!" My struggles were taken for part of the charade, and they weakened as I grew faint from lack of oxygen.

Then a voice rang out—a voice famous throughout the length of Egypt for its resonance and audibility. It reassured, it inspired me; my strength returned, my struggles were renewed. The grip that held me loosened. I felt myself flying through the air; reached out, groping and blinded; braced myself for the impact I knew must follow...And struck a solid but yielding surface with a force that drove the last of the straining breath from my lungs. I clutched at it; it recoiled from me with a grunt of effort and then, recovering, caught and held me.

I opened my eyes. I had not needed to see him to know whose arms enclosed me, but the sight of the beloved face—crimson with choler, eyes blazing like sapphires—left me too weak to speak. Emerson drew a deep, shuddering breath. "Damnation!" he roared. "Can't I leave you alone for five minutes, Peabody?"

CHAPTER 4

"No woman really wants a man to carry her off; she only wants him to want to do it."

Why didn't you pursue the fellow?" I demanded.

Emerson kicked the bedroom door shut and dropped me unceremoniously onto the bed. He had carried me straight upstairs and he was breathing rather heavily. Our rooms were on the third floor, but I fancied it was exasperation rather than exertion that had quickened his breath. The tone in which he replied further strengthened this theory.

"Don't ask stupid questions, Peabody! He threw you straight at me, like a bundle of laundry. Would you rather I had let you fall to the floor? Even if I had been so cold-blooded, I reacted instinctively; and by the time I had recovered myself he was long gone."

I sat up and began to straighten my disheveled hair. Somewhere along the way I had lost my pith helmet. I reminded myself to search for it next day; it was a new one and very expensive.

"The implied reproach was unfair, Emerson. I

apologize. It would take him only a minute to achieve anonymity by divesting himself of his robes. They were not an exact copy of yours but they were close enough."

"Confounded fancy dress!" Emerson had divested himself of *his* robe; he tossed it into a corner and plucked the headdress from his head. I let out a cry.

"Is that blood on your face? Come here and let me see."

After some masculine grumbling he consented to let me have a look. (He likes being fussed over but refuses to admit it.) There was only a small trace of blood on his temple but it marked a tender spot that would no doubt blossom into a purple bruise before morning. "What the devil have you been up to?" I asked.

Emerson stretched out on the bed. "I had a little adventure of my own. You don't suppose it was Divine Guidance that brought me to your rescue in the traditional nick of time, do you?"

"I could believe in Divine Guidance, my dear. Are you not always at my side when danger threatens?"

Leaning over him, I pressed my lips to the wound. "Ouch," said Emerson.

"What happened?"

"I had gone out for a smoke and some intelligent conversation," Emerson explained.

"Out of the hotel?"

"No one in the hotel—saving your presence, my dear—is capable of intelligent conversation. I thought Abdul or Ali might be hanging about. As I strolled innocently through the gardens, three men jumped me."

"Three? Was that all?"

Emerson frowned. "It was rather odd," he said.

"The fellows were, I believe, ordinary Cairene thugs. If they had intended to murder me, they might have done some damage, for as you know, they all carry knives. They never used them, only their bare hands."

"Bare hands did not inflict this wound," I said, indicating his temple.

"One of them had a club. The confounded headdress was of some use, it deflected the blow. I became a trifle annoyed then, and after I had disposed of two of them, the third fled. I would have questioned them, but it occurred to me that you might be in similar straits and that I had better see what you were up to."

I got up and went to look for my medical kit. "Why should you suppose that? Your enemies are not necessarily mine, and I must say, Emerson, that over the years you have attracted quite a number of...Where the devil did I put that box of bandages? The safragi has mixed up the luggage; nothing is where I left it."

Emerson sat up. "What makes you think it was the safragi?"

I finally found the medicine box; it was in the original container, but not in the original place. Emerson, who had been searching his own luggage, straightened. "Nothing appears to have been taken."

I nodded agreement. He was holding an article I had not seen before—a long narrow box of heavy cardboard. "Has something been added? Be careful opening it, Emerson!"

"No, this is my property. Ours, I should say." He removed the lid, and I saw a glitter of gold and a rich azure glow. "Good heavens," I cried. "It is the regalia

Nefret carried away with her from the Holy Mountain—
the royal scepters. Why did you bring them?"

One scepter was shaped like a shepherd's crook,
symbolizing the care of the king for his people. The
materials were gold and lapis lazuli in alternating rings.
The other object consisted of a short staff made of gold
foil and dark-blue glass over a bronze core, from which
depended three flexible thongs of the same materials,
gold beads alternating with blue, and ending in cylin-
drical rods of solid gold. The flail represented (as I have
always believed) the other aspect of rule: power and
domination. It certainly would have inflicted a painful
blow if it had been made of more durable materials, as
the original whip undoubtedly was. No such objects
had ever been found in Egypt, though they were
known from countless paintings and reliefs.

"We agreed, did we not," said Emerson, "that it
would be unconscionable to keep these remarkable
objects from scholars. They are unique, and they are
two thousand years old if they are a day—treasured rel-
ics. They belong not to us but to the world."

"Well, yes—we did agree in theory, and I am of the
same mind still; but we cannot display them without
explaining where we found them."

"Precisely. We will find them. This season."

I caught my breath. "It is an ingenious idea, Emerson. Brilliant, even. No one is better able than you to
arrange a convincing if misleading ambience."

Emerson fingered the cleft in his chin and looked
a trifle uncomfortable. "Dishonesty goes against the
grain, Peabody, I confess it; but what else are we to
do? Thebes seems the most likely place for such a—

er—discovery; the Cushite conquerors of the Twenty-Sixth Dynasty remained there for some time. We must account in some way for the information about ancient Meroitic culture we acquired last winter. Sooner or later one of us, or Walter, will let something slip; it is not humanly possible to write about the subject without displaying information we ought not to have."

"I agree. In fact, the article you sent to the *Zeitschrift* in June—"

"Devil take it, Peabody, I said nothing revealing in that article!"

"In any case," I said soothingly, "it will not be published for some time."

"These scholarly journals are always behind schedule," Emerson agreed. "So you are thinking along the same lines, Peabody?"

"What lines?" I began rummaging in my box of medical supplies.

"I am surprised at you, Peabody. Usually you are the first to find portents of danger all around, and although I admit there are a number of individuals who have reason to dislike us, recent incidents are beginning to suggest quite a different theory."

He sat down on the edge of the bed. I brushed the hair from his brow and applied antiseptic to his wound. Absorbed in his theory, he ignored attentions he was not ordinarily willing to receive without complaint.

"Our luggage appears to have been searched. Theft was not the object; nothing was taken. Tonight we were both attacked. Murder was not the object; we must assume, I think, that abduction of one or both of us was. For what purpose?"

"Some of our old enemies may want to carry us off and watch gloatingly while hideous tortures are inflicted upon us," I suggested.

"Always cheerful, Peabody," Emerson said, grinning. "What are you doing? I won't have any confounded bandages."

I cut off a bit of sticking plaster. "Out with it, Emerson. You are beating around the bush."

"Not at all. I am simply admitting that the evidence is inconclusive. It is suggestive, though, don't you think?"

"I think this time it is your imagination that has got out of hand." I sat down next to him. "Unless you know something you haven't told me."

"I don't know anything," Emerson said irritably. "If I did, I would not be dithering like a nervous old spinster. All the same... We covered our tracks as well as we could, Peabody, but there are several weak spots in the fictional fabric we wove. A good hard shove at any one of them would leave a gaping hole of speculation."

"Are you by any chance referring to the Church of the Saints of the Son of God as a weak spot? Curse it, Emerson, I had to invent a religious sect; if we had claimed Nefret's kindly foster parents were Baptists or Lutherans or Roman Catholics, the most cursory inquiry would prove no such family existed."

"Especially if you had claimed they were Roman Catholics," Emerson said. Seeing my expression, he added hastily, "It was very clever of you, my dear."

"Don't patronize me, Emerson! I cannot imagine what has got you into this morbid state of mind. The story I—we—invented is no more unbelievable than many true...I do wish you would stop mumbling under your breath. It is very rude. Speak up!"

"Map," said Emerson.

"Willoughby Forth's maps? You heard how Maspero and the others laughed at them the other night—"

"The map," said Emerson loudly, "that Reginald Forthright showed to half the bloo——blooming officers at Sanam Abu Dom. Everyone from General Rundle to the lowest subaltern knew when he went after his uncle that he had more to go on than vague rumors. He never came back; but WE did, with Forth's daughter. How long do you suppose it will take some inventive journalist to concoct a thrilling scenario out of those facts? I am only surprised your friend O'Connell hasn't already done so. His imagination is almost as rampageous as—"

"The implication is insulting and undeserved—especially coming from YOU. I have never heard such... You are muttering again, Emerson. What did you say?"

With a shrug and a smile Emerson turned and answered, not the question but the underlying emotion that had prompted it and my other (I admit) unfair accusations. A soft answer turneth away wrath, as the Scripture says, but Emerson's methods were even more efficacious.

I had hoped to spend the rest of the week in Cairo enjoying the amenities of the hotel, but Emerson suddenly took it into his head to visit Meidum. I had no objection, though I wished he had given me a little more notice.

We had spent the morning in the sûk; after lunching

at the hotel, Emerson left me reading and resting while he went off on some errand of his own. Upon his return he calmly announced we would take the evening train. "So hurry up and get your gear together, Peabody."

I dropped my copy of Erman's *Ägyptische Grammatik*. "What gear? There is no hotel at Rikka."

Emerson began, "I have a friend—"

"I will not stay with any of your Egyptian friends. They are delightful people, but they have no notion of sanitation."

"I thought you might feel that way. I have prepared a little surprise for you, Peabody. What has happened to your sense of adventure?"

I was unable to resist the challenge, or Emerson's smile. As I packed a small bag with changes of clothing and toilet articles, my spirits began to soar. This was like the old days—Emerson and I, alone together in the wilderness!

Once we had fought our way through the confusion at the railroad station and found seats on the train, Emerson relaxed, but none of my attempts at conversation seemed to please him.

"I hope that poor fellow who collapsed in the sûk will be all right," was my first attempt. "You should have let me examine him, Emerson."

"His—er—friends were there to attend to him," Emerson said shortly.

After a while I tried again. "*Our* friends will be surprised to find we have gone! It was good of so many of them to come round this morning to express their concern."

Emerson grunted.

"I am inclined to believe Mr. Neville's theory was the right one," I went on. "How amusingly he put it: 'Some young fellow flushed with wine and inspired by your charms, Mrs. E., playing a silly trick.'"

"And my charms inspired the attentions of the three young fellows in the garden," said Emerson, with ineffable sarcasm.

"The timing of the two events may have been pure coincidence."

"Pure balderdash," growled Emerson. "Peabody, why do you insist on discussing our private affairs in public?"

The only other occupants of the carriage were a group of German university students, who were carrying on a loud conversation in their own language; but I took the hint.

By the time we reached Rikka my enthusiasm had dimmed somewhat. Darkness was complete, and we were the only non-Egyptians to disembark there. I stumbled over a stone and Emerson, whose spirits had improved in inverse ratio to the lowering of mine, caught my arm. "There he is. Hi, Abdullah!"

"I should have known," I muttered, seeing the white shape that hovered, ghostlike, at the end of the small platform.

"Quite," said Emerson cheerfully. "We can always count on good old Abdullah, eh? I sent a message to him this afternoon."

After the appropriate greetings had been exchanged, not only with Abdullah but with his sons Feisal and Selim and his nephew Daoud, we mounted the donkeys they had waiting and set out. How the devil the donkeys saw where they were going I do not know; I certainly could not, even after the moon rose, for it was on the wane and gave little light. The gait of some donkeys is very uneasy when they break into a trot. I got the distinct impression these donkeys did not like being out at that hour.

After a hideously uncomfortable ride across the cultivated fields I saw the light of a fire ahead on the edge of the desert. Two more of our men were waiting for us. The little camp they had set up was better than Abdullah's usual efforts along those lines; I was relieved to see that there was a proper tent for us, and the welcome aroma of fresh-brewed coffee reached my nostrils.

Emerson lifted me off my donkey. "Do you remember I once threatened to snatch you up and carry you off into the desert?"

I looked from Abdullah to Feisal to Daoud to Selim to Mahmud to Ali to Mohammed. They stood round us in an interested circle, their faces beaming. "You are such a romantic, Emerson," I said.

However, when I emerged from the tent the following morning I was in a better humor, and the scene before me roused the old thrill of archaeological fever.

Meidum is one of the most attractive sites in Egypt. The remains of the cemetery are situated on the edge of the low bluff that marks the beginning of the desert; toward the east the emerald carpet of the cultivated land stretched out toward the river, whose waters were stained rosy pink by the rays of the rising sun. On the bluff, rising high against the sky, was the pyramid, though I must confess it does not look much like one. The Egyptians call it El Haram el-Kaddâb, "The False Pyramid," for it more resembles a square tower of three diminishing stages. Once there were seven stages, like those of a step pyramid. The angles between them had been filled in with stone to give a smooth slope, but these filling stones and the upper stages had long since collapsed, forming a frame of detritus all around the giant tomb.

Like the pyramids of Dahshoor and Giza, it was uninscribed. I have never understood why the kings who went to so much trouble to erect these grandiose structures did not bother to put their names on them, for humility was not a notable characteristic of Egyptian pharaohs. It is also uncharacteristic of tourists, ancient or modern. As soon as the great art of writing was invented, certain individuals made use of it to deface monuments and works of art. Three thousand years before our time, an Egyptian tourist came to Meidum to visit the "beautiful temple of King Snefru," and left an inscription, or graffito, to that effect on one of the walls of the temple. Snefru was known to have had two such tombs; we had worked at one of them, the north pyramid of Dahshoor. Petrie, who had discovered the graffito in question, decided that this must be Snefru's second pyramid.

"Bah," said Emerson. "One graffito does not constitute proof of ownership. The temple was already a thousand years old when the confounded scribbler visited it; the guides of that remote era were probably as ignorant as those of the present day. Snefru's two pyramids are the ones at Dahshoor."

When Emerson speaks in that dogmatic tone, few care to contradict him. I am one of those few; but since I agreed with his views I did not do so on that occasion.

For the next two days we busied ourselves with
the private tombs. There were several groups of them
north, south and west of the pyramid—for the cultivated land eastward was of course unsuitable for tombs.
We had ample help. I had never really expected to be
alone with Emerson; the presence of strangers always
attracts local villagers demanding baksheesh or asking for work or simply satisfying their curiosity. They
began wandering in while we were at breakfast the first
day, and after interviewing them Emerson set some to
work under Abdullah's direction.

I always say that if one cannot have a pyramid, a
nice deep tomb is the next best thing. All the pyramids had cemeteries around them—tombs of courtiers
and princes, nobles and high officials, who were given
the privilege of spending eternity in proximity to the
god-king they had served in life. These Old Kingdom
tombs were called mastabas because the superstructure
resembled the flat-topped, sloping-sided benches found
outside modern Egyptian houses. The superstructures,
built of stone or mud-brick, had often disappeared or
collapsed into shapeless mounds; but they were not
the parts that interested me. Under the mastabas were
shafts and stairs descending deep into the rock beneath
and culminating in the burial chamber. Some of the
richer tombs had substructures almost as delightfully
dark, tortuous and bat-ridden as those of the pyramids.

Emerson very kindly allowed me to go into one such
tomb (because he knew I would do it anyway). The
steeply sloping entrance ramp was littered with debris
and only four feet high. It ended in a shaft, which I was
obliged to descend by means of a rope held by Selim,

who, at Emerson's insistence, had followed me down. I usually employed Selim for such work, since he was the youngest and slimmest of the trained men; one was always encountering holes through which a larger body could not easily pass, and of course the low ceilings presented a difficulty for taller individuals. Emerson was not particularly fond of tombs like these; he kept banging his head and getting stuck in holes.

But I must not allow my enthusiasm to lead me to a more detailed description, which might bore my duller readers and which is not really relevant to the tale I am telling. Suffice it to say that when I emerged, gasping for breath (the air in the lowest portions of such tombs is extremely hot and very close) and covered with a sort of paste compounded of perspiration, stone dust, and bat droppings, I could hardly contain my appreciation.

"It was delightful, Emerson! To be sure, the wall paintings are of poor quality, but I saw scraps of wood and linen wrappings among the debris in the burial chamber. I am sure we ought—"

Emerson had been waiting at the entrance to pull me out. Having done so, he hastily backed away, wrinkling his nose.

"Not now, Peabody. This was intended to be a survey; we haven't the manpower or the time to excavate. Why don't you amuse yourself with the pyramid?"

So I did. It was quite a nice pyramid in its own way, though the passageways were not so extensive or interesting as the ones in the Giza and Dahshoor monuments. Like them, it had been opened by earlier explorers who found it had been completely looted in antiquity.

On the afternoon of the second day came a further addition to what had now become something of a small mob—a pair of what Emerson refers to as cursed tourists. He unbent a trifle, however, when one of them introduced himself as Herr Eberfelt, a German scholar with whom Emerson had corresponded. He was a virtual caricature of a Prussian, monocled, stiff as a board, and very formal in his manner. Herr Schmidt, the young fellow with him, was one of his students—a plump, pleasant chap who would have been quite handsome had it not been for the ugly dueling scar that disfigured one cheek. German students take great pride in these scars, which they consider evidences of courage rather than of stupidity, which in fact they are. I am told the students even employ various painful and unsanitary methods of preventing the wounds from healing so that the scars will be as conspicuous as possible.

Herr Schmidt's manners were as faultless as his face was not. He addressed me in broken but delightful English and appeared more than ready to accept the cup of tea I offered. However, Emerson insisted on showing them around the site and the young man obediently followed his superior.

I had finished my tea and was about to go after them when one of the workmen sidled up, glancing shyly at me from under his thick lashes. Like the other men, he had stripped off his robe while working and was attired only in a wrapped loincloth. His sleek, smooth body shone with perspiration.

"I have found a tomb, honored Sitt," he whispered. "Will you come, before the others find it and claim a share of the baksheesh?"

I looked around. Emerson must have taken the visitors into the pyramid; they were nowhere in sight. Daoud was directing a group of workers who were investigating the tombs next to the causeway that led from the pyramid to the river.

"Where is it?" I asked.

"Not far, honored Sitt. Near the Tomb of the Geese."

He was referring to one of the most famous tombs of Meidum, from which had come the lovely painting now in the Cairo Museum. It was located in the mastaba field almost due north of the pyramid. A crew under Abdullah was at work in the area, searching for other tomb entrances; this man must be part of that crew. His surreptitious manner and look of suppressed excitement suggested that he had come on something remarkable enough to merit a sizable reward. Naturally he did not want to share it with the others.

Anticipation thrilled through my limbs as I pictured marvels equaling the geese, or even the life-sized painted statues of a noble couple that had been found in another mastaba in the same cemetery. Rising, I gestured to him to lead on.

The guttural chanting of Daoud's crew gradually faded as we scrambled over the fallen rocks and rough ground at the base of the pyramid. We were close to the northeast corner of the structure when my guide stopped. He held out his hand. "Sitt," he began.

"No," I said in Arabic. "No baksheesh until you have shown me the tomb."

He took a step toward me, smiling as sweetly as a shy maiden.

Then I heard a sound like the sharp crack of a whip. A rolling rumble of falling stone followed, as a rain of rocks and pebbles struck the ground behind me. My guide took to his heels. I could hardly blame him. Looking up in some annoyance, I saw a round, alarmed face peering down from the top of the slope, which was almost fifty feet above me at that point.

"*Ach, Himmel, Frau Professor—verzeihen Sie, bitte!* I did not see you. Are you damaged? Are you fainting with fear?"

He came scrambling down the slope as he spoke, waving his arms to keep his balance, and starting another miniature avalanche.

"Neither," I replied. "No thanks to you, Herr Schmidt. What the dev——That is, what were you shooting at? For pity's sake, put your revolver away before you drill a hole through me or yourself."

Coloring, the young man returned his weapon to its holster. "It was *eine Gazelle*—a... How do you call it?"

"Nonsense. It could not have been a gazelle, they are timid creatures who would not venture so close to humans. You tried to shoot some poor villager's goat, Herr Schmidt. Luckily for you, you missed it; the world's finest marksman could not hit such a distant target with a pistol."

My lecture was interrupted by Emerson, who came rushing toward us demanding to know who had shot at what and why. My explanation did nothing to relieve his tender anxiety; turning to his German colleague, who had been close on his heels, he burst into a storm of complaint.

"*Sie haben recht, Herr Professor,*" Schmidt murmured submissively. "*Ich bin ein vollendetes Rindvieh.*"

"You are making a great fuss about nothing, Emerson," I said. "The bullet came nowhere near me."

"In short, no harm was done or intended," said Professor Eberfelt, coming to the defense of his colleague.

"Except that my guide was frightened away," I added. "Let us see if we can find him and reassure him. He had found a new tomb which he was about to show me."

But neither the guide nor the tomb he had mentioned was to be found, though we searched for some time. "Perhaps he will return tomorrow, once he has got over his fright," I said at last. "He was young, and appeared to be very timid."

Our visitors did not linger; the boat they had hired awaited them, and they meant to return to Cairo that night. Watching the donkeys disappear into the darkening shadows of the east, Emerson stroked his chin, as was his habit when deep in thought.

"I think we have done enough here, Peabody," he said. "The Luxor-Cairo train stops at Rikka in the morning. Shall we be on it?"

I could see no reason why not.

My first act upon reaching the hotel was to request the safragi to run a nice hot bath for me. As I luxuriated in the scented water Emerson looked through the letters and messages that had arrived in our absence and reported their contents to me, with appropriate comments. "Will we dine with Lady Wallingford and her daughter? No, we will not. Captain and Mrs. Richardson look forward to the pleasure of our company at their soiree...They will look in vain. Mr. Vincey hopes we will do him the honor of lunching with him on Thursday...It is an honor he has not earned. The Solicitor General...Aha! A grain of wheat among all this chaff! A letter from Chalfont."

"Open it," I called. A ripping sound told me he had already done so.

The epistle was a sort of round-robin, begun by Evelyn and added to by the others. Evelyn's and Walter's contributions were short, intended only to reassure us that all was well with them and their charges. Nefret's brief message was something of a disappointment to me; it sounded like a duty note from a child to a relation she does not much like. I reminded myself that I ought not to have expected anything else. She had been taught to read and write English by her father, but she had not had much occasion to practice that skill. It would be some time before she learned to express herself gracefully and at length.

Ramses's contribution made up for any deficiency in the latter quality at least. I could see why he had asked to be the last to write, for his comments were, to say the least, more candid than those of his aunt.

"Rose does not like it here. She does not say that, but her mouth always looks as if she has been eating pickled onions. I think the difficulty is that she does not get on with Ellis. Ellis is Aunt Evelyn's new maid. She came from the gutter, like the others."

Emerson stopped to laugh, and I exclaimed, "Good heavens, where does that child pick up such language? Out of the goodness of her heart Evelyn employs unfortunate young women whose lives have not been what they ought, but—"

"The description gains in pungency what it lacks in propriety," said Emerson. "He goes on:

"Rose says she does not hold this against Ellis. I certainly would not, though I am not precisely certain what the term implies. But I do not get on with Ellis either. She is always following Nefret trying to get her to change her clothing and curl her hair.

"Wilkins [our former butler, now employed by Evelyn and Walter] *has not been well since we arrived. He seems very nervous. The least little thing makes him start. When I let the lion out of its cage yesterday..."*

My body lost its purchase on the surface of the tub and my head went under water. When I emerged, sputtering and choking, I found that Emerson had continued reading.

"...no danger, since as you know I had been acquainted with the lion since it was a cub and had taken pains to renew the acquaintance whenever possible. Uncle Walter was not nervous but his remarks were pejorative in the extreme and he set me an additional ten pages of Caesar to construe. He added that he was sorry I was too old to spank. He has agreed to build a larger cage for the lion."

I will spare my Reader Ramses's detailed descriptions of the health and habits of the other servants

(I had not been aware of the cook's fondness for gin, nor, I imagine, had Evelyn). He saved HER for last.

> *"She has improved in health and spirits since we came here, I believe, though in my opinion [As I later discovered, Ramses had scratched the last three words out, but Emerson read them anyhow] she spends too much time at her studies. I have come round to your view that mens sana in corpore sano is a good rule, and have adopted it myself. Toward that end I determined to take up the sport of archery. It is a sport in which young ladies are encouraged to participate. Aunt Evelyn agreed with me and Uncle Walter, who can be obliging when he chooses, set up the butts for us. I discovered that Nefret is already acquainted with that sport. She has agreed to instruct me. In return I am teaching her to ride and to fence."*

"He doesn't know how to fence," I exclaimed indignantly.

"Er," said Emerson.

I decided not to pursue the subject. I had suspected Emerson was taking fencing lessons on the sly, but he never likes admitting he needs instruction in anything, and his original motive for taking up this sport was not to his credit, for it arose out of jealousy of an individual concerning whom he had not the slightest cause to feel that emotion. I had to admit his skill had proved useful on several occasions thereafter, though. Apparently he had allowed Ramses to be instructed as well. He knew I would not have approved; the idea of Ramses's wielding a long, flexible, sharp instrument made my blood run cold.

Two more paragraphs described Nefret's activities in far more detail than they merited. After Emerson had finished he remarked, in tones fatuous with parental pride, "How well he writes. Quite literary, upon my word."

"It sounds as if things are going well," I replied. "Hand me that towel, Emerson, will you please?"

Emerson handed me the towel. He then returned to the sitting room to peruse the remainder of the post.

"Well, where next?" Emerson inquired, as we sat down to dinner that evening. "Luxor or Amarna?"

"Have you eliminated Meidum?"

"No, not at all. But I feel we ought to look at the other possibilities before we make a decision."

"Very well."

"What is your preference?"

"It is a matter of complete indifference to me."

Emerson peered at me over the top of the ornate menu the waiter had handed him. "Are you annoyed about something, Peabody? Ramses's letter, perhaps? You have scarcely spoken to me since I read it."

"What possible cause for annoyance could I have?"

"I can think of none." He waited for a moment. When I did not respond he shrugged—one of those irritating masculine shrugs that dismisses a woman's behavior as incomprehensible and/or irrelevant—and resumed the discussion. "I suggest we go direct to Luxor, then. I am rather impatient to rid myself of certain objects as promptly as I can."

"That makes sense," I agreed. "Have you any ideas as to where we might—er—discover them?"

We discussed alternatives while we ate. It was still early when we finished, and I suggested a stroll along the Muski.

"We are not going out this evening," Emerson replied. "I have something else in mind I hope will please you."

It did. But when Emerson had settled into his usual sleeping position—flat on his back, arms folded across his breast like a statue of Osiris—I could not help remembering an occasion when the sight of me rising from the bath had prompted comparisons with Aphrodite. This afternoon he had simply handed me a towel.

The only invitation Emerson had not thrown away was one from Mr. George McKenzie. He was one of those eccentric individuals more common in the old days of archaeology than they are today: gifted amateurs who had excavated and studied Egyptology without the restrictions of government regulation. Some of them had done admirable work despite their lack of formal training, and McKenzie's massive three-volume work on ancient Egyptian culture was an invaluable source, for many of the reliefs and inscriptions he had copied in the 1850s had vanished forever. He was a very old man now, and seldom gave or accepted invitations. Even Emerson admitted this was a most flattering attention and an opportunity we ought not miss.

He refused to wear evening dress, but he looked very handsome in his frock coat and matching trousers. I wore my second-best gown of silver brocade woven with red roses and trimmed with silver lace at the bosom and the cuffs of the elbow-length net sleeves. I hope I may not be accused of vanity when I say that all eyes turned toward us as we crossed the terrace toward the waiting carriage. A brilliant sunset blazoned the western sky; the domes and minarets of old Cairo swam in a dreaming haze.

Old Cairo was our destination—the medieval city with the beautiful four-story houses and palaces from which the cruel Mamluk warriors had tyrannized over the city. Many dwellings had fallen into disrepair and were now inhabited by the poorer classes, whole families to a room; the elaborately carved latticework which had concealed the beauties of the harîm from envious eyes had been stripped away, and the laundered gala-beeyahs of the humble dropped disconsolately from the decayed screens of mashrabiyya alcoves. McKenzie's house had belonged, it was said, to Sultan Kait Bey himself, and its architectural features were well preserved. I quite looked forward to seeing it.

There are no street signs or house numbers in old Cairo. Finally the driver stopped his horses and admitted what I had suspected for some time, to wit, that he had no idea where he was going. When Emerson indicated a street, or rather an opening between two houses just ahead, the driver declared he could not go there. He knew that street; it narrowed even farther as it proceeded, and there would be no place in which to turn the horses.

"Wait for us here, then," Emerson said. As he helped me down from the carriage, he was unable to resist remarking, "I told you not to wear that frock, Peabody.

I thought it likely we would have to go partway on foot."

"Then why didn't you say so?" I demanded, hitching up my skirts. "You have been here before, haven't you?"

"Some years ago." Emerson offered me his arm and we started off. "Down this way, I think. McKenzie sent directions, but they were not…Ah, yes, here is the sabil he mentioned. First turning to the left."

We had not gone far when the passage narrowed even more, till there was scarcely room to walk abreast. It was like proceeding through a tunnel, for the high, secretive facades of the old houses rose sheer on either side and their jutting balconies almost met overhead. I said uneasily, "This cannot be right, Emerson. It is very dark and nasty here, and I haven't seen a soul since we left the fountain. Mr. McKenzie would not live in such a slum, surely."

"There are no architectural class distinctions here; the mansions of the wealthy adjoin the tenements of the poor." But Emerson's voice reflected my own doubts. He stopped. "Let us go back. There was a coffee shop near the sabil, we will ask directions there."

It was too late. The narrow way was lighted only by a lantern some considerate householder had hung over a door a few feet behind us, but it cast sufficient light to allow us to see, in the shadows beyond, the hulking forms of several men. Their turbans showed pale in the darkness.

"Damnation," said Emerson calmly. "Get behind me, Peabody."

"Back to back," I agreed, taking up that position. "Curse it, why did I come out without my belt of tools?"

"Try the door there," Emerson said.

"Locked. There are other men ahead," I added. "At least two. And this is only a flimsy evening parasol, made to match my gown, not the one I usually carry."

"Good Gad," Emerson exclaimed. "Without your parasol we dare not face them in the open street. A strategic retreat would seem to be in order." With a sudden movement he whirled and kicked out at the door I had tried. The lock gave with a crack, the door swung back; seizing me around the waist, Emerson thrust me within.

Squeals and flutters greeted my abrupt appearance. The two men who had occupied the room fled, leaving the narghila they had shared bubbling gently. Emerson followed me and slammed the door. "It won't hold them for long," he remarked. "The lock is broken and there is no piece of furniture heavy enough to serve as a barricade."

"There is surely another way out." I indicated the curtained doorway through which the men had gone.

"We will investigate that if we must." Emerson leaned against the door, his shoulders braced. "I don't fancy more dark alleys, though, and I would rather not rely on the kindness of strangers—especially the sort of strangers that inhabit a warren like this. Let us consider other options, now that we have achieved a momentary—"

He broke off as a sound from without reached us through the flimsy panels of the door. I started, and Emerson swore. "That was a woman's scream—or worse, that of a child."

I flung myself at him. "No, Emerson! Don't go out there. It may be a trick."

The cry came again—high, shrill, quavering. It rose to a falsetto shriek and broke off. Emerson tried to loosen my grip; I struggled to hold on, throwing my full weight against his.

"It is a ruse, I tell you! They know you, they know your chivalrous nature! Fearing to attack, they hope to lure you out of sanctuary. This is no simple attempt at robbery; we were deliberately led astray."

My speech was not so measured, for Emerson's hands had closed bruisingly over mine, and he was employing considerable force to free himself. It was not until a cry of pain burst from my lips that he desisted.

"The damage is done, whatever it was," he said breathlessly. "She is silent now... I am sorry, Peabody, if I hurt you."

His taut muscles had relaxed. I leaned against him, trying to control my own ragged breathing. My wrists felt as if they had been squeezed in a vise, but I was conscious of an odd, irrational thrill. "Never mind, my dear. I know you didn't mean to."

The silence without did not endure. The voice that broke it was the last I expected to hear—bold, unafraid, official—the voice of a man giving crisp orders in faulty Arabic.

"Another ruse," I exclaimed.

"I think not," said Emerson, listening. "That chap must be English; no Egyptian speaks his own language so badly. Have I your permission to open the door a crack, Peabody?"

He was being sarcastic. Since I knew he would do it anyway, I agreed.

By comparison to the darkness that had prevailed

earlier, the street was now brightly lit by lanterns and torches carried by men whose neat uniforms made their identity plain. One of them came toward us. Emerson had been correct; his ruddy complexion proclaimed his nationality just as his erect carriage and luxuriant mustache betrayed his military training.

"Was it you who screamed, madame?" he inquired, politely removing his cap. "I trust you and this gentleman are unharmed."

"I did not scream; but thanks to you and your men we are quite unharmed."

"Hmph," said Emerson. "What are you doing in this part of the city, Captain?"

"It is my duty, sir," was the stiff reply. "I am serving as an adviser to the Cairo police force. I might with better cause ask the same question of you."

Emerson replied that we were paying a social call. The incredulity this answer provoked was expressed, not in speech, but in the young man's pursed lips and raised eyebrows. Obviously he did not know who we were.

He offered to escort us back to our carriage. "Not necessary," said Emerson. "You seem to have cleared the way very neatly, sir. Not even a fallen body in sight. Did they all get away from you?"

"We did not pursue them," was the haughty reply. "The prisons are overflowing with such riffraff and we had nothing to charge them with."

"Screaming in public," Emerson suggested.

The fellow had a sense of humor after all; his lips twitched, but he replied sedately, "It must have been one of them who cried out, if the lady did not. They did not attack you, then?"

"We cannot charge them with anything," I admitted. "In fact, you could arrest us, Captain; we forced entry into this house and broke the door."

The officer smiled politely. Emerson took a handful of money from his pocket and tossed it onto the table. "That should take care of any complaints about the broken door. Come along, my dear, we are late for our appointment."

We had taken the wrong turning at the fountain. The proprietor of the coffee shop knew Mr. McKenzie's house very well; it was only a short distance away. But somehow I was not surprised when his servant informed us that he was not expecting guests that evening. In fact, he had already retired. He was, the servant said reproachfully, a very elderly man.

CHAPTER 5

"Men are frail creatures, it is true; one does not expect them to demonstrate the steadfastness of women."

N ot so cursed elderly he had forgotten where he lives," Emerson remarked. "The directions are clear. Left at the sabil."

He tossed the crumpled paper onto the breakfast table. It fell into the cream jug; by the time I had fished it out, the writing was so blurred as to be indecipherable.

"I will take your word for it," I said, putting the soggy wad onto a clean saucer. "Nor will I claim that even a young man might suffer a momentary lapse of memory or an inadvertent slip of the pen. The fact that the wrong turning led us into an ambush is proof positive that the misdirection was intentional. Have you ever done anything to offend Mr. McKenzie?"

"I presume," said my husband, distorting his handsome face into a hideous scowl, "that you are attempting to be facetious, Amelia. The invitation did not come from McKenzie."

He had not answered the question. It was a safe assumption that at some time or other he had offended Mr. McKenzie, because there were few people he had not offended. The reaction seemed somewhat extreme, however.

"How do you know it did not come from him?"

"I don't," Emerson admitted. "I sent round this morning to inquire, but the messenger has not yet returned."

"He will deny it in any case."

"True." Emerson brooded like a pensive sphinx over the muffin he was buttering. "There are some curious stories about McKenzie. His age and the passage of time have given him an air of respectability he did not always deserve. In his youth he swaggered around in Turkish costume—silken robes and a huge turban—and by all accounts behaved like a Turk in—er—other ways."

I knew he was referring to women. Emerson is absurdly shy about such matters—with me, at any rate. I had some reason to suspect he was not so reticent with other men, or with *some* women.

"Did he keep a harîm?" I inquired curiously.

"Oh, well." Emerson looked uncomfortable. "It was not uncommon at that time for wild young men encountering a strange culture to adopt some of its customs. Early archaeologists were no more scrupulous about the monuments than they were about—er—other things. McKenzie's private collection of antiquities is said to be—"

"He never married, I believe," I mused. "Perhaps it was not women he favored. There is one Turkish custom—"

"Good Gad, Peabody!" Emerson shouted, crimsoning. "A well-bred woman has no business knowing about such things, much less talking of them. I was speaking of McKenzie's collection."

But I was not to hear of Mr. McKenzie's collection at that time. The safragi entered to announce a visitor.

Mr. Vincey and his cat came in together, the great brindled feline leashed and walking beside his master like...I was about to say a well-trained dog, but there was nothing of canine subservience in the cat's manner; it was rather as if he had trained Mr. Vincey to take him for a walk instead of the reverse.

I offered Mr. Vincey coffee, which he accepted, but when I poured a little cream into a saucer for Anubis he sniffed it and then gave me a contemptuous look before sitting down at Vincey's feet and curling his tail around his haunches. Mr. Vincey apologized at quite excessive length for his pet's rudeness.

"Cats are never rude," I said. "They act according to their natures, with a candor humans might well emulate. Many grown cats don't care for milk."

"This one certainly has the air of a carnivore," added Emerson. He is more courteous to cats than to people; he went on, "Well, Vincey, what can we do for you? We were about to go out."

Mr. Vincey explained that he had called to inquire whether I had fully recovered from my unfortunate adventure. I was about to reply when a fit of coughing and a pointed stare from Emerson reminded me that Vincey must be referring to the affair of the masked ball, for our most recent experience could not be known to him. I assured him I was in perfect health and spirits. Emerson began to fidget, and after a few more courteous exchanges Mr. Vincey took the hint. It was not until he rose and picked up the leash that I realized the cat was not attached to the other end of it. The collar dangled empty.

With an exclamation of amused chagrin Mr. Vincey surveyed the room. "Now where has he got to? He seems determined to embarrass me with you, Mrs. Emerson; I assure you he has never done this before. If you will forgive me . . ." Puckering his lips, he let out a shrill, sweet whistle.

The cat promptly emerged from under the breakfast table. Avoiding Vincey's outstretched hand, it jumped onto my lap, where it settled down and began to purr. It was clear that efforts to remove it without damage to my skirt would be in vain, for Mr. Vincey's first attempt resulted in a low growl and a delicate but definite insertion of sharp claws. I scratched it behind its ear; releasing its grip, it rolled its head back and let out a reverberant purr.

"The creature demonstrates excellent taste," said Emerson dryly.

"I have never seen him behave this way," Mr. Vincey murmured, staring. "Almost I am emboldened to ask a favor of you."

"We are not adopting any more animals," Emerson declared firmly. He tickled the cat under its chin. It licked his fingers. "Not under any circumstances whatever," Emerson went on. The cat butted its head against his hand.

"Oh, I would never give up my faithful friend," Vincey exclaimed. "But I am about to leave Egypt—

a short journey to Damascus, where a friend of mine has requested my assistance in a personal matter. I have been wondering where to find a temporary home for Anubis. I have not so many friends to impose upon."

There was no self-pity in the last statement, only a manly fortitude. It moved me. Vanity also had some part in my response. The approval of a cat cannot but flatter the recipient.

"We could take charge of Anubis for a few weeks, couldn't we, Emerson? I find I miss the cat Bastet more than I had expected."

"Impossible," Emerson declared. "We are about to leave Cairo. We can't carry a cat to Luxor."

Once the matter was settled, the cat made no further objection to being removed. It was almost as if it had understood and approved the arrangements. Mr. Vincey was leaving the following day; he promised to deliver Anubis next morning. This duly transpired, and that evening Emerson and I and the cat took the overnight train to Luxor.

The cat was no trouble. It sat bolt upright on the seat opposite ours, staring out the window like a polite fellow passenger pretending not to eavesdrop on our conversation. This conversation was not, I am sorry to say, as free of acrimony as it might have been. I admit the fault was mine. I was in an irritable mood. This had nothing to do with my discovery, upon arriving at the station, that Emerson had, unbeknownst to me, invited Abdullah and Daoud to accompany us. Our experienced foreman could be of great assistance, especially at Luxor, where he had been born and in which city he still had hordes of relations. There was no sensible reason why I should resent Abdullah's presence. After they had helped us with our luggage, he and Daoud went off to find their own places.

"I don't understand why you were in such a hurry to get off," I said. "Mr. Vandergelt will be arriving in Cairo in a few days' time; we might have waited and traveled with him."

"You made that point earlier, Peabody. And I replied that I could see no sense in hanging around Cairo for an indefinite period. Vandergelt is a hopeless gad; he will want to attend dinner parties and make eyes at the ladies. Besides, he will travel south on his cursed dahabeeyah."

"It was kind of him to offer us his house while we are in Luxor."

"It costs him nothing."

"How ungracious you are!"

And so on. Nothing of further interest occurred, even after the porter had made up our berths, for the surroundings were not conducive to a display of conjugal affection and Emerson claimed the cat was watching.

"It is on the floor, Emerson. It can't possibly see us—or you it."

"I can *feel* it watching," said Emerson.

However, I woke early to see the kiss of the sunrise summoning a rosy flush to the western cliffs, a sight that never fails to raise my spirits. An exchange of affectionate greetings with my husband (who took the precaution of draping a sheet over the sleeping cat before proceeding) completed the cure. We went directly from the station to the quay and hired a boat to take us and our gear across to the west bank.

Only an individual devoid of imagination and completely deficient in artistic appreciation could fail to be moved by the sight that met my eyes as I sat in the prow with the great sails billowing above and the morning breeze ruffling my hair. On the opposite bank an emerald ribbon of fields and foliage bordered the river; beyond lay the desert, the Red Land of the ancient texts, and beyond that pale and sterile stretch rose the cliffs of the High Desert, through which the Nile had cut its path in prehistoric times. Gradually there appeared out of the mists shapes more visible perhaps to the imagination than the sight: magic castles rising from the foam, as the poet has put it—the ruined but majestic walls of the ancient temples.

(Upon further investigation I find the quotation is not entirely accurate. However, my version better captures the impression I was endeavoring to convey.)

Foremost among the temples, at least in my opinion, were the columned collonades of Deir el Bahri, the mortuary temple of the great female pharaoh Hatshepsut. Not far from it was a more modern structure, invisible to my eyes but only too clear in my memory: Baskerville House, the scene of one of our most extraordinary detective adventures.* It was now a forlorn and abandoned ruin, for the present Lord Baskerville had declined to preserve it; and small wonder, considering the horrible fate his predecessor had met while in residence. He had offered it to Cyrus Vandergelt, but the latter's memories of the ill-fated house were no more pleasant than his. "I wouldn't set foot in the consarned

---

* *The Curse of the Pharaohs*

place for a million dollars," was how Cyrus put it in his quaint American idiom.

Cyrus had built a house of his own near the entrance to the Valley of the Kings. Money was no object to him, and I must say that his home was more notable for extravagance than good taste. It stood on a towering eminence overlooking the Valley; as our carriage approached, Emerson studied the turrets and towers and balconies in disgust, and remarked, "It is a positive monument to extravagance and bad taste. I trust you won't take it as a model, Amelia."

"Mr. Vandergelt was inspired, I expect, by Crusaders' castles. There are a number of them in the Middle East."

"That is no excuse. Well, I suppose I must put up with it."

Personally I did not find it difficult to "put up with" clean comfortable rooms and excellent service. Cyrus kept a skeleton staff always in residence; the caretaker greeted us with the assurance that we were expected, and that our rooms were ready. They were as elegantly appointed as in any modern hotel. Fine Oriental rugs covered the floors. Windows and doors were fitted with netting to keep out insects, and the rooms were kept cool by a method known since the Middle Ages— porous earthenware jars in the mashrabiyya alcoves behind the windows.

After asking when we would like luncheon to be served, the majordomo bowed himself out and I began to strip off my travel-stained garments. Emerson prowled around opening wardrobe doors and investigating cabinets. He gave a grunt of satisfaction. "Vandergelt is no fool, if he is an American. There is a good solid lock on this cupboard. Just what I hoped to find."

From the small travel case he had carried in his own hand from Cairo he took the box containing the scepters and stowed it carefully away, putting the key in his trouser pocket after he had locked the cabinet. I heard the splash of water from the adjoining bathroom; the servants were not done filling the tub, so I wrapped myself in a robe and sat down to wait till they had finished. Cool drinks and an assortment of little cakes had been brought to us; I poured a glass of soda water.

"What a fuss you are making about those scepters! If I had had any idea they would prey on your mind as they seem to I would have suggested we 'discover' them last spring while we were at Napata. That is the most logical place for them to be found, after all."

"Do you suppose I did not consider that? I am not such a fool as you believe."

"Now, Emerson, be calm. I did not mean to imply—"

"Such a discovery at Napata would have drawn every treasure hunter in Africa and aroused the cupidity of the natives. They would have torn the pyramids to bits."

"There isn't much left of them now," I pointed out.

Emerson ignored this. Pacing furiously, hands clasped behind his back, he went on, "There was another consideration. I wanted the 'discovery' to be separated in time from Nefret's reappearance. If these objects are found at Thebes they cannot possibly be connected with Willy Forth's lost city."

I saw the sense of his reasoning and candidly confessed

as much. This put him in a better humor; and, a tap at the door having announced that my bath was ready, I proceeded to take it.

After luncheon we assumed our working attire and set out for the Valley, accompanied by Abdullah and Daoud and the cat. Abdullah was not a particular admirer of cats, and he viewed this one askance. Anubis responded, as cats will, by lavishing attention on poor Abdullah—twining around his ankles, leaping at him out of hiding in kittenish fashion, pretending (I believe he was pretending) to attack the hem of his robe. Abdullah tried several times to kick him (he did it when he thought I was not looking, but I was). Needless to say, his foot never connected.

Though I would have preferred to dispense with Abdullah and Daoud, not to mention the cat, the expedition could not but delight me. To see Emerson in the costume that becomes him best, his waving black locks shining in the sun, his tanned and muscular forearms displayed by the rolled sleeves of his shirt; to walk stride by stride with him, agile in my comfortable trousers; to hear the musical clash of the tools depending from my belt and clasp the sturdy handle of my parasol...Mere words cannot capture the exhilaration of that experience.

Instead of following the tourist road, we set off along a curving track that led northwest. The Valley of the Kings—Biban el Muluk, literally "Gates of the Kings" in Arabic—is not one valley but two. The one most frequently visited is the eastern valley, where the majority of the royal tombs of the Empire are located. It has been popular with tourists and explorers since

Greek times, and in our own time it had become too crowded for comfort, thanks to such enterprising merchants as Mr. Cook, whose steamers brought hundreds of idle visitors to Luxor each season.

It would require more than unsuitably clad, garrulous crowds to rob the eastern valley of its grandeur; but to my mind the western valley is even more impressive. "Valley" is not really an appropriate word, suggesting as it does the green and fertile depression watered by a river or stream. These canyons, or "wadis," as the Arabs call them, are as rocky and bare as the desert itself. We followed a twisting path that led through fantastic rock formations into a cup or bowl, floored with fine white sand and enclosed by rugged limestone cliffs. The only color was that of the blue sky high above; no green growing thing, not even a weed or a blade of grass, refreshed the eye.

Yet there was once water to spare in this arid amphitheater. The wadis were cut through the soft limestone of the cliffs in prehistoric times, when the desert bloomed like the rose and floods cascaded down the Theban hills toward the river. They are still subject to rare but violent flash floods which wash debris down the valleys and into the tombs.

A scorpion scuttled away from my foot; the insect, and a hawk hovering high above, were the only other living creatures in sight, though dark stains, clearly visible against the sun-whitened limestone, marked the nesting places of bats. The rock walls rose steep but not smooth; hundreds, nay thousands, of pockets and crevices, bays and caves turned the cliffs into a ragged fretwork of stone. The silence was absolute, for the sand muted even the sound of footsteps. One had an eerie reluctance to break that silence.

I broke it, but not until after Abdullah and Daoud had gone off to investigate a promising crevice. Neither of them knew our real purpose that day. We had not taken our loyal men with us to Nubia—it would have been impossible to provide transport and supplies for a large group in that troubled region—and they knew no more of our activities the previous winter than was known to the general public. The chances of keeping a secret increase in inverse ratio to the number of people who are acquainted with that secret.

"The place is certainly remote and private enough for our purposes," I said. "But is it a likely spot in which to find Cushite royal scepters?"

"Egyptology is full of unsolved mysteries," Emerson replied sententiously. "We will give our colleagues another, and let them debate endlessly as to how these remarkable objects could have found their way to a crevice in the rock."

"Thieves' loot," I suggested, my imagination fired. "Hidden by an unscrupulous robber who did not want his associates to share in the proceeds, and who was prevented, by accident or arrest, from returning to get them."

"That will be the accepted explanation, no doubt. But where did the thieves find them? I can hear Petrie and Maspero arguing that question for the next twenty years."

His eyes sparkled with enjoyment. I felt he was beginning to enjoy his trick a little too much. "It is a pity we must do this," I said.

Emerson "wiped the grin off his face," as the expressive American phrase has it. "You don't suppose I enjoy it, do you?" He did not give me a chance to reply, but went on, "Truth is impossible in this case, nor does it always suffice to end foolish speculation. Don't forget the mummy in the royal tomb at Amarna. I gave Newberry the facts of that matter the other night, but I don't suppose for a moment that will end speculation. Mark my words, scholarly journals for years to come will repeat the rumor that Akhenaton's mummy was found at Amarna. And furthermore—"

"Yes, my dear," I said soothingly, for I recognized the symptoms of one who doth protest too much. Deceit was anathema to that clear, candid brain, but he was right; what else could he do? "What will be your theory?" I inquired.

"Another cache of royal mummies, my dear Peabody. Two have been located so far, as well as a collection of high priests from the later dynasties. However, we are still deficient in priestesses. Where are the burials of the Gods' Wives of Amon—the Adorers of the God—who ruled in Thebes during the Twenty-Fifth and Twenty-Sixth Dynasties? Several of them were Cushite princesses." Emerson turned, shading his eyes with his hand, and surveyed the cliffs that enclosed the Valley like the splintered, broken sides of a gigantic bowl. "This is not an unlikely location for the original tombs."

"No late tombs have been found here," I objected. "And aren't we postulating a reburial, a group of mummies hidden away after their tombs had been violated by thieves? The other caches were located near Deir el Bahri."

"The other reburials were done in the Twenty-First and Twenty-Second Dynasties," Emerson retorted. "The Cushites didn't turn up until much later. What do you keep raising objections for? We've got to do something with the cursed things, and unless you can suggest a better alternative..."

In such stimulating if morally questionable debate we passed the next hours, inspecting the contours of the base of the cliffs, scrambling over rocky slopes. The heat was intense, and we consumed quantities of the cold tea Daoud carried with him. Anubis refused even the water we had also brought, but managed to knock Abdullah's cup out of his hand and deluge his skirts with tea. The cat went off after that to explore on his own, or, more likely, to hunt.

Emerson had brought along copies of the plans of the Valley made by earlier scholars. He enjoyed himself very much finding errors in them. Abdullah and Daoud searched for signs of unknown tombs. Like most treasure hunts, it was both endlessly enticing and relatively hopeless, for the rock was as riddled with holes as a sieve. Some individuals have, or develop, a seemingly uncanny instinct for such things; Belzoni, the flamboyant Italian strongman who had been one of the first to work in the Valley of the Kings, had an extraordinary talent for locating hidden tomb entrances. He had been a hydraulics engineer and was one of the first to realize that the floods, which were more common in his day than now, could leave evidence of subsidence and displacement. Abdullah and Daoud were not engineers, but they were descendants of the master tomb robbers of Gurnah, who have located more tombs than all archaeologists combined. Any hollow among the rocks might indicate a tomb entrance—or it might indicate only a natural hollow. We probed several such hollows and investigated a heap of stones like the one Belzoni had mentioned in his description of the discovery of the tomb of King Ay, in this very valley—all without result, which was what we had expected.

"Shall we have another look at Ay's tomb?" Emerson asked, indicating the opening that gaped forlornly above.

"The sight would only depress me. It was in wretched condition last time we visited it, and I am sure it has deteriorated even more. But that can be said of every tomb and every monument in Egypt. It is difficult to decide where to concentrate our efforts, there is so much to be done."

Not until sunset stretched glowing fingers across the sky did we turn our steps back toward the house. (It rejoiced, I must add, in the resounding name of "House of the Doors of the Kings," but this appellation appeared only on Cyrus's notepaper. Europeans referred to it as "Vandergelt's place," and Egyptians as "The Castle of the Amerikâni.")

The main valley was deserted; tourists and guides had left for the landing where boats would carry them across to their hotels on the east bank. Shadows thickened. Emerson quickened his pace. I heard a rattle of pebbles, and a strangled Arabic oath from Abdullah, trotting behind us; it included the word for "cat," so I deduced that Anubis had caused him to stumble. The animal's tawny-gray fur blended so well with the twilight that he was almost invisible.

He must have gone ahead after that, for he was waiting for us on the doorstep. "You see," I exclaimed. "My method was effective after all."

"Hmph," said Emerson. He had jeered at me when I rubbed the cat's paws with butter during luncheon in the time-honored and traditional method of training it to stay in a new home. He had also pointed out that Vandergelt might not thank us if we turned Anubis into a permanent resident. I replied that we would deal with that difficulty when and if it arose.

I had requested that dinner be served early, since I hoped to persuade Emerson into a moonlit stroll—without Abdullah and Daoud. However, when I proposed it he declined. We retired to the library, therefore—Vandergelt had one of the finest collections of Egyptological works in the country—and Emerson took out his pipe.

"Peabody," he said. "Will you come here?"

He had seated himself on the sofa, a large structure in the Turkish style, with a quantity of soft pillows. I had chosen a straight-backed chair and taken up a book.

"No, thank you, Emerson, I prefer this chair."

Emerson rose. Picking up the chair, with me in it, he carried it to the end of the sofa and set it down with a thud. "I bow to your wishes, my dear Peabody."

"Oh, Emerson," I began; and then, as he loomed over me, fists on his hips and lips curving, I could not but smile. I got up and took my place on the sofa.

"That is better," said Emerson, joining me and putting his arm around my shoulders. "Much more friendly. Besides, I don't want to be overheard."

The cat jumped up onto the other end of the sofa

and sat down. Its wide green eyes regarded us unwinkingly. "Anubis is listening," I said.

"Be serious, Peabody. I want you to promise me something. I do not order you, I ask you."

"Certainly, my dear Emerson. What is it?"

"Give me your solemn word that you will not go wandering around the cliffs, or anywhere else, alone. If you receive a message asking for your help, or offering to show you where a valuable antiquity is hidden—"

"Why, Emerson, you make me sound like some silly Gothic heroine instead of the sensible, rational woman you know me to be. When have I ever done such a thing?"

Emerson's lips parted and indignation furrowed his noble brow; but experience had taught him that contradicting my statements led only to further argument, not to the agreement he wanted. "Let me put it this way. You have an unnerving self-confidence, Peabody; when armed with your parasol you consider yourself capable of defeating any number of adversaries. Have I your word?"

"If you will give me yours, to the same effect." Emerson's brows drew together. I went on, "You have an unnerving self-confidence, Emerson; you consider yourself capable—"

Laughing, Emerson stopped my speech in a manner I find particularly pleasant. It was a rather short embrace, however; the unwinking stare of the cat seemed to disturb him, for he glanced uneasily at it before speaking again.

"The cases are hardly the same, Peabody, but I am willing to take some precautions. I hope you do not suppose I declined your invitation to walk in the moonlight because the idea was unpleasant to me? No. We are not going out at night until this matter is settled."

"What matter?"

"Oh, come, Peabody. You are usually the first to find ominous portents and harbingers of disaster in the accidents that befall us. At the time we first discussed the situation, the evidence was inconclusive; but it is beginning to mount up. The search of our room, three attempts at assault or abduction in less than a week—"

"Three? I can only think of two."

Emerson removed his arm and leaned forward, reaching for his pipe. "The incident at Meidum had certain interesting features."

At first I could not think what he meant. Then I laughed. "That foolish young German shooting at a gazelle? I told you, Emerson, the bullet came nowhere near me. Consider, as well, that only a madman would try to murder me in broad daylight with witnesses all around. Success would have been tantamount to suicide for the killer; that hasty temper of yours would have moved you to exact retribution on the spot. Oh, it is too absurd."

"I am rather inclined to regard the young man as a guardian angel," Emerson said slowly. "What became of the workman who promised you an unknown tomb, Peabody? We never saw him again."

"He was frightened."

"Bah. It seems to be you, my dear, these unknown individuals are after."

"The three men who attacked you in the garden—"

"I told you, they were uncommonly gentle," Emerson said impatiently. "That attack may have been designed to make sure I was out of the way when my double made off with you. There must be some underlying motive for all these events, and I can't think of anything we have done recently to inspire the interest of the criminal element—except find Willy Forth's lost city of gold."

"Surely you are jumping to unwarranted conclusions, Emerson. You or I might be able to weave together vague hints and scattered clues, and arrive at the correct conclusion: that Willoughby Forth's fantasies were true, and that we had located his treasure hoard. But who else is capable of such brilliant reasoning?"

Slowly Emerson's head turned, exactly as Bastet's head turns when she is planning to jump on some unconscious victim. He looked straight into my eyes.

"No, Emerson," I exclaimed. "It cannot be. We have not seen or heard from him for years."

"Only a man," said Emerson, "who has far-flung sources of information covering the world—like a spider's web, I believe you once said; who is familiar with the world of archaeology, its practitioners, its history and its legends; who has good cause to hate one of us and even better cause to—"

"My abductor was not the Master Criminal, Emerson. I could hardly be mistaken; after all, I was in intimate if unwilling proximity to the fellow for quite some time."*

It was not, I admit, the most tactful thing I could have said. Emerson's response consisted of a string of

* *Lion in the Valley*

expletives, including several that were unfamiliar to me. It took me considerable time and effort to calm him. My efforts succeeded so well that I was forced to remind him, after an interval, that the windows were uncurtained and that the servants had not gone to bed.

"Let us set them an example, then," said Emerson, drawing me to my feet. As we proceeded up the stairs he said thoughtfully, "Perhaps you are right, Peabody. I am still inclined to see the dread hand—another of your literary phrases, is it not?—the dread hand of Sethos everywhere. I may be mistaken as to the identity of our opponent, but my theory as to the motive behind these attentions is unshaken. It would take an archaeologist or a keen student of archaeology to put those clues together."

"I am sure it was not Mr. Budge who tried carry me off, Emerson."

My little joke had the desired effect. With a smile, Emerson led me into our room and closed the door.

For the next three days we worked in the West Valley. They were halcyon days; nothing disturbed the peaceful productivity of our work except an occasional archaeological visitor who had heard of our presence and—as Emerson put it—came to find out what we were up to; and the cat Anubis, who seemed intent on driving Abullah to felinocide. I endeavored to comfort our afflicted foreman.

"He likes you, Abdullah. It is quite a compliment. The cat Bastet never paid you such attentions."

Rubbing his head—which had come into painful contact with a rock when the cat had suddenly jumped onto his shoulder—Abdullah remained unconvinced. "She is not an ordinary cat, as we all know; does not she speak with the young master, and heed his commands? This one is a servant of evil, as the cat Bastet is a servant of good. Its very name is a bad omen; was not Anubis the god of cemeteries?"

Emerson's vigilance gradually relaxed as the days passed without any alarming incident. For all its isolation, the West Valley was safer than any city. No one could approach without being observed long before he came close to us.

At the end of the third day Emerson announced that we had almost completed the task for which we had come. We had corrected numerous errors in the existing plan of the Valley and located several promising sites that warranted further investigation—including one that offered a suitable hiding place for the scepters. Abdullah was pleased to learn we were nearly finished. Mapmaking was not a favorite activity of Abdullah's. Like his master, he preferred to dig.

"How much longer?" he asked, as we started back.

"A week at the outside," Emerson replied. Glancing at me, he added provocatively, "Vandergelt Effendi is coming soon. I want to be out of his house before he arrives."

We had received a telegram from Cyrus the day before, announcing his imminent arrival in Cairo and saying that he looked forward to seeing us shortly.

"Perhaps," said Abdullah hopefully, "the cat will stay here with the Effendi."

"That is a difficulty," Emerson agreed. "We will be camping out at Amarna; we cannot be bothered feeding and caring for him."

A rattle of rock and a pathetically abbreviated squeak nearby preceded the appearance of Anubis, with a limp brown shape in his mouth. "You needn't worry about feeding him," I said.

Abdullah said something under his breath. Daoud, a big silent man, whose placidity was seldom ruffled, glanced uneasily at the cat; his fingers twitched in a ritual gesture designed to ward off evil.

The cat disappeared with its prey and we went on in silence for a time. Then Abdullah said, "There is a fantasia tonight at the house of the brother of my father. It is in honor of my visit to the home of my ancestors; but it would be a greater honor if the Father of Curses and you, Sitt Hakim, would come."

"It would honor us," Emerson replied, as courtesy demanded. "What do you say, Peabody?"

The idea appealed to me. I was anxious to meet Abdullah's uncle, who had a certain reputation in the Luxor area; born and raised in Gurnah, the notorious village of hereditary tomb robbers on the west bank, he had acquired, by means no one cared to investigate, wealth enough to purchase a fine house on the east bank outside Luxor. Family pride would require him to hire the finest entertainers for his fantasia.

The entertainment at these celebrations consists primarily of music and dancing. In the beginning I had found Egyptian music painful to my ears; the singers' voices slide up and down a rather limited scale, and the musical instruments are primitive by Western standards. As with most art forms, however, prolonged exposure increases appreciation. I could now listen with relative enjoyment to the nasal singing and the accompaniment of flute and zither, tambourine and zemr (a form of oboe). The insistent rhythm of the drums (of which there were many varieties) had a particularly interesting effect.

I accepted the invitation with proper expressions of gratitude. Taking Emerson's arm, I let the others draw ahead before I said in a low voice, "Have you canceled your interdict against evening activities, then? Nothing has occurred since we arrived in Luxor—"

"I have made certain it would not," Emerson replied haughtily. "However, this is not the sort of evening activity I was concerned about. I defy the boldest of abductors to snatch you away when you have three such defenders." Seeing my expression—for he knows how I dislike being regarded as a helpless female—he added, "We might have dinner at the hotel and drop in on the performance later. Carter is in Luxor; I would like to have a chat with him, and prepare him for the great discovery we are about to make."

So it was arranged. We sent a message across to Howard inviting him to dine with us at the Luxor Hotel, and as the sun was setting we stepped on board the felucca that would take us across the river. Abdullah and Daoud looked like emirs in their best robes and most enormous turbans; the former's long white beard had been laundered till it shone like snow. It was incumbent on us to put on an equally impressive show; Emerson accepted the necessity of this, though he remarked grumpily, as I was tying his cravat, that he felt like a little boy being taken to visit wealthy godparents.

The gangplank, which served as an oar in times of diminished wind, had been pulled in and we were gliding away from the quay when a long sinuous form leapt into the boat. In the gathering dusk it was difficult to make out immediately what it was; Emerson let out an oath and tried to push me down onto the filthy bottom of the boat, and Abdullah would have toppled off the seat if Daoud had not caught him. I resisted Emerson's efforts, for I had of course immediately identified the latest passenger.

"It is only the cat," I said loudly. "Abdullah, for pity's sake, stop thrashing around. You will muss your beautiful robe."

Abdullah had never cursed in my presence. He did not do so now, but he sounded as if he were strangling on repressed epithets.

"Damnation," said Emerson. "What a nuisance. I refuse to take a cat to dine at the Luxor, Amelia."

"Throw it overboard," Abdullah offered.

I ignored this suggestion, as Abdullah no doubt expected I would. "We haven't time to take it back to the house. Perhaps the boatman has a bit of rope we can use as a lead."

"I don't approve of dragging cats around on a lead as one does a dog," Emerson declared firmly. "They are independent creatures who do not deserve such treatment." The cat walked along the bench, balancing like an acrobat, and settled down next to him. "Such a fuss over a cat," Emerson grumbled, scratching Anubis under his chin. "If he wanders away, he will simply have to fend for himself."

Emerson and I often attract considerable attention when we appear in public. I hope I may not be accused of vanity when I say that on this occasion it was no wonder all eyes were drawn to us as, arm in arm, we swept into the dining salon of the hotel. Emerson's splendid height and ruggedly handsome features were set off by the stark black-and-white of his evening dress, and he walked like a king. I fancied I looked rather well myself. However, I suspected that some of the wide-eyed stares focused on us—and the smothered laughter that rippled through the room—were occasioned by something other than admiration. Anubis had refused to stay in the cloakroom. He stalked along behind us with a dignity equal to Emerson's—tail erect, eyes straight ahead. His expression also bore a striking resemblance to that of Emerson. The phrase "well-bred sneer" comes to mind.

He was better behaved than some of the guests. A party of young male persons (they did not merit the name of "gentlemen") at a nearby table had clearly taken too much to drink. One of them leaned so far out of his chair to watch the cat that he fell to the floor. His companions were more amused than embarrassed by this performance; with cheers and comments in the accents of brash young America, they hauled him upright and restored him to his place. "Attaboy, Fred," said one of them. "Show these folks how a sport takes a fall!"

Howard arrived in time to see the end of this performance. "Perhaps Mrs. Emerson would like to move to another table," he suggested, eyeing the raucous party askance.

"Mrs. Emerson is not to be disturbed on account of rowdies," said Emerson, beckoning the waiter. He addressed this individual in tones loud enough to be heard throughout the dining salon. "Kindly inform the manager that if he does not remove the people over there at once, I will remove them myself."

The young men were duly removed. "There, you see," said Emerson, smiling at Howard in a kindly fashion. "That is the way to deal with such things."

We had to explain Anubis, who made his presence known to Carter by sniffing loudly at his trouser leg. I suppose the sound and the accompanying sensation must have been a trifle startling to one who was unaware that there was a cat under the table. Once the situation was made clear, Howard laughed and shook his head. "I should have learned not to be surprised at anything you and the professor do, Mrs. Emerson. It is like you to take charge of poor Vincey's pet. He is fanatically attached to it, and it does not get on with most people."

"Since you refer to him as 'poor Vincey,' I take it you are of the opinion that he was treated unjustly?" I inquired.

Howard looked a little uncomfortable. "I don't know the truth of the matter. I doubt that anyone does. He is a pleasant chap—very likable; I know nothing to his discredit except...But that is just gossip, and not the sort of thing I should mention in your presence, Mrs. Emerson."

"Ah," I said, motioning to the waiter to refill the young man's glass. "*Cherchez la femme!* Or is it *les femmes*?"

"The plural, decidedly," said Howard. He caught Emerson's eye and added quickly, "Idle gossip, as I said. Er—tell me how you are getting on in the Valley. Any new tombs?"

For the rest of the meal we confined ourselves to professional gossip. Emerson enjoyed himself, tantalizing our young friend with mysterious hints and refusing to elaborate on them. Howard was about to explode with curiosity when Emerson took out his watch and begged he would excuse us. "One of our friends is giving a fantasia in our honor," he explained, stretching the truth a little. "We must not be too late."

We parted at the door of the hotel. Howard set off on foot, whistling cheerfully, and we bargained for a carriage. The main street of Luxor, lined with modern hotels and ancient ruins, runs along the river; behind it is a typical village, with streets of bare dirt and clustered huts.

No premonition of disaster troubled my mind. I was more concerned about my thin evening slippers and trailing skirts, and with the distance we had to travel. This does not prove, as some claim, that such forebodings are only superstition; it proves that on some occasions they fail one. I could have wished mine had chosen another occasion on which to fail.

We left the lights of the hotels behind us and turned onto a narrow lane between fields of sugarcane, higher than a tall man's head. The leaves whispered softly in the night breeze. From time to time lights from country houses twinkled through the stalks. The night air was cool and refreshing; the mingled odors that mark an Egyptian town—the smell of donkeys, charcoal fires, and lack of sanitation—faded, to be replaced by a more salubrious scent of green growing crops and fresh earth. The carriage was open; the night air cooled my face; the rhythmic clop of the horses' hooves, the creak of the leather seats blended into a magical mood of romance. I leaned against Emerson's shoulder; his arm was around me. Not even the fixed regard of the cat, on the seat opposite, could mar the moment.

The drive was popular with visitors to Luxor, for it was one of the few country roads wide enough to take carriages. We met one or two others and had to pull off to let them by.

The driver glanced back, cursing in Arabic. I could not see what was behind us, but I had already heard the sounds: the pound of galloping hooves and a blurred chorus of voices. Someone was overtaking us, and presumably they meant to pass us, for the noise swelled rapidly.

"Good Gad!" I exclaimed, trying to look over the high back of the seat.

"It is just a party of young idiot tourists," Emerson said. "They race on this stretch all the time." He leaned forward and tapped the driver's shoulder. "Let them go by," he said in Arabic. "There is a space there ahead, beyond the wall."

The driver obeyed, pulling over in the nick of time, and the other carriage thundered past. Shouts and cheers and a snatch of raucous song hailed us, and someone waved a bottle. Then the carriage lights disappeared around a curve in the road.

"They will have themselves in the ditch if they go on at that pace," Emerson said, settling back.

We proceeded on our way, coming at last into a more thickly settled area. It was a strange blend of humble huts and walled houses, with open fields between.

"Not far now," said Emerson. "By Gad, I was right! There is the carriage that passed us. In the ditch."

"Shall we not stop and offer assistance?" I asked.

"Why the devil should we? Let them walk back, it will sober them."

He had already ascertained, as had I, that the horse was not injured. It stood patiently by the road, while the men tried to right the carriage. They were laughing and cursing; it was clear that no one had been hurt.

We had left them some distance behind when suddenly the cat sat up on the seat and stared intently at the side of the road. We were passing a large building of some sort; it looked like an abandoned warehouse or factory. Before I could see what had attracted the cat's attention, it gathered itself together and sprang out of the carriage.

"Confound the confounded beast!" Emerson shouted. "*Ukaf*, driver—stop at once."

"Oh, dear, we will never find it in the dark," I lamented. "Here, Anubis. Here, kitty, kitty."

Two eerily glowing orbs appeared, at ground level. "There he is," Emerson said. "That is a door behind him; he is looking for mice, no doubt. Stay here, Peabody. I'll go after him."

Before I could stop him, he had jumped out of the carriage. Then—when it was too late—the recognition of peril struck me like a blow in the face. For as Emerson reached down to take the cat into his arms, the door behind it swung open. I saw Emerson fall forward and heard the sickening thud of the club that had struck his bowed head. Wild with apprehension as to

his fate, I could not go to his assistance, for I was fully
occupied in fending off the two men who had rushed
at the carriage. The driver was face-down in the road; a
third man held the head of the terrified horse. My evening parasol—curse my vanity!—broke as I brought it
down on the turban of one of my assailants. It did no
more than annoy him. Hard hands captured mine and
dragged me out of the carriage.

I screamed—something I seldom do, but the situation seemed to warrant it. I did not expect a response.
It was with incredulous relief that I heard, through the
extremely filthy bag that had been pulled over my head,
an answering voice. No—voices! Rescue was approaching! I renewed my struggles; the man who held me had
to release one of my hands in order to hold the bag in
place, and I clawed blindly but effectively at his face. He
cried out and called me something rude in Arabic.

"Choke the witch and keep her quiet," exclaimed
another voice. "Hurry, they are—"

He broke off with a pained grunt and the man who
held me let me go so suddenly that I fell to the ground.
The bag was twisted around my head, I could not get
it off; when hands seized me again I struck out as hard
as I could.

"Ouch!" was the response—a good, familiar English "ouch." I ceased my resistance and concentrated
on removing the bag. A voice continued plaintively,
"Confound it, ma'am, that's not a ladylike thing to do
to a fellow when he was only trying to help."

I did not reply. I did not thank him or stop to see
who he was. Leaping to my feet, I snatched a lantern

from the hand of another individual who stood nearby and dashed toward the door of the warehouse.

It gaped open and empty. The darkness within was not complete; moonlight entering through holes in the ruined roof streaked the floor. Calling and rushing back and forth, I swept every foot of that floor with the lantern beam before I was forced to admit the truth. The place was deserted. There was no trace of Emerson—except for a damp spot, where some liquid darker and more viscous than water had soaked into the dirty floor.

CHAPTER 6

"I do not scruple to employ mendacity and a fictitious appearance of female incompetence when the occasion demands it."

I fear my behavior thereafter did me no credit. The sight of the cat strolling toward me sent me into a frenzy; I snatched it up and shook it, and I think I shouted at it, demanding to know what it had done with Emerson. This action appeared to surprise it; instead of struggling and scratching, it hung limp in my hands and let out an inquiring mew. When its mouth opened I saw there was something caught on one tooth. It was a shred of dirty cotton that might have come from a native robe.

After a time I heard one of my rescuers remark in a worried voice, "Say, boys, the lady's gone off her head. She'll hurt herself tearing around like that; how about I give her a little sock on the jaw?"

"You can't sock a lady, you lummox," was the equally worried reply. "Damned if I know what to do."

The words penetrated the fog of horror that had

enveloped me. Shame overcame me; common sense returned. I was shaking from head to foot; the lantern swayed in my hand; but I believe my voice was fairly steady when I spoke.

"I am not 'tearing around,' gentlemen; I am searching for my husband. He was here. He is not here now. They have carried him off. There is another door—they must have gone that way. Pray don't stop me"—for one of them had taken hold of my arm—"let me go after them. I must find him!"

My rescuers were none other than the young Americans who had behaved in so ungentlemanly a manner at the hotel. They had been in the carriage that had passed us. Falling into the ditch must have sobered them, for they were quick to understand and respond to my plea, and very kind, in their peculiar American fashion. Two of them immediately went off to follow the trail of the kidnappers and another insisted I return to the carriage.

"You can't go running around the fields dressed like that, ma'am," he said, when I would have resisted. "Leave it to Pat and Mike, they're as good as coon hounds on a trail. How about a nip of brandy? For medicinal purposes, you know."

Perhaps it was the brandy that cleared my head. I prefer to believe it was the resurgence of my indomitable will. Though every nerve in my body ached to join the search, I saw the strength of his argument, and it then occurred to me that there was better help close at hand. One of the young men—there were five of them in all—agreed to go to the house of Abdullah's uncle and tell our reis what had transpired. It was not long, though it seemed an interminable interlude to me, before Abdullah and Daoud were with me. I came perilously close to breaking down when I saw Abdullah's familiar face, distorted by worry and disbelief; Emerson had seemed to him like a god, immune to ordinary danger.

Assisted by the young Americans and a posse of their relatives, Abdullah and Daoud searched the fields and the nearby houses, ignoring the (legitimate) complaints of their occupants. But too much time had passed. He had been carried off and by now could be miles away. The dusty road kept its secret; too much traffic had passed along it.

Dawn was pale in the sky before I could be persuaded to return to the Castle. The driver had only been struck unconscious; restored by brandy and baksheesh, he turned the horse and the carriage. Daoud and the cat went with me. Abdullah would not leave the spot. I believe I had the courtesy to thank the Americans. It was not entirely their fault if they regarded the business as an exciting adventure.

I find it difficult to recall my sensations during the succeeding days. Events stand out in my memory sharp and clear as detailed engravings, but it was as if I were enveloped by a shell of clear cold ice that impeded neither vision nor touch nor hearing, but through which nothing could penetrate.

When the news of Emerson's disappearance became known, I was overwhelmed with offers of assistance. This should have touched me. It did not; nothing could touch me then. I wanted action, not sympathy. The local authorities were hustled and badgered into a show of efficiency uncommon to them; they arrested and questioned every man in Luxor who had cause to hold a grudge against my husband. The list was fairly extensive. At one time half the population of Gurnah, whose inhabitants resented Emerson's war against their tomb-robbing habits, were in the local prison. Hearing of this from Abdullah (several of whose distant kin were among the prisoners), I was able to bring about their release. Abdullah had his own methods of dealing with the men of Gurnah, and I knew Emerson would himself have interfered to forbid the kinds of interrogation the local police employed. Beating the soles of the feet with splintered reeds was a favorite method.

Our friends rallied around. Howard Carter visited me almost daily. Despite the differences of opinion that had often marked his relationship with Emerson, Neville was the first to offer his crew to help in the search. Telegrams arrived from Cairo; and from Cairo came, in person, Cyrus Vandergelt. He had abandoned his beloved dahabeeyah; he had not even waited for the regular train. Ordering a special, he had set out as soon as it was ready, leaving his luggage behind, and his first words to me were words of comfort and reassurance.

"Don't you fret, Mrs. Amelia. We'll get him back if we have to tear this two-bit town apart. Some good old American know-how is what is wanted here; and Cyrus Vandergelt, U.S.A., is the man to supply it!"

The years had been kind to my friend. There might be a few more silver threads in his hair and goatee, but their sun-bleached fairness looked just the same. His stride was as athletic and vigorous, the clasp of his hand as strong, and his wits as keen as ever. He brought to our problem a cynical intelligence and a knowledge of the world no one had been able to supply. When, in answer to his questions, I described the imprisonment of the Gurnah thieves, he shook his head impatiently.

"Sure, I know those Gurnah crooks detest my old pal, but this isn't their style. They're more inclined to throw knives or rocks. This smacks of something more sinister. What have you and the professor been up to lately, Mrs. Amelia? Or has that young rascal Ramses pulled another shady deal?"

I was tempted to tell him what I suspected, but I did not dare. I cleared Ramses, as was only proper, but replied that I could not explain the event.

Cyrus was too shrewd to accept this—or perhaps he knew me so well he sensed my hesitation. He was also too much of a gentleman to question my word. "Well, I'll tell you what I think. He isn't dead. They'd have found the ... er ... found him by now. This has got to be a question of ransom. Why else would they hold him prisoner?"

"There are other reasons," I replied, repressing a shudder.

"Now put that out of your head, Mrs. Amelia. Money is a lot more powerful incentive than revenge. I'll bet you you'll get a ransom note. If you don't, why, we'll offer a reward."

It was something to do, at least. The following day every tree and wall in Luxor bore the hastily printed placards. For reasons of my own which I could not explain to Cyrus, I did not expect results; and indeed, the message that arrived that evening was only indirectly related, if at all, to the offer.

It was carried by a ragged fellah, whose willingness to be detained supported his claim of innocence. He was a messenger only; the man who had given him the letter, with a modest tip and an assurance of greater reward upon delivery, had been a stranger to him. Few people are good observers, but it seemed evident from the messenger's confused description that there had been nothing distinctive about the man's dress or appearance.

We sent the messenger away with promises of untold riches if he was able to supply any further information. I thought he was honest. But if he was not, we were more likely to win him over by bribes than by punishment.

Cyrus and I had been in the library. After the messenger had gone, I sat turning the letter over and over in my hands. It was addressed to me, in large printed letters. The envelope bore the name of one of the Luxor hotels.

"If you would like to be alone when you read it..." Cyrus began. He had asked my permission to smoke and held one of his long thin cheroots.

"That is not why I hesitate," I admitted. "I am afraid to open it, Cyrus. It is the first ray of hope I have beheld. If it proves false... But such cowardice does not become me."

With a firm hand I reached for a letter opener.

I read through the letter twice. Cyrus held his tongue; the effort must have been difficult, for when I looked at him he was leaning forward, his face drawn with suspense. Silently I handed him the letter.

I might have given it to an individual I trusted less than I did my old friend without fear of betraying the deadly secret. It was the most suavely villainous, discreetly threatening epistle I have ever read. I felt contaminated by the mere touch of the paper.

Your husband is disinclined to confide in us [it began], He claims his memory is faulty. It seems incredible that a man could forget so remarkable a journey in so short a period of time; but recent experiences may well have had an adverse effect upon his mind as well as his body. I do not doubt your recollection is more accurate, and that you would be more than pleased to share it with us, in writing or in person. I will be sitting on the terrace of the Winter Palace Hotel tomorrow evening at five, in the hope that you will join me for an aperitif. Let me add only that, as one of your greatest admirers, I would be gravely disappointed if you sent a substitute.

Cyrus flung the paper to the floor. "Amelia," he cried in poignant accents. "You aren't going, are you? You wouldn't be such a blamed fool?"

"Why, Cyrus!" I exclaimed.

My friend shook out an enormous snowy-white linen handkerchief and mopped his forehead. "Pardon me. I took a liberty."

"By using my first name? Dear Cyrus, no one is better entitled than you. You have been a pillar of strength."

"No, but see here," Cyrus insisted. "You're as smart at reading between the lines as I am. I don't know what it is this dirty yellow dog wants, but sure as shooting he isn't going to exchange poor old Emerson for anything in writing. How'd he know you were telling the truth? This is just a trick to get ahold of you. Emerson's a tough nut and stubborner than any mule. You couldn't get him to talk if you stuck his feet in the fire or pulled out his...Oh, shucks, honey, I'm sorry. They aren't going to do anything like that, they know it wouldn't work. But if they had you in their filthy hands, he'd spill the beans all right."

"As would I, rather than be forced to watch while they..." I could not complete the sentence.

"You've got the idea. This ugly cuss needs both of you. That was a cute stunt of Emerson's, pretending to have amnesia, but it won't hold up for five seconds after he sets eyes on you. You can't take the chance, Amelia. It's for Emerson's sake as well as yours; they won't damage him permanently so long as you're on the loose."

"I realize that, my dear Cyrus. But how can I not go? It is our first, our only lead. You noted that the—dirty yellow dog seems a fitting description—that he gave no clue as to how I might identify him. That implies that he is someone I know."

Cyrus slapped his knee. "I've said it before and I'll say it again—you're the sharpest little lady of my acquaintance. But we've got to give this a lot of thought, Amelia. If I were running this scam, I wouldn't be at the Winter Palace. I'd have some innocent bystander pass you a note instructing you to go someplace else—someplace not so safe. You'd do it, too. Wouldn't you?"

I could not, did not, deny it. "But," I argued, "if I were accompanied—not by you, Cyrus, you are too recognizable—but by Abdullah and his friends—"

"Abdullah is as easily recognizable as I am. And be sure, my dear, that you would be led on and on by one means or another until you were beyond the reach of friends."

I bowed my head. I don't believe I had ever felt such an agonizing sense of helplessness. By risking capture I would endanger not only myself but Emerson. Our unknown enemy would have no recourse but to murder us once we had told him what he wanted to know. Only by remaining free could I preserve a life dearer to me than my own. And the loathsome letter had given me that much comfort at least. He lived.

Cyrus's voice broke in on my painful thoughts. "I haven't asked for your confidence, Amelia, and I won't. But if you could tell me what it is this devil wants, I might be able to come up with an idea."

I shook my head. "It would not help, and it might endanger you as well. Only two other people . . ."

It was like a hammer smashing through the shell of frozen calm that had enclosed me. My only excuse is that I had been so absorbed with Emerson I had neglected other, if lesser, responsibilies. They now came crashing in upon me. With a shriek that echoed among the rafters, I leapt to my feet.

"Ramses! And Nefret! Oh, heaven, what I have I done—or, to be more accurate, neglected to do? A telegram! Cyrus, I must send a telegram at once!"

I was rushing toward the door when Cyrus caught me up. Taking me by the shoulders, he strove to restrain me. "Don't go riding off in all directions! You shall send your telegram; sit down, compose it, while I find a man to take it over to Luxor." Leading me to the desk, he thrust pen and paper into my hands.

Desperation and remorse gave me the strength to write. When Cyrus returned I had finished the message. I handed it to him. Without looking at the paper he took it to the servant waiting at the door.

"It will be in London tomorrow," he said, returning.

"If it traveled on the wings of the wind, it could not arrive too soon for me," I cried. "How could I have failed to realize ... But it was not until now that I knew for certain."

"I prescribe a little brandy," Cyrus said.

"I believe ..." I had to stop to collect myself before I went on. "I believe I would prefer a whiskey and soda, please."

When Cyrus brought it to me, he dropped onto one knee like a medieval page serving his master. "You're not only the sharpest little lady I know, but the coolest and bravest," he said gently. "Don't give way now. I reckon I've an idea now what this is all about. You and Emerson, young Ramses and the girl—Willy Forth's daughter, isn't she? Uh-huh. Say no more, Mrs. Amelia, my dear. And don't worry about the kiddies. If half of what I've heard about that son of yours is true, he can take care of himself—and the girl too."

I always say there is nothing like a whiskey and soda to calm the nerves. After a few sips I was able to speak more composedly. "What a comfort you are, Cyrus. No doubt you are right. All the same, I don't know how I am going to endure the suspense until I hear from them. It will take at least three days to get a reply."

But a benevolent Providence spared me that suspense. No doubt It felt I had quite enough to bear already. When Cyrus's servant returned from Luxor he carried another telegram with him. I had already retired to my rooms, but I was not asleep. Cyrus himself brought the message to my door. How long it had been sitting in the telegraph office I never determined; Egyptians do not share our Western concern about haste. It was addressed to Emerson, but I did not let that deter me from opening it, for I had seen whence it came.

"Warning received and acted upon," Walter had written. "All is well. Guard yourselves. Letter follows. Guard yourselves."

I handed it to Cyrus. He had refused the chair I offered him and stood by the door, hands behind his back, looking extremely uncomfortable. What Puritans these Americans are, I thought in amusement. Only affectionate concern could have brought him to the room of an unchaperoned married lady after nightfall. And I in deshabille, too! I had snatched up the first garment that came to hand when I heard his knock; it was a particularly frivolous, ruffled, beribboned, lace-trimmed peignoir of yellow silk.

The message made Cyrus forget the ruffles and ribbons. "Thank heaven," he said sincerely. "That relieves one source of anxiety. 'All is well,' he says."

"Evidently I am more skilled at reading between the lines than you, Cyrus. Why does he repeat 'Guard yourselves?' Something must have happened."

"Now that is just your mother's anxiety, my dear. You don't know what Emerson said in *his* message. He must have sent a telegram to his brother some days ago, warning him of danger."

"Apparently that is the case. He did not tell me he had done so; no doubt he supposed I would jeer at his concern, as I did on the occasions when he tried to convince me of our peril. How cruelly Heaven has punished me for failing to heed him!" Cyrus's eyes followed me as I paced back and forth, the skirts of my robe swirling around me. "I will take what comfort I can from Walter's reassurance," I went on. "There is nothing more I can do."

"Get some sleep," Cyrus said kindly. "And don't worry. I will do whatever I can to serve you."

But it was not he who served me best.

Needless to say, I did not sleep. I lay awake as I had done every night since it happened—not tossing and turning, for that is an exhibition of weakness I do not allow myself—but trying to discover a possible course of action. At least this night I had new information to consider. I went over and over every word, every phrase, every comma, even, in that malevolent missive. Every word and every phrase contained sly threats all the more terrifying for being left to the imagination of the reader. (Especially an imagination as active as mine.) The man who had composed them must be a veritable fiend.

And an arrogant fiend. He had not even bothered to conceal his nationality; his English was as good, his syntax as elegant, as my own. I felt confident he was not a guest at the hotel. Anyone could have stolen stationery from the writing room. As for his aim in proposing a rendezvous…Well, Cyrus's reasoning was irrefutable. It agreed with my own. Even if I were cad enough to break my word and betray a helpless people in exchange for my husband's life . . .

But, oh, Reader! You know little of the human heart if you suppose that honor is stronger than affection or that cool reason can overcome loving fear. If the villain had stood before me at that moment with one hand outstretched and the other holding the key to Emerson's prison, I would have thrown myself at his feet and begged him to take what he wanted.

Emerson's suspicions had been logical but unsubstantiated. The letter had turned them from surmise into certainty. It was the location of the Lost Oasis the fiend was after. But what, precisely, would satisfy his demands?

A map? THE map? Either he knew it existed, or he had deduced that it must. The journey we had made led into the waterless, featureless desert, and only a madman would set out unless he had precise directions. The dirty yellow dog must know we had followed a map of some kind.

To the best of my knowledge, only one copy was still in existence. There had been five to begin with, and to complicate the matter still further, two of the five had been deliberately, fatally inaccurate. I had destroyed mine—one of the false maps. Ramses's copy, the one we had used to reach the oasis, had been lost or mislaid during our rather precipitate departure from the place. Emerson's copy had disappeared even before we left Nubia. That left two, one accurate, one false.

The other false copy had belonged to Reggie Forthright. He had left it with me when he set off on his expedition into the desert, and, as he had requested, I had passed it on to the military authorities, together with his last will and testament, before we went into the desert. Presumably these documents had been sent to his sole heir, his grandfather, when he failed to return. This copy of the map did not concern me, for it would only have led the one who followed it to a very dry, prolonged, and unpleasant death.

The original copy of the map had been in the possession of Lord Blacktower, Reggie's grandfather. It was now in Emerson's strongbox in the library at Amarna House. Blacktower had given it up, along with the guardianship of Nefret, at Emerson's emphatic request. I had urged that it be destroyed, but Emerson had overruled me. One never knew, he had said. There might come a time, he had said...

Had it come? For the second and, I am happy to say, last time, my integrity wavered under the impact of overpowering affection. I had to bite down hard on the linen pillowcase before reason again prevailed.

I could not trust the honor of a man who clearly had none. Nor would he trust mine. He could not afford to release his hostage until he was certain the information I had given him was accurate—and how could he know that until he had made the journey and returned? I could not have retraced our route or remembered the compass readings, but I did not doubt that Emerson could. He had held the compass and followed the directions. The villain did not need a map if he could force Emerson to speak.

No, the rendezvous was a ruse. Our only hope was to find Emerson and free him before...

Where could he be? Somewhere in the vicinity of
Luxor still, I felt sure. The search had been intensive
and was proceeding, but it could not penetrate into
every room in every house, especially the houses of foreign residents. Egypt enjoyed the blessings of British
law, which proclaims that a man's home is his castle. A
noble ideal, and one with which I thoroughly agree—
in principle. Noble ideals are often inconvenient. I
well remembered the story of how Wallis Budge had
smuggled his boxes of illegal antiquities away while the
police waited outside his house, unable to enter until
the warrant arrived from Cairo.

We needed a warrant, and for that we must have
grounds. That was what my devoted friends were trying to obtain—talking with their informants in the villages, following up gossip about strangers in the city,
investigating rumors of unusual activity—and I pinned
my hopes on their endeavors.

I had especially counted on Abdullah and his influence with the men of Gurnah, who were reputed to
know every secret in Luxor; but as I lay sleepless in
the dark, I had to confess I was sorely disappointed in
him. I had seen very little of him in the past few days. I
knew one reason why he avoided the house; he looked
like a white-bearded, turbaned John Knox when he
saw me and Cyrus together. Not that Abdullah would
have insulted me by supposing I had the least interest
in another man. He was jealous of Cyrus on his own
account, resenting anyone who wanted to assist me and
Emerson in the slightest way, and resenting Cyrus all
the more because his own efforts had proved futile.

Poor Abdullah. He was old, and this had been a terrible blow to him. I doubted he would ever fully recover.

God forgive me for such doubts. For it was Abdullah who served me best.

Cyrus and I were seated at luncheon next day, discussing how we should deal with the matter of the proposed rendezvous, when one of the servants entered and said that Abdullah wanted to speak with me.

"Have him come in," I said.

The servant looked scandalized. Servants, I have found, are greater snobs than their masters. I repeated the order; with a shrug the man went out and then returned to report Abdullah would not come in. He wished to speak to me in private.

"I can't imagine what he has to say that he could not say in front of you," I said, rising.

Cyrus smiled. "He wants to be your sole prop and defender, my dear. Such loyalty is touching, but blamed aggravating. Go ahead."

Abdullah was waiting in the hall, exchanging sour glances—and I think low-voiced insults—with the doorkeeper. He would not speak until I had followed him out onto the veranda.

When he turned to face me, I caught my breath. His sour frown had vanished, to be replaced by a glow of pride and joy that made him look half his age.

"I have found him, Sitt," he said.

"You must not tell the Amerikâni!" Abdullah took hold of my sleeve and held me back when I would have rushed back into the house with the news. Drawing me farther away from the door, he went on in an urgent whisper, "He would not let you go. It is dangerous, Sitt Hakim. I have not told you all."

"Then for God's sake, tell me! Have you seen him? Where is he?"

Abdullah's story gave me pause and forced me to curb my raging impatience. He did not need to caution me that we must move with the utmost discretion—especially since he had not yet set eyes on his master.

"But what other closely guarded prisoner could there be, so close to Luxor? The house is outside the town, near to the village of El Bayadiya. It is rented by a foreigner, an Alemâni or Feransâwi. A tall black-bearded man, an invalid, it is said, for he is pale and walks with a cane when he goes out, which is not often. His name is Schlange. Do you know him, Sitt?"

"No. But it is surely not his real name, nor, perhaps, his true appearance. Never mind that now, Abdullah. You have a plan, I know. Tell me."

His plan was the very one I would have proposed myself. We could not demand entry to the house until we were certain Emerson was there, and we could not be certain until we had entered it. "So we will go ourselves," said Abdullah. "You and I, Sitt. Not the Amerikâni."

He went on to list all the reasons why Cyrus should not make one of the party. Obviously he was reluctant to share the glory, but his arguments had merit. The strongest of them was that Cyrus would try to prevent me from going—and that was unthinkable. I would go mad if I had to sit waiting for news like some feeble heroine of romantic fiction, and I could trust no one but myself to act with the ruthlessness and determination the situation might well demand.

I arranged to meet Abdullah in an hour, in the garden behind the house, and assured him I would find a way of deceiving Cyrus. Do I sound calm and collected? I was—then. I knew I had to be. When I returned to the table where Cyrus awaited me, I gave one of my most convincing performances—a brave, sad smile, a forced cheerfulness.

"He is still pursuing idle rumors," I said, taking up my napkin. "I am sorry I was so long, Cyrus, but I had to comfort him and make him feel his efforts were useful. Poor Abdullah! He takes this very much to heart."

We returned to discussing our plans (only his part in them, had he but known) for the afternoon. I allowed myself to become increasingly agitated as he continued to insist I not keep the appointment. "Someone must go," I cried at last. "I could not bear it if we failed to pursue even the frailest hope."

"Why, sure, my dear. I have it all figured out. I'll go in person to direct operations, as soon as you promise me you'll not leave the house till I get back."

"Very well. I yield only because I must—and because I know it is the safest course, for him. I shall go to my room now, Cyrus, and stay there, with the door locked, until you return. I think I may take a little something to make me sleep; otherwise the minutes will drag too slowly. Godspeed and good fortune, my friend."

Cyrus patted me clumsily on the shoulder. Handkerchief to my eyes, I fluttered out of the room.

When I reached my room I found Anubis stretched out on the bed. How he had got there I did not know;

he came and went as he pleased, as mysteriously as the afreet the servants believed him to be. Abdullah hated him as much as he feared him, blaming the poor creature for Emerson's capture. Of course that was nonsense. Cats cannot be held guilty for their actions, since they have no morals to speak of. If I had been given to superstitious fancies, I would have imagined Anubis regretted his inadvertent involvement in the disaster. He spent a good deal of time wandering about the house as if in search of something—or someone?—and he was often in my room, tolerating and even inviting my caresses. The feel of a compliant cat's fur has a surprisingly soothing effect.

After greeting the cat in an appropriate if hurried manner, I hastened to change. I dared not wait until after Cyrus had left the house; Abdullah and I had to cross the river and travel a considerable distance, and I wanted to reach the suspected house before nightfall. A surreptitious entry into unfamiliar territory is hazardous in the dark. It took only a few minutes to rip off my ruffled gown and replace it with my working costume. I reached automatically for my belt; a voice audible only to my inner ear stopped me. "You jangle like a German brass band, Peabody," it reminded me. Sternly repressing the emotion that threatened to overcome me, I abandoned my belt, slipping revolver and knife into my handy pockets. I locked my door—making certain Anubis was inside—and went onto the balcony. The cursed vine I had counted upon to assist my descent proved to be too far away. I had to hang by my hands and drop a considerable distance. Fortunately there was a flower bed below. Cyrus's petunias and hollyhocks cushioned my fall nicely.

Abdullah was waiting. I did not question or commend at that time the arrangements he had made—the donkeys, the felucca ready to sail, the horses waiting on the other side. One thought permeated every cell in my frame. Soon I would see him—touch him—feel his arms around me. For, as I am sure I need not say, I did not mean to content myself with a cautious reconnoiter and strategic withdrawal. My fingers touched the pistol in my pocket. If he was there, I would have him out, that day, that instant, no matter what or who stood between us.

The path Abdullah took followed an irrigation ditch through fields of cabbages and cotton. Half-naked workers straightened and stared after us as we galloped past; children playing in the courtyard of a house waved and called. Abdullah slackened speed for neither man nor beast. When a careless billy goat—whose goatee and long face gave it a certain resemblance to my friend Cyrus—wandered out into the road, Abdullah dug his bare heels into the horse's flank and soared over the goat. I followed his example.

He drew rein at last amid a huddle of huts, where another path crossed ours. Following his example, I dismounted. The place was strangely deserted; only a few men, drinking coffee at tables under a rude shelter, were to be seen. One of them came to us and handed Abdullah a bundle of cloth before leading the horses away.

"We must go on foot from here," said Abdullah. "Will you wear this, Sitt?"

He shook out the bundle—a woman's enveloping robe of somber black, with the accompanying burko, or face veil. After I had put it on, he nodded approval. "It is good. You must walk behind me, Sitt, and not stride like a man. Can you remember?"

His bearded lips were twitching. I smiled back at him. "If I forget, Abdullah, you must beat me. But I will not forget."

"No. Come then. It is not far."

As we walked, I glanced at the sun. After so many years in Egypt I had learned to read its position as readily as the hands of a clock; even now Cyrus's agents must be in their positions on the terrace of the Winter Palace Hotel. Was he there, the unknown villain who had laid such a dastardly plot? I prayed he was. If he was absent from his house, our mission of rescue would be easier.

My heart gave a great leap when I saw a high mud-brick wall ahead. Palms and dusty-leaved acacias surrounded it, and the tiled roof of a house showed over the top. It was a sizable establishment—an estate, in Egyptian terms—house, gardens and subsidiary buildings surrounded by an enclosure wall for privacy and protection. Abdullah passed it without breaking stride; I shuffled humbly after him, my head bowed and my heart thudding. Out of the corner of my eye I noted that the wall was high and the wooden gate was closed.

When we reached the end of the wall, some sixty feet farther on, Abdullah darted a quick glance over his shoulder and turned aside, pulling me after him. The wall continued now at right angles to the road. Another turn brought us to the third side of the enclosing wall, and after a short distance Abdullah stopped, gesturing.

His meaning was plain, and I could only approve his decision. Behind us a field of sugarcane formed a green wall that hid us from casual passersby. We were now at the back of the estate, as far from the main house as was possible. Mud-brick, the ubiquitous building material of Upper Egypt, is convenient but impermanent; the bricks and their plastered outer surface had crumbled, leaving chinks and crevices.

"I will go first," he whispered.

"No, you will not," I replied. "We must reconnoiter before we attempt to enter, and I am younger...that is, I am a lighter weight than you. Give me a hand up."

I threw off the muffling black robe and veil. No disguise would save us if we were discovered inside. I put the toe of my boot into a convenient hole; Abdullah—who had learned early on that it was a waste of time to argue with me—cupped his hands under the other boot and lifted me till I could see over the wall.

I had hoped to see a garden, with shrubs and trees that could offer concealment. No such amenities appeared, only a bare open space littered with the usual household discards—scraps of broken pots, rusty bits of metal, rotting melon rinds and orange peel. Of such detritus are formed the kitchen middens dear to the hearts of archaeologists, and they are still in the process of formation in Egypt, for householders commonly dump their trash casually in their yards. This was as nasty a place as any I had seen—clear evidence that the present occupant of the house was a transient, unconcerned about sanitation or appearance. The only unusual feature was the absence of animal life. No chickens scratched in the dirt, no goats or donkeys nibbled at the scanty weeds.

An open shed roofed with bundles of reeds had once
served as an animal shelter, to judge by the scattered
straw and other evidence. A row of straggling, dusty
tamarisk trees half-hid the back of the mansion. There
was one other structure visible: a small, windowless
building some ten feet square. Unlike the rest of the
place, it showed signs of recent repair. There were no
gaps in those walls; every chink had been filled with
fresh plaster that showed pale against the older gray-
brown surface. The flat roof was solid, not the usual
covering of reeds overlaid with mortar.

Something of value must be within, or the owner
of the property would not have taken such precautions. Hope renewed weakened my limbs; Abdullah
gave a pained grunt as my weight pressed heavily on his
hands. I was on the verge of completing the ascent, for
exultation had momentarily overcome prudence, when
a dampening thought occurred to me. Surely something so valuable would not be left unguarded? I could
only see the back and one side of the building. There
were no windows, but there must be a door on one of
the walls I could not see.

I motioned to Abdullah to lower me. He was glad to
do so, I believe. He was perspiring heavily, and not only
from my weight; suspense gnawed at his vitals as it did
at mine.

Quickly I described what I had seen. "We must
assume there is a guard," I whispered. "Can you move
like a shadow, Abdullah?"

The old man's hand went to the breast of his robe. "I
will deal with the guard, Sitt."

"No, no! Not unless we must. He may cry out and

summon others. We will have to get on the roof. There is an opening of some kind there—"

"I will go first," said Abdullah, his hand still at the breast of his robe.

This time I did not argue.

The evening breeze had arisen, rustling through the cane and stirring the leaves. The small sounds blended with the equally soft noises we could not avoid making, but they were few; for all his size Abdullah glided up the wall and over it like the shadow I had mentioned. He was waiting to lift me down when I reached the top; without pausing we crept toward the building. It was low—a kennel for a dog or some other beast. Abdullah lifted me up and followed me onto the roof.

There was a guard. Silently though we had moved, something must have alerted him; I heard a mutter and the rustle of fabric as he rose and then the soft pad of bare feet. We flattened ourselves behind the low parapet and held our breaths. He went round the perimeter of the building, but it was a perfunctory performance and he did not look up; people seldom do when they are searching. Finally he settled down again and lit a cigarette. The smoke rose in a thin gray curl, wavering in the breeze like a writhing serpent. Then and only then did we dare crawl toward the opening. It was closed by a rusted grille whose crossbars were set so close together that a finger could barely be inserted in the gaps.

I have not described my sensations, nor will I attempt to do so. The greatest of literary giants could not begin to capture their intensity. I pressed my face to the rusty metal surface of the grille.

The interior of the place was not entirely dark. There was another opening, a narrow slit over the door on the wall opposite the one we had climbed. Through it enough light entered to enable me to see the interior of the reeking den. The walls were bare and windowless, the floor was of beaten earth. There was no rug or carpet, only a flat square shape that might have been a piece of matting. The furnishings consisted of a table holding a few jars and pots and other objects I could not identify, a single chair—shockingly out of place in that setting, for it was a comfortable armchair of European style, upholstered in red plush—and a low bed. On it lay the motionless form of a man.

Abdullah's face was so close to mine I felt his breath hot against my cheek. Then the sinking sun sent a golden arm through the gap over the door, illumining the interior. I had not needed light to know him. I would have known that outline, that presence, in the darkest night. But if there had been breath in my lungs I would not have been able to restrain a cry when I saw the familiar features—familiar, yet so dreadfully changed.

The beard banished by my decree had returned, blurring the firm lines of jaw and chin, spreading up his cheeks toward his hairline. His closed eyes were sunken and his cheekbones stood out like spars. His shirt had been opened, baring his throat and breast...

The memory of another time, another place, assaulted me with such force my brain reeled. Was THIS how a mocking Providence had answered my unspoken appeal for a return to those thrilling days of yesteryear, when Emerson and I had been all in all to one another—before Ramses? So had he appeared on that never-to-be-forgotten day when I entered the tomb at Amarna and found him fevered and delirious. I had fought death to save him then, and won. But now... he lay so still, his features pinched and immobile as yellowed wax. Only eyes as desperately affectionate as my own could have marked the almost imperceptible rise and fall of his breast. What had they done to reduce a man of his strength to such a state in only a few days?

The dying light, glinting off an object on the table, gave me the answer. It was a hypodermic needle.

Scarce had the horror of that sight penetrated my mind when I saw something else. I had observed that his arms were stretched over his head in a stiff, unnatural position. Now I realized why. From the manacles on his wrists a chain looped over and through the bars of the headboard of the narrow bed.

I cannot explain why that detail affected me so powerfully. It was certainly a reasonable precaution; in fact, anyone who wished to keep Emerson in a place where he did not care to remain would have been a fool to neglect such restraints. Nevertheless, it did upset me a great deal, and perhaps the intensity of my outrage accounts for what—as I am told—happened next.

I had been vaguely aware of voices at the door. The guard had been joined by another man; they were talking loudly and, I suppose, telling improper stories, for there was a good deal of raucous laughter. The sounds faded into a dim insect-buzzing. A black cloud enveloped me, and a roaring fury filled my ears.

I came back to my senses to find Abdullah's alarmed face nose-to-nose with mine. One of his hands was clamped over my mouth. "The guards have gone, to fetch beer, but they will return," he hissed. "Do you hear me, Sitt? Has the demon departed?"

I could not speak, so I blinked at him. Finger by finger, watching me nervously, he loosened his grip. I became aware of a sharp, shooting pain in my hands. Looking down, I saw that I had seized the heavy grille and lifted it up out of the framework on which it rested. My fingers were torn and bleeding.

Abullah was muttering in Arabic—spells and incantations, designed to ward off the powers of evil.

"The—er—demon has gone," I whispered. "How very curious. This is the second time such a thing has happened, I believe. I laughed at Emerson when he told me of the first occasion. I must tell him, and apologize for doubting him, when he . . . when we . . ."

To my consternation, I found I could not control my voice. I lowered my head onto my folded arms.

A hand, gentle as a woman's, stroked my hair. "My daughter, do not weep. Dost thou believe I would dare to call myself a man and a friend if I left him to lie there? I have made a plan."

Abdullah had never spoken to me except with formal respect, nor used a term of endearment. I had known the depth of his regard for Emerson; "love" would not be too strong a word, had not that word been corrupted by European romanticism; but I had not been aware that in his own fashion Abdullah loved me too. Infinitely moved, I replied in kind.

"My father, I thank thee and bless thee. But what shall we do? He is drugged or sick; he cannot move. I had counted on his strength to help us."

"I feared we would find him thus," Abdullah

replied. "One does not chain the lion without clipping his claws, or cage the hawk without—"

"Abdullah, I love and honor thee as a father, but if thou dost not get to the point I am going to scream."

The old man's bearded jaws opened in a smile. "The Sitt is herself again. We must go quickly, before the guards return. My men wait at the crossroads."

"What men?"

"Daoud and the sons and grandsons of my uncles. They all have many sons," Abdullah added proudly. "The sun is setting; it is a good time to attack, at nightfall."

It did not occur to me for a moment to protest this dangerous and illegal procedure, but when he tugged at my sleeve I resisted. "I cannot leave him, Abdullah. They may carry him away or kill him if they are attacked."

"But, Sitt, Emerson will have my heart to eat if you—"

"So long as he is alive to eat it. Hurry, Abdullah. And—take care, my dear friend."

His hand gripped mine for a moment and then he was gone. I twisted around to watch, and saw him vanish over the wall as silently as he had come.

I had, of course, no intention of remaining on the roof. My normal strength might not have sufficed to lift the grille; fortunately that little matter had been taken care of. One side of the heavy metal square now rested on the lip of the opening; I had only to push it aside. The opening was, I thought, just large enough to admit my body. It would have to, for I meant to get in by one means or another.

Before I could carry out this scheme I heard the men returning. Their voices were more subdued this time, and after a moment another voice broke in. It spoke Arabic, but I knew from the accent and the tone of command that the speaker was not an Arab. Fear—for my husband, not for myself—and fury strengthened every sinew. He was here—the leader, the unknown villain who had perpetrated this foul deed.

The group paused outside the door and I hesitated, hands clenched on the metal, scarcely feeling the pain of my bleeding fingers. I must not act prematurely. They had no reason as yet to suspect rescue was imminent.

Then the speaker switched to English. "Wait here until I come for you. I want him wide awake and rational when he sees you."

To my astonishment the voice that responded, in the same language, was that of a woman. "I tell you, he is not so easily deceived. He will know I am not—"

"That, my dear, is the point of this exercise—to test the truth of his claim of amnesia. In that costume and in the gloom, with a gag hiding the lower part of your face, you look enough like her to deceive an affectionate spouse—for long enough, at least, to win a betraying cry of alarm from him. That will tell me what I want to know. And if he believes you are she, I will have at last the means of persuading him to tell me what I want to know."

A wordless murmur from the woman brought a mocking laugh from the leader. "The threat will be enough, I believe. If not—well, my dear, I won't damage you any more than I can help."

Every violent emotion I had repressed during the

days of waiting now boiled within me, with raging curiosity added to the mix. I had an inkling of what the villain planned, and I was on fire to see my double. His despicable trick might succeed, if the copy was faithful enough.

The door swung open, admitting a glow of light. It did not come from the sun, which was now below the horizon. The man who entered carried a lamp. You may believe, Reader, I studied his face intently. His voice had been familiar, but the features I saw did not match the appearance I expected. They were distorted by shadows, and masked by a heavy black mustache and imperial. It might be he; I could not be certain.

Putting the lamp on the table, he bent over Emerson and shook him roughly. There was no response. Straightening, the monster swore under his breath and turned toward the door.

"I told you to keep out!"

The woman's voice was almost inaudible. "He lies so still."

"The last dose of opium must have been too strong. Never mind, I'll have him awake and cursing in a moment."

He picked up the needle and plunged it into a bottle. The whisper came again.

"You use too much. He will die."

"Not until it suits my purpose," was the calloused response. "Now get back. He'll come round before long."

I forced myself to watch and remain passive. The needle went into a vein, with a careless skill that suggested some medical expertise. I made a note of this, even while my skin crawled with loathing and hatred. Whatever the substance was, it was effective. Moments later Emerson stirred. His first word was a feeble but heartfelt oath. Tears came to my eyes, and I promised myself I would never again complain of any language he chose to employ.

His adversary laughed. "Awake, are we? Another word or two, if you please; I want to be certain you are able to appreciate the treat I have for you."

Emerson obliged with a pithy description of his captor's presumed parentage. The fellow laughed again.

"Excellent. I presume you are still unwilling to admit me to your confidence?"

"Your conversation has become tedious," said Emerson. "How many times must I repeat that I have not the faintest idea what you are talking about? Even if I were able to supply the information you want I would not; I have taken a dislike to you."

"Give up any hope of rescue." The other man's voice hardened. His toe nudged the square object, which I now saw to be a wooden hatch or cover. "Have you also forgotten what lies beneath this?"

"Again you repeat yourself," was the bored reply. "I don't know where you get these melodramatic notions. Out of some novel, I suppose."

This comment seemed to madden the villain. He darted forward; for a moment I thought he would strike his helpless prisoner. Mastering himself with an effort that made his upraised hand quiver, he hissed, "The well is at least forty feet deep. If anyone attempts to force his way in here, the guard will see that you have the opportunity to measure its precise depth."

"Yes, yes, you said that." Emerson yawned.

"Very well. Let us see if I have found a means of persuading you to change your mind."

Leaving the lamp on the table, he went to the door. Emerson's eyes followed him; the pupils were so dilated they looked black instead of blue. After a moment the door opened again and the man entered, pushing a slighter form before him.

She would have deceived ME. The costume she wore was an exact copy of my old working uniform—Turkish trousers, boots, and all—even a belt hung with tools. Her hair was the same jet-black; it tumbled over her shoulders, as if it had been loosened in a struggle. Her supposed captor's arm pinned hers to her sides and held her back out of the light, so that her features would have been hard to make out even if a white cloth had not covered the lower part of her face.

"A visitor to see you, sir," said the unknown, in a mocking parody of a butler's announcement. "Haven't you an affectionate greeting for your wife?"

Emerson's face was impassive. Only his eyes moved, from the top of the woman's head to her boots, and back again. "She does appear to be female," he said, in an offensive drawl. "Hard to tell at first, in that outlandish garb..."

"You claim you don't recognize your own wife?"

"I don't have a wife," Emerson said patiently. "I seem to have forgotten a good many things, but of that I am certain."

"You contradict yourself, Professor. How can you be certain if you claim to be suffering from amnesia?"

A gasp of laughter came from Emerson's cracked

lips. "Whatever else may have slipped my mind, I could hardly forget something so monumentally stupid. Never in my weakest moment would I be damned fool enough to saddle myself with a wife." Narrowing his eyes, he went on, "Is she, by any chance, the female who brought me food and water yesterday...or the day before...can't remember..."

His eyes closed. The woman had bowed her head— in shame, I hoped. The man who held her loosened his grasp. She shrank back against the wall and pulled the gag from her face.

"He is fainting," she whispered. "Let me give him something—water, at least..."

Fists on his hips, the villain studied her with a sardonic smile. "'O Woman! in our hours of ease, Uncertain, coy, and hard to please...When pain and anguish wring the brow, A ministering angel thou!' Minister, then. If he dies before I can get that damned woman into my hands I'll have no means of persuading *her* to talk." He turned to the door, adding, over his shoulder, "Don't be long."

She waited until the door had slammed before relaxing. A long sigh issued from her lips.

"I have never understood the female sex," said a voice from the bed. "Why do you tolerate such treatment?"

She spun around to face him. "You are awake? I thought so. You only pretended...."

"Not...entirely," said Emerson.

She knelt by the bed, holding a cup of water to his lips and supporting his head while he drank thirstily. He thanked her, in a stronger voice. She lowered his head gently onto the hard mattress and stared at her stained fingers.

"It will not heal," she murmured. "Does it pain you?"

"I have the devil of a headache," Emerson admitted.

"And your poor hands..." Her fingers slid slowly up his right arm and touched the swollen, bloody flesh of his wrist.

"It would be pleasant to stretch a bit." His voice had changed. I knew that purring note, and a shiver ran through me. I dislike, even now, admitting the emotion that prompted it. I believe it is not necessary for me to do so.

Emerson went on, in the same tone, "If my arms were free I could better express the appreciation I feel for your kindness."

She let out a little laugh, in which coquetry and defiance were mingled. "Well, why not? You cannot pass the guards, you are not strong enough; and if you think you can win freedom by holding me hostage you deceive yourself. No English gentleman would harm a woman. He knows that."

The key to his manacles were on the table. I appreciated the refinement of cruelty that left freedom in sight, but unattainable. As she bent over him to unlock them a tress of her hair brushed his face.

Well! I would like to believe I could have held firm, even in the face of what was obviously about to transpire; but I had seized the edge of the grille with both hands and my muscles were tensed, when there was an outcry from the direction of the house. Voices shouting, the rattle of gunfire! My faithful Abdullah and his valiant friends had arrived! Rescue was at hand! The time for action had come!

One heave of my shoulders pushed the grille aside. I inserted my feet into the opening and...and stuck, at a region I prefer not to specify. There was not a moment to lose; gritting my teeth, I squeezed myself through, landing with bent knees, upright and ready. Pulling out my pistol, I leveled it at the door.

In the nick of time! And I might not have been in time, owing to that moment of delay, had she not flung herself at the yielding door. Her strength was not great enough; even as I aimed my pistol she was crushed behind the opened panel. The sounds of combat rose in pitch and a dark form rushed in, intent on obeying his leader's dastardly command.

There was no time for a reasonable discussion. I fired.

I could hardly avoid hitting him, for his body filled the doorway, but the wound was not mortal; his cry, as he recoiled, held more surprise than pain. Curse it, I thought, and fired again. I believe I missed him entirely on that occasion. However, the effect was gratifying. With another howl, he fled. These hired thugs are never reliable.

I now turned my attention to the woman, who had emerged from behind the door and stood watching me. It gave me an odd sensation to see her—the shadowy image of myself.

Emerson had swung his feet to the floor and sat up. Further effort was obviously beyond him; his face was ashen and his arms hung awkwardly at his sides. The very act of moving them must have been unutterably painful. He looked from me to the woman at the door and back to me, but he did not speak.

"Let me go," she whispered. "If your people catch me I will go to prison...or worse...Please, Sitt! I have tried to help him."

"Go, then," I said. "Close the door after you."

With one last, flashing look at Emerson, she obeyed.

Then, at last, at last, I could go where I yearned to go. I rushed to his side and knelt beside him. Emotion stifled breath and speech.

He stared blankly at me, a faint frown furrowing his brow. "One female in trousers is confusing enough, but two is a bit much for a man in my condition. If you will excuse me, madam, I believe I will take advantage of my freedom from restraint to...Oh, damnation!"

It was his last word, a bitter acknowledgment of his inability to do as he had planned. He fell to his knees and collapsed face-down onto the floor.

I was too numbed by shock to prevent it. The pistol dropped from my nerveless hand. But I was holding it leveled at the door, and cradling Emerson's unconscious head in the other arm, when Abdullah's shout informed me that our saviors had arrived. He burst through the door and stopped short, horror replacing the triumph on his face.

"You weep, Sitt! Allah be merciful—he is not..."

"No, Abdullah, no. It is worse than that! Oh, Abdullah—he does not know me!"

CHAPTER 7

"Marriage should be a balanced stalemate between equal adversaries."

Of course I did not mean what I said to Abdullah. There may be conditions worse than death, but there are few, if any, as irreversible. Gladly would I have searched the length and breadth of Egypt for my husband's dismembered body, as Isis did for Osiris; cheerfully I would have taken up my Orphean lyre and descended into the nethermost pits of Hades to fetch him back—had such deeds been possible. Unfortunately they were not; fortunately they were not necessary. There was a light at the end of this Stygian tunnel. So long as he lived, anything was possible. And if a thing is possible, Amelia P. Emerson will tackle the job.

It took a while to sort things out. My first task was to comfort Abdullah; he sat down on the ground and blubbered like a child, with relief and with distress at seeing his hero laid so low. Then he wanted to rush out and kill a few more people, but there were none; our victory had been complete, and since our men had not been concerned with taking prisoners, the survivors of the battle had run or crawled or crept away. Among the fugitives, I was chagrined to learn, was the leader.

"But we will find him," said Abdullah, grinding his teeth. "I saw him in the fight, before he ran away; it was a bullet from his weapon that wounded Daoud. I will remember him. And Emerson will know..."

He broke off, with a doubtful glance at me. "Yes," I said firmly. "He will. Now, Abdullah, stop ranting and be sensible. Daoud is not seriously injured, I hope? And your other men?"

Miraculously, none of our defenders had been killed, though several had been wounded. Daoud, who soon joined us, bore his bloody sleeve like a badge of honor and insisted on helping to carry the litter on which Emerson was borne away. I hated to move him, but the alternatives would have been more dangerous; we could not remain there, and the village offered no accommodations in which I would have put a sick dog. Emerson was deeply unconscious and did not stir, not even when the cart Abdullah had commandeered jolted along the path to the riverbank.

It goes without saying that I did not leave his side for an instant. Though I had not brought my medical kit, my expertise (derided though it often had been by Emerson) assured me that his heart beat strong and steady and his breathing, though shallow, showed no evidence of distress. The drugs he had been given were enough to account for his present state, though I had reason to suspect he had been kept short of food and water as well. His injuries were superficial except for the wound on the back of his head. That concerned me most, for it must be connected with his loss of memory.

What I had taken to be a clever ruse to avoid questioning was the terrible truth. He had not been delirious or off his head; his remarks had been rational, his mind clear. Except in one rather important particular.

As we approached the Castle I saw that it was lit from cellar to attics. I ran on ahead, in order to lose as little time as possible in making Emerson comfortable. When I reached the gate Cyrus was waiting.

I will not endeavor to reproduce his remarks. American profanity is apparently unrelated to the mother tongue or to any other language known to me. Determined as I was to make myself heard, I could not stop the flow of his eloquence. Not until the litter bearers came in sight with their precious burden did Cyrus break off, with a sound that must have hurt his throat.

Taking advantage of his momentary paralysis of speech, I said, "No questions now, Cyrus. Help me get him to bed. And make sure the doctor is admitted at once. I sent Daoud to fetch him when we passed through Luxor."

After I had put my stricken spouse to bed (for I would permit no other than myself to perform that tender duty), Cyrus joined me. Arms folded, he stood looking down at Emerson. Then he leaned forward and lifted one sunken eyelid.

"Drugged."

"Yes."

"What else is wrong with him?"

I had done all I could. Tucking in the last end of the

bandages I had wrapped around his lacerated wrists, I sat back and nerved myself to admit the painful truth.

"Apparently they realized, as anyone who knows Emerson must realize, that torture would only stiffen his resistance. He is not seriously injured, except...We agreed, you remember, after we had read the message, that he must be pretending to have amnesia. He was not pretending, Cyrus. He—he did not know me."

Cyrus sucked in his breath. Then he said, "Opium produces strange delusions."

"He was perfectly rational. His replies were sensible—sensible for Emerson, that is. Hurling insults and sarcastic remarks at a man who holds one a chained prisoner is not, perhaps, very wise."

Cyrus let out a brief bark of laughter. "Sounds like Emerson, all right. Still—"

"There can be no mistake, Cyrus. Would that there were! Not only did he look me straight in the face and call me 'madam,' but earlier he said...he said he would never be damned fool enough to saddle himself with a wife."

Cyrus's efforts to comfort me were interrupted by the arrival of the doctor. He was not the pompous little Frenchman with whose medical inexpertise I had been forced to deal on a previous occasion,* but an Englishman who had retired, for reasons of health, to a warmer clime. Evidently the desired effect had been achieved; though his beard was gray and his body cadaverously thin, he moved with the vigor of a young man, and his diagnosis assured me that we were fortunate to have found him.

* *Curse of the Pharaohs*

We could only wait, he said, for the effects of the
opium to dissipate. Though the dosage had been large,
the patient had not been under its influence for long; there
was every hope, given his splendid physique, that the process of recovery would be neither prolonged nor unduly
arduous. The only serious injury was the wound on the
back of the head, but this concerned Dr. Wallingford
less than it had me. "There is no fracture of the skull,"
he murmured, probing the area with sensitive fingers. "A
concussion, perhaps...We cannot assess that until the
patient has recovered consciousness."

"His loss of memory," I began.

"My dear lady, it would be a wonder if his memory
were not confused, after such a blow on the head and
daily doses of opium! Be of good heart; I have no doubt
he will make a full recovery."

He left after promising to return the following day
and after giving me directions I did not need but which
further reassured me, since they agreed in every particular with my own intentions: Keep the patient warm
and quiet, try to get him to take nourishment.

"Chicken broth," I murmured abstractedly.

A murmurous, musical mew sounded, as if in agreement. The cat Anubis had entered, as silently as the
shadow he resembled. I stiffened as the animal jumped
onto the bed and inspected Emerson from feet to head,
pausing to sniff curiously at his face. Abdullah's antipa-
thy toward the beast was based on ignorance and superstition, but—weary and worried as I then was—I found
myself beginning to sympathize with him. Had the
bearded blackguard who held Emerson captive been
Anubis's master? I had not been able to make out his

features. The voice had reminded me of Vincey's, but I could not be certain even of that, for its sneering tone had been quite unlike the gentle, well-bred accents of the man I had known so briefly. Anubis returned to the foot of the bed, where he lay down and began washing his whiskers. I relaxed, feeling a trifle foolish.

Cyrus returned after showing the doctor out. He announced that the cook was boiling a chicken and asked what else he could do to help me.

"Nothing, thank you. He has taken a little water; that is a good sign. I am very impressed with Dr. Wallingford."

"He has an excellent reputation. But if you would like to send to Cairo—"

"We will wait awhile, I think. I expect you are full of questions, Cyrus. I will answer some of them now if you like."

"I know most of the story. I gave myself the pleasure of a little chat with Abdullah." Seating himself in an armchair, Cyrus took out one of his cheroots and asked my permission to smoke.

"By all means. Emerson loves his nasty pipe; the smell of tobacco smoke may rouse him. I hope you were not too hard on Abdullah."

"I couldn't bawl him out, could I, for succeeding when I failed? Nor for letting you bully him into going along. You've got him right under your little thumb, Amelia."

"It was his devotion to Emerson that inspired him. But, yes, I think he is fond of me too. I never realized that. It was a touching moment when he opened his heart to me as he had never done before."

"Huh," said Cyrus. "I suppose I can't persuade you to get some rest while I keep an eye on my old pal."

"You suppose correctly. How could I sleep? Go to bed, Cyrus. You must be tired. I need not ask if your mission to the hotel was unsuccessful."

"I'm plumb wore out, it's true; but what did it was coming back here and finding you gone. I was afraid the message had been a stunt to get me out of the way so they could carry you off. I don't want to spend another couple of hours like those."

"Dear Cyrus. But all's well that ends well, you see."

"Let's hope so." Cyrus crushed out the cheroot. His hand was a trifle unsteady, and this evidence of affectionate concern moved me deeply. "Well, I'll leave you to your vigil. Call me if…Oh, shucks, I almost forgot. The mail came this afternoon. There's a letter for you from Chalfont."

"The promised letter!" I cried. "Where is it?"

Cyrus indicated a pile of letters on the table. The one on top was the one I wanted; its bulk suggested that the writer had quite a story to tell, and so it proved. A brief note from Walter introduced the missive.

I have decided to let young Ramses have his say; his epistolatory style has a panache mine lacks. You know your son well enough not to be misled by his tendency toward exaggeration. Have no fear for us, we have taken all precautions, as you will see. It is for you, dear brother and sister, that we are anxious. Please keep us informed.

There followed several pages closely written in a hand with which I was only too familiar. I can do no better than copy out this extraordinary document in its entirety, for it is impossible to summarize Ramses.

> *Dearest Mama and Papa [it began]. I trust this finds you well. We are all well. Aunt Evelyn assures me my hair will soon grow back.*

After I had recovered from the effect of this startling statement, I read on.

> *Your telegram was of great assistance in preventing a more serious event than actually occurred, but I already had reasons for suspecting that a game of some sort was afoot. While making my usual rounds of the estate in order to run off poachers and look for traps, I came upon a roughly dressed individual who, instead of running away when I challenged him, ran at me with the evident intention of taking hold of me. Retreating, as discretion seemed to indicate (for he was approximately twice my bulk), I led him through a thorn thicket and left him hopelessly entangled in the branches my lesser height and greater knowledge of the terrain enabled me to avoid. He was shouting loudly and profanely as I departed the scene, but when Uncle Walter and I and two of the footmen returned, he had fled.*
> *Uncle Walter, I regret to report, scoffed at my claim that the fellow's behavior roused the direst suspicions as to his motives for being there. After Papa's telegram arrived, however, Uncle Walter was gentlemanly enough to apologize and*

intelligent enough to reconsider the case. After a council of war we determined to take defensive measures. As I pointed out, it was safer to err on the side of excess than to fail from lack of caution.

Aunt Evelyn wanted to call the constable. She is a very kind person, but not practical. Uncle Walter and I persuaded her that we had no grounds for requesting official assistance, and that in order to convince officialdom of the validity of our reasons for concern we would have to disclose matters we had sworn to keep secret. Our defensive force, therefore, consists of the following:

1. Gargery. He was very pleased to be asked.

2. Bob and Jerry. As you know, they are the strongest of the footmen, and familiar with our habits. You will recall that Bob was of great assistance in our attack on Mauldy Manor, when I was fortunate enough to effect your escape from the dungeon.*

3. Inspector Cuff. I should say, "former Inspector Cuff," since he has retired from the force and is growing roses in Dorking. I spoke to him personally on the telephone (a most useful device; we must install one at Amarna House), and after he stopped sputtering and listened to what I had to say he was persuaded to join us. I believe he is bored with roses. Do not fear, Mama and Papa, we did not disclose the SECRET. I flatter myself that the Inspector has enough confidence in my humble self to believe my assurance that the matter is serious. Uncle Walter's

* Deeds of the Disturber

confirmation was of some small assistance in this regard.

It was fortunate (or, if you will permit me to say so, farsighted) that these measures were instituted; for Inspector Cuff, the last to arrive, had not been in the house twenty-four hours before the anticipated attack occurred.

It came about in this wise.

Finally! I thought, turning the page—and ground my teeth when instead of telling me what I ached to know, Ramses went off on another tangent.

If I have not mentioned Nefret you may be certain it is not because she was inactive or deficient in courage and intelligence. She is... [Here several words had been scratched out. Either Ramses's vocabulary had been inadequate to express his feelings, or he had repented of having expressed those feelings so openly.] She is a remarkable person. She... But perhaps an account of what occurred will demonstrate her qualities more effectively than mere words of mine could do.

I had anticipated—erroneously, as it turned out, but not without reason—that Nefret would be the person most in need of protection. For, if Papa's hints in his telegram and my own deductions based on those hints were correct, she was the one most directly connected with the aforesaid SECRET. It is true that my theory ignored the fact that the disheveled gentleman had apparently been intent on seizing ME, so perhaps chivalry had clouded my ordinarily acute reasoning powers. I once remember

*thinking that being a little gentleman seemed more
trouble than it was worth. The incident I am about
to relate confirmed that opinion, as you will see.*

"I certainly hope so," I muttered, wishing I had the
little "gentleman" with me so I could shake him and
force him to get to the point.

*Nefret had set out in the carriage that day as
usual, to go to the vicarage for a Latin lesson and
religious instruction. She was attended not only by
Gargery, who insisted on driving, but by Bob and
Jerry as well. Uncle Walter felt this would be protection enough, but I had a certain foreboding (such
as Mama often has) about the expedition, and so I
took one of the horses and went after them, remaining at a discreet distance, for I had reason to suppose that Gargery, Bob, Jerry, and perhaps Nefret
herself, would object to this procedure.*

*They had let their guard down, as they later
admitted, when they were almost at their destination.
After passing along that deserted stretch of road (you
remember it) where ambush might be expected and
where nothing of the sort ensued, they were within a
hundred yards of the first house of the village when
another carriage appeared around the curve in the
road, coming toward them at a considerable speed.
Gargery drew to one side to let them by. Instead of
doing so the driver pulled up and even before the wheels
had stopped rolling, men burst out of the carriage.*

*I saw everything that transpired, for the road
runs straight at that point and nothing impeded*

*my vision. I am sure I need not tell you I reacted
promptly and swiftly, urging my steed to a gal-
lop. Before I was able to reach the scene of action,
Gargery had taken a cudgel (his favorite weapon)
from under his coat and smashed it down on the
head of the individual who was attempting to pull
him from the seat. Bob and Jerry were grappling
with three other miscreants. A fifth man tugged at
the door of the carriage.*

*A cry burst from me at this terrible sight and I
fear I so forgot myself as to kick poor Mazeppa in an
attempt to induce greater speed. This turned out to
be unwise as well as unkind. Unaccustomed to such
treatment, Mazeppa came to a sudden halt, and I
fell off. I landed on my head. Undaunted, despite
the blood that flowed freely from the wound, I was
crawling toward the scene of battle when rough
hands seized me and a voice shouted, "I've got him!
Come on, lads, hold 'em off!"*

*Or words to that effect. The lads held them off
with such success that my captor reached the criminous carriage and transferred his grip to the back
of my neck and the seat of my trousers, preparatory,
one must suppose, to pitching me inside.*

*At that moment, when all seemed lost, I heard
an odd whistling sound, followed by a soft thud. The
man in whose grip I hung helpless and dizzy (for
a blow on the head, as you know, has the effect of
disorienting the recipient to a considerable degree)
shrieked aloud and dropped me. I am happy to
report that discretion prevailed over the lust for
battle that had brought me to my predicament. I*

rolled under the carriage, out the opposite side, and into a convenient ditch.

I was plucked from this refuge a few moments later by Gargery, in time to see the miscreants' vehicle retreating in a cloud of dust. My knees were a trifle unsteady, so Gargery very kindly held me up by my collar, while my eyes sought the object of my chief concern. "Nefret?" I gurgled. (I had swallowed a quantity of rather muddy water.)

She was there, leaning over me, an angelic vision…[Ramses had crossed this out, but the words were legible.]…her face pale with concern…for ME.

"Dear brother," she cried in poignant accents. "You are wounded! You are bleeding!" And with her own hand, careless of the mud and gore that stained her spotless white gloves, she parted the hair on my brow.

It was not my injury but the sight of what she held in her other hand that struck me dumb (a state, Mama might claim, that is uncommon with me). The object was a bow.

Swooning, I was carried away by Gargery and we soon found ourselves safe at home. Unfortunately I came back to my senses before the doctor stitched up my head. It was cursed painful. That was when some of my hair was cut off, but Aunt Evelyn says it will soon grow back. Everyone else was unhurt except for bumps and bruises.

It was Nefret herself, as you may have deduced, who saved the day. The villain who was attempting to open the carriage door went sprawling, his nose *bloodied, when she slammed it into his face, and the villain who carried me off was deterred by an arrow directed with a skill worthy of Robin Hood himself (if legend is to be trusted, which I doubt it is).*

The bow she had concealed under her heavy cloak (the weather being quite chilly) was the one she had brought with her from Nubia. Unlike the composite bows carried by the military, hers is a single-staff weapon only twenty-nine inches long, employed ordinarily for hunting. But why, one might ask, had she deemed it expedient to carry such a weapon? I did in fact ask; and she answered the question after my affectionate friends had gathered around my bedside for a council of war.

"I have kept a weapon close at hand ever since the Professor's telegram arrived," she explained coolly. "He is not a man to start at shadows, and although I am deeply grateful for the loyal protection of our friends, it is not in my nature to cower in a corner while others risk their lives in my defense. The Professor made it clear that Ramses and I were the ones in danger, not of assassination but of abduction. We know what the abductors want. Who could give them that information? Only your mother and father, Ramses; they alone know the way to the place the villains seek."

"I could retrace my steps—" I began with some indignation.

She raised a finger to her lips. "I know that, dear brother. But in this world children are treated like pet animals, without sense or memory, and you are one of the few who could do what you claim. I could not. *If they want you, it can only be as a hostage, to wring information from those who love you.*"

"And you," I hastened to assure her.

"Those who threaten us may reason so. Fear not, I will defend myself; I carry a knife as well as a bow and will use either if I must." Her face grew grave. "It is not for us I fear, but for the Professor and Aunt Amelia. They have not our strong protectors. They are in the greatest danger."

Her wise words made me realize, dear Mama and Papa, that in my concern for her I had not given enough attention to your predicament. I should be at your side. I proposed this to Uncle Walter, but he absolutely refused to buy a steamship ticket for me, and since I only possess one pound eleven shillings sixpence I cannot carry out the transaction without his financial assistance. Please telegraph at once and tell him to let me come. I am reluctant to leave Nefret, but the duty (and of course affection) of a son supersedes all other responsibilities. Besides, she has Gargery and the others. Besides, she does very well without me. Please telegraph immediately. Please be careful.

Your loving (and at this point in time extremely anxious) son,

Ramses.

P.S. Gargery was very disappointed that he could not rescue Nefret like Sir Galahad.

P.P.S. If you telegraph immediately I can be with you in ten days' time.

P.P.P.S. Or thirteen at the most.

P.P.P.P.S. Please be careful.

It would have required a great deal to turn my attention from Emerson at that moment, but this astonishing epistle almost succeeded. I recalled having mentioned to Ramses, on one occasion, that literary flourishes were best restricted to the written form. Obviously he had taken the suggestion to heart; but his questionable literary devices (swooning, indeed! What had the child been reading?) did not conceal his genuine emotion. Poor Ramses! To be rescued instead of rescuer—to fall off a horse, to be dragged out of a ditch and held up like a sack of dirty laundry, dripping with muddy water, before the eyes of the girl he yearned to impress...His humiliation had been complete.

And he had taken it like a man and an Emerson! He had only praise for her whose achievements had cast his into the shade. And how touching to a maternal heart was that piteous admission: "She does very well without me." Poor Ramses indeed.

As for Nefret, her behavior confirmed my initial impression of her character and convinced me that she would be a worthy addition to our little family. She had acted with the same vigor and independence I would have displayed, and as effectively. I am not accustomed to cower in corners either.

The very idea of Ramses at my side trying to protect me chilled the blood in my veins, and I only hoped Walter could prevent him from robbing a bank or playing highwayman in order to get the money. Not that I doubted the sincerity of his protestations. I must remember to telegraph next day, though how precisely to couch the message presented some difficulty. To inform without alarming them...

At that moment the rustle of linen brought me flying to Emerson's side. He had turned his head! It was only a slight movement and he did not stir again, but I hovered over him the rest of the night counting every breath and tracing every line of that beloved face with gentle fingers.

The beard would have to go, of course. Unlike his hair, Emerson's beard is very stiff and prickly. I objected to it as well on aesthetic grounds, for it hid the admirable contours of his jaw and chin, as well as the cleft in the latter organ.

In time of emotional distress the mind tends to focus on petty details. That is a well-known fact and accounts, I believe, for my failure to consider several problems rather more important than Emerson's beard. They were brought to my attention the following morning, when Cyrus entered to fetch me a breakfast tray and inquire how we had passed the night. I persuaded him—without difficulty—to join me in a cup of coffee, and entertained him by reading excerpts from Ramses's letter.

"I must telegraph at once, to reassure them," I said. "The question is, how much shall I tell them? They know nothing of what has transpired—"

"My dear Amelia!" Cyrus, who had been chuckling and shaking his head over the letter, immediately sobered. "If they don't know already, they soon will. We made no secret of his disappearance—heck, we plastered the whole town with notices. Unless I miss my guess, the English newspapers will get wind of the story from their Cairo correspondents and then we'll be in the headlines. You and your husband are news, you know."

The seriousness of the matter was immediately apparent to me. With Cyrus's help I determined on a course of action. We must telegraph at once, assuring our loved ones that Emerson had been found and that we were both safe and well, and warning them not to believe anything they read in the newspapers. "For I shudder to think what garbled versions of the facts those confounded journalists will report," I said bitterly. "Curse it, Cyrus, I ought to have anticipated this. I have had enough unpleasant encounters with the 'gentlemen' of the press."

"You had other things on your mind, my dear. The most important thing is to get poor old Emerson back on his feet and in possession of his senses. He'll take care of the reporters."

"No one does it better," I replied, with a lingering glance at the still face of my spouse. "But the danger is not over. The man responsible for this dastardly act got clean away. We dare not assume he will abandon the scheme. We cannot relax our vigilance for an instant, especially while Emerson lies helpless."

"Don't worry about that." Cyrus stroked his goatee. "Abdullah's relatives have surrounded the place like a band of Apaches besieging a fort. They've already man-handled my cook and beat up a date peddler."

With my mind at ease on this point, and the tele-gram having been dispatched, I could return my atten-tion to where my heart already lay. It was a trying time, for as the effects of the opium wore off, other, more alarming, symptoms appeared. They were due, Dr. Wallingford thought, to the other drugs Emerson had been given, but treatment was impossible since we did not know what they were.

Abdullah had returned to the prison to find the place swept clean. The police denied having taken anything away, and I was prepared to believe them, since they would not have had the sense to search the scene of the crime. It was evident that the kidnapper had returned to remove any evidence that might incriminate him. This was an ominous sign; but I had no leisure to consider the ramifications or contend with the reporters who, as Cyrus had predicted, besieged us, clamoring for news. Dr. Wallingford moved into one of the guest rooms and concentrated on his most interesting patient. His full attention was required, for coma was succeeded by delirium, and for two days it required all our efforts to prevent Emerson from harming himself or us.

"At least we know his physical strength is not seriously impaired," I remarked, picking myself up off the floor where Emerson's flailing arm had flung me.

"It is the unnatural strength of mania," declared Dr. Wallingford, rubbing his bruised shoulder.

"Nevertheless, I find it reassuring," I said. "I have seen him this way before. It is my own fault, I ought to have known better than...Get hold of his feet, Cyrus, he is trying to get out of bed again!"

Anubis had prudently retired to the top of the dresser, where he squatted, watching with wide green eyes. In the brief lull that followed Emerson's fit of agitation I became aware of a low rumbling sound. The cat was purring! Abdullah would have taken it for another sign of diabolical intelligence, but I felt a strange, irrational surge of renewed hope—as if the creature's purr were a good omen rather than the reverse.

I needed all the encouragement I could find during the dreadful hours that followed, but finally, after midnight on the third night, I dared to believe the worst was over. At last Emerson lay still. The rest of us sat round the bed, nursing our bruises and catching our breath. My eyes blurred; I was giddy and light-headed from lack of sleep. The scene was unreal, like a two-dimensional photograph of some past event—the smoky lamplight casting its shadows over the strained faces of the watchers and the emaciated features of the sick man, the silence unbroken except for the rustle of leaves outside the open window and Emerson's slow, regular breathing.

My senses did not dare to register that sign at first. When I rose and tiptoed to the bed, Dr. Wallingford came with me. His examination was brief. When he straightened, his tired face wore a smile.

"It is sleep—sound, natural sleep. Get some rest now, Mrs. Emerson. He will want to see you smiling and well when he wakes in the morning."

I would have resisted, but I could not; Cyrus had to half-carry me into the adjoining dressing room, where a cot had been placed for me. The unconscious mind—in which I firmly believe, despite its questionable status— knew I could now abandon my vigil, and I slept like the dead for six hours. Waking, filled with energy, I bounded from bed and rushed to the next room.

At least such was my intention. I was brought to a sudden stop by an apparition that appeared before me—shockingly pale, dreadfully disheveled, wild-eyed and unkempt. It was several seconds before I recognized my own image, reflected in the mirror over the dressing table.

A quick glance into the adjoining chamber assured me that Emerson still slept and that the good doctor, eyeglasses askew and cravat loosened, dozed in the chair next to the bed. Hastily I set about making a few essential repairs, smoothing my hair, pinching color into my cheeks, assuming my most elaborately ruffled and beribboned dressing gown. My hands shook; I was as tremulous as a young girl preparing for an assignation with her lover.

Sounds from the next room brought me flying to the door, for I recognized the querulous grunts and groans with which Emerson was wont to greet the day. If he was not himself again, he was producing a good imitation.

Cyrus, who must have been listening outside the door, entered when I did. Dr. Wallingford waved us back. Leaning over the bed, he said, "Do you know who you are?"

He was weary, poor fellow, or no doubt he would have found more felicitous phraseology. Emerson stared at him. "What a damned fool question," he replied. "Of course I know who I am. More to the point, sir, who the devil are you?"

"Please, Professor," Wallingford exclaimed. "Your language! There is a lady present."

Emerson's eyes swept the room in a slow survey and came to rest on me where I stood with hands clasped to my breast in order to still the telltale flutter of the ruffles that betrayed my wildly beating heart. "If she doesn't care for my language she can leave the room. I did not invite her."

Cyrus could contain himself no longer. "You blamed fool," he burst out, clenching his fists. "Don't you recognize her? If she had not dropped in uninvited a few days ago, you wouldn't be alive and blaspheming this morning."

"Another confounded intruder," Emerson muttered, glowering at Cyrus. He looked back at me... And this time there could be no mistake. The brilliant blue orbs were clear and conscious, and cool with indifference. They narrowed and his brows drew together. "Wait, though—the features are familiar, though the costume is not. Is she the unsuitably attired female who popped into my pleasant little room last night, like a cork forced into a bottle, and then proceeded to pepper the empty doorway with bullets? Females should not be allowed to handle firearms."

"It wasn't last night, it was three days ago," snapped Cyrus, his goatee quivering. "She saved your life with that pistol, you—you—" He broke off, with an apologetic glance at me.

A gleam of white teeth appeared amid the tangle of Emerson's beard. "I do not know you, sir, but you appear to be a hot-tempered fellow—unlike myself. I am always calm and reasonable. Reason compels me to confess that the doorway may not have been empty, and that this lady may have rendered me some small assistance. Thank you, madam. Now go away."

His eyes closed. A peremptory gesture from the doctor sent both of us from the room. Cyrus, still quivering with indignation, put a protective arm around me. Gently but decisively I removed it.

"I am quite composed, Cyrus. I do not require to be soothed."

"Your courage amazes me," Cyrus exclaimed. "To hear him deny you—sneer at your devotion and daring—"

"Well, you see," I said with a faint smile, "it isn't the first time I have heard such remarks from Emerson. I had hoped, Cyrus, but I had not really expected anything else. Having nerved myself to expect the worst, I was prepared for it."

In silence he placed his hand on my shoulder. I allowed it to remain; and neither of us spoke again until the doctor emerged from Emerson's room.

"I am sorry, Mrs. Emerson," he said gently. "Pray don't be disheartened. He has not forgotten everything. He knows his name and his profession. He asked after his brother Walter, and declared his intention of proceeding at once to his excavations."

"Where?" I asked intently. "Did he say where he intended to work this season?"

"Amarna," was the reply. "Is that important?"

"It was at Amarna that he was working when we became . . . well acquainted."

"Hmmm. Yes. You may have found the clue, Mrs. Emerson. His memory of events is clear and precise up to a period approximately thirteen years ago. He remembers nothing that has happened since that time."

"Since the day we . . . became acquainted," I said thoughtfully.

The doctor put his hand on my other shoulder. Men seem to think this gesture has a soothing effect. "Don't despair, Mrs. Emerson. He is out of danger, but he is still much weaker than his—er—peremptory manner might lead you to believe. It may be that his memory will return as his health improves."

"And maybe it won't," muttered Cyrus. "You're pretty doggoned nonchalant about it, Doc; isn't there anything you can do?"

"I am not a specialist in nervous disorders," was the huffy reply. "I would certainly welcome a second opinion."

"No offense meant," Cyrus said quickly. "I guess we're all pretty tired and short-tempered. A specialist in nervous disorders, you said...Hey! Wait a minute!"

His face lit up and he stopped twisting his goatee, which had gone quite limp under his attentions. "I guess the good Lord must be on our side after all. One of the world's greatest experts in mental disorders is on his way to Luxor at this very moment, if he is not already here. Talk about the luck of the devil!"

"What is his name?" the doctor asked skeptically.

"Schadenfreude. Sigismund Schadenfreude. He's a crackerjack, take my word for it."

"The Viennese specialist? His theories are somewhat unorthodox—"

"But they work," Cyrus declared enthusiastically. "I was a patient of his myself a few years ago."

"You, Cyrus?" I exclaimed.

Cyrus looked down and shuffled his feet like a guilty schoolboy. "You remember, Amelia—that business with Lady Baskerville? I gave my heart to that woman, and she smashed it to smithereens. I went around like a droopy-eared hound dog for quite a while, and then

I heard about Schadenfreude. He set me straight in a matter of weeks."

"I am very sorry, Cyrus. I had no idea."

"Water over the dam, my dear. I've been footloose and fancy-free ever since. I told Schadenfreude when we parted company to let me know if he was ever in Egypt and I'd show him what an archaeological dig was like. He must have arrived in Cairo right after I left. Got his letter a few days ago—paid no attention to it at the time—other things on my mind—but if I remember rightly, he planned to be in Luxor sometime this week. What do you say I run over and see if he's available?"

Of course the matter was not so easily arranged as Cyrus's sympathetic enthusiasm led him to hope. It was evening before he returned, towing the famous Viennese physician along like a pet dog.

Schadenfreude was a curious figure—very thin in the face and very round in the stomach, his cheeks so pink they looked rouged, his beard so silvery-bright it suggested a halo that had slipped its moorings. Myopic brown eyes peered uncertainly through his thick spectacles. There was nothing uncertain about his professional manner, however.

"A most interrrresting case, to be sure," he declared. "Herr Vandergelt has given me some of the particulars. You have not forced yourself upon him, *gnädige Frau*?"

I stiffened with indignation; but a wink and a nod from Cyrus reminded me that the famous doctor's imperfect command of English must be responsible for this rude question.

"He has slept most of the day," I replied. "I have not

insisted upon my relationship with him, if that is what you mean. Dr. Wallingford felt that might be unwise, at this stage."

"*Sehr gut, sehr gut.*" Schadenfreude rubbed his hands together and showed me a set of perfect white teeth. "I will alone the patient examine. You permit, Frau Professor?"

He did not wait for my permission, but flung the door open and vanished within, closing said door with a slam.

"Peculiar little guy, isn't he?" Cyrus said proudly, as if Schadenfreude's eccentricities proved his medical prowess.

"Er—quite. Cyrus, are you certain—"

"My dear, he's a wonder. I'm a living testimonial to his talents."

Schadenfreude was inside quite a long time. Not a sound emerged—not even the shouts I fully expected to hear from Emerson—and I was getting rather fidgety before the door finally opened.

"*Nein, nein, gnädige Frau,*" said Schadenfreude, holding me back when I would have entered. "It is a discussion we must have before you speak so much as a single word to the afflicted one. Lead us, Herr Vandergelt, to a place of discussion and supply, *bitte*, something of refreshment for the lady."

We retired to my sitting room. I refused the brandy the doctor tried to press upon me—the situation was too serious for the temporary consolation of spirits— and he applied himself to the beer he had requested with such gusto that when he emerged from the glass his mustache was frosted with foam. However, when he began to speak I had no inclination to laugh at him.

Many people at that time were skeptical about the theories of psychotherapy. My own mind is always receptive to new ideas, however repellent they may be, and I had read with interest the works of psychologists such as William James and Wilhelm Wundt. Since some of their axioms—particularly Herbart's concept of the threshold of consciousness—agreed with my own observations of human nature, I was inclined to believe that the discipline, when refined and developed, might offer useful insights. Herr Doktor Schadenfreude's theories were certainly unorthodox, but I found them horribly plausible.

"The immediate cause of your husband's amnesia is physical trauma—a blow on the head. Has he often suffered injury to that region?"

"Why—not to an excessive degree," I began.

"I don't know about that," Cyrus demurred. "I can remember at least two occasions during the few weeks we were together at Baskerville House. There's something about my old pal that makes people want to beat him over the head."

"He does not avoid physical encounters when he is defending the helpless or righting a wrong," I declared.

"*Also!* But the blow was only the catalyst, the immediate cause. It broke not only his head but the invisible membrane of the unconscious mind; and from this rent, this weakened part of the fabric, rushed fears and desires long suppressed by the conscious will. In short—in lay terms, *gnädige Frau und Herr Vandergelt*—he has forgotten the things he does not want to remember!"

"You mean," I said painfully, "he does not want to remember ME."

"Not you as yourself, Frau Emerson. It is the symbol he rejects."

When a man gets to talking about his own subject he is inclined to be verbose. I will therefore summarize the doctor's lecture. (I must warn the Reader that some of his statements were quite shocking.)

Man and woman, he declared, were natural enemies. Marriage was at best an armed truce between individuals whose basic natures were totally opposed. The need of Woman, the homemaker, was for peace and security. The need of Man, the hunter, was for the freedom to prey upon his fellowmen and upon women (the doctor put this more politely, but I caught his meaning). Society aimed to control these natural desires of man; religion forbade them. But the walls of constraint were constantly under attack by the brute nature of Man, and when there was a rent in the fabric, the brute burst forth.

"Good gracious," I murmured, when the doctor paused to wipe his perspiring brow.

Cyrus had gone beet-red and was biting his lip to repress strangled noises of indignation and denial. "Doggone it, Doctor, I have to object to your language in the presence of Mrs. Emerson—and to your slur upon the masculine gender. We aren't all—er— ravening beasts. You did say 'ravening,' didn't you?"

"Ravening and lusting," said Schadenfreude happily. "Yes, yes, that is the nature of man. Some of you repress your true natures successfully, *mein Freund*;

but beware! The greater the control, the more the pressure builds, and if there is a rent in the fabric of the walls—BOOM!"

Cyrus jumped. "Now see here, Doc—"

"Be calm, Cyrus," I urged. "The doctor is not being rude; he is being scientific. I am not offended, and indeed, I find some sense in his diagnosis. However, I am not so much interested in a diagnosis as in a cure. To employ your own metaphor, Doctor (and a striking one it is), how do we force the—er—beast back behind the wall and what kind of plaster do we use to mend it?"

Schadenfreude beamed approvingly at me. "You have an almost masculine directness, Frau Emerson. The procedure is obvious. One does not employ brute force against brute force; the ensuing struggle might wound both combatants mortally."

"Striking as the metaphor is, I would prefer a more practical suggestion," I said. "What am I to do? Would hypnosis—"

Schadenfreude shook a playful finger at me. "Aha, Frau Emerson! You have been reading the works of my more imaginative colleagues. Breuer and Freud are correct in stating that the operative force of the idea which was not abreacted by allowing its strangulated effect to find a way out in speech or action must be relived—brought back, in other words—to its status nascendi. But hypnosis is only a showman's toy that may do more harm than good by substituting the practitioner's own preconceptions for the psychical processes of the patient."

I believe I have rendered accurately the general sense of his discourse. He had to pause for breath at this point—not surprisingly—and when he went on, it was in more specific terms.

"The memory is like a lovely flower, *gnädige Frau*; it cannot be brought into existence fully formed, it must grow slowly and naturally from the seed. The seed is there in his mind. Return him to the scenes he does remember. Do not force memories upon him. Do not insist on facts he honestly, sincerely, believes to be false. This would be disastrous in his case, for if I read his character correctly, he is the sort of man who will insist on doing precisely the opposite of what you have told him to do."

"You've got that right," Cyrus agreed.

"But your suggestions are still too general," I complained. "Are you saying that we ought to take him back to Amarna?"

"*Nein, nein!* You *take* him nowhere. He goes where he wishes to go, and you accompany him. Amarna was the place he kept mentioning. An archaeological site, is it?"

"It's just about the most remote, desolate site in Egypt," Cyrus said slowly. "I don't think it would be such a smart idea for—for various reasons."

The doctor folded his delicate hands across his rounded stomach and smiled placidly at us. "You have no choice, my friend Vandergelt. Short of imprisonment, which is against the law, your only alternative is to have him declared incompetent. No reputable physician would sign such papers. I would not. He is not incompetent. He is not insane, within the legal definition of the word. If it is the unavailability of medical attention at this place—Amarna—that concerns you, do not be concerned. Physically he is on the road to recovery and will soon be himself again. There is no danger of a recurrence."

There was danger, however, though not of the sort of recurrence the good doctor meant. After he had departed Cyrus burst out, "I'm sadly disappointed in Schadenfreude. Of all the insulting theories...He never told *me* I was a ravening beast."

"He is an enthusiast. Enthusiasts tend to exaggerate. But I am forced to agree with some of his theories. What he said about marriage being a truce..."

"Hmph. That's not my notion of what the wedded state ought to be, but I guess you know more about the condition than a sorry old bachelor like me. But I'm dead-set against Amarna. You and Emerson would be like ducks in a shooting gallery out in that wilderness."

"I disagree, Cyrus. It is easier to guard oneself in a howling wilderness than in a teeming metropolis."

"In some ways, maybe. But—"

"Now, Cyrus, argument is a waste of time. As the doctor said, we have no choice. It will be good," I mused, "to see dear Amarna again."

Cyrus's stern face softened. "You don't fool me, Amelia. You are the bravest little woman I know, and that stiff upper lip of yours is a credit to the whole British nation; but it isn't healthy, my dear, to suppress your feelings this way. I've got a pretty broad shoulder if you want one to cry on."

I declined the offer, with proper expressions of gratitude. But if Cyrus had seen me later that night, he would not have had such a high opinion of my courage. Huddled on the floor of the bath chamber, with the door locked and a towel pressed to my face to muffle my sobs, I wept until I could weep no more. It did me good, I suppose. Finally I rose shakily to my feet and went to the window. The first pale streaks of dawn outlined the eastern mountains. Drained and exhausted, I leaned on the sill looking out; and as the light strengthened I felt a slow renewing trickle of the courage and hope that had temporarily abandoned me. My fists clenched, my lips tightened. I had won the first battle; against all odds, I had found him and brought him back to me. If other battles had to be fought, I would fight and win them too.

CHAPTER 8

"When one is striding bravely into the future, one cannot watch one's footing."

Years had passed since I last beheld the plain of Amarna, yet in eternal Egypt a decade is no more than the blink of an eye. Nothing had changed—the same wretched villages, the same narrow strip of green along the riverbank, the same empty arid plain behind, enclosed by frowning cliffs like the fingers of a cupped, stony hand.

It might have been only yesterday that my eyes last rested upon the scene, and this impression was further strengthened by the fact that I saw it from the deck of a dahabeeyah—not my beloved *Philae*, on which I had traveled during my first visit to Egypt, but an even grander and more luxuriously appointed sailing vessel.

These graceful floating apartments, once the most popular means of travel for well-to-do tourists, were fast disappearing. Cook's steamers plied the river; the railroad offered quick if uncomfortable travel between Cairo and Luxor. The spirit of the new century was already upon us, and although modern devices were no doubt more convenient, it was with a sigh that I contemplated the loss of dignity, leisure, and charm the dahabeeyahs had exemplified.

A few traditionalists clung to the old customs. The Reverend Mr. Sayce's boat was still a familiar sight along the river, and Cyrus also preferred the comfort of a dahabeeyah when traveling and when visiting sites where suitable accommodations were lacking. In fact, there was not a clean, much less comfortable, hotel to be found between Cairo and Luxor. Visitors who wished to stay at Amarna overnight had to camp out or request the hospitality of the local magistrate. This individual's house was only a little larger and hardly less filthy than those of the fellahin, so I was extremely pleased when Cyrus announced he had ordered his reis to bring his dahabeeyah to Luxor so that we might travel on it to Amarna.

I had seen *The Valley of the Kings*, as his boat was named, before; so you may conceive of my surprise when I beheld a new and astonishing sailing vessel awaiting us at the dock the day we left Luxor. Twice the length of the other boat, gleaming with fresh paint, it bore the name *Nefertiti* in elaborate gilt lettering on the prow.

"I figured it was time the old *Valley* was retired," Cyrus said negligently, after I had expressed my admiration. "Hope the decor meets with your approval, my dear; I had one suite fixed up to suit a lady's taste, in the hope that one day you might do me the honor of sailing with me."

I concealed a smile, for I doubted I was the only lady

Cyrus had hoped to entertain. He was, as he had once said, "a connoisseur, in the most respectable sense, of female loveliness." Certainly no female could have been other than delighted at the facilities this rough-hewn but gallant American had provided; from the lace-trimmed curtains at the wide windows to the daintily appointed dressing room adjoining the bath, everything was of the finest quality and most exquisite taste.

The other guest rooms—for the boat had eight—were equally splendid. After a silent, contemptuous survey of the accommodations, Emerson selected the smallest of the chambers.

He had not accepted this means of transport without a considerable fuss. The arguments of Dr. Wallingford, who insisted that a few more days' recuperation would be advisable, had their effect; so did the arguments of Cyrus, who had presented himself to Emerson as the financier of that season's work.

It was in matters such as these that my afflicted husband's loss of memory served to our advantage. He knew there were gaps in his memory; the (to him) overnight whitening of Abdullah's grizzled beard would have been proof enough had there been no other evidence. He dealt with this difficulty, as I might have expected Emerson to do, by coolly ignoring it. However, he was thus forced to accept certain statements as true because he could not assert they were false. It was quite the usual thing for wealthy individuals to finance archaeological expeditions. Emerson disapproved of the practice—and said so, rather emphatically—but being unaware of his own financial situation, he was forced in this case to agree.

Did I hope that the tranquil voyage, the moonlight rippling along the water, would bring back fond memories of our first such journey together—the journey that had culminated in that romantic moment when Emerson had asked me to be his? No, I did not. And it is just as well I didn't, for my dream would have been doomed to disappointment. In vain did I flaunt my crimson flounces and my low-cut gowns (for I thought it would not hurt to try). Emerson fled from them like a man pursued by pariah dogs. The only time he condescended to notice my existence was when I wore trousers and talked of archaeology.

I wore my new working costume at luncheon the day after we left Luxor (the crimson gown having had the aforesaid result the previous night). I was late joining the others, for I had, I admit, gone through my entire wardrobe before deciding what to wear. Cyrus got to his feet when I entered. Emerson was slow to follow his example, and he gave me a long look, from boots to neatly netted hair, before doing so.

"This is just the sort of inconsistency I object to," he remarked to Cyrus. "If she dresses like a man and insists on doing a man's work, why the devil should she expect me to jump to my feet when she enters a room? And," he added, anticipating the reproof that was hovering on Cyrus's lips, "why the devil can't I speak as I would to another fellow?"

"You can say anything you like," I replied, thanking Cyrus with a smile as he helped me into my chair. "And I will say what I like, so if *my* language offends *you*, you will have to put up with it. Times have changed, Professor Emerson."

Emerson grinned. "Professor, eh? Never mind the academic titles, they aren't worth—er—considering. Times certainly have changed, if, as Vandergelt here tells me, I have employed a female for the past several years. An artist, are you?"

Women had occasionally served in that capacity on archaeological digs; they were generally considered unfit for more intellectually taxing activities. I decided not to remind Emerson of the two ladies who had excavated the temple of Mut at Karnak a few years earlier, for even at the time he had been critical of their methods. But to do him and them justice, he was equally critical of the efforts of most male archaeologists.

Calmly I replied, "I am an excavator, like yourself. I am a fair draftsman, I am acquainted with the use of surveying instruments, and I can read the hieroglyphs. I speak Arabic. I am familiar with the principles of scientific excavation and I can tell a pre-dynastic pot from a piece of Meidum ware. In short, I can do anything you...or any other excavator...can do."

Emerson's eyes narrowed. "That," he said, "remains to be seen."

To my affectionate eyes he was still painfully thin, and his face had not regained its healthy tan. Not much of it was visible; he had irritably refused to trim his beard, and it had spread up his cheeks and formed a jetty bush around jaws and chin. It looked even worse than it had when I first met him. But his eyes had regained their old sapphirine fire; they shot a challenging look at me before he applied himself to his soup and relapsed into ominous silence.

No one broke it. Emerson might not be entirely himself again, but there was enough of him to dominate any group of which he made a part; and the two young men who were at the table with us shrank into near invisibility in his presence.

I beg leave to introduce to the Reader Mr. Charles H. Holly and M. René D'Arcy, two of Cyrus's assistants. If I have not presented them before, it is because I had never met either of them; they were of the new generation of archaeologists, and this was Charlie's first season in Egypt. A mining engineer by profession, he was a ruddy-cheeked cheerful young man with hair the color of Egyptian sand. At least he had been cheerful until Emerson got at him.

René, as pale and soulful-looking as a poet, was a graduate of the Sorbonne and a skilled draftsman. The ebon locks that fell gracefully over his brow matched the mustache that drooped with corresponding grace over his upper lip. He had a very pleasant smile. I had not seen the smile since Emerson got at him.

Emerson had quizzed them like students at a viva-voce examination, criticizing their translations of hieroglyphic texts, correcting their Arabic, and deriding their stumbling descriptions of excavation technique. One could hardly blame them for not coming off well under that blistering interrogation; I had heard distinguished scholars stutter like schoolboys when Emerson challenged their theories. The poor lads could not know that, and they took pains to avoid my husband thereafter. Neither of them knew the SECRET, as Ramses would have called it, but they were aware of the fact that the peril from which Emerson had escaped might still pursue us. Cyrus assured me they were devoted to him, and good men in a fight, as he put it.

Not until he had finished eating—with good appetite, I was happy to see—did Emerson speak again. Throwing down his napkin, he rose and fixed a stern look on me. "Come along, Miss—er—Peabody. It is time we had a little chat."

I followed him, smiling to myself. If Emerson thought to catch me out or intimidate me as he had the poor young men, he was in for a salutary shock.

The Reader may be surprised at my calm acceptance of a situation that should have induced the strongest feelings of anguish and distress. Fortitude in the face of adversity has always been my way; tears and hysteria are foreign to my nature. Could I ever forget that supreme accolade I had once received from Emerson himself? "One of the reasons I love you is that you are more inclined to whack people over the head with your parasol than fling yourself weeping onto your bed, like other women."

I had had my night of weeping—not on a comfortable bed, but on the hard floor of the bathroom at the Castle, huddled in a corner like a beaten dog. Never doubt that there were other moments of pain and despair. But what purpose would a description of them serve? None were as severe as that first uncontrolled outburst of anguish; I had purged myself of useless emotions that terrible night; now every nerve, every sinew, every thought, was bent on a single purpose. It was as if I had forced myself to lose those same years Emerson had lost—to return in my mind to the past.

In this I was following the dictates of Dr. Schaden-freude. "You," he had informed me, on the eve of our departure, "you, Frau Emerson, are the crux. My initial impression has been confirmed by all that I have seen since. It is from the bonds of matrimony that his memory retreats. In all else he is receptive; he accepts with relative equanimity what he is told. On that subject alone he remains obdurate. Follow him into the past. Recapture the indifference with which you once regarded him. Act upon it. And then...act upon what follows."

Cyrus had become sadly disenchanted with Dr. Schadenfreude since that distinguished gentleman expressed his views on marriage and the reprehensible habits of the male sex. Like most men, Cyrus was a secret romantic, and hopelessly naive about people. Women are more realistic—and I, I believe I may say without fear of contradiction, am a supreme realist. The doctor's advice appealed to certain elements of my character. I enjoy a challenge; the more difficult the task, the more eager I am to roll up my sleeves and pitch in. I had won Emerson's heart before, against considerable odds, for he had been a confirmed misogynist and I am not and have never been beautiful. If the spiritual bond between us, a bond transcending the limits of time and the flesh, was as strong as I believed, then I could win him again. If that bond existed only in my imagination...I would not, could not, concede it was so.

So with limbs atingle and brain alert I followed him to the saloon, which also served as a library and Cyrus's study. It was a symphony in crimson and cream, with touches of gold. Even the grand piano had been gilded—one of Cyrus's few descents into execrable trans-Atlantic taste. Emerson flung himself into an armchair and took out his pipe. While he was messing with it, I took up a manuscript from the table. It was the little fairy tale I had been reading in Cairo; I had taken it up again in order to distract my mind.

"It is my turn to be tested, I presume," I said composedly. "Shall I translate? This is 'The Doomed Prince,' a tale with which you are no doubt familiar."

Emerson glanced up from poking at his pipe. "You read hieratic?"

"Not well," I admitted. "This is Walt—er—Maspero's hieroglyphic transliteration." And without further ado I began, "There was once a king to whom no son was born. So he prayed the gods he served for a son, and they decreed that one should be born to him. Then the Hathors came to decree his destiny. They said, 'He shall die by the crocodile or the snake or the—' "

An invisible hand gripped my throat. Superstition is not a weakness to which I am prone, but the parallel suddenly struck me with such force I felt like the unhappy parents hearing the doom prophesied for their child.

At the beginning of our acquaintance at Amarna, Emerson and I had faced an adversary I had described as a veritable crocodile, waiting on the sandbank to destroy the lover seeking his sweetheart. Now another enemy threatened us—a man who had used the name Schlange. In German, Schlange means snake.

Nonsense, said the rational part of my much-tried brain. Fanciful you may be, but this is the grossest kind of pagan morbidity. Dismiss it! Let common sense prevail over the affectionate fear that has weakened the ratiocinative process!

Unaware of the painful struggle going on under his very eyes, Emerson said sarcastically, "Is that the extent of your preparation?"

"I can go on if you like."

"Never mind. I did not request a private interview in order to review your qualifications. If Vandergelt can be believed, I have already accepted them."

"You have."

"And you were present on the presumed expedition concerning which my gentle host was so curious?"

"I was."

"It did take place?"

"It did."

"At least she doesn't talk as incessantly as most women," Emerson muttered to himself. "Very well, then, Miss—er—Peabody. Where the devil did we go, and why? Vandergelt claims to be ignorant of those facts."

I told him.

Emerson's eyebrows performed a series of alarming movements. "Willie Forth? It seems only yesterday I spoke with him . . . You say he is dead?"

"And his wife. The details do not matter," I continued, for I was not anxious to recall some of those details. "What does matter is that someone has learned that Mr. Forth's lost civilization is not a fantasy, and that we alone can lead him to it. We swore we would never disclose its location—"

"Yes, yes, you explained that. Forgive me," Emerson continued, with poisonous politeness, "if I express a certain degree of skepticism about the whole affair. I told Willie Forth he was mad, and thus far I have seen no evidence that contradicts that judgment. You and your dear friend Vandergelt might have invented this story for reasons of your own."

"You still bear the evidence of someone's interest in your affairs," I said indignantly. "Your bruised head and that horrible beard—"

"What does my beard have to do with it?" Emerson clutched protectively at the appendage in question. "Leave my beard out of this, if you please. I grant you that someone appears to be taking an impertinent interest in my personal affairs, but he was not as specific as you—"

"How could he be? He knows nothing about the place except that it holds incredible riches—"

"Do you always interrupt people when they are talking?"

"No more than you. If people go on and on—"

"I never interrupt," Emerson shouted. "Pray allow me to finish the point I am endeavoring to make."

"Pray make it," I snapped.

Emerson drew a deep breath. "There are a number of individuals who hold grudges against me. I am not ashamed of that; indeed, it is a source of modest pride to me, for in all cases their resentment stems from my interference with their illegal or immoral activities. I am also, as you may have observed, close-mouthed—discreet—taciturn. I don't tell people everything I know. I don't trumpet my knowledge to the world. I never speak unless—"

"Oh, good Gad," I exclaimed, jumping to my feet. "I quite agree with the premise you are suggesting, at such unnecessary length: there are undoubtedly dozens of people who would like to murder you for dozens of different reasons. You want evidence that this particular individual is after one particular piece of information? I will give you evidence. Come with me."

He had no choice but to obey or leave his curiosity unsatisfied, for I was on my way to the door even as I spoke. Stamping heavily and muttering under his breath, he followed me until I reached my room and flung the door open.

"Here!" he exclaimed, starting back. "I refuse to—"

Exhilarated, amused, and exasperated, I got behind him and gave him a shove. "If I make a rude advance you can scream for help. When you see what I have to show you, you will understand why I prefer not to remove it from this room. Sit down."

Eyeing the canopied bed as if it might extend ruffled tentacles to grasp him, Emerson circled around it and lowered himself cautiously into a chair. He stiffened when I went to the bed, but relaxed a little after I had taken the box out from under the mattress and handed it to him.

The sight of the contents brought a soft whistle to his lips, but he did not comment until after he had examined both scepters thoroughly; and when he raised his eyes to my face they glittered with the old blue fire of archaeological fever. "If they are fakes they are the finest I have ever seen, and you and Vandergelt have gone to considerable trouble to deceive me."

"They are genuine. We are not deceiving you. Not even Cyrus has seen these, Emerson. He knows no more about the matter than does our unknown enemy, who put together the same clues Cyrus—"

"Unknown? Not to me."

"What?" I cried. "You recognized him?"

"Of course. He had grown a beard 'and dyed it and his hair, and he looked older...which," Emerson mused, "is only to be expected, since he *was* older. No doubt about it, though. Well, well. This explains why he was so bad-mannered. I could not imagine why he was put out with me, since I had been one of the few to defend him. What a sad world it is, when greed proves stronger than gratitude and the lust for gold overcomes friendship—"

"Men are so naive," I exclaimed. "The commonest reaction to favors rendered is resentment, not gratitude. He probably detests you even more than he does those who condemned him. So it was Mr. Vincey. I thought I recognized his voice."

"You know him?"

"Yes. That is his cat." I indicated Anubis, who was curled up on the sofa. "He asked us—curse his insolence!—to care for the animal while he went to Damascus."

"He certainly was not in Damascus," Emerson said. "Very well, let us get down to business instead of wandering all around the subject the way you women are inclined to do. Vincey is on the loose and it would be extremely careless of us to assume he has given up his little project. He has all the more reason to be vexed with me now, after I got away from him so neatly. I could...What's the matter? Something caught in your throat? Have a glass of water and don't distract me."

It did not seem an opportune moment to remind him that his escape had been neither neat nor due to his efforts. Choking on my indignation, I remained silent. Emerson went on thoughtfully, "I could track him down, I suppose, but I will be damned if I allow him to interfere with my professional activities any more than he already has. If he wants me, he will come after me. Yes, that will be best. I can get on with my work, and if he turns up, I'll settle the fellow."

I was meditating how best to respond to this complacent statement when I heard someone approaching. The steps were those of Cyrus; the rapidity of their pace made my scalp prickle with apprehension. He was almost running, and as he neared my door he began to call out.

"Amelia! Are you there?"

"Just a moment," I called, snatching the box from Emerson and hastening to restore it to its hiding place. "What is it, Cyrus? What has happened?"

"Big trouble, I opine. We have found a stowaway!"

As soon as I had the box concealed, I admitted Cyrus. In my excitement I had overlooked the fact that Emerson's presence might cause some embarrassment—particularly to Emerson—until I saw Cyrus's jaw drop and color flood his lean cheeks. Emerson had gone equally red in the face, but he decided to brazen it out.

"You are interrupting a professional discussion," he growled. "What's all the fuss about?"

"A stowaway," I reminded him. "Who? Where?"

"Here," Cyrus said.

One of the sailors pushed her into the room. One had to assume she was female from her dress, though the worn black robes completely covered her shape and the dusty veil hid all but a pair of terrified dark eyes.

"It is some poor village woman fleeing a cruel husband or tyrannical father," I cried, my sympathies immediately engaged.

"Hell and damnation," Emerson exclaimed.

Her eyes found him where he sat bold upright, hands clutching the arms of his chair. With a sudden effort she tore herself free and flung herself at his feet.

"Save me, O Father of Curses! I risked my life for you, and now it hangs by a thread."

Exaggeration seemed to be in the air that day, I thought to myself. She had tried to keep the murderous guard from entering Emerson's prison, but how could her dread master know of that? Was this even the same woman? Her voice sounded different—huskier, deeper, and with a distinct accent.

"You are safe with me," Emerson said, studying the bent black head with—I was happy to observe—a rather skeptical expression. "If you speak the truth."

"You doubt me?" Still on her knees, she sat back and wrenched the veil from her face.

I cried out in horror. No wonder I had not recognized her voice; the prints of fingers showed dark on her bruised throat. Her face was equally unrecognizable, swollen and stained by the marks of brutal blows.

"This is what he did to me when he learned you had escaped," she whispered.

Pity had not altogether wiped out my suspicions. "How did he learn..." I began.

Replacing the veil, she turned to me. "He beat me because I had shown compassion and because... because he was angry."

Emerson's face was impassive. Those who had never

beheld a demonstration of the seething sea of sentiment his sardonic exterior conceals might have believed
him to be unmoved; but I knew he was thinking of
the child-woman he had been unable to save from her
murderous father.* Nothing of this showed in his voice
when he said gruffly, "Find her a room, Vandergelt.
God knows you've enough useless space on this boat."

She kissed his hand, though he tried to stop her, and
followed Cyrus out. Frowning, Emerson took out his
pipe. I heard Cyrus summon his steward; after directing the fellow to show the lady (he stumbled a bit over
the word, but I had to give him credit for the effort) to
a vacant stateroom, he returned.

"Are you loony, Emerson? The da—er—darned
woman's a spy."

"And her bruises were incurred in an effort to give
verisimilitude to an otherwise unconvincing story?"
Emerson asked dryly. "How devotedly she must love
her tormentor."

Cyrus's lean face darkened. "That's not love. It's a
kind of fear you'll never know."

"You are right, Cyrus," I said. "Many women know
it—not only the helpless slaves of a society such as this,
but Englishwomen as well. Some of the girls Evelyn has
taken in off the streets... It does you credit, Cyrus, that
you can understand and sympathize with a condition
so alien from any you could ever have experienced."

"I was thinking of dogs," Cyrus said, blushing at my
praise but too honest to accept it when it was undeserved. "I've seen 'em come fawning back to the feet of

* Curse of the Pharaohs

the varmint that had beaten and kicked them. You can reduce a man to that state too, if you go about it right."

Emerson blew out a great cloud of blue smoke. "If you two have quite finished your philosophical discussion, we might try to settle this matter. The girl's arrival raises another point which I was about to make when Miss—er—Peabody got me off the track. Vincey may not be the only one involved."

Cyrus expressed surprise at the name, and I took it upon myself to explain. "I thought at the time his voice was familiar, Cyrus, but he had disguised his appearance so well I could not be certain. Emerson has just now confirmed my assumption, and I suppose he could hardly be mistaken. Do you know Mr. Vincey?"

"By reputation," Cyrus replied, frowning. "From what I've heard I wouldn't put such a trick past him."

"He certainly was not the only one involved," I went on. "Abdullah claims to have killed at least ten of the enemy."

This little sally produced a smile from Cyrus, but not from Emerson. "Local thugs," he said curtly. "Such men can be hired in any city in Egypt or in the world. The girl is another such tool. Vincey has an unsavory reputation as regards women."

"Women of the—of that class, you mean," I said, remembering Vincey's grave courtesy toward me, and remembering as well Howard's veiled hints about his reputation. Repressing my indignation, I went on, "I find your use of the word 'tool' interesting. She may still be serving him in that capacity. Cyrus is right—"

"I am not so naive"—Emerson shot me a malignant glance—"as to accept the girl's story unreservedly. If she is a spy, we can deal with her. If she is telling the truth, she needs help."

"Must have been a good-looking woman before he got to work on her," said Cyrus.

This apparent non sequitur, which was of course nothing of the kind, did not escape Emerson. His teeth showed in a particularly unpleasant smile. "She was, yes. And will be again. So behave yourself, Vandergelt; I don't allow distractions of that nature to interfere with my expeditions."

"If it were up to me, I'd kick her off the boat tonight," Cyrus declared indignantly.

"No, no. Where's that famous American gallantry? She stays." Emerson turned the singularly unpleasant smile on me. "She will be company for Miss Peabody."

After they had gone, I gathered up a few things and went to the woman's room. The door was locked from the outside, but the key was in the lock; I turned it, announced my presence, and entered.

She was sprawled across the bed, still swathed in her dusty black robe. It was with some difficulty that I persuaded her to discard it, and she refused to allow me to attend to her injuries; so I handed her the clean nightgown I had brought and allowed her to attend to her ablutions in private. When she emerged from the bathroom she seemed startled to see me still there. Averting her face and cringing like the dog with which Cyrus had compared her, she hurried to the bed and got under the covers.

"I don't know what we are to do about clothing," I said, hoping to put her more at ease by discussing a subject that seldom fails to interest females. "My traveling wardrobe is not extensive enough to equip you as well."

"Your gowns would not fit me," she muttered. "I am taller than you, and not—not so—"

"Hmph," I said. "I will procure fresh robes for you when we stop at the next town, then. This one is filthy."

"And a veil—please! It would hide me from watching eyes."

I doubted it would prove a sufficient disguise to deceive the man she feared so desperately, but since my aim was to soothe her and win her confidence, I decided not to raise unpleasant subjects. Under my tactful questioning she unbent so far as to tell me something of her history.

It was a sad story and, sadly, not uncommon. The child of a European father and an Egyptian mother, she had fared better than the offspring of most such alliances, for her German father had at least had the decency to provide a home for her until she reached the age of eighteen. His death left her at the mercy of his heirs, who disclaimed any responsibility and denied any relationship. Her efforts to support herself in a respectable occupation had been frustrated by her age and her sex; while employed as a housemaid she had been seduced by the eldest son of the family and cast out onto the street when his parents discovered the affair. Naturally they blamed her and not their child. She had used the last of her savings to return to the land of her birth, where she found her maternal relatives as hostile as those of her father; alone and despairing in Cairo, she had met...HIM.

Seeing she was trembling with fatigue and agitation, I bade her rest. Her reticence could not be allowed to continue indefinitely, of course. I was determined to know all she knew. But that could wait till another time and, perhaps, a more persuasive questioner.

When we tied up for the night I sent one of the servants to the village bazaar to purchase clothing for Bertha—for such, she claimed, was her name. It certainly did not suit her, conjuring up (to me at least) images of blond Germanic placidity.

I had not achieved my aim of picking Bertha's brain by the time we arrived at our destination. Emerson refused to have anything to do with the matter. "What can she tell us—that Vincey is a brute, a liar, and a seducer of women? His past activities, criminal or otherwise, are of no interest to me; I am not a police officer. His present address—even supposing he were fool enough to return to any location known to her—is equally irrelevant. When I want the bastard, I will find him. Just now I don't want him. I want to get on with my work, and I will do it, come hell or high water, miscellaneous criminals, or female busybodies!"

For a stretch of almost forty miles along the Nile in Middle Egypt the cliffs of the high Eastern Desert rise sheer from the water's edge except in a single spot where they curve back to form a semicircular bay some six miles long by three miles deep. The barren, level plain seems even more forbidding than do other abandoned sites, for this is a haunted place—the site of short-lived splendor, of a royal city now vanished forever from the face of the earth.

Here, equidistant from the ancient capitals of Thebes to the south and Memphis to the north, the most enigmatic of Egyptian pharaohs, Akhenaton, built a new city and named it Akhetaton after his god Aton—"the only one, beside whom there is no other." By pharaoh's order the temples of other gods were closed; even their names were obliterated from the monuments. His insistence on the uniqueness of his deity made him a heretic in ancient Egyptian terms—and in our terms the first monotheist in history.

The portraits of Akhenaton show a strange haggard face and an almost feminine body, with broad hips and fleshy torso. Yet he was not deficient in masculine attributes, as the existence of at least six children proves. Their mother was Akhenaton's queen Nefertiti—"lady of grace, sweet of hands, his beloved"; and his romantic attachment to this lovely lady, whose very name meant "the beautiful woman has come," is shown in numerous reliefs and paintings. Tenderly he turns to embrace her; gracefully she perches on his knee. These depictions of marital accord are unique in Egyptian art, and uncommon anywhere. They had a particular attraction for me; I do not believe it is necessary for me to explain why that was so.

Some scholars view Akhenaton as morally perverse and physically deformed, and decry his religious reformation as nothing more than a cynical political maneuver. This is nonsense, of course. I do not apologize for preferring a more uplifting interpretation.

I trust the Reader has not skipped over the preceding paragraphs. The aim of literature is to improve the understanding, not provide idle entertainment.

We were all at the rail on the day of our arrival, watching as the crewmen maneuvered the dahabeeyah in toward the dock at the village of Haggi Qandil. The period of rest had done Emerson good; tanned and bursting with energy, he was almost his old self again—except for the confounded beard. He was also in a high good humor for, though it had almost choked me to do it, I had not pressed him on the subject of Mr. Vincey and Bertha. However, Cyrus and I had discussed the matter at length and had agreed upon certain precautions.

Waiting on the quay were twenty of our faithful men from Aziyeh, the little village near Cairo which produced some of the most skilled diggers in Egypt. I had sent Abdullah to fetch them to Amarna, and the sight of their keen, smiling faces was more reassuring to me than that of a troop of soldiers would have been. They had worked for us for years; Emerson had trained them himself, and they were devoted to him body and soul.

Emerson climbed over the rail and jumped ashore. He was still thumping backs and shaking hands and submitting to fervent embraces when I joined the group. I was not the second one ashore, however. The cat Anubis preceded me down the gangplank.

Abdullah drew me aside and gestured at the cat, which was giving each set of sandaled feet a thorough inspection. "Have you not rid yourself of that four-footed afreet, Sitt Hakim? He was the betrayer of Emerson—"

"If he was, it was inadvertent, Abdullah. Cats cannot be trained to lead people into ambushes—or to do anything else they don't want to do. Anubis has become very attached to Emerson; he stayed with him, on the foot of his bed, all the while he was ill. Now, Abdullah, have you warned the other men that Emerson is still in danger from the man who called himself Schlange, and told them of the subjects they must not mention?"

"Such as the subject that you are the wife of the Father of Curses?" Abdullah spoke with a sarcasm worthy of Emerson himself, and his prominent hawklike nose wrinkled critically. "I have told them, Sitt. They will obey, as they would obey any command you gave, though they do not understand your reasons. Nor do I. To me, this is a foolish way of bringing back a man's memory."

"For once we see eye to eye, Abdullah," said Cyrus, joining us. "But I reckon we've got to go along. When the Sitt Hakim speaks, the whole world listens and obeys."

"No man knows that better than I," said Abdullah.

Emerson's shout brought us gathering around. "Abdullah has set up camp for us," he announced.

"And I have washed the donkeys," said Abdullah.

Emerson stared at him. "Washed the donkeys? What for?"

"He was following my orders," I said. "The little animals are always in wretched condition, covered with sores and inadequately tended. I do not allow…Well, that is beside the point. Will you now condescend to tell us where we are going and what you propose to do—and why we require a campsite when we have the dahabeeyah?"

Emerson turned the stare on me. "I have no intention of staying on that cursed boat. It is too far from the tombs."

"Which tombs?" I asked, stepping heavily on Cyrus's foot to still the objection he was about to make.

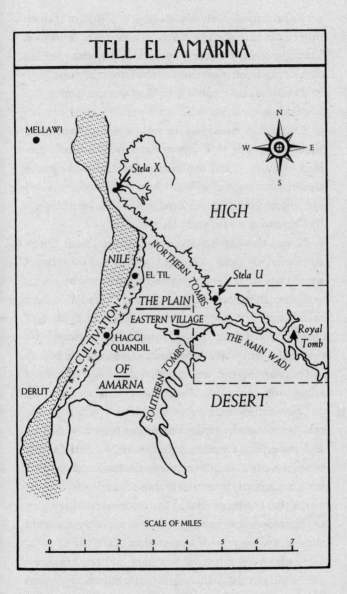

TELL EL AMARNA

MELLAWI

Stela X

N

W · E

S

HIGH

NILE

NORTHERN TOMBS

Stela U

EL TIL

THE PLAIN

EASTERN VILLAGE

CULTIVATION

Royal Tomb

HAGGI QUANDIL

THE MAIN WADI

OF

SOUTHERN TOMBS

AMARNA

DERUT

DESERT

SCALE OF MILES

0   1   2   3   4   5   6   7

"All the tombs. The southern group is a good three miles from here and the northern group is even farther. There is another interesting area in a hollow behind that low hill near the center of the arc of the cliffs."

"There are no tombs there," I objected. "Unless the brick-work—"

Emerson gestured impatiently. "I will make my final decision tonight. My object today is to make a preliminary survey, and the sooner you stop arguing, the sooner we can get at it. Well? Any further objections?" He wheeled suddenly on René, who had edged closer.

There were no further objections.

Before the day was over, any doubts as to Emerson's physical condition were removed. He declared we did not need the donkeys—a statement with which everyone disagreed but to which everyone except myself was too cowed to object. I knew perfectly well that he was testing us—me, especially—and so I did not object either. We must have walked almost twenty miles, counting the perpendicular distances we covered scrambling over piles of rocky scree and climbing up and down the cliffs.

The easiest way of describing this hegira is to envision the area as a semicircle, with the Nile forming the straight side. The cliffs of the high desert curve like a bow; at the extreme north and south ends they almost touch the riverbank. Haggi Qandil is somewhat south of the midpoint of the straight line, so we were a good three miles from the nearest section of the cliffs.

The path led through the village and the surrounding fields out onto the plain—an undulating, barren surface littered with pebbles and potsherds. The ruined foundations of Akhenaton's holy city lay under the drifted sand. It had stretched the entire distance from the north end of the plain to the south. The portion we had excavated during the years we worked at Amarna lay farther to the south, but I felt sure the slow, inexorable hand of nature had reclaimed the site and buried all evidence of our labor as it had that of the ancient builders.

Emerson struck briskly out across the plain. Quickening my pace, I caught up to him. "I take it, Emerson, that we are going to the northern tombs?"

"No," said Emerson.

I glanced at Cyrus, who shrugged and smiled and invited me, with a gesture, to walk with him. We allowed Emerson to forge ahead, with only Abdullah close on his heels. No one else seemed eager for his company.

We did, in fact, visit some of the northern tombs, but not until after Emerson had indicated another kind of monument he wanted to examine in detail that season.

Around the rocky perimeter of his city Akhenaton had carved a number of commemorative markers defining its boundaries and dedicating it to his god. Emerson and I had found and copied three of them ourselves. These stelae, as they are called, were similar in form: a central round-topped marker bearing a long hieroglyphic inscription under a scene in bas-relief that depicted the king and his family worshiping their god Aton, in the form of a sun-disk extending rays that ended in small human hands. Statues of the royal family stood on either side. Most of the boundary stelae were in ruinous condition; some portions had been deliberately destroyed by the royal heretic's enemies after his death and the restoration of the old gods he had denied.

"There are two series of inscriptions, one earlier in time than the other," said Emerson. Hands on his hips, bareheaded in the baking sunlight, he stood staring up at the cliff that towered over us. "This is one of the earlier; there are two princesses shown with their parents. The later stelae show three daughters."

Cyrus took off his solar topi and fanned himself with it. "How the dickens you make that out I don't know. The top of the darned thing has to be thirty feet off the ground and the cliff is absolutely sheer."

"It cannot be approached except from above," said Emerson. He turned. Charlie was trying to hide behind Abdullah, whose tall form and voluminous robes offered a good-sized shelter, but Emerson's eyes went straight to him. With ferocious good humor Emerson said, "The boundary stela are your responsibility, Holly. A healthy young fellow like you should enjoy the challenge of copying texts while you dangle at the end of a rope."

A precipitous path led us up to the ledge on which the northern group of nobles' tombs were located. Once they had gaped open, vulnerable to the depredations of time and tomb-robbers. Recently the Antiquities Department had put up iron gates at the entrances to the most interesting of them. Emerson studied these gates, which had not been there in our time, with critical curiosity.

"Isn't there an American saying about locking the barn door after the horse is stolen? Ah, well; better late than never, I suppose. Who has the keys?"

"I can get them," Cyrus replied. "Since I did not know—"

"I may want them later," was the curt reply.

He refused to say more until we had reached Abdullah's campsite. Knowing Abdullah, I was not surprised to see that his efforts had consisted of putting up a few tents and gathering camel dung for a fire.

"Very nice, Abdullah," I said. The reis, who had been watching me out of the corner of his eye, relaxed, and then stiffened again as I went on, "Of course nothing is as commodious as a nice, convenient tomb. Why can't we—"

"Because we are not going to work at the tombs," said Emerson. "This site is equidistant between the two groups, northern and southern."

"Site?" Cyrus repeated indignantly. "What the dev——the dickens do you want to waste your time on this area for? There can't be any houses out here, so far from the main city, and no one has found any evidence of tomb shafts."

Emerson's well-shaped lips—now, alas, virtually hidden from my fond eyes by bristling black hair—curled in a sneer. "Most of my colleagues couldn't find a tomb shaft if they fell into it. I told you, Vandergelt, explanations will have to wait till this evening. We have quite a distance yet to cover; follow me."

The sun was now directly overhead and we had been walking (to use that term loosely) for several hours. "Lead on," I said, taking a firm grip on my parasol.

Emerson had already eyed this appendage askance, but had not asked about it, so I saw no reason to explain that a parasol is one of the most useful objects an individual can carry on such an expedition. Not only does it provide shade, but it can be used as a walking stick or, if need be, as a weapon. My parasols had frequently been employed in the latter capacity. They were specially made, with a heavy steel shaft and a pointed tip.

Like the gallant gentleman he was, Cyrus came to my rescue. "No, sir," he declared. "It's high noon and I'm famished. I want my lunch before I stir another step."

Emerson was ungraciously pleased to agree.

The shade of the tents was welcome. One of Cyrus's servants unpacked the hampers his chef had provided, and we consumed a luncheon far more elegant than most field archaeologists enjoy. While we ate, Emerson condescended to lecture again. He directed most of his remarks at the two young men.

"The brickwork Miss—er—Peabody referred to is on the slopes and at the bottom of the hollow behind us. Some of it probably belongs to tomb chapels. The ruins on the floor of the hollow are clearly of another nature. I will start there tomorrow with a full crew. You, Vandergelt, and Miss—er—"

"If the title bothers you so much, you may dispense with it," I said calmly.

"Hmph," said Emerson. "You two will assist me. I trust this meets with your approval, MISS Peabody?"

"Quite," I said.

"Vandergelt?"

"I can hardly wait," said Cyrus, with a grimace.

"Very well." Emerson jumped to his feet. "We have dawdled long enough. Let us be off."

"Back to the dahabeeyah?" Cyrus asked hopefully. "Since you have decided where you mean to excavate—"

"Good God, man, there are a good six hours of daylight left, and we have seen less than half of the area. Hurry up, can't you?"

Enviously the others watched Cyrus's servant strike off toward the river with the empty hampers; then the procession formed again, with Emerson's entourage trailing after him.

I presumed he meant to complete the circuit of the cliffs, and my heart beat high at the thought of seeing again the southern tombs where we had dwelt for so many happy years. But somehow I was not surprised when he led us into the foothills toward an opening in the rocky ramparts. Cyrus, ever at my side, let out a stifled American oath.

"Great jumping Jehoshaphat! I had a horrible premonition about this. The royal wadi! It's a three-mile hike each way and I'll bet you the temperature is high enough to fry an egg on a rock."

"I'll bet you it is," I agreed.

As I have already explained, but will reiterate for the benefit of less attentive readers, the wadis are canyons cut through the high desert plateau by past floods. The entrance to this one was located midway between the southern and northern groups of tombs. Its proper name is the Wadi Abu Hasah el-Bahri; but for reasons that should be evident, it is commonly referred to as the main wadi. The royal wadi proper is a narrow offshoot of this larger canyon, approximately three miles from the entrance to the latter. Here, in a spot as remote and desolate as a lunar valley, Akhenaton had caused his own tomb to be built.

If the southern tombs brought back poignant memories, the royal tomb recalled scenes that had impressed themselves indelibly upon my heart. In the gloomy corridor of that sepulcher I had felt Emerson's arms about me for the first time; along the rubble-strewn floor of the wadi we had raced by moonlight to save those we loved from a hideous death. Every foot of the way was familiar to me, and the spot was as fraught with romance as a garden of roses might be to one who had led a more boring life.

Shortly after we entered it the valley curved, cutting off our view of the plain and the cultivation beyond. After approximately three miles the rocky sides closed in and smaller wadis opened up on either side. Emerson had already disappeared; following, we saw him trotting along one of the narrow side canyons, whose floor rose as it proceeded to the northeast.

"There it is," I said, in a voice pent with emotion. "Ahead and to the left."

Soon the others saw it too—a dark opening framed by masonry, above a scree of tumbled rock. Charlie groaned. His clean-shaven countenance already showed signs of what promised to be a painful sunburn. Even a hat cannot entirely protect those of fair complexion from the effects of Egypt's burning solar orb.

When we had climbed to the ledge in front of the tomb, Emerson was there, glowering at the iron gate that barred entry. "We will certainly need this key," he said to Cyrus. "Make sure I have it tomorrow morning."

By the time Emerson announced we were finished for the day, I was as much in the dark about his intentions as was Cyrus. He had scrambled around the foot of the cliffs to the north and south of the royal tomb for over an hour, poking into holes like a ferret after a rat.

"Where are we going?" Cyrus asked, as we trudged wearily back along the rock-strewn path. "See here, Emerson, there's no earthly reason why we can't spend the night on the dahabeeyah."

"I never said there was," said Emerson, with an air of innocent astonishment that left Cyrus gnashing his teeth.

When we reached the gangplank I saw that Anubis was waiting for us. Where he had been or how he had spent his time I could not imagine, but when we approached he rose, stretched, yawned, and accompanied us onto the boat.

"We will meet in the saloon in half an hour," said Emerson, heading for his room. The cat followed him. I heard him say "Nice kitty," as he stumbled over it.

I had barely time to bathe and change in the time he had arbitrarily allotted, but I managed it, hastily selecting a garment that required no prolonged process of hooking up, and no assistance with regard to buttons. (I cannot imagine how women lacking husbands or personal maids ever manage to get dressed. Gowns that fasten up the back are impossible except for a contortionist.)

Emerson was already there, brooding over a heap of papers and plans spread across the table. His eyebrows lifted when he saw my pink flounces and ruffles (the garment to which I have referred was a tea gown), but he made no comment, and only grunted when I ordered the steward to serve tea.

I was pouring when Cyrus came in, followed closely by the two young men. Apparently they felt there was safety in numbers. Poor Charlie was as red as an English brick, and René's mouth repeated the downward droop of his mustache.

Emerson sat tapping his fingers on the table and looking pointedly patient while I dispensed the genial beverage. Then he said, "If the cursed social amenities are concluded to your satisfaction, MISS Peabody, I would like to get on with it."

"Nothing has prevented you from doing so," I said mildly. "Take this to Professor Emerson, René, will you please?"

"I don't want any damned tea," said Emerson, taking the cup. "I thought you were all burning to know where we are going to excavate."

"You told us," Cyrus said, while Emerson sipped his tea. "The stelae—"

"No, no, they won't occupy us for the entire season," Emerson interrupted. "You American dilettantes are always after royal tombs. What do you say to the tomb of Nefertiti?"

CHAPTER 9

"Martyrdom is often the result of excessive gullibility."

Emerson enjoys making dramatic announcements. I fear the results of this one disappointed him. Instead of expressions of rapturous enthusiasm or scornful disbelief (he is quite happy with either), he got only a skeptical grunt from Cyrus. The two young men were afraid to commit themselves by speaking at all, and I raised my eyebrows and remarked, "She was buried in the royal tomb, with her husband and child."

Emerson had finished his tea. He held out his cup to be refilled and girded himself for the kind of battle he much enjoys and in which (I must confess) he generally triumphs.

"Fragments of his sarcophagus have been found, none that might have been hers. If Nefertiti died before her husband—"

"No one knows when she died," I said. "If she survived into the reign of Tutankhamon, she may have gone with him to Thebes and been buried—"

"Yes, yes," Emerson said impatiently. "All that is idle

speculation. But it was you who informed me that in recent years objects bearing her name have appeared on the antiquities market, and that there are rumors of fellahin carrying a golden coffin across the high desert behind the royal valley."

(It was Charlie who had informed him, actually, hoping to distract him from the evening inquisition by relating archaeological gossip. The distraction had not succeeded.)

"There are rumors like that about every site in Egypt," said Cyrus—but though his tone dismissed the story, the light in his eyes indicated his rising interest. To a man of Cyrus's romantic temperament there could be no more thrilling discovery than the last resting place of the heretic pharaoh's exquisite queen.

"Certainly," said Emerson. "And I put no great faith in the golden coffin. Such a unique object could not have been marketed without leaving signs of its passage through the dirty world of dealers and collectors. Note, however, the significant word 'gold.' Any artifact made of or covered with gold could start the gossip mills grinding and lead to the usual exaggeration that distinguishes their operation. The appearance of inscribed objects on the antiquities market is even more significant. That, if you recall, was how Maspero got onto the cache of royal mummies in 1883. The Gurnawis who had found the hiding place began marketing objects from it; the names on those objects indicated they must have come from a tomb unknown to archaeologists."

"Yes, but—" I began.

"But me no buts, MISS Peabody. There are other tombs in the royal wadi. I have known of some of them for years, and I feel certain there are others. The royal tomb itself has not been properly explored; are there passages and chambers as yet undiscovered? Certain of the existing ones seem strangely incomplete. Curse it, Akhenaton had thirteen years after his arrival at Amarna in which to prepare a tomb. It would have been one of his first acts. The boundary stelae mention his intention of doing so—"

"Those same inscriptions suggest that the queen shared his tomb," I interrupted. " 'There shall be made for me a tomb in the eastern mountain; my burial shall be therein...and the burial of the Great Royal Wife Nefertiti shall be therein—' "

"Ah, but does 'in it' refer to the tomb itself or to the eastern mountain?" Emerson leaned forward, his eyes glittering with the joy of argument—or, I should say, learned debate. "He goes on to say, 'If she (Nefertiti, that is) shall die in any town north, south, west or east, she shall be brought and buried in Akhetaton.' He does not say 'in my tomb in Akhetaton—' "

"There was no need for him to say it, given the context. He meant—"

"Will you two stop that?" Cyrus demanded. His goatee quivered with the muscular contractions of his jaws and chin. "The man's been dead for over three thousand years, and anyhow, his original intentions don't mean a curse. What I want to know is, where are those other tombs you were talking about, and why the—er—dickens haven't you excavated them?"

"You know my methods, Vandergelt," said Emerson. "Or at least you claim to. I never excavate unless I can finish the job without delay. Opening a site or a tomb invites the attentions of thieves, or of other archaeologists, who are almost as destructive. I have knowledge of or strong suspicions about at least six other sites..."

He let the words trail off. Then he said deliberately, "We will excuse you, Charles and René. No doubt you want to freshen up before dinner."

Two men cannot constitute a stampede, but they tried.

Emerson had reached for his pipe and was spilling tobacco all over his papers. As soon as the door closed he said, "I trust you have no objection to my dismissing your employees, Vandergelt?"

"It wouldn't do a whoop of good if I did object," said Cyrus. "But I think I see where you're heading, and the less those two innocents know about the other business, the better. Are you suggesting Vincey was trying to pick your brain about those unknown tombs?"

"Nonsense," I exclaimed. "We know exactly what Vincey wants, and it has nothing to do with—"

"May I remind you," said Emerson, in the growling purr that usually heralded a particularly devastating remark, "that it was I the gentleman questioned, not you."

"You need not remind me, since I was the first to observe the results of his questioning," I snapped. "But may *I* remind *you* that you have not seen fit to confide the details to me or to Cyrus. What the devil did he ask you?"

"My state of mind was a trifle confused," said Emerson, with one of those infuriating volte-faces men employ to avoid a direct answer. "The details elude me."

"Oh, really!" I exclaimed. "Now see here, Emerson—"

"Don't waste your time, my dear," said Cyrus, as Emerson grinned at me in a particularly trying fashion. "Can we get back to the question of the tombs in the royal wadi? I take it that is your real goal this season. So what's the point of messing around with that brickwork in the hollow?"

Emerson opened his eyes very wide. "Why, I intend to do both, of course. And copy the boundary stelae. We'll start in the hollow, as I said." He rose, stretching like a great cat. "I must change for dinner. I trust, MISS Peabody, that you intend to do the same; that garment seems more suitable to the boudoir than the dinner table. The proprieties must be observed, you know."

After he had gone, Cyrus and I stared silently at one another. His craggy face was soft with the sympathy he dared not express aloud, and since I felt no desire for sympathy I did not invite him to express it.

"Curse the man," I said pleasantly.

"You know what he is up to, I suppose."

"Oh, yes. Emerson's mind is an open book to me. His memory may be flawed, but his essential character is unaltered."

"What are you going to do about it?"

"As is my habit whenever possible, I am going to follow the advice set forth in Scripture. 'Sufficient unto the day is the evil thereof' is, in my opinion, one of the wisest statements in that wonderful Book. I will deal with Emerson's lunatic scheme when he tries to put it into effect. Who knows what may transpire before that time? And now, if you will excuse me—"

"Are you going to change?" Cyrus asked.

I smiled. "Certainly not."

* * *

I had left our uninvited guest to herself, since she had intimated that she did not find my company desirable. So far as I was aware, she had not emerged from her room. Her meals were carried to her and Cyrus insisted that her door be locked at night. That evening I decided that a serious discussion with the young woman could not be postponed any longer. I had hoped Emerson would want to question her, but to the best of my knowledge he had not done so. His intent was clear to me now. I had suspected from the moment he expressed it that his proclaimed intention of ignoring Vincey unless the latter again attempted to interfere with him was a flat-out lie. "If he turns up, I'll settle the fellow," indeed! He expected Vincey would "turn up"; he fully intended to "settle the fellow," and in order to hasten the confrontation he meant to leave the safety of the dahabeeyah and station himself somewhere in the desert, like a tethered goat staked out as a lure for a tiger, in the hope Vincey would initiate another assault. It was also clear to me that Emerson was still skeptical about the Lost Oasis. (I had to admit I would have doubted the story myself if I had not actually been there.) Hence his references to hidden tombs and Nefertiti's treasures. He would employ any means possible to intrigue an enemy and encourage him to attack. He meant to go his solitary, stubborn way without consulting the rest of us or taking us into his confidence. It left me with no choice but to do the same; and since I was cognizant of facts Emerson did not know and would not have admitted if he had, the burden was as usual on my shoulders.

Bertha was sitting by the open window. The cool night breeze stirred the muslin curtains. A single lamp burned by the bed. In its light I saw that she was wearing one of the robes I had purchased at a village bazaar. It was black—only young unmarried girls wore colors—but unlike her original garment it was clean and unworn. She looked like a giant crow huddling against an approaching storm, and as she turned toward me I saw her lower her hand from her face. The veil was in place.

"Why do you feel it necessary to hide your face from me?" I asked, seating myself in the chair next to hers.

"It is not a pretty sight."

"Still? The swelling should have gone down by now. Let me have a look."

"I do not need your medicine, Sitt Hakim. Only time—if you will allow me that."

"For your face to heal, yes. For other things—no. Not while the life of the Father of Curses is still in danger."

"And yours, Sitt Hakim." There was a strange note in her voice, as if she smiled as she spoke.

"Yes, I suppose so. Bertha"—I still stumbled over that inappropriate name—"we have left you in peace, to rest and recover your health. Now it is time for you to prove yourself. Mr. Vandergelt believes you were sent here to spy on us."

"I swear to you—"

"My dear girl, you are not speaking to some gullible man, but to another woman. I have excellent reasons, unknown to Mr. Vandergelt, for believing in your good intentions; but for your own sake as well as ours you must give me more active assistance."

"What do you want, then? I have told you all I know."

"You have told me nothing. I want dates, names, addresses, facts. We have learned—no thanks to you!—the identity of the man who was your master and your tormentor. Do you know him by his true name of Vincey, or only as Schlange, the name he used in Luxor? Were you in Cairo with him? When did he leave for Luxor? Where did he go after he was driven from the villa? Where is he now?"

I had brought pencil and notepaper. From the way she responded to my questions, I had the impression she was no stranger to official interrogation, but she answered me readily enough. Those answers confirmed what I already suspected, but were of little use in planning future strategy.

"Does a hammer driving nails into a piece of wood know the plan of the house?" she asked bitterly. "I was not good enough to share his apartment in Cairo. He called himself Schlange there too, I know him by no other name. He came to my house when he wanted... In Luxor I lived at the villa, it is true. No one knew him there, his reputation was not damaged by my presence, and he needed me to help him break the Father of Curses. After I left you that night I went to my room; I was packing my clothes when he came, and forced me to go with him. I had to leave everything, my jewelry, my money! We stayed for a week in a cheap hotel in Luxor; when he left it, which was seldom, he locked me in the room. I could not go out, I had nothing to wear but the clothes that were like yours, and I dared not appear in them on the streets of Luxor."

"A week, you said. But your bruises were fresh when you came to us. He did not abuse you at first?"

The veil quivered, as if her lips writhed under it. "No more than usual. He was waiting, I think, to see whether the Professor would recover, and to learn what you meant to do next. One day, when he returned, he brought the robe you saw me wearing and told me to put it on. We would go that night—"

"Where?"

"Does a man who carries a piece of luggage inform it of its destination? He was very angry. He had learned something—no, don't ask me what, how would I know?—something that drove him wild. He uttered only vile curses and threats, and complaints about those who had failed him. They, whoever they may have been, were not there. I was there. So…"

"Yes, I see." The news that had driven Vincey to violence must have been the failure of his people in England to kidnap Ramses and Nefret. Ramses's letter had reached me at about that time. "How did you get away from him?" I asked.

"He slept heavily that night," she said. "And the garments he had brought were the very disguise I would have chosen. Veiled and in black I looked like any woman of Luxor. He thought I would never have the will or the courage to leave him, but fear, when it reaches a certain point, can inspire courage. I knew that night what I had been unwilling to admit before: that one day he would kill me, out of rage or suspicion of betrayal."

She had spoken with a passion and seeming candor that could not fail to move a sympathetic hearer. The story made sense, too, as far as it went. I waited for a moment to allow her to calm herself, for her voice had grown hoarse and tremulous with remembered terror.

"You do not appear to be in a position to betray very much," I said. "You don't know where he intended to go, or what he intended to do. You cannot describe any of his friends or associates?"

"Only the men he hired in Luxor. They could not betray him either; they never knew his real name, only the one he used when he rented the villa."

"Schlange," I murmured. "I wonder why... Well. Is that all you can tell me, then?"

She nodded vehemently. "Do you believe me? You will not abandon me, unprotected and alone?"

"You don't mean to insult me, I suppose," I said calmly. "But if you imagine I would betray even an enemy to death or torture, you cannot be familiar with the moral code that guides a Briton. The beautiful tenets of the Christian faith require that we forgive our enemies. To that creed we all adhere... At least," I amended, remembering Emerson's unorthodox views on the subject of organized religion, "most of us do."

"You are right," she murmured, bowing her head submissively. "He would not abandon me."

I knew to whom she referred. "None of us would," I said somewhat sharply. "But we face a difficulty. Tomorrow we begin our excavations and for long hours, perhaps for days at a time, we will be away from the dahabeeyah. Are you afraid to stay here alone, with only the crew?"

She indicated, with considerable vehemence, that she was. "He is here, I know it! I have seen shadows moving in the night..."

"In your head, you mean. Our guards have seen nothing out of the way. Well, I suppose you will have to come with us. Though heaven knows what I am going to do with you."

In fact, when we left the boat the following morning she blended in quite well with the interested villagers who gathered around our little group. There were women among them; I would not have been able to distinguish her from the other black-robed figures had she not stayed close to me. I had expected she would dog Emerson's heels, but she did not, perhaps because she would have had to contend with the cat for that position.

Our entourage followed us as we passed through the village. Some of them hoped to be employed on the dig, others were drawn by idle curiosity. The people of Haggi Qandil had become more accustomed to visitors since the days when we had first worked there, for many of the tourist steamers stopped on their way upriver, but life in these small settlements is extremely dull; any new face, especially that of a foreigner, attracts a crowd. How these people had changed since our first visit! Fair dealing and kindly treatment had converted a once sullen population into ardent supporters; smiles and waves and Arabic greetings—and the conventional demands for baksheesh—followed us along the way. Even the lean, abused dogs slunk along behind at a safe distance; they had learned that visitors sometimes threw scraps of food to them. I always made a habit of doing so.

A number of men and children continued to follow as we left the village and headed for the cliffs. Emerson led the way as usual. The morning was pleasantly cool and he was still wearing his tweed jacket. I observed with a start of surprise that he had taken the cat up on his shoulder. Ramses had trained the cat Bastet to do the same, but owing to the meager dimensions of that portion of Ramses's anatomy Bastet had to drape herself around his neck. Emerson's frame suffered no such disadvantage; Anubis sat bolt upright, leaning slightly forward like the figurehead on a ship. I must say they presented an extremely odd appearance, and I wondered how Emerson had won the animal's confidence to such an extent.

Emerson glanced back at the ragtag, cheerful straggle of people and called to Abdullah, "We shan't want diggers and basket children till tomorrow or the next day. Tell them to go back; we will let them know when we intend to begin hiring."

"I am hiring today," said Cyrus, strolling along with his hands in his pockets.

Emerson slowed his steps and allowed Cyrus to catch him up. They made an amusing contrast, Cyrus in his immaculate white linen suit and solar topi, his lean cheeks closely shaved and his goatee as precisely barbered as the artificial beards worn by Egyptian pharaohs; Emerson in creased coat and trousers, his shirt open at the neck, his boots scuffed and dusty, his uncovered black head shining in the sunlight. The cat was much better groomed.

"May I inquire whom you are hiring, and for what purpose?" Emerson inquired politely.

"Allow me to surprise you," Cyrus replied with equal politeness.

As soon as we arrived at the site, Cyrus took his recruits aside and began lecturing them in ungrammatical but effective Arabic. It was not long before the results became apparent. Construction is quick and easy in Egypt, where the most common building material is mud, formed into sun-dried bricks or used as mortar over a foundation of reeds. The architectural techniques are equally simple, and have been employed since time immemorial. It does not require complex equipment to design a square flat-roofed house with a door and a few ventilation slits high up under the eaves. Wide windows are not an advantage in that climate; they admit heat rather than air, and allow the entrance of creatures with whom one would not care to share living quarters.

Emerson ostentatiously ignored the furious activity going on a short distance away, busying himself with a preliminary survey and plan of the area, nor did he refer to it immediately when we stopped for a spot of lunch. Accepting a plate from Bertha, who had appointed herself cook's helper, he spoke to her for the first time that day.

"Sit down and eat. Who told you to wait on us?"

"It was her own idea," I said, knowing full well whom he suspected of having given the order. "And I agree with her, that under the present circumstances anonymity is to be preferred to the equality of station I would otherwise insist upon."

"Hmph," said Emerson. Taking this for what it was—a tacit admission of the wisdom of my decision—Bertha quietly withdrew.

Cyrus watched her retreating form with narrowed

eyes. I had passed on to him the information, such as it was, Bertha had given me the night before. Now he said, "I still don't trust the darned woman. I want her watched day and night. I want her inside four walls where nobody can get at her without making a racket."

"Ah, it is a prison you are building," Emerson said, gesturing toward the rising walls.

"Cut it out, Emerson, I'm getting tired of your sarcasm. These darned tents aren't my idea of a proper headquarters; canvas walls won't keep out scorpions or sand fleas, much less thieves. If you won't spend the nights on the dahabeeyah—"

"Wherever did you get that idea?" Emerson asked.

"From you, you stubborn, bullheaded—"

"Language, Vandergelt! There are ladies present. You must have misunderstood me." He rose. "But go ahead and build your expedition house if you like. The rest of us have work to do. Charles—René—Abdullah—"

So we spent the next three nights on the dahabeeyah. Emerson's experienced eye had been right again; the bricks in the hollow were the foundations of houses—one house, at least—for by the end of the third day the men had uncovered most of it and found part of a thick enclosure wall that must have surrounded the entire area.

Evening social activities were negligible; the two young men were so exhausted they kept slumping forward onto the table during dinner, and sought their beds immediately thereafter. Cyrus avoided me, explaining ingenuously that Emerson had him in such a temper he could not speak civilly even to me. Emerson locked himself in his room and Bertha was locked into hers. I was, of course, perfectly fit and ready for any interesting activity that presented itself, so for me the evenings were extremely tedious—not even an attempted burglary or armed attack to break the monotony.

I was therefore delighted when Cyrus joined me in the saloon on the third evening, looking very elegant in the evening kit he always wore in my honor, and with an expression that suggested his mood had improved. "The mail-boy has just arrived from Derut," he announced, his smile anticipating the pleasure he hoped to bestow upon me.

The thick packet he handed me did indeed bear the Chalfont crest. I hastened to open it, but I suspected my pleasure might not be entirely unalloyed.

There had been a frantic flurry of telegrams before we departed from Luxor. Unhappily, my message announcing Emerson's rescue did not arrive in England until after our dear ones had learned of his disappearance, and the first telegram I received from them was so agitated as to be virtually unintelligible. A second message announced the arrival of mine, expressed relief, and demanded further details. These I supplied as best I could, given the limitations of the medium and the necessity for reticence. I knew perfectly well that the telegraph operators in Luxor were susceptible to bribery, and that the jackals of the press were well aware of this deplorable habit—which is, however, only to be expected in a country whose inhabitants do not possess the advantages of British moral training, or a living wage.

I had promised to write, and had, of course, done

so. However, I doubted my letter could have arrived by this time; certainly it had not arrived in time to elicit a response from Ramses. He must have written this even before the dreadful news of his father's disappearance became known to him.

In this last assumption I was mistaken, as the date heading the letter proved. I looked up at Cyrus, who was still on his feet, unwilling to seat himself until I had invited him to do so, but fairly quivering with the curiosity he was too courteous to express.

"Stay, dear friend," I said. "I have no secrets from you. But first tell me how this missive reached me so quickly. It is dated only eight days ago, and the mail boat takes eleven to reach Port Sa'id. Have you a genie in your employ, or have you hired an inventor to perfect one of those flying machines I have read about? For I know it must be to your good offices, in some manner or other, that I owe this—er—treat."

Cyrus looked embarrassed, as he always did when I praised him. "It must have come overland to Marseilles or Naples; the express takes one or two days, and a fast boat can reach Alexandria in another three. I asked a friend in Cairo to collect your mail the instant it arrived and send it off by the next train."

"And the mail-boy who travels to and from Derut is one of your servants? Dear Cyrus!"

"I'm as curious as you are," Cyrus said, blushing. "Even more so, I reckon; aren't you anxious to read it?"

"I am torn between anticipation and apprehension," I admitted. "Where Ramses's activities are concerned, the latter emotion tends to predominate, and this appears to be a long...Ah, but not so long as I had thought; Ramses has enclosed a batch of clippings from the London newspapers. Confound them! 'Famed Egyptologist Missing, Feared Dead...' 'The Archaeological Community Mourns the Loss of Its Most Notorious...' Notorious! I am surprised at the *Times*; the *Mirror*, perhaps, or...Oh, curse it! The *Mirror* describes me as hysterical with grief, under a doctor's care; the *World* has a sketch of the 'murder scene,' complete with a huge pool of blood; the *Daily Yell*..." The papers drifted from my palsied hand. In a hollow voice I said, "The account in the *Daily Yell* was written by Kevin O'Connell. I cannot read it, Cyrus, indeed I cannot; Kevin's journalistic style has often inspired me to homicidal fury. I shudder to think what he has written this time."

"Don't read it, then," said Cyrus, bending to collect the scattered papers. "Let's hear what your son has to say."

"His literary style is not much of an improvement on Kevin's," I said gloomily.

In fact, the only part of the letter that calmed my nerves was the salutation.

"Dearest Mama and Papa: My hand trembles with mingled joy and dread as I inscribe that last word; for the space of a few endless hours I feared I might never again be privileged to employ it in direct address. Endless, I say, and so they seemed, though in fact less than twelve of them elapsed before Mama's telegram brought renewed hope to hearts sunk deep in the depths of woe. Uncle Walter bore the news with manly fortitude, though he aged

a year for every hour that passed; Aunt Evelyn wept unceasingly; Jerry and Bob had to be restored by copious applications of beer, Rose by copious applications of cold water and smelling salts. I cannot speak of Nefret's pallid, silent, suffering grief, and words fail me when I attempt to describe my own. Only Gargery remained steadfast. 'I don't believe it,' he declared stoutly. 'It ain't true.' (I quote Gargery literally, dear parents; excessive emotion always has an adverse effect upon his grammar.) 'They couldn't kill the professor, not even if they run over him with a locomotive, which are scarce in Egypt anyhow, I am told. And if they did, madam wouldn't be under no doctor's care, she'd be rampaging up and down the country breaking heads and shooting people. It ain't true. You can't believe nothing you read in those newspapers.'"

My reading of this remarkable literary effort was interrupted by a series of strangled sounds from Cyrus. Taking out his handkerchief, he applied it to his streaming eyes and gasped, "I beg your pardon, my dear; I couldn't help it. He is—he really is—does he talk that way too?"

"He used to," I said, clenching my teeth. "He has not lost his loquacity, only turned it into written form. Shall I go on?"

"Please."

"And you see, dear Mama and Papa, that of us all Gargery was the only one to discern the truth. I had certain reservations, of course, regarding the accu-

racy of journalistic reporting, but filial affection quite overcame my reason at that point.

"We had our first intimation of incipient tragedy the day before the newspaper accounts appeared, when certain more responsible journalists endeavored to inquire of us concerning the accuracy of their reports. After the first inquiry, from the Times, which Uncle Walter flatly denied, we refused to communicate by telephone. The result was an onslaught of unauthorized visitors waving press credentials and demanding entry. Needless to say, they were repelled by our gallant forces. But concern continued to grow, and when the newspapers arrived next morning we were forced to concede their truth, since they quoted reputable sources in Cairo and Luxor. Not until evening did a messenger succeed in delivering your telegram. Ah, then what a scene ensued! Aunt Evelyn cried harder than ever. Rose went into hysterics. Uncle Walter and Gargery shook hands and kept on shaking them for ten minutes. Nefret and I . . ."

I held the letter closer to my eyes. "He has scratched something out here," I said, frowning. "I think he wrote 'flew into one another's arms,' and then replaced it with 'expressed our emotions in a suitable fashion.'"

"So that's the way the land lies, is it?" Cyrus was no longer amused. "I hope you won't take offense, Amelia, if I say that the only thing that could deter a man from the honor of asking you to be his wife would be the prospect of having to be a father to that boy."

"Emerson is the only one up to that challenge," I

replied. "And thank heaven there is no need to consider another candidate. Let me see . . . Oh, damnation!"

"Amelia!" Cyrus exclaimed.

"I beg your pardon," I said, almost as shocked as he at my inexcusable lapse. "But really, Ramses is enough to drive a saint to profanity. He spends four pages describing in disgustingly fulsome detail emotional reactions that are of only academic interest at this stage, and then devotes one paragraph to a really horrifying piece of news. Listen to this:

"The only unfortunate consequence of the happiness following the receipt of your telegram was that Bob and Jerry (our gallant gatekeepers) slept rather too soundly that night, owing, as they explained, not to an excess of beer but to the fatigue of joyful relief. Whatever the cause (and I see no reason to doubt the word of such loyal friends who are, moreover, in a better position than I to evaluate the effect of large quantities of beer), they did not hear the men climbing over the wall, and it was not until those individuals were discovered by the dogs that the barking of the said dogs roused Bob and Jerry. They arrived on the scene in time to drive off the would-be burglars, to the great disappointment of the dogs, who had been trying to induce the visitors to throw sticks for them. Do not worry, Mama and Papa, I have thought of a way of ensuring that this will not occur again.

"In conclusion, let me say that I am all the more determined to join you and offer the affectionate assistance only a son can render. I now have three pounds eighteen shillings.

"Curse it!"

"Why does he say...Oh," said Cyrus.

"The expletive was mine," I admitted. "Ramses is saving his money to buy a steamship ticket."

"Now don't worry, my dear. A child can't purchase a ticket, or travel alone; someone would catch him before the boat left the dock."

"I dare not hope that difficulty has not occurred to Ramses. He probably intends to persuade Gargery to buy the tickets and accompany him. Gargery is a weak vessel, I fear; not only would he aid and abet Ramses in any wild scheme the latter proposed, but he is a hopeless romantic. I must telegraph at once, forbidding him to do any such thing."

"A telegram to your butler?" Cyrus inquired, raising his eyebrows.

"Why not, if the circumstances require it? I must warn Walter as well; he is too innocent to anticipate the diabolical machinations of which Ramses and Gargery are capable."

"The boy will take your messages whenever you like, Amelia. There is a telegraph office at Minia."

"It can wait till morning. I will get a letter off as well. First I had better see what lies the newspapers have printed; I can contradict them at least, if I cannot tell the truth, the whole truth and nothing but the truth."

Immediately Cyrus brought me a stiff whiskey and soda. Thus fortified, I was able to peruse the accounts in relative calm. I left Kevin's till last.

The brash young Irish journalist and I had had a rather up-and-down relationship. On the occasion of our first meeting his impertinent questions had so infuriated Emerson that my hot-tempered spouse had kicked him down the stairs at Shepheard's. It was not a propitious beginning for a friendship; but Kevin had stood valiantly at our side on several occasions when danger threatened. He was at heart a gentleman and a sentimental one at that; unfortunately the gentleman and the sentimentalist were both submerged, at times, by the professional journalist.

Thanks to the whiskey (which Cyrus thoughtfully kept replenishing) I got through the first part of Kevin's story without undue stress. "It could be worse," I muttered. "I suppose it was impossible for Kevin to resist dragging in hints of curses and 'doom falling at last on the head of one who had too long defied the ancient gods of Egypt.' I am not altogether happy about his reference to . . . Oh, good Gad!"

I leapt to my feet. "What is it?" Cyrus asked apprehensively.

"Listen to this. 'Our correspondent is leaving immediately for Egypt, where he hopes to interview Professor and Mrs. Emerson in order to ascertain the true facts behind this strange affair. That there are mysteries yet to be uncovered he does not doubt.'"

I crumpled the newspaper into a ball and threw it on the floor. Anubis pounced on it and began batting it back and forth.

Ordinarily this kittenish behavior on the part of a particularly large and dignified animal would have entertained me. On this occasion I was too distraught to pay him any heed. Pacing furiously, I went on, "This is disastrous news! At all costs we must prevent Kevin from speaking with Emerson."

"Well, sure, if we can. But he's just another consarned reporter."

"You don't understand, Cyrus. Isolated as we are, and with Abdullah on guard, we can fend off other journalists. Kevin's acquaintance with our habits and his cursed Irish charm render him a more formidable opponent. Have you forgotten that it was Kevin who turned the death of Lord Baskerville into 'The Curse of the Pharaohs'? It was Kevin whose journalistic joie de vivre inflated the death of a night watchman into the case of the British Museum mummy. He is familiar with archaeological matters; he spent some weeks with the Sudan Expeditionary Force, talking with the officers who..." I stopped short and raised a trembling hand to my brow. The idea that had come to me had the awful inevitability of a mathematical equation. "No," I whispered. "No. Surely not Kevin!"

Cyrus hurried to my side and put a respectful arm around me. "What ails you, my dear? You are as white as the driven snow. Sit down. Have another whiskey."

"There are some situations too serious even for whiskey and soda," I said, slipping out of his embrace with a casual air that—I hoped—gave no offense. "My idea was absurd, unjust. I will dismiss it. But at the least, Cyrus, Kevin is bound to ferret out the truth of Emerson's amnesia. He has known him too long and too well to miss evidences of that."

"I never could understand why you were so set on keeping it secret, even from the family," Cyrus said. "Seems to me his brother, at least, is entitled to know the truth."

"You know not whereof you speak, Cyrus! Five

minutes after Walter found out, everyone in the house would know it, and the whole lot of them would rush off to catch the first boat—including Gargery! Have you forgotten Dr. Schadenfreude's advice, Cyrus? We must not force Emerson's memory; we must wait for it to grow and blossom, like a flower."

"Huh," said Cyrus, in a tone as skeptical as the one Emerson would probably have employed.

"I know you dislike the doctor's theories, Cyrus, but he is unquestionably an authority in his field, and his analysis of Emerson's character was brilliantly accurate. It is imperative that we give Schadenfreude's methods a fair chance. That would be impossible if our family and friends descended on us en masse. None of them is capable of the iron self-control that has guided *my* behavior—and can you imagine the effect on Emerson of coming face-to-face with Ramses? An eleven-year-old son would be enough of a shock for a man who doesn't even know he is married, and a son like Ramses—"

"It might be the catalyst that would restore Emerson's memory, though," Cyrus said, watching me steadily. "The sight of his son—"

"He has known me longer than he has Ramses," I said. "And under circumstances that ought, if any could...I perceive no purpose in discussing it, Cyrus; you must let me be the judge of what is best for Emerson."

"As always, you think of him and not of yourself. I wish you would let me—"

"I don't care to discuss it," I said, softening the blunt words with an affectionate smile. "If you will excuse me, Cyrus, I believe I will take a turn around the deck before retiring. No, my friend, don't come with me; your men are on guard, and I would like some time for solitary reflection."

It required longer than I had expected for cool reflection to calm the agitated waters of distress. The suspicion I had entertained, if only briefly, was truly dreadful.

Emerson and I had discussed the qualities an enemy must possess in order to ferret out the secret of the Lost Oasis. Kevin had them all—even a smattering of archaeological training. He also had the insatiable curiosity and the rampageous imagination (as Emerson would have put it) that would enable an individual to weave the disparate strands of the puzzle into a meaningful whole.

Nothing can crush the spirit so much as the treachery of a friend. Certain of Kevin's newspaper articles had, in my opinion, stretched our friendship to the limit, but at worst they had only threatened our reputations. This was another matter entirely—a cold-blooded attack on life, limb and sanity. In my mind's eye I pictured Kevin's smiling, freckled face, his candid blue eyes, his crop of flaming hair. In my inner ear I heard his caressing Irish voice repeat the compliments and assurances of affection whose sincerity I had never doubted.

I would not doubt it now! As my agitation subsided I reminded myself that Kevin was not the only individual who had the expert knowledge to solve the puzzle. Nor could I believe that the desire for a journalistic sensation—which the story of the Lost Oasis would certainly constitute—was a strong enough motive to make a man turn on his friends and his own nature.

However, the danger posed by his ordinary journalistic instincts was real enough. I knew I had not convinced Cyrus that Emerson's mental condition had to be kept secret, though the reasons I had given him were perfectly sound. Why distress our loved ones unnecessarily? Why give them an excuse to rush en masse to Egypt and drive me to distraction? Yet I knew, as had my perceptive and understanding friend, that that was not my only reason.

I decided not to think about it. The important thing was to keep Kevin away from Emerson. I began calculating schedules. If he had taken the fastest possible means of transportation and pushed himself to the limit, he might even now have arrived in Cairo. Would he be clever enough to make inquiries there concerning our present whereabouts instead of following our original trail to Luxor? Several of our archaeological friends knew we had gone to Amarna; it had been necessary to appeal to them in order to obtain permission to excavate. M. Maspero's kindly concern and powerful influence had been of enormous help in cutting through the red tape, and he was not the only one who knew. If Kevin came directly to Amarna he could be here in a few days.

"Sufficient unto the day is the evil thereof," I reminded myself. At least I was now forewarned. I would deal with Kevin when—I felt sure it was "when," not "if"—he appeared.

The lovely night of Egypt had worked its magic; I was calmer now. The moon was waxing; soon it would reach the full and hang like a globe of living light over the cliffs, washing their pale limestone with silver. As I strolled the deck, the rustle of my skirts blending with the soft lap of water and the murmur of palm fronds stirring in the night breeze, I thought of the last full moon I had watched from the deck of another boat. Less than a month ago...With what high hopes and breathless anticipation had I viewed that silvery orb! Emerson had been with me, his strong hand holding mine, his arm circling my waist. Now I was alone, and he was farther distant from me than he had ever been, though only a few feet of actual space separated us.

The windows of the bedchambers opened onto the deck. His were lighted; the thin gauze of the curtains proved no impediment to vision. Glancing in as I walked past, I saw him sitting at a table strewn with books and papers. His back was to me, his head was bent over his work. He did not look up, though he must have heard the click of my heels. The temptation to stop and contemplate the sight so familiar and so beloved—the smooth stretch of muscle across those broad shoulders, the thick tumbled hair curling around his ears—was well-nigh irresistible, but I conquered it. Dignity forbade that I should risk being discovered peeping in at him, like a lovesick girl.

As I went on without pausing, there was movement in the shadows next to Emerson's window; a low voice murmured a greeting in Arabic and I gestured a silent acknowledgment. I could not see which of the men it was; in the dark, their silhouettes were all alike, for they all wore the same turbans and flowing robes. They were a fine, upstanding lot, and seemed devoted to their employer. No doubt he paid them well. (I do not mean to be cynical; no reasonable individual can feel loyalty toward a man who underpays him.)

Other anonymous shadows greeted me as I proceeded. The fellow squatting near my window, his back against the wall, was smoking; the glowing end of his cigarette swooped like a giant firefly as he raised his hand to his brow and breast.

The windows of the rooms inhabited by the two young men were dark; from René's I heard a rumble of bass snoring, positively astonishing from such a delicate, aesthetic-looking young fellow. Bertha's window was also dark. No doubt she was weary; the walk to and from the dig would tire a city girl like her, unaccustomed to healthful exercise. I recognized the man who guarded her window by his size; he was the tallest and strongest of the crewmen. Cyrus was taking no chances.

I glanced at his window as I strolled by and saw it too was unlighted. Perhaps he was still in the saloon, which opened onto the upper deck.

I need not have strolled alone in the moonlight. Since only the silent watchers could see me, I permitted myself to smile and shake my head. Dr. Schadenfreude's treatment had not cured Cyrus of his romantic weakness. Being something of an amateur psychologist myself, I wondered if the bluff American's tendency to fall in love with wholly unsuitable ladies was born of his unconscious desire to remain a bachelor. Modest woman that I am, I could not help having observed his increasingly soft glances and his chivalrous indignation on my behalf, but I was well aware that his growing attachment was based solely on friendship and on the rough-hewn gallantry for which Americans are well-known. Any "lady in distress" between the ages of eighteen and forty-eight would have aroused the same instincts. Cyrus knew he was perfectly safe from the toils of matrimony with me, not only while Emerson lived but ever after. Could I, having known such a man, be the bride of another?

The moonlight was making me morbid. Moonlight has that effect when one enjoys it alone. I went to my room, wrote out the telegrams to Gargery and Walter, penned a peremptory letter to my son, and put the notes I had taken on the dig that day into proper form. By the time I finished, my eyelids were heavy; nevertheless, I gave my hair the usual hundred strokes, took a long (cold) bath, and applied cream to my skin. (This is not vanity but necessity in Egypt, where sun and sand have a frightful effect on the complexion.) I had hoped energetic employment would prevent me from dreaming. However, it did not. I am sure I need not specify the theme of those dreams to the sympathetic Reader.

To a female in the pink of condition, as I always am, a disturbed night is of no consequence. I arose fresh and alert, ready to face the difficulties I felt sure were about to ensue. Emerson had been biding his time, trying to get us off guard by performing his archaeological duties; but he is not a patient man, and I suspected he was about to carry out his ridiculous plan. There was no way I could prevent him from doing so, for reasoned argument has no effect whatever on him when he has got some silly idea into his head. All I could do was anticipate the worst and take steps to prevent it from happening. There was one advantage to his scheme; the farther we went from the river, the more difficult it would be for Kevin O'Connell to get at us.

My first sight of Emerson that morning strengthened my hunch that today was the day. He was eating his breakfast with the air of a man stoking himself with food in anticipation of strenuous activity ahead, and he was in a suspiciously genial mood, complimenting René on the quickness with which he was learning excavation methods, and praising Charlie's plan of the site. From time to time he tossed a scrap of sausage to Anubis, who snapped it out of the air like a trout rising to a fly. I wished the confounded beard did not hide his mouth. Emerson's mouth always gives him away when he is contemplating something underhanded; he cannot control the corners of it.

He saw me staring. "Does something offend you, MISS Peabody? Crumbs in my beard, are there? Or is it the beard itself? Come, come; don't be shy of expressing your opinion."

"Since you ask," I began.

"I do, I do. Having strong opinions myself, I can hardly object to others' possessing them."

"Ha!" I said. "Well, then, I must say that yours is one of the most unprepossessing examples of an unattractive appendage I have ever beheld. Beards are unsanitary, unsightly, hot—or so I would suppose; dangerous—to smokers; and indicative of masculine insecurity. Men grow them only because women cannot, I believe."

Emerson's eyes narrowed with rage, but he could not speak at once because his mouth was full of egg and sausage. Before he could swallow, Cyrus—whose hand was plucking nervously at his goatee—exclaimed, "I never thought of it that way. Maybe I should—"

"Don't be a fawning fool, Vandergelt," Emerson growled. "She is talking nonsense in the hope of annoying ME. Who the devil began this talk of beards, anyway? Hurry and finish, all of you, I want to be off."

And he was off, leaving the door swinging wildly on its hinges. The young men jumped up and galloped after him. I buttered another piece of toast.

"I didn't mean you, Cyrus," I said, smiling at him. "That goatee is so much a part of you, I cannot imagine you without it."

I meant it as a compliment, but he did not seem pleased.

The air was still cool and pleasant when we went ashore. I lagged behind, talking with young Charlie, who had sought me out with the obvious intention of consulting me. It took him a while to get to the point; in fact, I had to ask him straight out what was worrying him.

"It's the stela," he admitted. "The one high up on the cliff—you remember?"

"Stela U," I said. "Don't concern yourself about it, Charles; it will be some time before Emerson turns his attention to the stelae."

"No, ma'am, it won't! He wants me to get at it today. And—er—I couldn't tell the professor, I didn't dare; but I can't—I have not—rather, I should say I have..."

"Fear of heights?"

He looked as guilty as if he had just confessed to murder.

"My dear Charles, that is nothing to be ashamed of. Scientific research indicates that such fears are weaknesses the sufferer cannot control. You must confess the truth; it would be dangerous, possibly fatal, for you to force yourself to a task you cannot perform." Charles did not appear to be cheered by this consoling diagnosis, so I went on, "If you like, I will tell Emerson."

The young chap squared his manly shoulders. "No, ma'am, I thank you, but that would be cowardly."

"Tell him yourself, then, but bear in mind that I will disclose the truth if you do not do so. Now hurry on, we are falling behind."

The others were already out of sight. As we hastened along the village street, returning the greetings of those who hailed us and stepping over dogs and chickens and children, a man came to meet us. I stifled an exclamation of impatience; it was the sheikh, the mayor of the village, and I could see from his manner that he was intent on delaying me. We had managed to avoid the time-consuming ceremonies of welcome which courtesy normally requires in such little communities, but I saw no way of getting out of it now without mortally offending the man.

The poor old mayor we had known was long dead; his successor was a man in the prime of life, who looked healthier and better-fed than most of the fellahin. He greeted me with the customary formula and I replied in kind. "Will the Sitt honor my house?" was the next question.

Knowing this visit might take an hour or more, I sought a courteous way of escape. "The honor is too great. I must follow Emerson Effendi who is my—er—

who is the leader of the work. He will be angry if I delay."

I had thought the argument would be persuasive in this male-dominated world, but the mayor's brow grew troubled. "The Sitt must hear me. I tried to speak with the Father of Curses, but he would not stop. He is a man without fear, but he should know. Mohammed has returned."

Mohammed is a very popular name in Egypt. It took me a moment to identify this one. "The son of the old mayor? I thought he had run away, after the affair of the mummy that was only an evil man."

"He ran away, yes. When you and the Father of Curses unmasked the evildoer, Mohammed knew he would go to prison for helping the bad man. Or that the Father of Curses would punish him, which would have been just as painful. He was gone from the village for many years; but he has returned, Sitt, for I saw him myself last night."

I wished, not for the first time, that some ineffable Power had not chosen to interpret my prayer so whimsically. Another ghost from the past! Would all our old enemies return to haunt us? While I pondered, the mayor went on with mounting agitation.

"We are honest people here, we respect the Father of Curses and his honored chief wife and all the Inglizi who hire us to work. But in every village there are a few who are not honest; I think Mohammed is trying to stir them up against the Father of Curses, for he was talking loudly in the coffee shop and the ones who listened were the evildoers among us. Warn the Father of Curses, Sitt, and take care for yourself. Mohammed holds you in equal blame for his disgrace. He hoped to be the sheikh after his father died."

And still hoped, I fancied. The mayor's concern for us was not entirely altruistic; Mohammed could be a potential rival. Nevertheless, he was an honest man, and I thanked him before hurrying on.

Emerson had named our excavation site the Eastern Village, overriding the objections of Cyrus, who claimed that one house and part of a wall did not a village make. He added that no one, not even an idiot like Akhenaton, would build a residential quarter so far from the river. (Cyrus was one of those who did not share my exalted view of the heretic pharaoh, but he generally kept his opinions to himself when I was present.)

They were arguing the matter when I arrived on the scene, for even at my best pace I could not catch Emerson up when he was in a hurry. Emerson had spread his plans out across a boulder. Taking his pipe from his mouth, he used the stem as a pointer. "These are ancient roads, Vandergelt; half a dozen of them converge at this point, which is midway between the southern and northern tombs. The house we finished uncovering yesterday is obviously one of a number of such dwellings; there is mud-brick of similar shape and material scattered all over the hollow. Oh, curse it, I can't be bothered to explain my reasoning now; why the devil should I? Go with Abdullah; he is following the face of the enclosure wall. He ought to come across a gate soon."

Muttering and shaking his head, Cyrus went off. Watching Abdullah and his trained men of Aziyeh was fascinating for an archaeological enthusiast; in some places only a skilled eye could distinguish between crumbled brick and the natural soil that had buried it. Cyrus was enthusiastic about the profession, mistake me not; but like many excavators he preferred royal and nobles' tombs to the dwellings of the humble, which these clearly were. The only artifacts we had uncovered were faience beads and a wooden spindle whorl.

"Emerson," I said urgently. "I must speak to you."

"Well, what is it?" He had rolled up the plan and was poised on one foot, impatient to get to work.

"The mayor told me an old enemy of ours—of yours—has returned to the village."

"What, another one?" Emerson let out a bark of laughter. He started off. I ran after him.

"You must listen to me. Mohammed has good reason to hold a grudge against us—you. He is a sneak and a coward—"

"Then he will have better sense than to bother me. I think," said Emerson consideringly, "that we will divide the work force. Charles seems to be getting the hang of it; with Feisal to help him, he can start on the southeast corner. I want to get an idea of how much diversity in plan…"

He trotted off, still talking.

As I had suspected, Emerson had only been teasing poor Charlie when he threatened to set him to work on the boundary stela. The subject was not mentioned again. By the time we stopped for luncheon, the partially uncovered walls of a second house had proved Emerson's theory, to his satisfaction, at least. My task, which was that of sifting through the fill removed from the site, had not proved onerous; there were few objects, and they were of poor quality. I was glad to stop, though; the sun was hot and there was little shade. How Bertha endured the heat in her muffling garments I could not imagine. I had enlisted her aid that morning; she had been quick and competent.

Emerson had graciously consented to allow his hard-pressed workers to rest during the hottest part of the day. This was customary on most digs, but Emerson always behaved as if he were making an enormous concession. That day he did not so much as mutter. After the others had gone off to find shelter from the sun, I kept my eye on Emerson.

He had stretched out on the ground, his hat shading his face. I occupied one of the tents, Cyrus another. The young men had gone to the house Cyrus had built. Where Bertha was I did not know, but I felt certain the man Cyrus had assigned to watch her did know.

Less than half an hour had passed when Emerson removed the hat from his face and sat up. He gave the tent where I lay concealed a long, suspicious survey before rising to his feet.

I waited until he was out of sight behind the ridge before I followed. As I had suspected, he was heading east, toward the cliffs and the entrance to the royal wadi.

The plain and the crumpled faces of the cliffs were utterly devoid of life. At this time of day even the desert animals sought their burrows. The only moving objects were a hawk, circling high in the sun-whitened sky, and the tall, erect figure ahead. My skin was prickling as I hurried after it. Emerson had—quite deliberately—given Mohammed or another adversary precisely the opportunity he wanted. Such a man would watch and follow, waiting in deadly patience for the moment when he might find his victim alone.

I waited until Emerson had almost reached the cleft in the cliff before I hailed him. I dared wait no longer; there were a hundred hiding places in the tumbled rock at their base, thousands among the narrowing walls of the wadi. He heard; he turned; an explosive comment floated to my ears. But he waited for me to join him.

"I ought to have anticipated this," he remarked, as, panting and perspiring, I came up to him. "Can't a man go for a peaceful stroll without you following like a hound on the scent? Return at once."

"Peaceful stroll?" I gasped. "Do you think I was fooled by all that nonsense about Nefertiti's tomb? I suppose you think you can order the rest of us to continue digging out that wretched village while you pretend to work in the royal wadi. You have no intention of wasting time there; the proposal is only a blind—a lure, rather, for an enemy stupid enough to believe your boasts about secret tombs—with yourself as the bait in the trap!"

"You are mixing your metaphors," said Emerson critically. His tone was mild, but I knew that soft purring voice, and there was a gleam in his eyes I had seen before—but never directed at me. "Now turn around and go back, MISS Peabody—or squat there, on a rock if you prefer, till I return—or I will put you over my shoulder and carry you back to your friend Vandergelt, who will make sure you don't wander off again."

He took a step toward me. I took a step back. I had not meant to.

"Cyrus would not do that," I said.

"I think he would."

I thought he would too. And there was no doubt in my mind that Emerson would do what he had threatened to do.

The idea had a certain attraction, but I put it aside. I could not stop Emerson, short of shooting him in the leg (an idea that had its own kind of attraction, but that might prove counterproductive in the long run). If I were to guard and protect him, craft and cunning were my only weapons. I proceeded to employ them, dropping down on the rock he had indicated and blinking my eyes furiously as if I were trying to hold back my tears.

"I will wait here," I said, sniffing.

"Oh," said Emerson. "Well, then. See that you do." After a moment he added gruffly, "I won't be long."

As I believe I have mentioned, the wadi takes a turn to the east almost immediately, and a spur of rock cuts off the explorer's view of the plain. Emerson passed around it. I waited, watching the spot over the handkerchief I had raised to my eyes. After a short time Emerson's head appeared, his narrowed eyes glaring at me. I bowed my head to hide my smile and pressed the handkerchief to my lips.

The head vanished, and I heard the crunch of rock under his feet as he walked on. As soon as the sounds faded I followed.

My heart was thudding as I hastened on, threading a path among the boulders that littered the floor of the canyon. The difficulty for me now was not concealment but a clear line of vision; the twists and turns of the path, the heaped-up detritus, gave me only flashing glimpses of Emerson's form as he proceeded. It was pure luck—or the blessing of Providence, as I prefer to believe—that one such glimpse showed me what I had feared to see.

The man emerged from behind a pile of boulders which Emerson had just passed. Noiseless on bare feet, his dirty white robe almost invisible against the pale limestone of the rock walls, he launched himself at Emerson's back. The sunlight struck blindingly from the knife in his hand.

"Emerson!" I screamed. "Behind you!"

The echoes rolled from cliff to cliff. Emerson spun around. Mohammed's upraised arm fell. The knife found a target; Emerson staggered back, raising his hand to his face. He kept his feet, though, and Mohammed, arm raised to strike again, circled warily around him. He was not fool enough to close with Emerson, weaponless and wounded as he was.

Needless to say, I had continued to move forward as fast as possible. I was of course carrying my parasol. It required no more than a second or two to realize it was not the weapon I wanted. I could never reach them in time to prevent another blow. Tucking the parasol under my arm, I pulled my revolver from my pocket, aimed, and fired.

By the time I came up to Emerson, Mohammed was long gone. Emerson was still on his feet, leaning against a spur of rock. His upraised arm was pressed against his cheek. Since he never has a handkerchief, I deduced he had substituted his shirt sleeve for that useful article, in an attempt to staunch the blood that was turning the left side of his beard into a sticky mass and dripping down onto his shirt front.

Between agitation, extreme speed of locomotion, and relief, I was panting too heavily to articulate. Somewhat to my surprise Emerson waited for me to speak first. Over his unspeakable sleeve his eyes regarded me curiously.

"Another shirt ruined," I gasped.

The intent blue orbs were veiled, momentarily, by lowered lids. After a moment Emerson muttered, "Not to mention my face. What were you shooting at?"

"Mohammed, of course."

"You missed by a good six yards."

"The shot achieved the desired effect."

"He got away."

"I resent the implied criticism. Sit down, you stubborn man, before you fall down, and take your dirty sleeve away from your face in order that I may assess the damage."

It was not as bad as I had feared, but it was bad enough. The cut ran from cheekbone to jaw, and it was still bleeding freely. My handkerchief was obviously inadequate for the task at hand. I unbuttoned my jacket.

"What the devil are you doing?" Emerson asked, alarm overcoming his momentary faintness as I cast the garment aside and began unfastening my blouse.

"Preparing bandages, obviously," I replied, removing the blouse. Emerson hastily closed his eyes; but I think he was looking through his lashes.

It was a deuced awkward wound to bandage. He looked rather like a half-finished mummy when I was done, but the flow of blood had almost stopped.

"At least you will balance now," I said, reaching for my jacket. "This will match the scar on your other cheek."

Emerson squinted at me through half-closed lids. "It will have to be stitched up at once," I went on. "And thoroughly disinfected."

Emerson sat bolt upright and glowered at me. He tried to say something, but the bandages I had wound around his jaws made articulation difficult. I understood the word, however.

"I fear I have no choice, Emerson. It is necessary to shave the scalp before treating a head wound, you know; the same is true of a wound on the face. But cheer up; I will only have to cut half of it off."

CHAPTER 10

"The worse a man is, the more profound his slumber; for if he had a conscience, he would not be a villain."

In the midday stillness the sound of the shots had echoed far, and, as I later learned, our friends had already noted our absence and begun searching for us. When we emerged from the entrance to the wadi I saw Abdullah approaching, at a speed I would never have believed he was capable of attaining. When he saw us he stopped and stared, and then crouched on the ground, covering his head with his arms. He remained in that position, motionless as a statue, until we came up to him.

"I have failed," said a sepulchral voice from under the folds of fabric. "I will go back to Aziyeh and sit in the sun with the other senile old men."

"Get up, you melodramatic old fool," growled Emerson. "How have you failed? I did not hire you as a nursemaid."

This is Emerson's idea of affectionate reassurance. He went on without waiting for a reply. The others were in sight now, led by Cyrus, so I allowed him to proceed without me. Slowly Abdullah rose to his full height. He does relish drama, as do most Egyptians, but I saw that his dignified face was drawn with shock and remorse. "Sitt Hakim," he began.

"Enough of that, my friend. Allah himself could not stop Emerson when he is determined to do something stupid. He owes you his life. I know that, and so does he; it is just that he has a rather unconventional way of expressing the gratitude and affection he feels for you."

Abdullah's face brightened. Finding the sonorous and dignified vocabulary of classical Arabic inadequate for my feelings, I added in English, "We will just have to watch him more closely, that is all. Curse the man, there are times when he is more trouble than Ramses!"

Fortunately Emerson was feeling rather feeble, so it only required ten minutes of concentrated shouting to persuade him to return to the dahabeeyah—though not until after he had lectured René and Charles about how to proceed with the excavation and insisted Abdullah stay with them to supervise. He would not lean on Cyrus or on me, but when Bertha approached him— any emotion she might have felt effectively concealed by her veil—he accepted the arm she offered.

In silent efficiency she assisted me in my medical endeavours until I began stitching the wound. Fortified by brandy and bullheadedness, Emerson uttered not a sound during this process, which I did not enjoy a great deal either. When I finished I saw the girl crouched in a corner with her back to me.

"Strange how squeamish some people are about

needles," I said musingly, cutting lengths of sticking plaster.

"Yes, isn't it," said Cyrus, turning around. "Why don't you let me finish that, Amelia? It can't have been a pleasant experience for you—"

"Ha," said Emerson, still supine.

"It will only take a moment," I replied. "You see how impossible it would have been to apply sticking plaster over all those whiskers, though."

Emerson immediately declared his intention of returning to work. After some rather noisy discussion he finally agreed to rest for the remainder of the day on condition we left him strictly alone. I closed his door, as he had requested, and then at last I allowed a sigh to escape my lips.

"My poor girl," Cyrus said gently. "How courageously you performed your painful duty."

"Oh, I am quite accustomed to stitching Emerson back together. But Cyrus—it was such a near thing! We cannot go on this way, fending off one attack after another. A good offense is the best defense. We must take the aggressive!"

Cyrus tugged at his goatee. "I was afraid you were going to say that. You're as bad as he is, Amelia. This is the second time you've snuck away and driven me to the brink of heart failure. I'm doing my level best to protect you—"

"I am aware of that, Cyrus, and appreciative of your concern, though if you will allow me to say so, the role of a poor little woman in need of male protection does not suit me."

It was Cyrus's turn to sigh. "Okay. Just do me the

favor of letting me in on your schemes, will you? What do you propose to do now?"

"I am going to the village."

"Then I am going with you."

We had a nice little chat with the mayor. He threw up his hands in horror when I told him what had occurred; invoking every saint in the Moslem calendar, starting with the Prophet himself, he protested his innocence and that of the village as a whole. I assured him we would never, as some tyrannical authorities had been known to do, punish an entire community for the misdeeds of one man. I then proceeded to make him an offer he could not refuse.

We were climbing down the bank toward the gangplank before Cyrus recovered his voice. "Dead or alive? A reward is a bully idea, Amelia, but did you have to say—"

"That was just Arabic rhetoric," I assured him. "It sounded more emphatic."

"It sure did. 'His head in a basket' carries a lot of punch."

"I made it clear I preferred him alive. But I will take what I can get."

Shaking his head, Cyrus went off to his quarters and I looked in on Emerson. He was sleeping soundly, which I had expected, because I had slipped a soupçon of laudanum into his water bottle. With my mind at ease on that point I proceeded to my room, not to rest, as I had promised Cyrus, but to consider my next move.

I had my strategy worked out by the time the weary workers returned from the dig. The most difficult part was to decide whom to take into my confidence, and to what extent. I did not count on any cooperation whatever from Emerson, but I hoped by one means or another to induce him to discuss his intentions with regard to the excavation. Cyrus, I feared, had not entirely abandoned his charming but absurd idea of protecting me, so I would have to find means of eluding his attentions when it did not suit me to accept them. Men are frightful nuisances at times; how much simpler life would be if we women did not have to make allowances for their little peculiarities.

Simpler, but not nearly so interesting. The sight of my now-beardless spouse, scowling at me across the dinner table, caused a thrill to run through my limbs and reminded me that no effort was too great to preserve him from peril. To my regret I had been forced to cover up the dimple in Emerson's chin, which he detests and which I cherish; strips of sticking plaster also disfigured the bridge of his nose and his upper lip. But the strong jaw was at last exposed; the magnificent modeling of one cheek at least was visible to my fond gaze.

I was about to compliment him on the improvement in his appearance when Cyrus entered, apologizing for his tardiness and looking rather sheepish. I dropped my napkin.

"Cyrus! You have shaved off your goatee!"

"A gesture of sympathy," said the American, glancing at Emerson.

"Wasted," said Emerson. "You ought to have stuck to your guns, Vandergelt, as you Americans say. You look ridiculous."

"Not at all," I said, considering the effect. "I

approve, Cyrus. You have a fine, well-shaped chin. Indeed, you look ten years younger."

Emerson immediately changed the subject, demanding of René an account of the afternoon's work.

"You were right, Professor," René said. "The second structure appears to be exactly the same size as the one adjoining it, five meters wide by ten deep. The plans are identical—four rooms in all. Into one room, where we found a hearth with a patch of smoke-blackened plaster above it, a part of the ceiling had fallen. It was of matting covered with mud plaster—"

"The roof, not the ceiling," snapped Emerson. "The houses had only one story. Stairs led to the roof, which was open but used for additional living and storage space. Charles—what about the other house?"

Again Emerson's surmise had been accurate. The structure was larger and more complex in plan than the smaller houses; the enclosure wall formed its south and east sides. After further discussion Emerson announced, "There can be no question about it. The larger house is that of an overseer or official. What we have is a workman's village surrounded by an outer wall and laid out with a regularity that indicates it was designed and built as a unit instead of growing haphazardly like ordinary towns. Petrie found a similar arrangement at Lahun; as I told him, it must have been occupied by the men who constructed and maintained the pyramid near it." Attempting to curl his lip at Cyrus—a gesture whose effect was somewhat mitigated by the strips of sticking plaster framing that part of his face—he added, "You see, Vandergelt, Akhenaton was not such a fool after all. Our village was inhabited by the workmen who decorated the tombs, and by necropolis guards, and the location could not have been bettered—midway between the two groups of nobles' tombs and not far from the entrance to the wadi where Akhenaton's own sepulcher was located."

This dogmatic pronouncement (which later excavations proved to be entirely correct) provoked no contradiction, but neither did it inspire enthusiasm in the hearers. Cyrus expressed the general reaction when he remarked, "Shucks, Emerson, we're not going to find anything interesting in a poor workers' village. I hope to goodness you don't want to excavate the whole place. It would take all winter."

"A typical dilettante's opinion," said Emerson with his usual tact. "We know almost nothing about ancient Egyptian domestic architecture, even less about how the ordinary people lived. Historically a discovery of this nature is far more important than a looted tomb, of which we already have too many examples."

"I quite agree," I said. "Having once begun, we ought to do the job properly, and produce a definitive publication which would include a comparison of our village with the one at Lahun."

I knew Emerson had no intention of doing this, but that he would go on arguing so long as Cyrus differed with him. Rather than find himself in agreement with me, he was forced to backtrack.

"I never intended the excavation of the village to be other than exploratory," he said with a frown. "As soon as the overseer's house has been cleared and properly recorded, we will move elsewhere."

Charles shriveled visibly. I gave him a reassuring

smile. "The boundary stelae?" I inquired. "That should certainly be our next project."

"Oh, you think so, do you?" Emerson glowered at me. "The boundary stelae can wait. I intend to work next in the royal wadi."

He obviously expected me to protest, so I did. Men are so easy to manipulate, poor things. When I gave in, with poor grace, Emerson thought he had won his point, whereas I knew I had won mine. Whither he went, we would go—all of us. There is safety in numbers—a trite saying, but like most trite sayings, right on the mark.

After dinner Charles and René asked permission to go to the village. It boasted a coffee shop of sorts, where the men spent the evenings, fahddling and lounging around; here, Charles explained with charming candor, he and René hoped to improve their command of the language and strengthen friendly relations with the villagers. I gave them a brief motherly lecture on the dangers of excessive friendliness with a certain section of the population. It embarrassed them very much, but I would have felt negligent in my duty had I not done so.

Cyrus and I retired to the saloon for a council of war. I invited Emerson to join us, but he declined and went stamping off to his room, which was what I had intended. He had lost a considerable quantity of blood and needed to rest. Besides, I wanted to discuss certain subjects with Cyrus in private.

"I have decided to take you fully into my confidence, Cyrus," I began. "I hope you believe that I have not been deterred by lack of faith in your discretion or in your friendship. I have sworn an oath of secrecy which

I cannot and will not break; but the facts I am about to impart to you will, I suspect, tell you nothing you have not already deduced."

With equal gravity he responded, "Let me set your conscience at rest, Amelia, by telling you what I already know. I guess I'm not the only one to have figured it out, either. Those of us who were acquainted with Willie Forth knew about his lost civilization. Heck, the problem was to keep him from boring us to death talking about it. Then you and Emerson come back from Nubia last spring with a young female who you announce is Willy's daughter. By itself that doesn't mean shoot; she could have grown up among poor harmless missionaries, as you claimed. But when some character goes to the trouble of snatching Emerson and makes references to a recent trip you folks made, I reckon he's not looking for directions to a Baptist mission. Add to that his wanting to collect you and young Ramses and the girl, and a shrewd operator like Cyrus Vandergelt can't avoid the conclusion that maybe poor old crazy Willie Forth wasn't crazy after all."

"Expressed with your customary acumen, Cyrus," I exclaimed. "It would be disingenuous and disloyal of me to deny the fact itself, though I can give you no further details."

"Unbelievable," Cyrus murmured. There was a faraway gleam in his eye. "I thought it must be true, but to hear you say so...And the place is all Willie claimed it was—a treasure house of antiquities and golden ornaments?"

"It holds enough, at least, to make it worth looting.

That is why Emerson and I swore never to betray its location."

"Yes, of course," Cyrus said abstractedly.

"We know the identity of the man responsible for our present difficulty, and I have some idea as to how he obtained the information that prompted his attack on us. But I suspect he is not working alone. In fact, I know he is not; he must have enlisted Mohammed, the man who assaulted Emerson today, for it is surely too much of a coincidence to assume that incident is unrelated to the others. Mohammed has been absent from the village for years, and if I read his character aright, he is not the sort of man to risk injury or imprisonment for the sake of an old grievance."

Cyrus stroked his chin reflectively. "Emerson's got a lot of enemies."

"True." I removed a sheet of paper from the portfolio I had brought with me. "I composed a brief list this afternoon."

Cyrus's jaw dropped. "One, two, three...Twelve people who are thirsting for Emerson's blood? He's been a busy little bee, hasn't he?"

"The list may not be complete," I admitted. "Emerson was a busy little bee even before I met him; new candidates keep turning up. These are the individuals of whom I have personal knowledge. Oh, wait—I forgot Mr. Vincey. That makes thirteen."

"I hope you're not superstitious," Cyrus muttered.

"I?" I laughed lightly. "The number is meaningless in any case. There is a strong probability that several of these people are dead or incarcerated. Alberto"—I

inscribed a neat interrogation point after the name—
"Alberto certainly *was* in prison. I used to drop in for a
visit when I passed through Cairo, but I have neglected
to do so for the last few years. Habib—you remember
Habib—"

"Oh, yes. He tried to brain my old buddy once
before."

"He did not appear to be in good health, and that
was some years ago. He may have passed on. But it
is imperative that we attempt to discover the present
whereabouts of these individuals. If any have been
recently released from prison, or have suddenly disappeared from their usual haunts..."

"It won't do any harm to ask," said Cyrus. He was
obviously unconvinced by my reasoning, which was,
I admit, based on somewhat slender evidence. I have
found that my instincts for criminal behavior are a
more reliable guide than logic, but I sensed that argument would not carry any more weight with Cyrus
than it ever had with Emerson, though Cyrus would
have expressed his reservations more diplomatically.

His brow furrowed, Cyrus ran his finger down the
list. It did not pause at the particular name I had feared
might rouse painful memories, and I was of course too
tactful to point it out. "Reginald Forthright," Cyrus
read. "Is he old Willie's nephew, the one the newspaper
stories mentioned? Sacrificed his brave young life in the
search for his uncle? I thought he was dead."

"Disappeared in the desert," I corrected. "However,
I consider it unlikely that he is involved. For one thing,
he knows...But I will say no more. Besides, Tarek
would have...I believe I have said all I ought to say."

"Your acquaintances sure have unusual names," Cyrus murmured. "Charity Jones, Ahmed the Louse . . . Sethos? I thought he was dead too."

"You are making a little joke," I said, smiling appreciatively. "The name does not refer to the pharaoh of the same name, who has indeed been dead for several thousand years. Have you never heard that name in a modern context, Cyrus? Perhaps you know him better by his sobriquet 'the Master Criminal.'"

"Can't say I do," Cyrus replied, raising his eyebrows. "Sounds more like a character out of a dime novel. But—hey, wait a minute. I did hear that name once from Jacques de Morgan, the former Director of Antiquities. He'd imbibed rather freely of the flowing bowl that evening; he also claimed your son had been possessed by an afreet, so when he started babbling about master criminals I kind of stopped listening."

"Sethos is no afreet, though he shares certain of their characteristics," I said. "For years he controlled the illegal antiquities market in Egypt. Nameless except for his noms de guerre, a master of disguise whose true face no one has seen, a veritable genius of crime . . ."

"Oh, really," said Cyrus.

"Yes, really. He is without a doubt the most formidable of our old adversaries, and logic would deem him the most likely suspect. He is well-versed in Egyptology. He commands a large criminal organization. His intellect is superior and poetic; the quest for the Lost Oasis is precisely the sort of thing that would fire his imagination. And he has a—a particular grudge against my husband."

"Not only the most likely suspect," Cyrus said slowly, "but ahead of the rest of the field by ten furlongs."

"I hope not, for our chance of finding him is almost nil. The others we may track down, but not Sethos. Furthermore..."

"Yes?"

"It is irrelevant," I murmured. "At least Emerson would say it was, and perhaps he would be right. I don't want Emerson to see this list, Cyrus."

"Not much point, if he doesn't remember any of them. It's just between you and me, Amelia." Cyrus's face reflected his pleasure in being able to assist me. "We will get the authorities on the trail of these ladies and gents. Might as well go straight to the top; if you will give me a copy of your list I will telegraph the British Consul-General, Sir Evelyn Baring, with whom I am slightly acquainted. He is the most powerful man in Egypt, and—"

"I know him well, Cyrus. He was a friend of my father's and has always been most obliging. I have already written him a letter; that mode of communication seemed best, since the situation is complex enough to require some explanation. Selim or Ali can catch the train tomorrow and deliver the letter by hand."

"As usual, you are right square on top of the business, my dear. But I hope you don't object if I make a few inquiries of my own?"

"You are very kind."

"That's what a pal is for," Cyrus declared.

I accepted his invitation to take a turn about the deck. The night was calm and peaceful; the brilliant stars of Egypt blazed overhead. But though I strove to open my senses to a scene that had never before failed to inspire and soothe me—though my companion's steps were slowed to match mine and his sympathetic silence answered to my mood—the attempt was a failure. How could I lose myself in the magic of the night when another than Emerson walked at my side? It was not long before I declared my intention of retiring and bade Cyrus an affectionate good night.

On the way to my room I stopped at Emerson's door, thinking he might be in need of some medication to help him sleep. Apparently he was not. There was no answer to my knock.

I hesitated, cursing the bizarre circumstances that prevented me from following the dictates of duty and affection. I feared to venture in without his permission, yet I could not leave without assuring myself he was not in a swoon or in pain his fortitude would not allow him to express.

Eavesdropping is a contemptible act to which I would never stoop. The fringes of my shawl somehow got caught in the door hinge. The fringe was very long and silky, and it took some time to untangle it without breaking the threads. As I worked at it I listened for the sounds of snores or groans. There was only silence.

Something pushed against my knee. I let out a muted exclamation of surprise and turned to see the cat Anubis sitting on my skirt, butting his head against me. Next to the cat was a pair of feet wearing curly-toed native slippers. The feet were not those of an Egyptian, however. I knew those members, as I knew every other inch of that particular anatomy.

Emerson stood over me, arms folded, eyebrows elevated. He was clad in one of the loose Egyptian robes.

"Where have you been?" I cried, surprise overcoming

my awareness of the fact that this question would only elicit a sarcastic and uninformative reply.

"Out," said Emerson. "Now I propose to go in, if I may impose on you to get out of my way."

"Certainly," I said, stepping back.

"Good night," said Emerson, opening the door.

He had entered—preceded by the cat—and slammed the door before I could reply, but not before I had observed that the bandage, which had covered half his face, had been reduced to a patch only three inches square. It had been very neatly done, so I knew he had not done it. The person responsible must have had slim, deft fingers.

Our messenger left before dawn to catch the train to Cairo. Cyrus had suggested we send one of his men instead of Selim, and I was glad to accept the offer. I would need every loyal man from now on if Emerson carried out his scheme of working in the wadi.

When we assembled for breakfast I studied my companions with the interest of a general taking stock of her forces. The countenances of Charles and René aroused some concern; the combination of sunken eyes and faint smiles was highly suspicious. However, the recuperative powers of the young are great, and I did not doubt they would respond to my orders with vigor and alacrity.

I had not yet accustomed myself to seeing Cyrus without his beard, but I approved the change; I have always thought a goatee a particularly ridiculous form of facial adornment. As always, he looked fresh and alert.

Need I remark that my eyes lingered longest on the

face of Emerson? I was pleased to observe that he had shaved that morning; I had expected he would let his beard grow again in order to annoy me. The exposed, shallowest part of the knife wound seemed to be healing nicely. One long strip of sticking plaster adorned the noble curve of his nose, but the cleft in his chin was visible to my admiring eyes. His mouth was visible as well; as he met my gaze the corners compressed in an expression that aroused the direst of forebodings, but he did not speak.

I had no proof that he had been with Bertha. I had not inquired. I preferred not to inquire.

When she joined us on the deck I observed that she had made a slight alteration in her attire. Her robe was the same discreet black, but the veil now covered only the lower part of her face, and it was of filmy, almost transparent fabric, through which the rounded contours of her cheeks and the delicate shape of her nose could be seen. The swelling seemed to have disappeared, and though she kept them modestly lowered, her long-lashed dark eyes were clear.

Some authorities claim that charms half-hidden are the most seductive. Bertha's veiled charms certainly seemed to have a powerful effect on René. (French gentlemen are particularly susceptible, according to those same authorities.) His chivalrous instincts had already been touched by her sad story; on several occasions he had approached her to offer the support of his arm or the consolation of a friendly greeting. As we climbed the path up from the riverbank I saw that he had relieved her of the bundle she carried, and was walking beside her.

I began to feel a certain sympathy for Emerson's views about females on archaeological expeditions. Something would have to be done about Bertha. Even if she was victim instead of spy, she was quite capable of turning the heads of both young men, setting them one against the other, and decreasing their efficiency.

As we left the cultivated fields and set off along the desert track I saw the smoke that betokened the approach of a steamer. Not all of them stopped at Amarna, but apparently this one was about to do so.

"Confound it," I said to Cyrus, who was at my side. "Emerson's temper is not at its best just now, and tourists have a bad effect on him. I hope this lot will leave us alone."

"They stop here only long enough to see the pavement Mr. Petrie found," Cyrus assured me.

"It is so like Petrie to leave the painting open and exposed to tourists and other vandals," I said critically. "After having had one lovely section of pavement destroyed, we made a point of covering up or removing the bits we found. That is the only proper way to proceed."

Cyrus of course agreed with me.

I kept an eye on the steamer, whose location was easily ascertained by the smoke from its funnels. None of the "cursed tourists" came near us. After a few hours the steady column wavered and moved away, and I dismissed the boat from my mind. I had not supposed Kevin would be among the passengers; he would come by the fastest conveyance, probably the train. But Vincey—devious, devilish adversary that he was— might make use of an unlikely means of transportation simply because it *was* unlikely.

Emerson had set the entire crew at work on the foreman's house, leaving me and Ali to finish clearing the last few inches of debris from the second of the smaller ones. It was here that small objects were most likely to be found, and the work had to be done slowly and delicately. Some of the objects, especially those made of the glassy faience, were extremely fragile; others, such as bead necklaces, still showed the original pattern even though the string had rotted away. It was a demonstration of his increasing confidence in my skill at this finicky task that Emerson had assigned me to it and I believe I may say, without undue modesty, that his confidence was deserved.

The walls surrounding the room in which I was working had survived to a height of a meter or more, so I could not see what was going on in the southwest corner of the site. I could hear, though. Most of the remarks came from Emerson, most were profane, and many were directed against Abdullah. Our devoted reis stuck to Emerson like a shadow, and Emerson, whose movements were inclined to be abrupt, kept bumping into him.

It was Abdullah who first saw the men approaching. His shout of "Sitt Hakim!" brought me instantly to my feet and his gestures directed my eyes toward the forms that had occasioned the warning.

There were two of them, both wearing European clothing. The shorter and stouter of the pair had fallen behind, for his companion advanced with long strides. A pith helmet covered his hair and shaded his features, but there was something about that tall straight body that made my senses quiver with alarm. Scrambling over the wall, I ran to intercept Abdullah, who had started toward the newcomers, a long knife in his hand.

"Wait," I said, catching hold of him to emphasize the order. "And keep calm. There are only two of them, and they would not approach so openly if they—"

A cry from Abdullah and a sudden movement, not from either of the men ahead, but from behind me, stopped my speech. Abdullah fought to free his arm from my grasp. "Let me kill it, Sitt," he gasped. "It is a demon, an afreet, as I told you. See—it goes to greet its master."

The cat had leapt from the wall where it had been sleeping in the sunlight. The man stooped to greet it as it ran up to him. It butted its head against his hand, but when he would have picked it up it avoided his grasp and sat down a few feet away.

I reached for my pistol. "Stand perfectly still, Abdullah," I ordered. "An impetuous advance might bring you into the line of fire."

"Excellent advice," said a voice behind me. "Though the only safe place is flat on the ground behind a large rock. Put the gun away, Peabody, before you shoot someone."

"I intend to shoot someone, if he gives me the slightest excuse to do so. What the devil does he mean, walking coolly up to us this way? You know who it is, don't you?"

"Certainly," said Emerson. "I beg you won't shoot him until we hear what he has to say. I am immensely curious."

Cyrus and the other men had gathered around. "Me too," said Cyrus. His voice was flat and level, his eyes were narrowed, his hand was in his pocket. "Let him talk, Amelia. I've got the drop on him."

"So have I," I replied, aiming at the center of Vincey's chest. He had stopped ten feet away, his empty hands extended.

"I am unarmed," he said quietly. "You may search me if you like. Only allow me to speak—to clear away the misapprehensions under which you understandably labor. I only learned of them a few days ago, and I have spent every hour since then gathering the evidence which will prove I am not the man you believe me to be."

"Impossible," I cried. "I saw you with my own eyes."

"You could not have seen me. I was in Damascus, as I told you. I have brought my alibi with me."

He indicated the second man, who had now caught him up. His face was round and red and adorned with a set of superb mustaches curled like the horns of a water buffalo. Whipping off his helmet, he bent at the waist in a stiff formal bow.

"*Guten Morgen, meine Freunde.* To greet you at last is my pleasure. I could not in Cairo do so, for I was in Damascus."

"Karl von Bork!" I exclaimed. "But I thought you were in Berlin, working with Professor Sethe."

"So it was," Karl said, bowing again. "Until the summer, when a position with the Damascus expedition to me offered was. Egyptian reliefs had been found—"

"Yes, now I remember," I interrupted, for Karl, like my son, would go on talking until someone stopped him. "Someone—the Reverend Sayce, I believe—mentioned it when we dined with him in Cairo. Are you telling me that Mr. Vincey was with you?"

"*Ja, ja, das ist recht.* With a fever I was ill, and I feared I would not be soon recovered. A substitute was necessary to carry on my work. The good God sent me health sooner than I had hoped; and when Herr Vincey telegraphed to me that the police had accused him of terrible crimes I hurried at once to clear his name. I had heard, with what shock and distress my tongue fails me to say, of the Herr Professor's accident, but never would I have supposed—"

"Yes, Karl, thank you," I said. "Then the police have accepted your story? I wonder they have not informed me."

"It was only yesterday they told me I was no longer under suspicion," Vincey said. "We set out at once for Amarna, for I was even more anxious to clear myself with you than with the police." He started to reach for his pocket, and then gave me a quizzical smile. "You will allow me? I brought other evidence—train tickets, dated and stamped, a receipt from the Sultana Hotel, affidavits from other members of the expedition."

"Karl's evidence is good enough for me," I said. "He is an old friend whom we have known for years—"

"Hmph," said Emerson, who of course had no recollection of ever having seen Karl before.

"All the same," I went on. "I trust Karl will not take offense if I call another witness, and if I request Cyrus to keep you covered (that is the phrase, I believe?) while I go in search of her."

"Good idea," said Cyrus. "Not that I doubt your

word, von Bork, but this is the doggonedest story I ever heard. If it wasn't Vincey, then who—"

"That will all be gone into at the proper time," I said. "First—where is Bertha?"

There was no need to search for her; she was there, a few feet behind us. René was at her side, his arm encircling her slim shoulders. "There is nothing to fear," he assured her. "This villain, this scum, cannot hurt you now."

"But it is not he," Bertha said.

"I would like to beat him as he—" René's jaw dropped. "What is it you say?"

"He is not the one." Bertha moved slowly forward, out of the protective circle of his arm. Her wide dark eyes were fixed on Vincey. "They are alike as sons of the same mother, but this is not the same man. Who would know better than I?"

"So it was Sethos after all," I said.

We had retired to the shade and I had asked Selim to brew tea. With such overwhelming evidence to support his claim it hardly seemed fair to exclude Mr. Vincey from our company, but I noticed Cyrus kept his right hand in his pocket and held his cup in his left.

"The conclusion is forced upon us," I continued. "Who else but a master of disguise, as we know the Master Criminal to be, could have imitated Mr. Vincey's appearance so precisely?"

In a dangerously soft voice Emerson requested elucidation of this speech. I obliged in general terms, omitting certain details of our former encounters with

Sethos. When I had finished, Emerson studied me pensively before speaking.

"I had begun to believe you suffered less from woolly-mindedness than other members of your sex, Peabody. I would be sorry to learn I was mistaken, but this farrago of nonsense, this piece of sensational fiction—"

"There is such a man," Vincey said. Emerson's critical gaze moved to him and he flushed faintly. "Anyone who has been involved with the illegal antiquities trade knows of him. The unfortunate incident in my past, which I bitterly regret and which I have endeavored ever since to live down, brought me in contact with that trade."

"*Ja, ja,*" Karl nodded vigorously. "I too have heard such stories. One is inclined, *natürlich,* to dismiss them as idle rumor, but no less a distinguished individual than M. de Morgan—"

"Balderdash!" Emerson shouted, his countenance reddening. "It seems necessary to admit that someone took advantage of Vincey's absence, but let me hear no more nonsense about master criminals. You credulous fools may sit here and spin fairy tales all day if you like; I am going back to work."

And off he went, with Abdullah close on his heels and the cat close on the heels of Abdullah. Vincey smiled ruefully. "I have lost the allegiance of Anubis, it seems. Cats are unforgiving creatures; he blames me for leaving him, I suppose, and will accept no excuses. I hope, Mrs. Emerson, that you are more merciful. You do believe me?"

"No reasonable individual could doubt your evidence," I replied, glancing from the little pile of receipts and statements—which I had of course examined carefully—to the solemn face of Karl von Bork. "And the misunderstanding has given me the pleasure of seeing Karl again. How is Mary, Karl? We heard she had been ill."

"She is better, I thank you. But—the Herr Professor...It is true, then, what we heard from friends? He did not seem to know me."

"He has suffered a temporary loss of memory in some areas," I admitted—since it would have been folly to deny it. "But that fact is not generally known, and I hope you will be discreet about mentioning it—especially to Walter, if you have occasion to write to him."

"We communicate less often than I would like," Karl said. "A scholar of the most profound brilliance is Mr. Walter Emerson; in my own field of philology he is the brightest star. He does not know of his most distinguished brother's—"

"We expect a complete recovery," I said firmly. "There is no need to distress Walter. Much as I would enjoy chatting with you, Karl, I had better return to my duties. Will I see you later? Perhaps you will both dine with us this evening on Mr. Vandergelt's dahabeeyah."

I glanced at Cyrus for confirmation of the invitation. Still preoccupied with the problem of drinking tea left-handed, he nodded brusquely.

"It would be better not, I think," said Vincey. "You are a kind, just woman, Mrs. Emerson, but you cannot be wholly comfortable in my presence just now; it must recall too many painful memories. We will spend the night at Minia and be on our way next morning. Karl must return to the dig; he has already given too much of his time to my affairs. As for me, I am at your disposal at any time and for any purpose."

"Where will you be?" I asked.

"At my apartment in Cairo, engaged in the same business as yourself." His face hardened. "My good name has been tarnished, my reputation impugned. That stain will remain until the blackguard who defamed me is caught and punished. My motive for tracking him down is not as compelling as yours, but I hope it will comfort you to know that I am bent on the same object."

I embraced Karl, which made him blush and stammer, and shook Mr. Vincey's hand. Cyrus did neither. He did not remove his hand from his pocket until the two retreating forms were blurred by distance and blowing sand into ghostly images of men. Then he said, "I guess I'm just a hardheaded old Yankee, Amelia, but I'd just as soon not turn my back on that fellow Vincey."

"You have known Karl as long as I. I would no more doubt his word than I would that of Howard Carter or Mr. Newberry."

"The more honest a man, the easier he can be bamboozled," Cyrus grunted. "Just promise me, Amelia, that if Vincey asks you to meet him in some dark alley you won't accept the invitation."

"Now, Cyrus, you know I would never do such a silly thing."

When I returned to the little faience ring I had been carefully removing from its position, I saw that the cat Anubis was stretched out along the wall. I had forgotten it until that moment, and so, evidently, had Mr. Vincey. Evidently his "faithful companion" was not so faithful as he had believed. Not that I blamed the intelligent animal for preferring Emerson's and my company.

With brushes and tiny probes I freed the ring from the matrix of hardened mud that held it. Emerson came loping over to see how I was getting on, and I handed him the ring—or, to be more accurate, the bezel of a ring. These common objects, made of cheap fragile faience, had usually lost the thinner shank portion when we found them; it may have been because they were broken that they had been discarded. Sometimes they bore the name of the reigning pharaoh and were worn as a token of loyalty; in other cases the bezel was ornamented with the image of a god favored by the wearer. "Bes," I said.

"Hmph," said Emerson. "So Akhenaton's devotion to his 'sole god' was not emulated by all the citizens of Amarna."

"The appeal of the homely little gods of the household must have been difficult to combat." I sat back on my haunches and rubbed my aching shoulders. "Witness the popularity of certain saints in Catholic countries. Bes, being the patron of jovial entertainment and—er—conjugal felicity—"

"Hmph," said Emerson again. "All right, Peabody, don't dawdle. There is a good-sized heap of sand to be sifted."

I noted the ring on the record sheet and put it into the appropriate box, which had been labeled with the numbers assigned to the square, the house, and the particular room. As I bent again to my task, I was conscious of a strange sense of depression. I ought to have been encouraged by Emerson's use of that loved and loving appellation—i.e., my maiden name, sans title. He was using it now as he had originally, with sarcastic intent, but even that was a step forward, for it tacitly awarded me the same equality he would have given a fellow worker who happened to be male.

It was not Emerson who had affected my mood, or even the startling discovery of Mr. Vincey's innocence; though the knowledge that we now had to deal, not with an ordinary criminal, but with that enigmatic and unknown genius of crime who had evaded capture so often, was certainly discouraging. What disturbed me most was being forced to acknowledge I had been mistaken in my assessment of Sethos's character. I had been gullible enough to believe in that strange man's honor—to trust his word that never again would he impinge upon my life. Obviously he was no more to be trusted in that area than in any other. I ought not to have been surprised or disappointed. But I was.

The swollen globe of the sun hung low over the river, veiled by the rising mist of evening, when we started back to the dahabeeyah. Emerson had driven the men unmercifully and himself just as hard—and me even harder. I was so stiff and cramped with squatting I was glad to accept the offer of Cyrus's arm. René had given his to Bertha; watching the oddly assorted pair—the slim, dapper young man and the perambulating bundle of shapeless cloth beside him—I said thoughtfully, "I have never been one to interfere with romantic attachments, Cyrus, but I do not approve of that relationship. His intentions cannot be serious—in the way of matrimony, I mean."

"I hope not," Cyrus exclaimed. "His mother is a member of some noble French house; the old lady would have a fit if he brought home a squashed blossom like that."

"Please don't mention that to Emerson. He is as prejudiced against the aristocracy as he is against young lovers. However, Cyrus, I cannot approve of an unlicensed attachment; it is not fair to the girl."

"I suppose you've got her future all planned," Cyrus said, the corners of his mouth twitching. "Are you going to give her any say in the matter?"

"Your sense of humor is delightful, dear Cyrus. I haven't had time to consider the matter seriously; first I will have to ascertain what talents she has, and how best to employ them. But I certainly will not allow her to fall back into the life of degradation and abuse she has experienced thus far. Honorable marriage or an honorable profession—what other choices are there for any woman who is given the opportunity to choose?"

Cyrus's hand went to his chin. Finding no goatee on which to tug, as was his habit when perplexed or perturbed, he rubbed his chin. "I reckon you're a better judge than I am," he replied.

"I reckon I am," I said, laughing. "I know what you are thinking, Cyrus; I am a married woman, not an inexperienced girl. But you are wrong. Men always believe what they want to believe, and one of their least attractive delusions concerns the—er—the . . ."

While I was considering how best to express this

delicate matter (and really, there is no way of expressing it delicately), I saw the black-robed form of Bertha sway closer to René, and her head tilt toward him. I caught my breath.

"Never mind, my dear, I get your drift," said Cyrus with a smile.

However, it was not embarrassment that had caused me to lose track of what I had been saying. The girl's sinuous, swaying movement had roused a long-forgotten memory. I had known another woman whose gestures had that serpentine grace. Her name was one of those on the list I had sent to Sir Evelyn Baring.

The mayor was waiting for me when Cyrus and I reached the village square. His dour expression told me, before he spoke, what news he had to give.

"No sign of Mohammed yet?" I inquired.

"He has not returned to the village, Sitt, and some of the men searched the cliffs all day. Hassan ibn Mahmud believes he has run away again."

"I would like to speak with Hassan." I sweetened the request with a few coins, adding, "There will be the same for Hassan if he comes at once."

Hassan promptly appeared; he had been watching from behind a wall. He frankly admitted that he was one of those Mohammed had asked to join him. "But I would never do such a thing, honored Sitt," he exclaimed, opening his eyes as wide as they would go. The effect was not convincing; like those of many Egyptians, Hassan's eyelids were inflamed by recurrent infections, and his other features were not precisely prepossessing.

"I am glad to hear that, Hassan," I remarked pleasantly. "For if I believed you meant to harm the Father of Curses, I would tear the soul out of your body by means of my magic, and leave it shrieking in the fires of Gehenna. But perhaps you agreed to go along with Mohammed yesterday in order to prevent him from carrying out his evil plan?"

"The honored Sitt reads the hearts of men!" exclaimed Hassan. "It is as the honored Sitt has said. But before we could act, the Sitt appeared, shooting and shrieking, and we knew the Father of Curses was saved. So we all ran away."

Of course I did not believe a word of this fantasy, and Hassan knew I did not. His cowardly allies had waited in concealment to see how Mohammed made out before risking their own precious hides, but if I had not come when I did, they would have been on Emerson like a pack of jackals on a wounded lion. Mastering my contempt and anger, I took out a few more coins and jingled them carelessly in my hand. "What was Mohammed's plan?"

I had to listen to a good many more protestations of innocence before I could winnow the few grains of wheat from among the chaff of Hassan's lies. He insisted that murder was not Mohammed's aim—and that I did believe. Once their victim was subdued and helpless, they would carry him to a place Mohammed knew of and leave him there. Hassan insisted he knew nothing more—and I believed that too. He and his friends were only hired thugs—tools, to be used for a specific purpose and discarded.

"And now," Hassan concluded sadly, "Mohammed

has run away. One of your bullets struck him, Sitt, for he bled as he ran, and I think he will not come back. I would be glad if he would."

I assured him the reward was still in effect, offered lesser amounts for any additional information, and sent him on his way—not rejoicing, but in a more cheerful frame of mind.

Twilight crept along the ground like a woman trailing long gray veils. Golden flowers of lamplight blossomed in the windows of the houses. "If I were not in the company of a lady," said Cyrus, "I would spit. I have a bad taste in my mouth."

I took his arm. "For that affliction I usually prescribe a whiskey and soda. And if you pressed me to join you, Cyrus, I would not say no."

"Don't give way to discouragement, my dear." Cyrus squeezed my hand. "You handled that rascal just right. If Mohammed hasn't already skipped the country his pals will be hot on his trail. I don't think we have to worry about him bothering us again."

"But who will be next?" We had reached the shore; warm, welcoming lights glowed from the dahabeeyah and the aroma of roasting mutton wafted to our nostrils. Across the river the western cliffs were crowned with a single brilliant star.

I stopped. "Will you think me foolish, Cyrus, if I confess a weakness I scarcely dare admit to myself? May I confide in you? For I feel the need of unburdening myself to a listener who is sensitive to my feelings and will not reproach me for them."

In a voice gruff with emotion, Cyrus assured me he would be honored by my confidence. Darkness, I have found, assists confession; the softness of the night, the silent attention of a friend lent eloquence to my tongue, and I told him of my selfish, contemptible yearning to return to the past.

"Can you blame me," I demanded passionately, "for feeling as if some evil genie intercepted the prayer I had the temerity to address to a benevolent Creator? Legends and myths tell us how such selfish wishes are twisted to harm instead of help the wisher. You remember Midas and the golden touch. The past has come back, not to help but to haunt me. Old enemies and old friends—"

"Right," Cyrus interrupted. "Amelia, dear, you're too sensible a lady to believe that stuff. I figure what you want from me isn't so much sympathy as a jolt of common sense. These people haven't been lying around in some eternal museum waiting to be wound up and set on your trail all at once; you've seen Karl off and on over the years, and me, and Carter, and a lot of other folks. Old enemies are bound to turn up too—along with plenty of new ones, considering how you and Emerson operate. It's impossible to go back, Amelia. This is now, not then, and the only direction you can go is forward."

I drew a deep, steadying breath. "Thank you, Cyrus. I needed that."

His warm, firm fingers tightened around mine. He leaned toward me.

"That whiskey and soda you mentioned will complete the cure," I said. "We had better go on; the others will be wondering what has become of us."

That evening Emerson informed us we would begin work next day in the royal wadi, and that he intended to remain there for several days and nights. The rest of us could do as we pleased; if we preferred to return to the dahabeeyah each evening, he would allow us to stop work early.

Cyrus looked at me. I smiled. Cyrus rolled his eyes heavenward and went off to make the necessary arrangements.

CHAPTER 11

"All is fair in love, war, and journalism."

I dreamed last night I returned to the royal wadi again. Moonlight transformed the ragged cliffs to icy silver sculptures of ruined palaces and crumbled colossi. The silence was absolute, unbroken even by the sound of my footsteps as I glided on, disembodied as the spirit I felt myself to be. Shadows sharp-limned as ink stains reached out and then retreated as I moved on. Darkness filled the narrow cleft toward which I drifted, and something moved to meet me—a shape of pale light, crowned with moonbeams and swathed in white linen. The deep-set eyes were sunk in shadow. The mouth was set in a grimace of pain. I held out my arms in pity and appeal, but he paid no heed. He passed on into eternal night, condemned to oblivion by the gods he had tried to destroy. Forever will he wander and forever, no doubt, will I return in dreams to that haunted place which draws my spirit as it does his.

*   *   *

"You appear a trifle hollow-eyed this morning, Peabody," Emerson remarked. "Didn't you sleep well? Something on your conscience, perhaps."

We were alone on deck, waiting for the others to collect their gear. A considerable quantity of supplies would be required if we were to remain in the remote wadi for several days; Emerson had of course left the complex arrangements to Cyrus, and had already complained about the delay.

Ignoring the provocation (for it was nothing less and certainly nothing more), I said, "I want to change that bandage before we go. You have got it wet."

He fussed and protested but I persisted, and at last he consented to follow me to my room. I left the door ostentatiously ajar.

"Are you sure you are willing to abandon your luxurious quarters for a tent among the rocks?" Emerson inquired, with a contemptuous survey of the elegant room. "You have my permission to return to the dahabeeyah at night if you prefer. It is only a three-hour walk each—ouch!"

This ejaculation was wrung from him by my brisk removal of the sticking plaster. "I thought you angels of mercy prided yourselves on the delicacy of your touch," Emerson went on, between his teeth.

"Not at all. We pride ourselves on our efficiency. Stop squirming or you will get a mouthful of antiseptic. It is not meant to be taken internally."

"It stings," Emerson grumbled.

"There is some localized infection. I expected that. The healing process is proceeding nicely, however." My voice was steady, I believe, though the sight of the ugly, inflamed wound made my heart contract.

"As for returning to the dahabeeyah every night, that would of course be the most sensible procedure," I said, cutting strips of sticking plaster. "But if you are determined to perch in the wadi like a bird in the wilderness, the rest of us must—"

The voice of Cyrus calling my name interrupted me before Emerson could do so, as his expression indicated he fully intended. "There you are," said Cyrus, in the doorway. "I was looking for you."

"You have a positive genius for stating the obvious, Vandergelt," said Emerson. He pushed my hand away. "That will do. Collect your bottles and paint and jars and other female flapdoodle and let's be off."

Brushing rudely past Cyrus, he went out. I packed away my medical supplies and tucked the box into my knapsack.

"Is that all you are taking?" Cyrus asked. "Someone can come back for anything you have forgotten, of course."

"That will not be necessary. I have everything I need." I tucked my parasol under my arm.

The donkeys were being loaded when we crossed over to the riverbank. Emerson had gone on, the cat riding on his shoulder. I stopped to talk to Feisal, who was supervising the donkey men.

"They have been washed, Sitt Hakim," he assured me. He was referring to the donkeys, not the men, though their appearance certainly could have been improved by a little soap and water.

"Good." I took a handful of dates from my pocket and fed them to the donkeys. One of the lean pariah dogs slunk toward us, its tail between its legs. I tossed it the scraps of meat I had saved from breakfast.

"Poor dumb creatures," said Cyrus. "It's a waste of time feeding them, though, my dear; there are too many of them, and all half-starved."

"One scrap of food is better than none," I replied. "At least that is my philosophy. But Cyrus, what is all this baggage? We are setting up a temporary camp, not a luxury hotel."

"Lord only knows how long your bullheaded husband will want to stay in the wadi," Cyrus replied. "You won't leave the place so long as he's there, so I figured we might as well be comfortable. I ordered up a few extra donkeys, in case you wanted to ride."

I declined this thoughtful offer, but René helped Bertha mount one of the little beasts and walked beside her as we set out. It took about an hour for our caravan to cross the plain; unless it is beaten, which I never permit, a donkey's pace is not much faster than that of a man. I kept a watchful eye on Emerson, some distance ahead. Abdullah and several of his sons were in close attendance, to Emerson's audible annoyance. Sound carries quite a distance in the desert.

Mounting into the foothills, we reached the entrance to the wadi, where Emerson was waiting. He was rolling his eyes and tapping his foot and exhibiting other ostentatious signs of impatience, but even he, I think, was glad to rest and catch his breath for a moment. We were high enough to see a stretch of the river sparkling in the morning sunlight beyond the soft green of cultivated fields and palm trees. It was with a sense of impending doom—and a corresponding stiffening of nerve and sinew—that I turned to contemplate the dark opening in the cliffs.

The reality was grim enough, though of course it looked nothing like the fantasy that was to haunt my dreams for years to come. Sterile, bare and dead; not a blade of grass, not a trickle of moisture. The rocky faces on either side were cracked, horizontally and vertically, like crumbling ruins; the sloping detritus below them and the pebbles and boulders littering the Valley floor were ominous evidence of constant rockfalls, and of the rare but violent flash floods that had helped to shape the wadi.

When we passed into the Valley, only the heights of the left-hand cliffs shone with sunlight. The Valley floor was still deep in shadow. Gradually the light crept down the cliffs and moved toward us as we followed a path winding among the tumbled rocks, until at last the full force of the sun struck down like a blast from a furnace. The barren ground quivered with heat. The only sounds that broke the silence were the gasping breaths of men and donkeys, the crunch of rock under their feet, and the cheerful jingle of the accouterments dangling from my belt.

Never had I been so grateful for my comfortable new trousers and neat knee-high boots. Even the bloomer-rationals I had worn on my first visit to Egypt, improvement though they were over trailing skirts and bulky bustles, had not permitted such ease of movement. The only thing I envied the men was their ability to remove more clothing than I could properly do. Emerson, of course, had his coat off and his shirt sleeves rolled to the elbow before we had gone a mile, and as the sunlight enveloped our perspiring forms even Cyrus, with an apologetic glance at me, removed his linen jacket and loosened his cravat. The cotton robes the Egyptians wore were better suited to the climate than European clothing. I had wondered at first how they managed to scramble around so easily without tripping over their skirts, but I soon realized they had no compunction about tucking them up or stripping off the robes altogether when this was expedient.

After approximately three miles the rocky walls began to close in and narrower canyons opened up to the right and left. Emerson stopped. "We will camp here."

"The royal tomb is farther on," Cyrus said, mopping his wet forehead. "Up that wadi to the north—"

"There is not enough level space for your confounded tents in the royal wadi itself. Furthermore, the other tombs I mentioned are nearby. There is at least one in that small valley to the south."

Cyrus made no further objection. The word "tombs" had the same effect on him that the mention of "pyramids" has on me. From Emerson's ironical expression I suspected he knew what I anticipated would be the case: that the other tombs would be even more ruined and empty of objects than the abandoned sepulcher of Akhenaton. However, hope springs eternal, as the saying goes, and I sympathized with Cyrus's feelings. It is much more sensible to be an optimist instead of a pessimist, for if one is doomed to disappointment, why experience it in advance?

We left the men to set up camp—no easy task on

ground so littered with debris—and went on another hundred yards to where the royal wadi led northward. A few minutes' walking brought us to the spot.

After a moment Cyrus spoke in a soft, contemplative voice. "There is something about the place . . . What was he really like, that strange, enigmatic figure? What did he really believe?"

I knew by Emerson's expression that he was not unmoved, but when he replied his voice was harshly practical. "More to the point are the mysteries of the tomb itself. Akhenaton was interred there, I would stake my reputation upon it. Fragments of his burial equipment, including the sarcophagus, have been found. That massive, hard stone object was smashed to bits; few of the pieces are larger than five centimeters across. No tomb robber would expend such effort. The vandals must have been enemies of the king, driven by hatred and the desire for revenge. Did they also destroy his mummy, or had it been transferred to a safer place, along with the rest of his burial equipment, when the city was abandoned?

"The second of his daughters died young, before there was time to prepare a separate tomb for her. Fragments of another sarcophagus which must have been hers have also been found here. I don't doubt she was buried in the rooms which were decorated with the scenes of her parents mourning over her body.

"But what of Nefertiti? There is only one sarcophagus emplacement in the burial chamber. The separate suite of rooms leading off from the entrance corridor may have been meant for her burial, but it was never completed and not a fragment of her funerary equipment has turned up in or near the tomb."

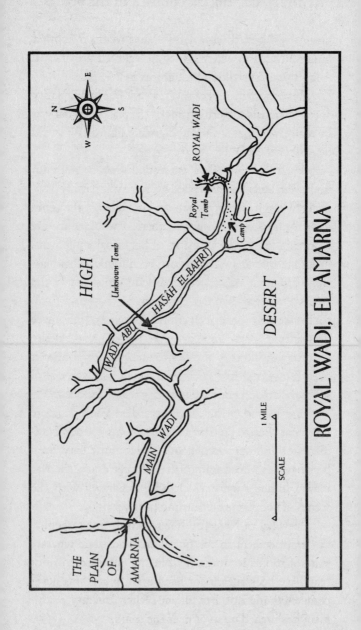

ROYAL WADI, EL AMARNA

"What about the jewelry Mond bought in 1883?" Cyrus asked. "There was a ring with her name—"

"That," said Emerson dogmatically, "was part—a very minute part—of her husband's rich equipment. Those bits and pieces were pocketed—I speak figuratively, of course—by one of those who transferred the mummy of Akhenaton to another tomb or by the vandals who destroyed the sarcophagus. The former hypothesis seems most likely to me. The sarcophagus was too heavy to be moved, but the coffined body and the equipment buried with it—jars of oil and food, clothing, furniture, ornaments—were taken away. The jewelry acquired by Mond was purchased from local villagers. The ancient thief hid his loot somewhere in the wadi, meaning to come back for it later, but he never did. The cache was undoubtedly discovered by modern thieves."

"Then you believe her tomb—" Cyrus began.

"May yet be found," Emerson said. "But the royal tomb should be our first enterprise. I want the place completely cleared out, down to bare rock. The fill in the shaft will have to be removed and sifted. Floors and ceilings and walls should be probed to make certain no hidden doorways exist. Where the devil is—hell and damnation, Abdullah, will you stop treading on my heels?"

"I follow to be ready when the Father of Curses commands," said Abdullah.

"I command you not to walk so close behind, then. Go fetch Ali and four—no, five—of the others. I want only trained men to work here. You know what to look for, Abdullah."

"We start now?" Abdullah inquired, rolling his eyes heavenward. High above, the cloudless sky shimmered with heat.

"It is almost midday," I said, before Emerson could reply. "And the trip has been long and arduous. We will rest and eat before starting work, Abdullah."

"As for you," said Emerson, fixing me with a critical blue stare, "you can take your treasure-hunting friend Vandergelt back to the main wadi and start looking for other tombs."

"We haven't the manpower," Cyrus objected. "There are tons of rock and sand to be shifted."

"Get workers from the village."

"For pity's sake, Emerson," I exclaimed. "Are you out of your mind?"

"So you keep telling me," Emerson replied mildly.

"We dare not admit strangers to our group," I insisted. "Some of the men of Haggi Qandil were hiding in the cliffs when Mohammed attacked you, ready to carry you off if his plan succeeded. Most of them are honest, I believe, but a few—"

"Hire the honest ones, then," said Emerson impatiently. "Why the devil can't you use a little initiative instead of depending on my advice for everything?"

Naturally I paid no attention to Emerson's attempt to divide our forces. "If you want to concentrate on the royal tomb, then let us concentrate," I said firmly. "In addition to the tasks you mentioned this morning, we ought to make a more accurate plan of the entire tomb and copy the remaining reliefs. Bouriant's copies are invaluable because they show sections that have now disappeared, but they are not entirely accurate, and—"

"Damn it, woman, don't lecture me!" Emerson bellowed. He fumbled at his chin. Finding no beard on which to tug, he rubbed the member in question until it turned pink. "I intended, of course, to do all the things you gratuitously suggested. Since you anticipated me, you may have the pleasure of copying the reliefs."

I felt certain I knew what had motivated this suggestion. He was getting even with me for the beard. The inner chambers of the tomb were as hot as the pits of the infernal regions.

"Certainly," I said calmly. "What method had you in mind? Dry squeezes or tracings?"

"Both," said Emerson, his lips curving in an expression that hardly deserved to be called a smile. "I want every scratch on those walls recorded. One technique may show details the other missed. After you have compared the two and made a master drawing, you will take it back into the tomb and check it against the wall itself. You may have René to assist you. Begin in room E and make sure you cover every inch of every wall."

Room E was the burial chamber—the deepest, most remote, hottest part of the tomb.

"Certainly," I said again. Emerson went off, smirking. While he was haranguing the men on how he wanted them to proceed, I took Abdullah aside.

"I don't know what he is up to, Abdullah, but he has just ordered me into the deepest and most distant part of the tomb, where I can't keep an eye on him. He has not said what he means to do, but I fear the worst. I rely on you, my friend. Watch him! Don't let him wander off alone."

"Have no fear, Sitt. Since the last time he eluded us I have made sure someone watches over him even when he sleeps, or seems to sleep. He will not escape us again."

"Excellent. I trust you as I would myself."

I was turning away when the old man said hesitatingly, "Sitt Hakim..."

"Yes, Abdullah?"

"I would not have you think your safety is a lesser matter to us."

"You need not tell me that, old friend," I said warmly. "You and I understand one another's hearts, I think. We both know that the Father of Curses is in greater need of protection than I; he is the bravest of men, but he does take foolish chances." Adjusting my belt, I added, "I can take care of myself."

Abdullah's bearded lips quivered. "Yes, Sitt. But I hope I do not offend if I say that as you trust in me, I trust in the rich American who is also your friend. He will not let harm come to you if he can prevent it."

"Mr. Vandergelt is a true friend," I said. "We are fortunate to have such loyal friends—and you chief among them, Abdullah."

The courtesies and the dictates of affection having been satisfied, Abdullah set off in pursuit of Emerson and I found René and instructed him to gather our equipment.

Cyrus of course offered to assist me, but I could see he was not interested in such painstaking, plodding work—nor had he the training for it. When I assured him I would get on very well without him he did not insist. He already had his eye on a pile of debris across the wadi, near the place where other explorers, including Emerson, had found evidence of a possible tomb opening, and I could see he was itching to start digging.

René and I carried our rolls of paper and pencils down the long shafts and stairs, over the half-filled shaft (which had been bridged by planks) and down a short ramp into the burial chamber.

It was about thirty feet on either side (10.36 by 10.40 meters, to be precise) with two square pillars and a raised plinth that had once supported the sarcophagus. The floor was covered with hardened mud set solid as plaster. The surfaces of walls and pillars had been decorated with painted reliefs modeled on a layer of plaster which had been applied to the rock surface. Here, where the heretic's own body had rested, the full fury of his enemies had been expended. Most of the plaster was gone. However, some of the figures had been roughly delineated on the underlying rock before the plaster was applied, and these rude outlines still survived.

"We will start with the back wall," I said to René. "I at the right-hand corner, you at the left. Watch me first; I am sure you are familiar with the technique, but I have my own methods."

The process of dry squeezing consists of pressing a thin sheet of paper over the carvings with the fingertips. Wet squeezes would of course give a more precise copy, but they often damaged the crumbling reliefs and removed the last traces of any remaining paint. The technique of rubbing should be self-explanatory; soft pencils and a steady, even pressure were necessary. It was hard on the arm and hand muscles to maintain this, especially when working on a perpendicular surface.

I will not elaborate on the working conditions. Imagine the hottest, dustiest, deadest, driest climate your mind can conceive, and double it; that will give some idea of what René and I endured that afternoon. I was determined to stick to it till I dropped and René was determined not to be outdone by a mere woman (though of course he knew better than to voice this sentiment aloud). For his sake rather than my own I decreed occasional breaks for rest, air, and refreshment. Copious consumption of water was essential to ward off dehydration. Each time we emerged my eyes sought Emerson. Each time he was in a different place—remeasuring a room Charlie had already measured, and telling him he had done it wrong, criticizing Abdullah for overlooking a scrap of pottery in a crack in the floor, or hectoring the small work force he had assigned to Cyrus. He left me and René strictly alone most of the afternoon; when he finally came thumping down the passage, it was to tell us to stop for the day.

A faint moan came from René. I said, "As soon as I finish this sheet of paper."

Emerson picked up one of the rubbings I had completed and held it near the lamp. "Hmph," he said, and thumped off.

The valley was sunk in blue shadows when we emerged. René collapsed on the ledge, gasping. I handed him my canteen; the water was hot enough to have been used for tea, but it gave him strength enough to go on. I had to help him descend the slope, however.

"What luck?" I inquired of Cyrus, who was waiting below.

"Not much. Emerson insists we pick through every confounded square inch of sand. At this rate it will take two weeks to reach bedrock. So far we have found a diorite maul, the kind the ancients used to break rock, and four pieces of pottery." Cyrus wiped the perspiration from his brow with his sleeve and then blinked at me. "But my poor dear girl—you look as if you have spent the day in a steam bath. You must be exhausted."

"Not at all. A nice hot cup of tea and a nice warm cup of water with which to bathe my face, and I will be fully restored."

"We can do better than that," Cyrus said, taking my arm. "Come and see what my fellows have done."

What they had accomplished was little short of a miracle. The area was quite unsuitable for a camp. The central space was so narrow the tents and shelters had to be arranged in a long line instead of clustering together. To clear the ground entirely of rock would have taken weeks, but the men had rolled away many of the larger boulders and prepared relatively flat surfaces on which tents could be erected. Rugs and matting softened the pebbly ground, and folding cots offered promise of comfortable rest. Even the wood and dried camel dung for a fire had to be brought with us, for there was not so much as a twig to be gathered. Several fires burned bright in the dusk, and lanterns hung near the tents. Water jars, bowls and towels had been arranged outside each of them.

"No wonder you wanted so many donkeys," I said to Cyrus as, with glances admiring on my part and modestly proud on his, we surveyed the scene. "You sent them back after they were unloaded?"

"Figured I might as well. In rough terrain like this a man can scramble around as fast as a donkey can move." He hesitated for a moment, and then said, "I hope Emerson isn't going to throw a fit when he finds out I ordered some of my own men to stay. They don't know much about excavating, but they have sharp eyes and suspicious natures."

"Let him throw a fit if he likes. I approve, and I believe I can still bully—persuade, I mean—Emerson to accept the inevitable. How did you manage to convince your crewmen to take on the duties of guards?"

"Money is a great persuader, my dear. We'll speak no more of that; have a look at your quarters and see if I have forgotten anything you need or want."

The only fault I could find was that there was an excess of unnecessary luxuries, including soft cushions and a pretty china tea set. "It won't do, Cyrus," I said, smiling. "Emerson will wax sarcastic when he sees those ruffled pillows."

"Let him," was the sulky reply.

"More to the point," I continued, "there is not room for a second cot. Bertha will have to share my tent, Cyrus. No"—for he was on the verge of objecting—"there is no alternative, I fear. Far be it from me to cast aspersions on the character of any young gentleman, but I cannot allow the slightest breath of scandal to tarnish an expedition of which I am a part. Gossip of that sort, true or false, would hinder the advancement of females in the profession, and that advancement, as you know, is a matter of great concern to me. Furthermore—"

"I take your point," said Cyrus with a sigh. "If that's what you want, Amelia, that's how it's going to be."

Cyrus's cook was among those who had consented to stay with us. I could only assume Cyrus had bribed him extravagantly, for good chefs can easily find employment and do not have to endure conditions like the ones under which he labored.

I was pouring tea by the fire when Charlie staggered into camp. The poor young American was a sight to behold. His shirt was as wet as if he had stood under a waterfall, and his hair was dripping.

"So how did it go?" I inquired cheerfully. "You have been working on the plan of the tomb, I believe?"

"Part of the time," said Charlie, in a voice hoarse with fatigue and dust. "I believe I have by now practiced every possible aspect of the archaeologist's trade. If the professor—"

He was interrupted by the professor himself, who had gone off to inspect the camp. He now came storming up to us, brandishing some object like a club. It was so dark that I did not identify the object until he got close to the fire.

"What the devil do you mean by this, Vandergelt?" he demanded, thrusting the rifle—for so it proved to be—into Cyrus's face.

"For heaven's sake, Emerson, point it the other way," I exclaimed in some alarm.

"It is not loaded," said Emerson, pitching the weapon away. "But the ammunition is there, along with a half dozen other rifles. What the devil—"

"If you will give me a chance, I will answer you," said Cyrus coolly. "Nobody is forcing you to pack a six-shooter, but I'll be consarned if I am going to neglect such an obvious means of self-defense. These are Mauser Gewehrs, with 7.92-millimeter cartridges and a five-round magazine. A sharp shot, which I am, can blow a man's head off at two hundred yards. And if I see a head I don't recognize, that's what I intend to do, with your permission or without it."

Emerson's teeth gleamed in the firelight. "I'm sure your speech has made a great impression on the ladies, Vandergelt. It doesn't impress me; but then that was not your purpose, was it? I hope your eyesight is good. It would be a pity if you happened to shoot Abdullah or me by mistake."

Hearing Cyrus's teeth grinding, I hastened to intervene. "No more squabbling, if you please. Supper will be ready soon; go and wash."

"Yes, Mama," said Emerson. He has rather large, very white teeth; the reflection of the firelight off their surfaces presented a horrifying picture.

Bertha glided off to assist the chef. When the group reassembled, tempers had improved somewhat—I refer primarily to the temper of Emerson—and the consumption of an excellent meal put everyone into a more relaxed frame of mind. In relative affability we compared notes on the activities of the day and discussed plans for the morrow. The only discordant note was introduced by—whom else?—Emerson, who inquired why I was lounging around the fire instead of collating the copies I had made that day.

With perfect calm I replied, "It is impossible to do

it properly under these conditions. The light is inadequate, there is not a flat surface large enough to spread the papers out—"

"Bah," said Emerson.

It was not long before yawns and lengthening silences interrupted speech, and I decreed that it was time to retire. It had been a long hard day for most of us.

Bertha was not pleased to learn that she was to share my tent. Not that she said so—she was a very silent creature, at least with me—but she was very adept at conveying her feelings without the use of words. Removing only her outer robe and veil, she rolled herself in a blanket and within a few minutes her regular breathing indicated that she had fallen asleep. I had intended to ask her a few questions, but I was unusually tired myself. I felt my eyelids droop...

How long it took me to realize that my drowsiness was unnatural I cannot say. I am particularly resistant to drugs and hypnosis; it is not so much physical immunity as something in my character, I believe. For an indeterminate time I lay in a semi-stupor, dozing off and waking, hearing the low voices of the workmen and the clatter of cooking pots gradually fade into silence. It was well past midnight, I think, when the sleepless sentinel within my brain finally made itself heard. "This is no natural repose," it cried. "Arouse yourself and act!"

It was easier said (or thought) than done. My limbs felt as limp as boneless tentacles. But the remedy was close at hand. I had employed it before in a similar situation, and thanks to the rearrangement of the tent made necessary by the addition of Bertha's cot, all my equipment was nearby. I had only to stretch out my hand.

My fingers were as clumsy as an animal's paws, but at last I managed to open the box of medical supplies and extract my smelling salts. A good whiff of them not only cleared my head, it left the distinct impression that the top of that appendage had been blown off. I sat up and put my feet on the floor. I had taken off my boots and jacket and my belt of accounterments before retiring. The boots, at least, I must reassume before proceeding to investigate. Not only was the ground uneven and painful to stockinged feet, but there were scorpions and other stinging creatures to be avoided.

I was still fumbling for my boots—for I did not deem it expedient to strike a light—when I heard a soft rattle of pebbles from without, and realized that a similar sound must have alerted my sleepless sentinel. An animal might have caused it, or a man abroad on some harmless errand. But I thought not. Leaping to my feet, I promptly fell flat onto the floor—or, to be more accurate, onto Bertha's cot. The sudden impact was too much for the frail structure; it collapsed, with Bertha still on it.

Though I had not planned it that way, the incident had the desired effect, i.e., to alarm the camp. My startled shout was answered by a louder cry. Rocks crunched and rolled under running feet. A shot rang out.

I managed to extract myself from the mass of tumbled blankets and bits of broken cot. Bertha had not stirred. If I had had any doubts about being drugged, her immobility would have removed them; normal sleep would surely have been interrupted by the collapse of the bed and the impact of my body. First I located my parasol; then, finding my knees were still too unsteady to permit a more erect posture, I crawled toward the entrance of the tent. When I raised the flap the first thing my hazed eyes beheld was a gigantic firefly, wavering back and forth in drunken flight. With some effort I focused my vision. The light was that of a lantern. Emerson was holding it. Seeing me he said, "Hell and damnation!" but he said no more, for his knees buckled and he sat down suddenly on the ground—on a sharp rock, to judge by the equally profane outcry that followed.

"It is most interesting," I remarked somewhat later, "to observe the varying effects of a particular drug on different people."

"Urgh," said Emerson. He had irritably refused the offer of my smelling salts, and was drinking cup after cup of strong coffee.

"You," I continued, "may have acquired a certain immunity as a result of—er—your recent experiences. Cyrus was less affected than René and Charles—"

"Argh," said Cyrus.

"While Bertha was the most susceptible of all."

"Will she be all right?" Heavy-eyed and pale, René looked anxiously at me.

"Yes, certainly. She will have a good night's sleep, which is more than can be said of the rest of us. The guard," I continued, "appears to have been relatively unaffected. Of course we don't know how the laudanum was administered, so we cannot be certain of how much each person consumed."

"It was in the food," Emerson muttered.

"Or drink. But which dish? Everyone got some of it, not only ourselves, but the Egyptians. Even the guard admits he was dozing when he heard me cry out. The question is one of some importance, you must agree, since we must determine who had the opportunity to add the opium to our food. We have a traitor in our midst, gentlemen!"

Emerson gave me a critical look over the rim of his coffee cup. "Allowing for the excessive melodrama of your speech patterns, Peabody, it appears you are correct. The chef is the most obvious suspect."

"Too obvious," I said. "You know how he cooks—pots simmering for hours on a fire, out in the open, with people constantly coming and going—and staying to gossip. We must interrogate the servants—"

"Rot," Emerson growled. "There is no way we can determine who is responsible for this. The filthy stuff may have been added to one of the water jars before we ever left the village. Anyone could have done it." His eyes raked the watching faces with sapphirine intensity, and he repeated with slow emphasis, "Anyone."

Charles immediately looked so guilty, my old friend Inspector Cuff would have arrested him on the spot. It led to a strong presumption of his innocence.

But after we had finally dispersed I asked myself what I really knew about the two young archaeologists. René had been with Cyrus for several years, but even old acquaintance could not clear a man of suspicion in this case. The lure of treasure and of discovery is strong enough to seduce those of weak character. Aside from our men from Aziyeh, there were only three who could be considered above suspicion: Emerson, Cyrus and myself. As for Bertha...Her drug-induced sleep was genuine. I had applied a number of tests, the results of which left no doubt in my mind. But only the stupidest of conspirators would fail to include himself—or herself—among the victims in such a case. I did not think Bertha was that stupid.

In the clear light of morning we were able to determine that only the area near my tent showed signs of uninvited guests. The partial prints of bare feet were visible in two places where none of our men had trod.

When we started out for the royal wadi, Cyrus was carrying a rifle. Emerson's eyebrows climbed when he saw it, but he made no objection, even when Cyrus said coolly, "Don't get het up if you see someone above, on the plateau. I sent a couple of my boys up there to keep a lookout."

Like Cyrus, I had determined to take a few precautions of my own. Over Emerson's violent objections (which I of course ignored) to the depletion of his work force, I had stationed Selim, Abdullah's youngest son, at the far end of the main wadi. Selim was Ramses's particular friend, a handsome boy barely sixteen years of age. Knowing the foolhardy courage of youth, I had been reluctant to assign him to this particular task; I only did so after Abdullah assured me that both he and Selim would feel dishonored if his offer were refused. I cautioned the boy as emphatically as I was able that his role was that of an observer only, and that he would fail in that role if he went on the attack. "Stay in hiding," I instructed him. "Fire a warning shot to alert us if you see anything that arouses your suspicions, but do not shoot at anyone. If you will not swear by the Prophet to obey my order, Selim, I will send someone else."

His big brown long-lashed eyes wide and candid, Selim swore. I did not like the loving way he handled the rifle, but with Abdullah beaming with paternal pride, I felt I had little choice. I only hoped that if he did shoot someone, it would be Mohammed and not the reporter from the *London Times*.

Or even Kevin O'Connell. It was he whom I expected, of course. I was only surprised he had not succeeded in tracking us down before this.

When we returned to camp that evening, after grueling hours in the heat and dry air of the burial chamber, I found Selim waiting. I had ordered him to come back and report to me at sunset. Not even to protect Emerson would I have allowed such an excitable lad to stay in his dangerous post after dark, when, as all Egyptians knew, demons and afreets came out of hiding. Selim's face was rapt with awe. He could hardly wait to tell me his news.

"He came, Sitt, as you foretold he would—the man himself, the very one you described to me. Truly you are the greatest of magicians! He said he had not told you of his coming. He said you would be glad to see him, though. He said he was a friend. He said—"

"He tried to persuade—or bribe?—you to let him pass," I said, thereby increasing my reputation for supernatural powers in the eyes of the innocent youth. "Did he send a message, as I—as my magic—foretold he would?"

"The Sitt knows all and sees all," Selim said reverently.

"Thank you, Selim," I said, taking the folded paper he handed me. "Now rest. You have done a man's work today."

Bertha had waked in the morning without ill effect, though she had been drowsy and sluggish all day. She had gone straight to our tent when we returned, but when I entered she rose and glided out. I did not attempt to detain her. Sitting down on the edge of the bed, I unfolded the note, which appeared to have been composed on the spot, for the writing was so uneven the paper must have been resting upon a rocky surface. That difficulty had not restrained Kevin's tendency toward verbosity or dimmed his ebullient Irish spirits.

After the usual florid compliments he went on:

> I look forward with a delight I cannot express in mere words to renewing my acquaintance with such admired friends as you and the Professor, and to expressing my felicitations on another miraculous escape. In fact I look forward to it so much I won't take no for an answer. I have taken up my abode in the pleasant little house someone (dare I hope it was you, in the expectation of my coming?) kindly constructed not far from the entrance to this canyon. One of the villagers has agreed to bring food and water for me daily, so I expect to be quite comfortable. I am an impatient fellow, though, as you know, so don't keep me waiting too long or I may be tempted to risk my neck crossing the plateau and climbing down to join you.

Further compliments followed. It was the closing words—an impertinent "*À bientôt*,"—that forced from my lips an expression of the outrage I had thus far suppressed.

"Curse it!" I cried.

Bertha's face appeared in the tent opening. Over her veil her eyes were wide with alarm. "Is something wrong? Is it from—from him?"

"No, no," I said. "Nothing is wrong—nothing that need concern you. You needn't stand outside, Bertha, though your courtesy is noted and appreciated." Folding the letter, I put it in my box and went out to splash water on my dusty and now even more heated face.

I did not join in the conversation around the fire as energetically as was my wont that evening; I was preoccupied with considering how I could meet Kevin and head him off. I did not doubt that if I failed to confront him he would do precisely what he had threatened to do; and if he did not break his neck climbing down the cliff face, one of Cyrus's guards would probably shoot him. A less honorable woman might have regarded that as an ideal solution, but I could not entertain such a reprehensible idea. Besides, there was always the chance that Kevin might elude the guard and accomplish the descent without damaging himself.

I must see him and speak with him, and hope that an appeal to the friendship he claimed to feel for me would persuade him to leave us alone. A little bribe, in the form of a promise of future interviews, might assist in achieving the desired end. But how was I to reach him alone and unescorted? Cyrus would insist on accompanying me if he knew what I planned, and Cyrus's critical presence would destroy the friendly, confidential atmosphere that was essential to any hope of success.

I would have to go during the midday rest period, I decided. It would have been folly to attempt the long, difficult walk in darkness, and I could not disappear for any length of time during working hours. The rest period usually lasted for two or three hours. There was no hope of being able to return before my absence was discovered, since the distance was almost three miles each way, but if I could deal with Kevin before they caught me up, I would have accomplished my purpose. It was feasible, I concluded. Certainly it was worth a try. And there could be no danger, for Selim would be on guard at the entrance to the wadi.

Having decided this, I applied myself to my dinner with good appetite. The others, I observed, were inclined to study each bite suspiciously before putting it into their mouths, but I had reasoned that the same trick would not be tried again so soon after the failure of the first attempt.

Such proved to be the case. I woke several times during night, feeling only normal drowsiness before I allowed myself to sleep again. Bertha seemed restless too, which further reassured me.

René and I put in a good morning's work in the Pillared Hall (i.e., the burial chamber), for I never allow mental distraction to interfere with my archaeological duties. We had almost finished the back wall; the lowest sections could not be accurately copied until the floor was cleared to bedrock. I pointed this out to Emerson when we stopped for luncheon.

"I don't suppose you want the men stirring up dust

while you are copying?" he inquired. "Leave that till later. You still have three walls and four sides of two pillars to go, I believe?"

René's face fell. He had hoped for a day or two off while the men worked.

I had considered slipping a little laudanum into the tea at lunch to ensure everyone would sleep soundly while I stole away. That did not seem quite cricket, so I only put it in Bertha's cup.

She dropped off almost at once. Though I was on fire to be up and away, for time was of the essence, I forced myself to remain recumbent a little longer in order to ensure that the others had followed her into the land of Morpheus. As I lay watching her I could not help but wonder what the future held for such a woman. What thoughts, what fears, what hopes lay concealed behind that smooth white brow and those enigmatic dark eyes? She had never confided in me, nor responded to my attempts to win her confidence. Yet I had seen her engaged in animated conversation with René, and less often with Charles; even Emerson had managed to induce, upon occasion, one of her rare silvery laughs. Some women do not get on with other women, but that could not be the cause of her reticence with me, because she was equally wary of Cyrus—who, I must admit, did not conceal his dislike of her. Was she still a willing slave of the man who had been so brutal to her? Had it been she who drugged our food?

She lay with her back to me. Rising slowly, impelled by an impulse I could not have explained, I bent over her. As if my intent regard had penetrated her slumber, she stirred and murmured. Quickly I drew back. Silence reigned without. It was time to go.

I had taken off my belt before I reclined. Much as I would have liked to take it with me, I dared not risk the noise. Thanking heaven and my own foresight for my useful pockets, I distributed several important tools among them. One of the most important, my handy little knife, provided me with a convenient exit from the tent. After cutting a long slit I returned the knife to my pocket, picked up my parasol, and exited.

Cyrus had placed my tent some distance from the others in a thoughtful attempt to give me as much privacy as the terrain allowed. It was not much, for at its greatest extent the wadi was only a few hundred feet wide. My tent backed up onto the slope of scree that bordered the cliffs. Carrying my boots, I crept along the base of it. Even our Egyptian friends wore sandals here, for the thick integument that years of going barefoot had developed on the soles of their feet was insufficient protection against the sharp-edged stones littering the floor of the canyon. My thick stocking served me no better, but I did not dare assume my boots until after I had gone some distance and was concealed from sight of the camp by a series of outcroppings.

It was extremely hot and very still. The only shade was high up on the steep, loose scree of the slope at the base of the cliff. Since haste was imperative, I had to follow the path winding among the boulders on the bottom, now in full sunlight. If I had not been in such a hurry I would have enjoyed the walk. It was the first time in many days I had been alone.

Naturally I kept a firm grip on my parasol and a sharp eye on the surroundings, but I was more inclined to trust that sixth sense that warns of lurking danger. Persons like myself, who are sensitive to atmosphere and who have been often subject to violent attack, develop this sense to an acute degree. It had seldom failed me.

I cannot explain why it failed on this occasion. No doubt I was preoccupied with composing the speech I meant to make to Kevin. The men must have been lying concealed and motionless for some time, for I certainly would have heard sounds of someone descending the slope.

They did not come out of hiding until after I had passed the first of them, so that when they emerged, simultaneously, I found retreat cut off. A second man popped out of a hole opposite me; two others appeared ahead. They looked very much alike in their turbans and grubby robes, but I recognized one of them. Mohammed had not run away after all. I had to admire his persistence, but I did not like the way he was grinning at me.

The cliff face was split by innumerable crevices and cracks. Some of the fallen boulders were big enough to conceal not one but several men. How many opponents must I defeat? Taking a firm grip on my parasol, I considered alternatives with a rapidity of thought my measured prose cannot attempt to convey.

Flight, in any direction, would have been folly. I could not scramble up the scree fast enough to escape those who would follow. A rapid advance would have sent me straight into the waiting arms of two adversaries, who were now advancing slowly toward me. Retreat— not flight, but a considered, deliberate withdrawal— eastward, in the direction from which I had come, appeared to offer the best hope. If I could dispose of the single man who barred my way...

But even as I shifted my parasol to my left hand and reached for my pistol, that hope was reduced by the rattle and crunch of rock. Another man was coming from the east to reinforce his confederate, and at considerable speed. There was not much chance, I feared, that I could incapacitate or elude two men. A hand weapon is inaccurate except at very close range, and I would be running as I fired. I would have to try, of course.

The second man came into view, and my fingers froze on the barrel of the pistol (which had shifted around in my pocket in a way I had not anticipated). Astonishment paralyzed every muscle. The man was Emerson, bareheaded, red-faced, and in extremely rapid motion. With a shout of, "Run, damn you!" he hurled himself at the surprised Egyptian, who collapsed onto the ground in a flurry of dirty fabric.

I took it that the order was addressed to me, and I was certainly in no position to object to the way it had been phrased. Emerson's sudden appearance and abrupt action had sent our opponents into momentary confusion; I had no difficulty in outstripping the man who was nearest to me. They were all close behind, though, and when Emerson caught my hand and fled, dragging me with him, I was in full agreement with his decision. I did wish he would get over his prejudice against firearms, however. A rifle would have been particularly useful just then.

We were over a mile from the camp and I did not see how we could reach it without being overtaken. Had he come alone? Was help on the way? Questions flooded my mind but I was too short of breath to articulate them, which is probably just as well, because Emerson was obviously in no mood to permit debate. After rounding an outcrop of rock he turned abruptly to the right, caught me round the waist, and threw me up onto the rocky slope. "Go on," he gasped, emphasizing the suggestion by a sharp slap on a convenient part of my anatomy. "Through that opening. Hurry!"

Looking up, I saw the opening he referred to—a black irregular hole in the cliff face. It was roughly triangular in shape, narrowing to a crack that turned at a sharp angle to meet the top of the slope. Only at its widest part was there room for the passage of a body. Mine passed, with little conscious volition on my part but with considerable assistance from Emerson, shoving from behind. I did not resist, though the prospect of dropping down into blackness, with no idea of what lay below and beyond, was not especially appealing. It was more appealing than the alternative, however.

I landed somewhat forcibly on an uneven surface about six feet below the opening. The floor was littered with stones and other objects which pressed painfully into my bare hands. As I struggled to my feet I heard a nasty crunching sound and a scream, followed by a rumble of falling rock. I deduced that Emerson had kicked one of our pursuers in the face. The ensuing confusion gave him time to make a more dignified entrance into the hole than I had managed; feet first, he dropped down beside me, and for a few moments he was too out of breath to do more than pant heavily.

The space in which we stood was quite small. Immediately behind us the floor sloped sharply up toward the ceiling. The width was no more than five or six feet, but from the relative regularity of the side walls I deduced it must be the entrance to one of the tombs Emerson had mentioned.

Emerson got his breath back. "Where is that ridiculous pistol of yours?" was his first question.

I produced it and handed it to him. Extending his arm out the opening, he pulled the trigger three times.

"Why are you wasting bullets?" I demanded. "There are only six in the pistol, and you didn't even—"

"I am summoning assistance," was the brusque reply.

Summoning assistance is not something Emerson often does. In this case it seemed the only sensible course. The entrance to the tomb-cave was so narrow and inconveniently located our adversaries could only pass through it one at a time—at the considerable risk of being knocked on the head, one at a time, by Emerson, as they did so—but neither could we get out while they were waiting for us. Emerson had—for once—accepted the inevitable, but he obviously did not like it.

"Oh," I said. "Then you came alone?"

"Yes," said Emerson, very softly. Then his voice rose to a roar that deafened my ears. "You damned-fool woman! What the devil possessed you to do such an idiotic thing?"

I started back, but I did not go very far; Emerson's hands shot out and gripped my shoulders. He shook me like a terrier with a rat, shouting all the while. Distorted by echoes, the words were relatively unintelligible, but I got the idea.

I do not *think* I would have hit him if—quite unintentionally, I feel sure—his violent shaking had not brought my head into painful contact with the wall behind me. I had lost my hat during our flight and my hair had come down, so there was nothing to cushion the blow. It hurt enough to remove any inhibitions I might have had about hurting him back. All the same, if I had not been in a state of considerable emotional excitability (for various reasons) I would not have done it. Except for playful gestures of quite another nature (which are irrelevant to this narrative) I had never struck Emerson. It would not have been playing the game to strike an opponent who is unable to hit back.

I certainly did not intend to hit him on the face. My wild blow landed square on his bandaged cheek.

The effect was remarkable. With a long gasping intake of pain (and, I presume, fury) he shifted his grip. One arm encircled my shoulders, the other my ribs. Pulling me to him, he pressed his lips to mine.

He had NEVER kissed me like that before. Between the steely strength of his arm and the pressure of his mouth, my head was bent back at an angle so acute that I felt my neck must snap. Between the unyielding barrier of the wall at my back and the hard muscles of his body, mine was crushed as if in a vise. What with constant practice and assiduous study, Emerson's natural talents at osculation had been honed to a fine pitch; but he had never kissed me like THAT before. (And I certainly hoped he had never kissed anyone ELSE like that before.) My senses were not gently wooed; they were assaulted, mastered, overcome.

When at last he let me go I would have fallen had it not been for the wall against which I leaned. As the roaring of blood in my ears subsided, I heard other voices, crying out in question and alarm. Rising above them all was a voice I took to be that of Cyrus, for it called my name, though I would scarcely have recognized it otherwise.

"We are here," Emerson shouted through the opening. "Safe and unharmed. Stand by, I will hand her out."

Then he turned to me. "I beg your pardon," he said quietly. "That was an unforgivable action for a gentleman—which, despite some eccentricities of behavior, I like to consider myself. You have my word of honor it will never happen again."

I was too shaken to reply, which is probably just as well; for if I had, I would have blurted out what I was thinking: "Oh, yes, it will—if I have anything to say about it!"

CHAPTER 12

"Once a man has taken refreshment in your home and a chair in your sitting room, you are less likely to pitch him into a pond."

There was nothing for it but to take Cyrus into my confidence.

"It was Kevin O'Connell I had to see," I explained. "I told you he would turn up, and so he has. Selim delivered a message from him yesterday."

I sat on a camp stool drinking tea, for I felt myself entitled to a mild restorative. Emerson, of course, had immediately returned to work. Cyrus had not followed him; he now lay sprawled on the rug at my feet like a fallen warrior, his face hidden in his arms.

I nudged him gently with my toe. "What you need," I said, "is a nice hot cup of tea."

Cyrus rolled over and sat up. His face was still flushed, though the livid color it had originally exhibited had faded somewhat. "I have never been a drinking man," he said, endeavoring to control his voice. "But I am beginning to understand how a man can be driven to drink. Never mind the darned tea. Where is that bottle of brandy?"

He was only joking, of course. I handed him a cup of tea. "Give me the benefit of your advice, Cyrus. What am I to do about Kevin?"

"Amelia, you are the most... You have an absolutely unparalleled... You—you—"

"We have already had that conversation, Cyrus. I said I was sorry to have worried you, but as you see, it has all turned out for the best. We have captured Mohammed! One enemy the less! And as soon as his broken nose heals we can question him and find out who hired him."

"One down," said Cyrus gloomily. "How many to go? If you are going to take risks like that to collect the rest of them, my heart is going to give way under the strain. Your lip is bleeding again, my dear; I can't stand the sight of it."

"The hot liquid must have opened the cut," I murmured, pressing my napkin to my mouth. "It is no injury incurred in the line of battle, you know, only a— a bitten lip."

For a moment we were both silent, thinking—I am sure—quite different thoughts. Then I gave myself a little shake and said briskly, "Now if we may return to the subject of Kevin..."

"I'd like to murder the young rascal," Cyrus muttered. "If it had not been for him... All right, Amelia, all right. Where is he, and what do you want me to do?"

I explained the situation. "So," I concluded, "we had better be off at once."

"Now?" Cyrus exclaimed.

"Certainly. If we hurry we can be back before dark. I do not anticipate another attack so soon; the men who got away can scarcely have had time to report the failure of this one. However, it is difficult walking in the dark."

With a wry smile Cyrus put down his cup and got to his feet. "Are you going to tell Emerson?"

"No, why should I? I am sure he has already cautioned you not to let me out of your sight."

"He didn't have to," Cyrus said, no longer smiling. There was no need for him to say more; his steady regard and firmly set lips proclaimed his resolution. The removal of the goatee had definitely been an improvement. He reminded me of those strong, silent sheriffs of whom one reads in American fiction.

He left me after promising he would be ready to go in five minutes. I did not require so much time. I put away the tea things and strapped on my belt; then I took from my pocket the small object my groping hands had encountered on the rock-strewn floor of the tomb. My touch has been trained by years of experience; I had known by the shape of it that it was not a stone but an object shaped by man, and the same trained instinct had prompted me to slip it into my pocket.

It was a ring bezel of cheap faience, like those I had found in the workmen's village and elsewhere. Some bore the name of the ruling pharaoh, others were adorned with the images of different gods. This was of the second variety. The image was that of Sobek—the crocodile god.

Not only Cyrus but two of his men accompanied me this time. All were armed. It was a needless precaution,

I felt sure, but men always enjoy marching around with weapons and flexing their figurative muscles, and I saw no reason to deny them this harmless exercise. As I had expected, the journey was without incident, and after hailing Selim, who had come out of hiding when he saw us, we emerged from the mouth of the wadi and walked the short distance to the little mud-brick house.

Kevin had certainly made himself comfortable. We found him sitting on a camel bag in the shade at the front of the house reading a yellowback novel, a glass in one hand and a cigarette in the other. He pretended to go on reading until we were almost upon him; then he leapt to his feet with a theatrical and unconvincing start of surprise.

"Sure an' it's one of those mirages I'm seeing—a vision of loveliness like the houris in the Moslem paradise! Top o' the afternoon to ye, Mrs. Emerson, me dear."

As he came to meet me the sun set his hair ablaze and reddened his sunburned cheeks. Freckles, snub nose, ingratiating grin, wide blue eyes made up an irresistible picture of a young Irish gentleman—and roused an irresistible urge in my breast. I did not try to resist it. I brought my parasol down on his outstretched arm.

"I am not your dear, and that brogue is as false as your professions of friendship!"

Kevin fell back, rubbing his arm, and Cyrus, unable to hide his smile, said, "I thought you were going to use gentle persuasion. If you wanted the guy beaten up, I could have done that for you."

"Oh, dear," I said, lowering the parasol. "I fear that in the stress of emotion I lost sight of my object. Stop cringing, Kevin, I won't hit you again. Unless you annoy me."

"I certainly would like to avoid doing so," said Kevin earnestly. "Would it annoy you if I offered you a chair—or a camel bag, rather? I'm afraid I have not enough seats for your escort."

Cyrus had already gestured his men to take up positions on either side of the little structure, where they could see in all directions. "I'll stand," he said curtly.

"You remember Mr. Vandergelt, of course," I said to Kevin, taking the seat he had offered.

"Ah, I thought he looked familiar. It has been a good many years, and I didn't know him at first without his goatee. How do you do, sir?" He started to offer his hand; Cyrus's frosty stare made him think better of it. "And how's the professor?" Kevin went on, squatting at my feet. "Fully recovered, I hope, from his—er—accident?"

"I give you credit, Kevin," I said. "You don't beat around the bush. It was no accident, as you well know. 'The curse of the ancient gods of Egypt' was how you put it, I believe. Surely your readers must be tiring of curses."

"Och—I mean, oh, no, ma'am. Readers never tire of mystery and sensationalism. You and I know better, to be sure, and I'd be glad to set them straight if I had the facts."

He continued to nurse his arm. I knew full well that Kevin would have considered a broken arm, much less one that was slightly bruised, as a fair exchange for the story he wanted, so I was unmoved by his look of hurt reproach.

"You will be the first to have the facts, I promise, as soon as they can be made public."

The reprehensible young man gave a crow of delight. "Aha! So there are facts as yet unknown. Never mind denying it, Mrs. Emerson, and don't be chewing on that pretty lip of yours; one particular fact, which cannot fail to capture the imagination of the reading public, is already known to me, for I spent several enlightening days in Cairo conversing with mutual friends."

It is an old trick of journalists and other villains to pretend to knowledge in order to trick the victim into an admission of it. I laughed lightly. "You are referring, I suppose, to the incident at the ball. That was a silly joke—"

"Let's not fence, Mrs. E. I am referring to the professor's loss of memory."

"Curse it," I exclaimed. "The few who knew were sworn to secrecy. Which—"

"Now you know I can't be giving away my sources." He had me now, and he knew it. His wide smile had the impertinent good humor of a wretched little Irish brownie.

In fact I had a good idea as to who had "spilled the beans," to use an American colloquialism. The only mutual friend of mine and Kevin's who knew the truth was Karl von Bork. Kevin's acquaintance with other archaeologists was superficial and for the most part antagonistic. Kevin had known Karl since the old days at Baskerville House, when Karl had won the girl they both wanted; and no doubt it had given Kevin a great deal of satisfaction to trick the intelligent but unworldly German into giving away more than he meant to.

Cyrus, who had listened in silence, now spoke. "It's getting late, Amelia. Send him away or let me knock him over the head. My fellows can hold him prisoner here till you decide—"

"Now let's not be losing our tempers," Kevin exclaimed, his eyes widening. "Mrs. Emerson, ma'am, you'd never allow—"

"When the stakes are so high, I might not only allow but encourage such a solution. I would hate to have Cyrus risk a lawsuit and a good deal of unpleasant publicity for my—for the sake of friendship; but I would commit acts even more contemptible to prevent this news from being made public. I wish I could appeal to your honor, but I fear you have none; I wish I could trust your word, but I cannot."

With an air of finality, I rose to my feet. Cyrus raised the rifle to his shoulder.

"He isn't going to shoot you," I explained, as Kevin gave a bleat of alarm. "At least I don't think he is. Cyrus, tell your men to treat him as gently as possible. I will come by now and then, Kevin, to see how you are getting on."

Kevin then proved himself the man I had always—despite some evidence to the contrary—believed him to be. He laughed. Considering the circumstances, it was a fairly convincing imitation of insouciant mirth.

"You win, Mrs. E. I don't think you mean it, but I would rather not take the chance. What must I do?"

There was really only one solution. If Kevin gave me his word to remain silent he would be entirely sincere—at the time. Like Ramses, and, I fear, a good many other people, he could always find a specious excuse for doing what he had promised not to do if he wanted badly enough to do it. He had to be kept in confinement, and the most secure prison available was the royal wadi itself.

I had to slow my steps to match Kevin's; he was not in such good training as he ought to have been. If I had not been so out of temper with him I would have given him a friendly little lecture on the advantages of physical fitness. At that time I confined my lecture to more important matters, and it was not at all friendly. I concluded by informing him that if he volunteered any information whatever to Emerson (for a flat interdiction seemed the simplest course) I would never speak to him or communicate with him again.

A look of sadness, a blush of shame spread over the young man's face. "You may believe it or not, Mrs. Emerson," he said, in a well-bred voice without the slightest trace of an accent, "but there are some acts too despicable even for me to commit. In our battles of wits we have been worthy opponents—and I include the professor, who has made a fool of me as often as I have embarrassed him. I have enjoyed matching wits with both of you, and although you may not admit it, I think you have enjoyed it too. But if I thought any act of mine would cause you grievous harm of mind or body, no promise of reward, however great, could induce me to commit it."

"I do believe you," I said. And at that moment, I did.

"Thank you. So, then," said Kevin, in quite his old manner, "how are you going to explain my presence?"

"That is a difficulty. Emerson may not remember you, but his opinion of journalists is of long standing.

You cannot pass as an archaeologist; you know nothing of excavation."

"I could say my arm was broken," Kevin suggested, giving me a meaningful look.

"You could have two broken arms and the like number of broken legs. Emerson would quiz you and you would betray your ignorance. Ah! I have it! The perfect answer!"

"A detective?" Emerson's voice rose on every syllable. "What the devil do we want a detective for?"

When he put it that way, I was hard-pressed to come up with a sensible answer. I therefore responded in a manner I felt certain would distract him.

"*You* certainly don't seem to be making much progress in solving our little mystery. All these interruptions are getting to be a nuisance."

It was delightful to watch Emerson trying to decide which provocation to counter first. I did not think he would be able to resist a play on the word "nuisance," applying it of course to me, but perhaps he was unable to compose a sufficiently stinging retort on the spur of the moment. Instead he went on the defensive, which, as I could have told him, is always a mistake.

"I caught one of the swine, didn't I?"

"'Caught' is hardly an appropriate word. You shouldn't have kicked him so hard. He cannot speak intelligibly with his nose and jaw immobilized, and furthermore—"

Emerson rolled his eyes, threw up his hands and stormed off. Kevin, who had prudently retired to a distance during the discussion, returned and sat down on the rug at my feet. "He seems quite his old self. Are you certain he—"

"I could hardly be mistaken. Remember what I told you. One slip of the tongue and I will let Cyrus deal with you as he proposed. And don't forget to call me Miss Peabody."

It might have been the sunset glow that softened the young journalist's features, but his voice was equally subdued as he said, "That must be the unkindest cut of all, ma'am. How he could forget a woman like yourself—"

"I do not want your sympathy, Kevin. I want—I insist upon—your cooperation."

"You have it, Mrs.... Miss Peabody. I suppose you have no objection to my chatting with the others—Abdullah, for instance? After all," he added winsomely, "if I am supposed to be a detective I ought to question people."

The point was well taken. Now that it was too late, I wished I had thought of a different persona for Kevin—that of an illiterate deaf-mute, for instance. "Oh, what a tangled web we weave, when first we practice to deceive!" Taking my baffled silence for consent, Kevin wandered off, hands in his pockets, a cheerful whistle issuing from his lips; and I considered this latest tangle and whither it might lead.

Kevin already knew the one fact I had been most anxious to keep from him. He seemed still to be in ignorance of other equally important facts, and these I was determined to keep from him at all costs. Kevin would fall on the story of the Lost Oasis like a dog on a ripe, smelly bone, for it was just the sort of fantastic tale in which he specialized. The slightest hint would be enough to set him off; he would not bother to substantiate it, for fiction was as good as truth by the standards of his profession. Rapidly I ran through the list of persons present to reassure myself there was no danger of exposure from any of them.

Emerson knew only what I had told him of the matter and he was not inclined to believe that. In any case, Kevin was the last person with whom he would have discussed the subject. Cyrus's discretion I did not doubt. René and Charles were unwitting, as was Abdullah. Bertha maintained her "master" had told her nothing. If she lied . . . well, then she had every reason to remain reticent on the subject. An admission of knowledge she claimed not to have would prove her false, and would betray the secret her master was no more anxious than we to have spread abroad.

My reasoning was irrefutable. Relieved of that anxiety (and would the others were so easily disposed of!) I went to have a look at my latest patient.

One of Cyrus's men stood on guard outside the shelter that had been set up for Mohammed. There was no need; the wretch was so full of laudanum he would not have roused if someone had set fire to his bed. I hated to waste my medical supplies on such a vile specimen, but he had been in acute pain and even if mercy had not tempered my wrath I could not have set his broken nose while he was writhing and screaming. His jaw, I thought, was only bruised, but since I could not be absolutely certain I had wound it round with bandages too.

He was a dreadful sight as he lay there on the pile of

rugs. Not even Christian charity and the ethics of the profession of which I count myself a formally unqualified but able practitioner could have forced me to touch the ragged, flea-infested robe or bathe the filthy body. The cast I had applied to his nose jutted out like the grotesque beak of some mythical monster; coarse black hairs bristled at odd angles from above and below the bandages covering most of the lower half of his face. A slit of white glistened under each eyelid. His mouth gaped open, displaying brown, rotting teeth. The light from my lantern cast shadows that intensified every ugly feature and made the open cavern of his mouth look like a black hole.

I took his pulse and listened to his breathing. There was nothing more I could do; only time, and a good deal of luck, would complete the cure. I prayed most sincerely for his recovery, but I am sorry to say that Christian charity had very little to do with that prayer.

When I emerged, dusk was far advanced, but the light of the lantern I carried showed a retreating form. The flutter of draperies betrayed her identity; none of the men walked as she did. I had not heard her address the guard, so she must have turned away as soon as she realized I was within.

I hurried after her. "Bertha! Wait, I wish to speak with you. What were you doing there?"

Her posture was submissive—hands clasped, head bowed. In a low voice she said, "I would help you nurse the man, Sitt. There is not much I can do to show my gratitude, but I am skilled at women's work."

It was as if she had deliberately cast off her European heritage. Voice, manner, speech were more and more

Egyptian with every passing day. Naturally I found this extremely irritating.

"There is *no* work a woman cannot do," I said. "We must have a little chat about that one day, Bertha. Just now you can help me best by continuing to search your memory. Anything you recall may be of importance, even if it seems meaningless to you."

"I am trying, Sitt," she murmured.

"And don't call me Sitt! Miss Peabody will do, if you cannot twist your tongue around my given name. Come away now. The injured man is in no need of services you can provide."

A little gasp of what sounded like amusement issued from her lips. It must have been a stifled cough, I concluded, for nothing I had said could have provoked laughter.

By the time we assembled for the evening meal, Kevin had already ingratiated himself with René and Charlie. I did not know how he had managed it with René, but he had won Charlie's heart by professing a passion for motor cars.

"They are the wave of the future," Kevin exclaimed enthusiastically. "Daimler's internal-combustion engine—"

"But have you seen the Panhard?" Charlie interrupted. "The sliding-gear transmission—"

They went on talking unintelligibly about things like clutches and gears, while Bertha hovered at René's shoulder and Emerson glowered impartially on all of us and I...I looked at Emerson. It seemed to make him rather nervous, but I saw no reason why that should deter me.

He had hardly spoken to me since that thrilling

encounter in the tomb, except when the loss of his temper over the advent of Kevin overcame his reticence. At first I had been a trifle discouraged by his apology and ensuing silence; I am something of a romantic myself, and I had hoped that that passionate embrace would burst the bonds that held his memory in thrall. Schadenfreude had said it would not; in fact, he had warned me, most vehemently, against applying any such procedure. Apparently the doctor had been correct.

However, as I thought back over the incident, I felt it offered some encouragement. It might be interpreted as marking a step forward in the relationship I was, according to the doctor's instructions, endeavoring to re-create. Annoyance had replaced Emerson's initial indifference; he was now sufficiently interested to follow after me and risk himself to save me. That he would have done the same for Abdullah or any of the other men I was prepared to admit; but no combination of relief and anger would have prompted him to behave to Abdullah as he had behaved to *me*.

However. The kiss might have meant less than I hoped. As I had good cause to know, Emerson is a hot-blooded individual. The mere proximity of a female who, if not irresistibly beautiful, has been regarded by some as worthy of admiration, might have been sufficient to inspire such a response in a man who was under considerable emotional stress.

Dare I admit the truth? I see no reason why I should not, since these journals will not be read by other eyes until I can find a publisher worthy of them (a more difficult procedure than I had believed) and then not until after considerable revision. I hoped and prayed

Emerson's memory might be restored, but what I really wanted restored was his love for me, whether it came by recollection or by being forged anew. That marriage of true minds, based on mutual trust and respect (and on another kind of attraction whose importance I would be the last to deny) was all in all to me. By one means or another I meant to regain it, and I did not really care how it was achieved. It might be a little difficult to explain to a man who has just proposed marriage for, as he believes, the first time, that he already has an eleven-year-old son. It would be an even greater shock to receive the full impact of Ramses all at once, instead of getting used to him a little at a time. However, I could and would deal with greater difficulties than that, if only . . .

So my emotions swung back and forth like the pendulum of a clock, now rising, now falling. So absorbed was I in my thoughts, and in contemplation of Emerson's splendid, scowling physiognomy, that I was unaware of Cyrus's approach until a gentle cough made me look up.

"A penny for your thoughts," he said. "Or whatever amount you ask; they must be distressing, to judge by your face."

"Only confusing," I said. "But I will straighten them out, Cyrus, never fear. Once Mohammed is able to speak, we may be on the way to a solution of our present difficulty. It is a pity his nose and mouth took the brunt of the blow."

Emerson, who had been openly eavesdropping, took this for another not-so-veiled criticism. Scowling even more fiercely, he rose and started to stalk away.

"Don't go far," I called. "Dinner will be served shortly."

There was no reply, not even a grunt.

"I have something that may cheer you up," Cyrus said. "My servant has been collecting the mail, as usual; he brought the most recent letters here this evening."

"All this way?" I took the packet he handed me. "Cyrus, you are the most thoughtful of men."

"Well, I figured you'd be keen to know what's going on back in jolly old England. I'm a little curious myself, so . . ."

"Of course. I have no secrets from you, Cyrus. But I see dinner is ready; I will wait to read this particular epistle until afterward, I think. Not only is it very bulky, but I fear it might spoil my appetite."

From Cyrus's admiring look I could see he took this as a demonstration of British phlegm. In fact I had a cowardly reluctance to read Ramses's latest literary offering, which I expected would only tell me a number of distressing things I could do absolutely nothing about. If anything serious had occurred, Walter would have telegraphed.

So after a meal no one except Kevin seemed anxious to eat, we dispersed. Emerson had not joined us; I concluded he had dined with Abdullah and the others. At my invitation, Cyrus followed me to my tent.

There were two letters from Chalfont in the packet. I recognized Evelyn's dainty, precise handwriting on one, and decided to save it for a treat—or an antidote— after I had read Ramses's.

"Dearest Mama and Papa. I am sorry to tell you that Gargery is still not a hero. However, we have another heroine.

"I never thought Aunt Evelyn had it in her. It has been a salutary if humbling experience for me and will teach me, I hope, to question even more rigorously the false stereotypes our society holds about the behavior and character of females. I had always believed myself free of such prejudices and certainly I ought to have been, with Mama's example of abnormality always before me. How curiously the human mind operates! It seems to be able to dismiss any evidence that conflicts, not only with its own desires, but with preconceived beliefs so deeply seated and unconsciously instilled that they are not recognized as irrational. Examined in the cold light of reason..."

Before turning the page—which ended with the last phrase I have quoted—I took a firm grip on my temper. It would serve no purpose to lose it, since the object of my wrath was out of reach. He must have been reading the articles on psychology I had strictly forbidden him...Or had I? I had certainly meant to, since some of the theories expressed were far too shocking for the innocent minds of children. However, I could not be certain. Telling Ramses what not to do was a time-consuming process, and it was almost impossible to keep up with him because he was always thinking of new atrocities to commit.

Realizing that I was letting my mind stray, just as Ramses had done, I went on reading.

"...*many of these beliefs do not stand up for a moment. They are, in fact, no more than mindless superstition. Whence, then, do they come? I confess I have not yet found an answer. It is particularly galling to discover them in a mind as rational as I have always considered mine to be.*

"*I would like to discuss this matter with you, dearest Mama and Papa, for it interests me a great deal; but perhaps this is not the appropriate time, for you must be wondering what particular incident prompted my speculations.*

"*You may recall that in my last letter I described the curious incident of the dogs that barked in the nighttime. Since barking was the extent of their assistance I determined, as I believe I mentioned, that I would take steps to provide a more effective variety of watch-animal. You see, I had a hideous foreboding...*"

I had one too. "Oh, no," I gasped.
"What?" Cyrus cried, hardly less agitated than I.

"...*a hideous foreboding that we had not seen the last of nocturnal invasions. I felt certain it would be impossible to convince Uncle Walter of the logic of my decision, so I had to carry it out myself, and it was cursed inconvenient having to wait for everyone to go to sleep before I crept out to let... [My voice broke.]...let...the lion...out of...*"

"By the Almighty!" Cyrus exclaimed. "For pity's sake, go on, Amelia, I can't stand the suspense!"

"...its cage, and then waking up at dawn to put it back before some other member of the household encountered it. Nefret very kindly assisted me..."

Again emotion overcame me. "Another one," I said hollowly. "I thought one was bad enough, and now... Forgive me, Cyrus. I will endeavor not to break down again.

"...assisted me on two occasions; she said I was a growing boy and needed my rest. I hardly need say, Mama and Papa, that I took this without resentment, in the spirit in which it was meant.

"Naturally I had shut up the dogs and warned Bob and Jerry to lock themselves into the lodge while the lion was out. They agreed this was a sensible procedure.

"Uncle Walter has insulted me mortally. His remarks on the subject of the lion were uncalled for, unfair, and extremely rude, particularly in view of the fact that my foresight prevented—or helped to prevent, at least—an incident that might have proved disastrous.

"Having anticipated such an occurrence, I was the first to wake when the piercing screams of a female in the last extremity of terror, mingled with the growls of a large feline, rent the night! I had been sleeping in my clothes, of course, in order to be fully prepared and ready for action; it was the work of a moment to snatch up the weapon I had put at hand (a poker from the fireplace) and rush down the stairs.

"*The moon cast a frosty light upon the lawn (which was, in fact, covered with frost, the night being cold). The forms of the great jungle beast and its prey stood out in sharp outline. Hastening toward the group, poker at the ready, I beheld a somewhat disconcerting sight. There was just enough light for me to make out the features of the individual lying supine between the lion's paws. With a start of chagrin, I recognized her as Ellis, Aunt Evelyn's new maid.*

"*In fact, the lion would probably not have harmed her. To be sure, it was growling, but the sound held a note of inquiry rather than ferocity. I had the distinct impression it did not know what to do next. Ellis had swooned, which was no doubt a sensible move on her part.*

"*While I was thinking how best to proceed, I saw Nefret running toward me, her little bare feet noiseless on the grass. Her unbound hair streamed out behind her, silver-gold in the pale light; her light nightdress billowed about her slender limbs. She was a vision of...* [Something had been scratched out here. Ramses went on.] *...of womanly efficiency. Her knife was in her hand.*

"*With her assistance I persuaded the lion to abandon his new toy. Grumbling under his breath he ambled off, with Nefret's fingers twisted affectionately in his mane. The literary allusions that occurred to me will doubtless occur to you, Mama, as well, so I will not take up paper describing them.*

"*I set to work restoring Ellis to consciousness, but I had not had time to slap her more than once* before I heard a considerable racket coming from the house. I had been expecting some reaction from that quarter; I was surprised it had not occurred before, but I suppose the actions I have described had taken only a few minutes. Astonishing, is it not, how quickly time passes when one is engaged in interesting activities?

"The sounds I heard suggested to me something rather more serious than the indignation of Uncle Walter at being awakened. These cries were high-pitched—female, I deduced. So abandoning Ellis, I hastened to ascertain their origin.

"As you know, the majority of the windows in the castle are narrow and small. Only the sitting room has been modernized; its windows open onto the rose garden. It was from this room that the noise issued, and as I came through the garden I was distressed to note that the windows stood open. The room was dark and at first I could not make out what was going on; rapid movements, gasps and exclamations of pain and exertion were all the evidence available to me. Then the combatants—for such they were—approached the window. The poker fell from my palsied hand when I identified them.

"One was a man, a hulking fellow wearing a short fustian jacket and a cap pulled low over his eyes. He held a cudgel or thick stick, with which he was warding off the blows directed at him by...

"But no doubt you have anticipated me. Her nightcap had come off and hung by its strings; her braided hair fell over one shoulder. Her face was set in a ferocious snarl quite unlike her normal sweet

*look, and the instrument with which she was bela-
boring the cowering villain appeared—and indeed
proved—to be a parasol.*

"*I recovered myself and my poker and rushed
to her assistance. She was not in need of it, but the
rascal might have got away from her if I had not
tripped him up. Together we subdued him. Tearing
off the sash of her dressing gown, Aunt Evelyn bade
me bind his arms.*

"*It was at this point that Uncle Walter arrived
on the scene, followed by Gargery and Bob, both of
whom carried lanterns. They had been wandering around the grounds, uncertain as to where
the action was taking place. (Wandering gives an
inaccurate impression, in fact, for it was obvious
from Uncle Walter's appearance that he had been
running as fast as he could, though to little effect.
Like Papa, he does not like being waked up suddenly
and is slow to react.)*

"*Bob lit the lamps and Gargery finished binding
the arms and legs of our burglar. This was at my
direction; I am sorry to say that Uncle Walter lost
his head completely. I have never seen him behave
so erratically. He rushed at Aunt Evelyn and shook
her very hard. Then he embraced her as fiercely as
ever I have seen*...[Another phrase was scratched
out. I knew what it must have been, though.]...
*others do. Then he shook her again. Strangely
enough, Aunt Evelyn did not seem to mind.*

"*I do not have another sheet of paper, and cannot get one, since Uncle Walter has confined me to
my room until further notice, so I am forced to be*

brief. Ellis was on her way to meet a friend, as she explained, when the lion intercepted her. (Rose says people like Ellis manage to find friends wherever they go. It is an endearing characteristic, I think.) The burglar claimed he was looking for valuables. Inspector Cuff has taken him off to London. Inspector Cuff is a very taciturn person. All he would say, before he left with his prisoner, was, 'I think I can be of greater use to you elsewhere, Master Ramses. You will hear from me in due course.' As for Aunt Evelyn, she says she has had the parasol for quite a long time. I have never seen her carry it. It is like yours, Mama, very heavy and plain, not her usual little ruffled ones. I wonder why she would have something like that if she never expected to need it? But that is another matter we can discuss at a future time.

"My paper tells me I must stop. Your loving son, Ramses.

"P.S. I know that Papa is very busy with his excavations, but it would comfort me a great deal to receive a message in his own hand."

Cyrus and I sat in silence for a few moments. Then he said, "Excuse me, Amelia. I will be right back."

When he returned he was carrying a bottle of brandy. I had a little sip. Cyrus had a little more.

"Comment," I said, "would be futile. Now let me read Evelyn's version."

But Evelyn made no reference to the events Ramses had described. After affectionate greetings and assurances that all were well, she explained that her chief reason for writing was to clarify in her own mind what might lie behind the mysterious events that had recently occurred.

My own poor powers of reasoning are so inferior to yours, dear Amelia, that I hesitate even to express thoughts that must long ago have been apparent to your clear, decisive mind. Yet I will venture to do so, in the hope that by sheer chance I may have stumbled on some notion that has not occurred to you.

I began as I believe you might have done, by asking how these terrible people could have learned the secret you were so careful to conceal. The story you gave out was plausible, so our enemies must have had sources of information not known to the public. Several possibilities have occurred to me; I list them in the neat order you would approve.

1. One of us might unwittingly have betrayed information that could only have come from a visit to the place mentioned by Mr. Forth. You would never be indiscreet enough to do this, dear Amelia; search my conscience as I might, I can think of no occasion on which I might have done so. I do not wish to ask Walter, for the very idea that he might be responsible, however innocently, for the troubles that have befallen us would break his noble heart. Yet I wonder: Did he or Radcliffe speak, in the articles they have written since your return, or to colleagues in archaeology, of things an expert might recognize as firsthand knowledge? The articles have not yet been published, but surely they have been read by the editors of the journals at least?

2. *One of the officers at the military camp may have had more information about the matter than you realize. Had Mr. Forthright befriended any of them? Had they been shown the map? You mentioned that there were compass readings on it. I know little of such matters, but it would seem to me that such precise details would arouse interest and intelligent speculation, particularly after you came back to Gebel Barkal with Nefret.*

3. *I hesitate to mention this, for it seems even more foolish than my other silly ideas; but I cannot help recalling the young man Nefret met at Miss McIntosh's school. An individual whose curiosity had already been aroused might seek her out with the intention of questioning her about her experiences. As we all know, it is very difficult to avoid slips of the tongue, and an innocent child is particularly unwary. I wonder—I can put it no more strongly than that—I wonder if that fleeting acquaintance might not have been renewed, or an attempt made to do so, if she had not already given him what he hoped to get? At my request she performed the Invocation to Isis for us one evening. (Do not fear, dear Amelia, I made certain she thought it was only for our amusement.) Walter could not contain his excitement. He recognized some of the phrases of the song, which he said were from an ancient ritual. And certainly no one could suppose that she learned that dance, or would have been permitted to perform it, at a Christian mission!*

So I questioned her, with equal tact, I assure you, about the young man she called Sir Henry. He had thick waving black hair, parted down the middle; a cavalry-style mustache; gray or pale-blue eyes and long lashes. He was of medium height and slender build, with a fair complexion and a rather pointed chin and narrow nose.

I know this description is too vague to be of much use (especially since, if my silly idea is right, a disguise might have been employed). However, I pass it on to you because another and very alarming thought has occurred to me. This person's failure to pursue the acquaintance with Nefret might stem from the fact that he is no longer in England. Your recent communications have attempted to reassure us, dear Amelia, but I know you very well, and I sense a formality and stiffness that suggests you are concealing something from us. I would not urge you to greater candor; I appreciate the tender affection that makes you reluctant to add to our concern. (Though I might add, my dear friend and sister, that speculation often conjures up fears far worse than the truth.) Logic also forces upon me the conclusion that if the children have been threatened, you and Radcliffe must be in even greater peril. Pray take care! Curb your courageous propensity to rush headlong into danger! And try to restrain Radcliffe—though I know that is no easy task. Remind him, as I remind you, that there are those to whom your health and safety are as important as their own. Chief among them is

   Your loving sister,
   Evelyn.

Tears blurred my vision as I read the last lines. How blessed I was in such affection! And how I had

underestimated Evelyn! Ramses's lecture on preconceptions had not been directed at me (at least I trusted
it had not), but everything he had written about himself could as well be applied to me. And I, of all people,
ought to have known better. Had I not seen Evelyn
coolly confront the hideous mummy? Had I not heard
her accept an offer that made every nerve quiver with
revulsion in the hope that by doing so she could save
those she loved? I was as guilty of prejudice against my
own sex as the blind, biased men I had condemned.

Evelyn had not said a word about her adventure.
Instead she had bent all her efforts on trying to find an
answer to the mystery. The analysis was brilliant; the
mind that had composed it was as keen as my own.

Cyrus had been rereading Ramses's letter. Sensitive
to every change in my expression, he said gently, "What
is it, Amelia? Some bad news Ramses did not mention?
I find it difficult to believe he could or would omit anything, but—"

"In that assumption you are correct. Evelyn is far
more considerate of my feelings than is my son." I
folded the letter and slipped it into my pocket. Let it
rest there, against my heart, to remind me of my good
fortune and my shame!

"I hope you will forgive me for not sharing this with
you, Cyrus," I went on. "It was the tender expressions
of affection it contains that brought the tears to my
eyes."

I was more than ready to follow his advice that I seek
my couch, for it had been a tiring day. Never has fatigue
prevented me from doing my duty, however. I first

inspected my patient, whose condition was unchanged, and then went in search of Bertha. The sooner I could find a suitable establishment for her, the better; it really was a nuisance having to play chaperone as well as perform my other duties.

Somehow I was not surprised to find her sitting by the dying fire, talking with Kevin. Knowing he would be all the more determined to speak to her if I made a mystery of her identity, I had simply described her as another victim of the villain who had attacked Emerson. I had expected Kevin would seek her out. No journalist could resist the mysteriously veiled, seductively gliding figure, and victimized women are particularly popular subjects. I could have composed the heading for his story myself; the words "love-slave" would undoubtedly appear. In the private pages of this journal I will admit that I was willing to throw poor Bertha to this Hibernian wolf of the press if her story would distract him from other aspects of the case.

However, there was no reason why I should go out of my way to accommodate Kevin, so I interrupted the discussion and sent Bertha off to bed. "You had better do the same, Kevin. We rise at dawn and it will be a long day."

"Not for me," said Kevin with a lazy smile. "We detectives keep our own hours. Wandering to and fro, questioning this one and that—"

"You will not be wandering. You will be with me, so I can keep my eye on you."

"Ah well, it was worth a try," Kevin murmured. "While I am with you, Mrs.—Miss Peabody, you can tell me all about your daring rescue of the professor.

It's bound to come out, you know," he added with a challenging smile. "Even now some of my more enterprising colleagues are interviewing various citizens of Luxor. From what I have heard, you cut rather a wide swath. Wouldn't you rather have the true facts published than the exaggerated fantasies some of my associates—"

"Oh, be quiet and go to bed," I snapped.

He went off, crooning some sentimental Irish melody in a way that was calculated to annoy me. When I reached my own tent, Bertha was already asleep, or pretending to be. I fully intended to ask her what she had talked about with Kevin, but at that time I had other matters on my mind. Having sought my couch, I had at last leisure to consider what Evelyn had proposed.

Her first two suggestions I had myself considered. The third, I confess, I had not, and chagrin threatened to overcome me when I realized how stupid I had been. That a young gentleman should appear at the school on the very day Nefret was expected there, and that he should insist on meeting some of the scholars—it was highly suspicious, and I could not think why I had not seen it at the time. Was it possible that maternal instincts I had never supposed I possessed had clouded my normally clear intellect?

Highly unlikely, I decided.

Evelyn's incisive outline had made clear to me something else I ought to have realized much earlier. No single suspicious circumstance but a combination of many—a piling up of confirmatory evidence—would be strong enough to induce an enemy to act with such violence and persistence. He might have been alerted in the first place by remembering a conversation with Willoughby Forth, who appeared to have babbled to every archaeologist in Egypt. Skillful questioning of the officers of the Sudan Expeditionary Force would add additional evidence. Greatly as I shrank from holding Walter culpable in the least degree, I had had to caution him more than once to be careful of appearing to know more than he should. He had several friendly rivals in the philological game; had he dropped hints to Frank Griffith, or another, that he was about to make a miraculous breakthrough in the decipherment of Meroitic? Griffith was honest, I had never suspected him; but he might have spoken of the matter to someone else.

Having by such means established a possibility, the villain would seek further confirmation—and what better source than Nefret herself? She was not nearly so naive and helpless as Evelyn believed, but Evelyn's view was shared—as Nefret had herself pointed out— by society. There were a number of ways in which an acquaintance thus begun might be continued; if all else failed, the good old reliable "accident outside the gates of the park" might serve. How surprised the injured young gentleman would be to recognize the charming girl he had met at Miss McIntosh's! How reluctant he would be to impose on our kindness! How gratefully he would accept my ministrations, the friendly attentions of the dear children!

It had not been necessary. Evelyn had hit the nail on the head. I had seen Nefret perform the Invocation to Isis, and there was no way on earth she could have learned it from a family of missionaries, or even in a native village while under the supervision of such a family. It would take a trained scholar to recognize its origins—but that was true of the other evidence as well.

Yet still our deadly foe had held his hand until he discovered the final proof—objects, artifacts, that could only have come from a place such as Willoughby Forth had postulated. He must have searched our rooms in Cairo and found the scepters. The attacks on us had not begun until after we had been in the city for several days.

Evelyn—my dear, sweet Evelyn, whose intelligence I had so sadly underrated—had been right in every particular. The villain was no longer in England. He was in Egypt—in our very camp. I had known there was a traitor among us. Now I knew who he was.

"Charlie?!"

I had been waiting for Cyrus when he emerged from his tent next morning—at a discreet distance, of course, lest I embarrass him by inadvertently observing his ablutions. The pleased smile with which he had greeted me vanished as he listened to my explanation, and the name burst from him with the force of incredulity.

"He is new with you this season, Cyrus. You had not known him before."

"No, but...I know his father, his family. I wouldn't hire a fellow without—"

"He may be the true Charles H. Holly. Engineers and archaeologists are no more immune to greed than members of other professions."

"May be the true...Excuse me, Amelia, sometimes I have a doggone hard time following your train of thought. You surely don't suspect Charlie of being your Master Criminal in disguise?"

"It is possible, but unlikely. I doubt that Sethos would dare face me again. I could not be in his presence for long without penetrating any disguise he might assume." I added, with some asperity—for his skeptical expression annoyed me—"My reasons for suspecting Charles have nothing to do with Sethos. He fits the description of a man whom I have reason to believe—"

"Uh-huh. So you said. You want to run through that again, my dear? I am afraid I didn't follow you the first time."

So I ran through it again, and finished by reading the description Evelyn had given.

"But—but," Cyrus stuttered, "that description doesn't match Charlie in any particular. It sounds more like René. Not that I believe he—"

"That is the point, Cyrus. 'Sir Henry' was obviously disguised. He would take care to change those aspects of his appearance when he came to us—the color of his hair, the mustache. The long chin and narrow nose match Charlie's, and Charlie is approximately the same age."

"Jimminy," Cyrus muttered. "How many men that age have long chins and narrow noses, do you suppose? Two million? Five million?"

"But only one of them is here," I cried impatiently. "And one of us is a spy for Sethos! Consider that not only was our food drugged, but that the ambush set for me yesterday must have been arranged by one who anticipated I would follow that path. He must have read the note from Kevin and realized I would respond as soon as I was able."

"An assumption that would certainly be made by anyone who had the honor of your acquaintance," said Cyrus, stroking his chin. "My dear girl, I am not denying there may be something in what you say. But you would be the first to agree I cannot condemn a man on such equivocal evidence."

"I am not suggesting we hold a marsupial court—"

"I beg your pardon?" said Cyrus, staring.

"It is an American term, I believe? Having to do with illegal trials?"

"Oh. Kangaroo court, you mean?"

"No doubt. You know me better, I hope, than to suppose I would leap to unwarranted conclusions or subvert the principles of British justice. In fact, I am inclined to agree that we ought to let him go on believing he is not under suspicion. Sooner or later he will betray himself and then we will have him! And perhaps his leader as well. An excellent idea, Cyrus. He will have to be watched closely, of course."

"I guess I could manage that," Cyrus said slowly.

"I am glad we are in agreement. Now go and get your coffee, Cyrus. You appear a trifle sluggish this morning. No offense taken, I hope?"

"None in the world, my dear. You will join me for breakfast, I hope?"

"First I must see how Mohammed is getting on. I confess I find myself postponing that task; his very presence—not to mention the varied insect life that pervades his person—makes my skin crawl. And don't suggest, Cyrus dear, that I leave the disgusting duty to another. That is not my way. Besides, it is possible that he may be able to speak today and I trust no one else to question him."

"I long ago gave up trying to talk you out of anything you had set your mind on," said Cyrus, smiling. "Your sense of duty is as remarkable as your boundless energy. Do you want me to come with you?"

I assured him it was not necessary, and he went off, shaking his head. It had become a habit of his recently.

I stopped outside the shelter to speak with the guard. He was one of Cyrus's crew, a stocky, dark-skinned fellow with the aquiline features that spoke of Berber or Touareg blood. Like the desert men, he wore a khafiya or headcloth instead of a turban. He assured me he had looked in on Mohammed at regular intervals during the night and had found no change.

Yet as soon as I pushed the curtained hanging aside I realized that there had been a change—the most final change of all. Mohammed lay in the same position in which I had last seen him, flat on his back, with his mouth ajar and his eyes half-closed. But now no breath of air stirred the bristling hairs of his beard, and blood had issued from his mouth to stain the bandages around his jaws a rusty brown.

CHAPTER 13

"Superstition has its practical uses."

Well, Sitt Hakim," said a voice behind me. "Will you admit this case is beyond even your skill?"

It was Emerson, of course, speaking in the annoying drawl that indicates he is trying to be sarcastic. I turned, holding the curtain aside.

"He is dead," I said. "How did you know?"

"It requires very little medical expertise to realize that a man cannot live long with a knife in his heart."

I had not seen the haft of the knife till then; I was a good deal more shaken than I would have admitted, especially to Emerson. "Not his heart," I said. "The knife is in the center of his chest. Many people make that mistake. The blade may have pierced a lung. A man in his condition would not survive even a slight wound."

Squaring my shoulders, I started toward Mohammed. Emerson pushed me rudely aside, and bent over the body. I made no objection. Revolting as Mohammed had been in life, he was even more disgusting dead.

After a few moments I heard a nasty sucking sound and Emerson straightened, the knife in his hand.

"He has only been dead for a few hours. The blood has dried, but there is no sign of stiffening in the jaw or extremities. The knife is the kind most of the men carry, with no distinctive features."

"We must search the place," I said firmly. "Let me pass. The killer may have left some clue."

Emerson took my arm and pushed me out of the shelter. "When you own a dog you are not supposed to bark, Peabody. Where is your tame detective?"

He was sitting by the fire with the others, calmly drinking tea. Surprise—and that short-lived—rather than horror was the general response to Emerson's terse announcement that Mohammed was no more. Charlie appeared to be as astonished as anyone, which only confirmed my suspicions. If a spy and a traitor does not learn how to counterfeit emotion convincingly, he does not last long in his profession.

Cyrus was the only one to comprehend instantly the seriousness of the blow. "Doggone it! Don't feel bad, my dear, you did all you could. A serious injury like that—"

"Even the great Sitt Hakim's talents could not have prevailed in this case," said Emerson. He had been holding the knife behind him; now he tossed it onto the ground. "Mohammed was murdered—and not by me. In the dark of night the deed was done, with that knife."

The others eyed the weapon as if it had been a snake coiled to strike. Charlie was the first to speak. "Then— then he was deliberately silenced! This is horrible! It means there is a traitor among us!"

He did it very well, I must say.

"We knew that," Emerson said impatiently. "And now that it is too late, we know that Mohammed was a danger to him or to his leader. How the devil did the killer get past your guard, Vandergelt?"

"I am going to find out pretty quick," said Cyrus grimly.

"Mr. O'Connell will wish to accompany you," said Emerson, as Cyrus got to his feet.

Kevin was not at all anxious to volunteer. "At least let me finish my breakfast," he pleaded. "If the fellow is dead, he can wait a few more minutes."

"You lack the dogged zeal that is supposed to characterize your profession, Mr. O'Connell," said Emerson. "I had expected you would be on fire to examine the body, study the ghastly face, probe the wound, search the bloodstained garments, crawl around the floor looking for clues. The fleas and lice and flies won't bother a man of your hardened nerve, but do watch out for scorpions."

Kevin's face had gone a trifle green. "Stop that, Emerson," I ordered. "Come, Kevin. I will go with you."

"*Chacun à son goût,*" remarked Emerson, taking a chair and reaching for the teapot.

As I had expected, Kevin was of no help at all. After one glance at Mohammed's motionless form he hastily turned his back and began scribbling in his notebook while I crawled around the floor and carried out the other actions Emerson had suggested. I did allow myself to omit one; probing the wound was not necessary, since the stains on the knife blade were sufficient indication of how deeply it had penetrated.

While I searched for clues Cyrus was interrogating the guard. I heard most of what was said, for Cyrus's voice was rather loud and the guard's voice rose in volume as he defended himself. He stoutly denied that anyone had approached during the night. Yes, he might have dozed off; no one had relieved him, and a man could not do without sleep indefinitely. But his body had blocked the entrance to the shelter and he swore he would have sprung instantly awake if anyone had tried to pass him.

"Never mind, Cyrus," I called. "The killer did not enter that way. Come here and see."

The slit in the canvas wall would have escaped my notice had I not been searching for something of the sort. It had been made by a very sharp knife—probably the same one that had penetrated Mohammed's scrawny chest.

"The killer would not even have to enter," I said. "Only insert an arm and strike. He must have known exactly where Mohammed's pallet was placed. And I had left a lamp burning, so that the guard could see inside. It was a waste of time looking for clues here. Let us see if he left footprints outside."

But of course he had not. The ground was too hard to take prints.

I dismissed Kevin, who was very glad to go. Taking Cyrus's arm, I held him back and let Kevin draw ahead.

"Now will you take the precaution I suggested?" I hissed. "Charlie must be put under restraint! You were willing to take such measures with Kevin—"

"And still am," Cyrus said grimly. "Archaeology is not the only profession whose members may be seduced by greed."

I believe I gasped aloud. "You don't mean—"

"Who would know better than the man who sent it that you had received an invitation you wouldn't resist? I thought from the start there was something funny about that; a die-hard like O'Connell would be more likely to sneak up on you than ask you to come to him. He practically goaded you into bringing him here, and now you see what has happened—the first night after he arrived."

"No," I said. "Surely not Kevin!"

It was not the first time those words had burst from my lips. Kevin could not have heard them, but at that very moment he turned his head and looked back. It might have been my overstrained nerves; it might have been the distorted angle at which I saw him; but on his face was a sly, secretive expression more sinister than any I had seen on that countenance before.

Ineptly assisted by Kevin, I interrogated the others in an attempt to establish alibis. I did not expect useful results, and I got none. Everyone claimed to have slept the sleep of the innocent and weary, and denied they had heard anything unusual. Charles swore René could not have left the tent they shared without awakening him; René swore the same about Charles. That meant nothing. I could—and did—say the same about Bertha. But the dastardly deed could have been accomplished in five minutes or less, and innocent or guilty, we had all been tired enough to sleep soundly.

Emerson watched me with a sour amusement he made no attempt to conceal. At last he said, "Satisfied, MISS Peabody? I could have told you this was a waste of time. Does anyone save myself intend to do any work today?"

Taking this for the order it undoubtedly was, René and Charles followed Emerson's example, and Emerson. So did the cat.

My spirits were rather low as I prepared my equipment—notepad and pencils, measuring rule and water flask, candles and matches. If the day went on as it had begun, I did not know how I could bear it. Emerson had returned to calling me MISS Peabody. He had not requested my assistance that day. Instead of progressing toward that greater understanding for which I had hoped, we were farther apart than before.

Mohammed's death, before he could speak, was discouraging too.

If I had needed anything else to lower my spirits, the knowledge of where we were working that day would have done the job. Cyrus was determined to investigate the new tomb. It had not been mentioned by any of the earlier visitors to the wadi, so it could truly be called unknown; and nothing fires the imagination of an excavator so much as the hope of being the first to enter such a sepulcher. To be sure, the place had obviously been known to Emerson, but as Cyrus dourly remarked, "That son of a gun knows a lot more than he's saying about a lot of things. He doesn't think there's anything worth finding or he'd have dug into the place himself a long time ago. But he's not the last word, consarn him! There's bound to be something there."

I had not told him of my discovery. The ring bezel was in my pocket even at that moment. I seemed to feel it pressing against my breast—which was nonsense, because it was very small and light. Had I followed the dictates of my archaeological conscience, I would have left it behind, safely enclosed in a box labeled with the location and date of the discovery. I cannot explain or defend the idle fancy that told me I must keep it close, like an amulet warding off danger.

The old demonic, animal-headed gods of Egypt had been proscribed by the heretic king, but it is easier to pass edicts than enforce them when that which is forbidden appeals to passionate, deep-seated human needs and desires. Our earlier excavation had turned up evidence that the common people had not abandoned their beloved household gods. Sobek was a crocodile god whose chief center of worship was in the Fayum, far to the north. It was the first time any representation of him had been found at Amarna, but his presence was no more surprising than that of Bes, the grotesque little patron of matrimony, and Thoueris, who protected pregnant women. But for me to come upon the crocodile god's image there, after narrowly escaping another deadly threat...Is it any wonder superstition fought with reason in my mind?

First the snake, now the crocodile. Did the third fate still threaten us? If the traditions of myth and folktale held true, it would be the most dangerous of all.

The men had to spend most of the day clearing the tomb entrance, which was choked with fallen rocks. Some were of considerable size, and the sloping scree had been hardened by repeated flooding and drying into the consistency of cement. It was I who pointed out to Cyrus that we must sift through this debris. Water must have poured into the tomb through the opening above, and through other apertures as yet undisclosed, on more than one occasion, and objects might have been flushed out onto the slope.

Only Cyrus's good manners—and, I would like to believe, his respect for my professional expertise— prevented him from objecting vigorously to this procedure, for it took a great deal of time. It was late in the day before the wisdom of my methods was proved. The broken fragment we discovered would certainly have been overlooked by careless excavators.

It was only a piece of alabaster (more properly calcite), five centimeters long and apparently shapeless. The credit for recognizing its importance must go to Feisal—who, of course, had been trained in my methods. He brought it to me, smiling in anticipation of praise. "There is writing on it, Sitt. You see the hieroglyphs."

The excitement that suffused every inch of my being when I read those few signs was enough to overcome, for the moment at least, all other considerations. Summoning Cyrus with a piercing cry, I indicated the broken inscription. "'The king's great wife Neferneferuaten Nefertiti.' It is part of a shawabti, Cyrus—a shawabti of Nefertiti!"

"A ushebti?" Cyrus snatched it from me. I forgave him this momentary lapse of courtesy; like myself, he understood the import of the words.

Ushebtis, or shawabtis, were strictly funerary in nature. They were images of the dead man (or woman), animated in the afterlife to perform services for him and work in his stead. The wealthier an individual, the more of these little statues he possessed. Fragments of many ushebtis bearing the name of Akhenaton had turned up; Emerson had found three more the previous day, in the royal tomb. But this was the first I had seen or heard of with the name of the queen.

"By the Almighty, Amelia, you're right," Cyrus exclaimed. "It's the lower legs and part of the feet of a ushebti. It can't have come from the royal tomb..."

"That is not necessarily true." Some scholars, I regret to say, concoct fantastic theories from inadequate evidence, but I have never been prone to this weakness and I felt I must caution Cyrus against overenthusiasm.

"Broken fragments of Akhenaton's funerary equipment, including ushebtis, must have been thrown out of his tomb," I went on. "And a violent flood could have washed them some distance down the wadi. But this was not part of *his* tomb furnishings. Her name appears on many objects along with his, but ushebtis were designed and named only for the dead person."

Cyrus held the battered fragment as gently as if it had been solid gold. "Then this must have come from her tomb. This tomb!"

"No," I said regretfully. "I think not. If she had a separate tomb it would surely have been nearer his. From what little we have seen of this one, it is small and unfinished. However, this is a remarkable discovery, Cyrus. I congratulate you."

"The credit goes to you, my dear."

"And Feisal."

"Oh, sure." Cyrus gave Abdullah's son a hearty slap

on the back. "Big baksheesh for you, my friend. Even bigger if you turn up any more pieces like this."

However, by the time sunset forced an end to the work, nothing more of interest had been discovered. The frustration of his hopes put Cyrus in a bad temper, though I must say it was a model of saintly forbearance compared to the demonstrations of which Emerson was capable. "I'm sure tired of trying to wash in a cupful of water," he grumbled, as we trudged along the dusty path. "If I don't get near a tub pretty soon, I won't be fit company for a mule, much less a lady."

"The lady is in no better case," I said with a smile. "I confess that of all the inconveniences of camping out, the absence of adequate means of ablution vexes me most. Unless I have lost count, tomorrow is Friday; the men will want their day of rest, so I presume Emerson intends to return to the river."

"You can't take anything for granted where that bull-headed billy goat is concerned," Cyrus said picturesquely.

I promised to see what I could do to convince Emerson. I hope no one will suppose that it was a lack of Spartan fortitude that made me favor a reprieve from our labors. A lady likes to be fresh and dainty at all times, and a lady who is attempting to win the heart of a gentleman cannot feel much confidence in her success when she looks like a dusty mummy and smells like a donkey. However, those were not my reasons (at least I think they were not) for wishing to leave the royal wadi. The place was beginning to oppress me. The rocky walls seemed to have edged in closer, the shadows were deeper. I had crawled on hands and knees through dusty tunnels and squirmed through holes scarcely large enough to admit my body without ever feeling the sense of claustrophobia that afflicted me now.

The others had returned from their work, so I went off to look for Abdullah. He and our other men had their own little camp; they were frightful snobs (as they had some reason to be, since they were the most sought-after trained workers in the country) and always refused to hobnob with lesser men. I had brought along my medical kit and when I saw the delighted smiles that greeted me I felt ashamed that I had not taken the time to fahddle with them, or even ask whether they needed attention.

I felt even more ashamed when they displayed a variety of minor injuries, ranging from a mashed finger to a bad case of ophthalmia. After I had washed out Daoud's eyes with a solution of boracic acid, and tended the other injuries, I scolded them for not coming to me at once.

"Tomorrow we will return to the river," I said. "My medical supplies are low, and we all need rest."

"Emerson will not go," said Abdullah gloomily.

"He will go willingly, or rolled in a rug and carried on our backs," I said.

The men grinned and nudged one another, and Abdullah's dour face brightened a trifle. But he shook his head. "You know why he came here, Sitt."

"Certainly I know. He hoped to entice our enemy into attacking him again, so that he could catch the fellow. So far only half that brilliant plan has succeeded. We have been attacked twice—"

"Not we, Sitt Hakim. You."

"And Mohammed. That is three attempts, and we are no nearer a solution than before."

"It has made Emerson very angry," said Abdullah. "He did very foolish things today, even more foolish than is his custom. Once he almost escaped me. Fortunately Ali saw him slip away and followed him. He was almost at the end of the wadi before Ali came up to him."

"What was he doing?" I demanded.

Abdullah spread his hands out and shrugged. "Who can follow the thoughts of the Father of Curses? Perhaps he hoped they were waiting to find him alone."

"All the more reason why we must persuade him to leave this place," I said firmly. "It is too dangerous. I will go now and find him."

"I will have the rug ready, Sitt," said Abdullah.

Emerson was not in his tent. It was getting dark; night gathered in the narrow cleft like black water filling a bowl. Stumbling over stones and swearing under my breath (an indication, if any were needed, that my state of mind was far from the calm that ordinarily marks it), I finally smelled tobacco and made out the red glow of his pipe. He was sitting on a boulder some distance from the fire. At first I took the dark shape at his feet for another rock. Then its outlines shifted, like shadows moving.

"Get up at once, Bertha," I said sharply. "A lady does not squat on the ground."

"I did offer her a rock," said Emerson mildly. "So spare me the lecture I feel sure you were about to deliver. She was in need of comfort and reassurance, as any normal female would be under these circumstances.

You would not expect an English gentleman like myself to turn away a lady in distress."

"She might have come to me." I fear my tone was still a trifle critical. "What is the matter, Bertha?"

"How can you ask?" She continued to crouch at his feet, and I thought she pressed closer to him, if that were possible. "He is out there, watching and waiting. I can feel his eyes upon me. He is toying with me, like a cat with a mouse. Your guards are useless, he can come and go as he likes, and when he wishes to strike at me, he will." She rose to her feet and stood swaying. Even in the dark I could see the agitated trembling of her draperies. "This is a horrible place! It closes in around us like a giant tomb, and every rock, every crevice hides an enemy. Are you made of ice or stone, that you cannot feel it?"

I would have slapped her soundly across the cheek if I had been able to locate that part of her body precisely. Reaching out blindly, I took hold of some part—an arm, I believe—and shook it vigorously. "Enough of that, Bertha. None of us is pleased to be here, but an exhibition of unwomanly hysteria won't help matters."

A voice from the dark repeated, "Unwomanly?"

Ignoring it, I went on, "You will only have to endure one more night here. We are leaving tomorrow."

"Do you mean it? Is it true?"

Emerson must have inadvertently inhaled a quantity of smoke. He began coughing violently. "Yes," I said loudly. "It is true. Now go and—and—oh, I don't care what the devil you do, only stop keening and wailing and getting everyone in a state of nerves."

She moved away, gliding over the uneven ground

as easily as if she could see in the dark. Emerson had got his breath under control. He remarked, "Nothing seems to affect your nerves, MISS Peabody. Or your monstrous self-confidence. So you have decided we are leaving, have you?"

"Circumstances that should be apparent to any reasonable individual demand a brief interlude for rest and reorganization. I cannot collate the rubbings and squeezes I made in the royal tomb under these conditions. The men are entitled to their day of rest, and I used most of my medical supplies on Mohammed, and furthermore...Good Gad, why am I arguing with you?"

"It would be a departure for you to deign to explain your decisions," Emerson replied, in the same ominously mild voice. "I take it you have subverted Abdullah and the other men, as well as your faithful follower Vandergelt? I cannot prevent you from doing as you like, but what is to stop me from remaining here?"

"Abdullah and the other men, as well as my faithful follower Vandergelt," I replied smartly. "Now come back to the fire. Don't sit here in the dark inviting someone to stab you in the back."

"I will sit where I like, MISS Peabody, for as long as I choose. Good evening to you."

No one tried to stab Emerson in the back, much to his disappointment, I felt certain. It was not long before he joined us at the fire. I waited for him before making my announcement, since it is not my habit to undermine his authority behind his back. Direct confrontation, and a brisk argument, saves time in the long run, I had found.

The argument did not ensue, nor did the news of our departure produce the surprise and pleasure I had expected. It appeared that everyone had taken it for granted.

"Friday is the Moslem holy day, after all," Charlie pointed out. "We figured an enlightened employer like Mr. Vandergelt would be sympathetic to the rights of the laboring man and agree we were entitled to the same." He gave his employer a cheeky grin.

Cyrus grunted, quite as Emerson might have done. Emerson did not even grunt.

I wondered what he was up to. A few moments of cogitation gave me an answer, however. He had hoped to entice our enemy out into the open. So far that enemy had declined to take the challenge, as any sensible person would. He had sent hired bullies and spies to do the dirty work, and if he had been on the scene it had been under cover of darkness. I doubted that he had. His modus operandi, if I may employ a technical term, was based on the principle of leading his regiment from behind. He had not dared face Emerson until the latter was chained and helpless.

Impatience is one of Emerson's most conspicuous failings, and although "stubborn" is too mild a word for him, he does not refuse to accept a conclusion when it is forced upon him. His stratagem had not succeeded, nor was it likely to. Of course I had realized this from the first, and if Emerson had been willing to listen to reason I would have told him so. He had not been willing to listen; the conclusion had now been forced upon him; and he was getting bored with fighting off attentions that distracted him from his archaeological work and yielded no effective results. The time had come to shift his ground.

At least, I reflected, it had not been a complete waste of time. The removal of Mohammed was a dubious blessing; I did not doubt Sethos could find as many scurvy assassins as he wanted. But we (I use the word editorially) had done some good work in the royal tomb, and gotten some ideas about promising sites for future excavation. Kevin was firmly in hand, not wandering around the country causing trouble; and whether Cyrus admitted it or not, which he did not, I knew that Charlie was the man to be watched. I was glad I had not yielded to my first unthinking impulse and put him under arrest. Secret surveillance of his movements might lead us to his master.

Most consoling of all—dare I admit it?—was the fact that we had survived two of the frightful fates mentioned in the antique tale. I did not dare admit it to anyone else, for fear of being laughed at, but as you will see, dear Reader, a woman's instincts are keener to discern the mysterious workings of Fate than is cold logic.

We were all in good spirits when we set out next morning. We were on foot; since we were leaving the tents and much of our equipment behind, there was no need for donkeys. Bertha's musical laugh echoed frequently from the rocky walls; it held a note of anticipation that made me realize she was, after all, very young. Inured as I am to the hardships of desert travel, I found myself looking forward with great anticipation to a bath and a change of clothing. I had brought three of my working suits with me; all were in a frightful state of dust and muss, for of course it had been impossible to rinse them out.

I felt as if some invisible burden had fallen from my shoulders when we emerged from the widening mouth of the wadi and saw the plain stretching out before us. Open air, sunlight, distance! They came as an indescribable relief after those days of confinement. The sun was high and the desert quivered with heat, but beyond it the cool green of the cultivation and the glitter of water refreshed the eyes.

Our path led along the north side of the low hills that enclosed the Eastern Village. No one suggested we stop to rest, though we had been walking for two hours; we were all anxious to press on. Emerson had forged ahead, as was his infuriating habit; the cat clung to his shoulder, and Abdullah was close on his heels. Bertha and the two young men had fallen behind. I am sure I need not say that Cyrus was beside me as he always was.

Only our voices broke the stillness. Gradually, however, I became aware of another sound, sharp-pitched and monotonous as the mechanical ringing of a bell. It rose in volume as we approached the end of the ridge. Ahead and to the left I saw the wall of the little house Cyrus had caused to be built. The sound might have been coming from it.

Emerson heard it too. He stopped, cocking his head. Lowering the cat to the ground he turned, heading for the house.

The sun beat down on my shoulders and head with the force of an open fire; but a sudden chill permeated every inch of my body. I had recognized the sound. It was the howling of a dog.

I shook Cyrus off and began to run. "Emerson!" I shrieked. "Don't go there! Emerson, stop!"

He glanced at me and went on.

Though Emerson dislikes displaying any of the softer emotions, he is as fond of animals as I. His efforts on behalf of abused and threatened creatures do not attain the extravagance to which his son is unfortunately prone, but he had often interfered to rescue foxes from hounds and hunters. The cries of the dog suggested it was in pain or distress. They drew Emerson as strongly as they would have drawn me—had I not had cause to anticipate danger from such a source.

I saved my breath for running. I can, when it is necessary, attain quite a rapid pace, but on this occasion I believe I broke my own record. Emerson had reached the house before I caught him up. He paused, his hand on the latch, and looked at me curiously.

"The creature has got shut up inside somehow. What is—"

Being unable to articulate for want of breath, I threw myself at him. It proved to be an error, but one for which I may be excused, I think. I had not observed his fingers had already pressed the latch.

Hearing our voices, the dog had begun hurling itself at the door. It burst open. Emerson staggered back against the wall, and I fell rather heavily onto the ground.

The pariah dogs of the villages are scrawny, starved creatures of indeterminate breed. They are not pets, but feral beasts who have good cause to fear and hate human beings. Those who survive the hardships of early life do so because they are tougher and more vicious than their peers. And this one was mad.

It would have gone straight for Emerson's throat if I had not shoved him aside. Now it attacked the first object it saw—my foot. Bloody foam flew in pink flecks from its jaws as it sank its teeth into my boot, shaking it, gnawing it. My parasol was still in my hand. I brought it down on the dog's head. The blow would have stunned an animal less frenzied. It only drove this one to a more furious attack.

Emerson snatched the parasol from me. Raising it over his head, he struck with all his strength. I heard the crack of bone and a last, agonized howl that will haunt my memory forever. The beast rolled over, thrashing and kicking. Emerson struck again. The sound was less sharply defined this time but equally sickening.

Emerson seized me under the arms and dragged me away from the body of the dog. His face was as white as the bandage on his cheek—whiter, if I must be accurate, for the bandage had got very dirty, and he had refused my offer to change it that morning. Abdullah stood nearby, his knife in his hand. He was as still as a statue, and he too had gone pale.

Kneeling beside me, Emerson reached up and took Abdullah's knife. "Start a fire," he said. Abdullah stared blankly at him for a moment, and then nodded.

There was fuel at hand, part of Kevin's supplies. I was vaguely aware of Abdullah's rapid movements, but most of my attention, I confess, was focused on my boot, at which Emerson was slashing. The laces were knotted and sticky with saliva, and the part of the boot around the ankle had been torn to shreds.

"Don't touch it!" I exclaimed. "Your hands are always scratched and cut; an open wound—"

I broke off with a cry of pain I could not repress, as Emerson seized the boot in a savage grip and wrenched it off. Cyrus came round the corner of the house in time to hear my exclamation. Fury darkened his brow and he was, I think, about to hurl himself on Emerson when he saw the body of the dog. The color drained from his face as, with his usual quick intelligence, he grasped the significance of the scene.

"God in heaven!" he cried. "Did it—"

"That is what I am trying to ascertain, you damned fool," said Emerson, inspecting my dirty stocking with the intense concentration of a scientist peering through a microscope. "Keep them back," he added, as the others hurried up, exclaiming in question and in alarm. "And don't touch the—"

The sound that issued from his lips was not a gasp or a groan. It was a muttered expletive. I had seen it too—such a small rent, barely an inch long. But it was large enough to mean my death.

Carefully Emerson stripped the stocking off and took my bare foot in his hand.

It is not proper to be vain about one's personal appearance, and heaven knows I had little cause; but in the privacy of these pages I will confess I had always believed I had rather pretty feet. Small and narrow, with high arches, they had been described in appreciative terms by no less an authority than Emerson himself. Now he stared fixedly, not at the appendage but at the tiny scratch on my ankle. The skin had barely been broken. There were only a few drops of blood.

For a moment no one spoke. Then Abdullah said, "The fire burns well, Father of Curses." He held out his hand. I thought it trembled a little.

Emerson gave him the knife.

If Ramses had been there, he would already have been talking. Kevin was almost as perniciously loquacious as my son, so I was not surprised when he was the first to break the silence. His freckles stood out dark against the pallor of his face. "It is only the merest scratch. Perhaps the dog was not mad. Perhaps—"

"If someone does not silence that babbling idiot of an Irishman I will knock him down," said Emerson.

"We cannot afford to take the chance, Kevin," I said. "I am going to sit up now—"

"You are not going to sit up now," said Emerson, in the same remote voice. "Vandergelt, make yourself useful. Put your knapsack under her head and see if you can locate a bottle of brandy."

"I always carry a flask of brandy," I said, fumbling at my belt. "For medicinal purposes, of course. There is water in this other flask."

Emerson took the brandy from me and wrenched off the top. I swigged it down like a hardened drunkard, for unnecessary martyrdom is not something I court. I only wished I could drink enough of the horrid stuff to render myself intoxicated and unconscious, but I knew if I consumed it too quickly I would only be sick.

Better sick, drunk, or in pain than dead. Hydrophobia is inevitably fatal, and it would be difficult to think of a more unpleasant way in which to die.

When Abdullah returned, my head was already spinning and I was glad to lie back against the support Cyrus had prepared. He knelt beside me, his face a mask of sympathetic anguish, and took my hand in his. The blade of the knife glowed cherry-red with heat. Abdullah had wrapped a cloth around the handle. Emerson took it from him.

It is quite an uncomfortable sensation, of course. Oddly enough the thing I minded most was the hiss and the stench of burning flesh. Someone cried out. Most probably it was I.

When I recovered my senses I felt someone's arms holding me. They were not Emerson's; blinking blurrily, I saw him standing nearby, with his back turned.

"It is all over, dearest Amelia," said Cyrus, pressing me closer. "Over, and safe, thank God."

"Excellent," I said, and fainted again.

The next time I woke I did not need to look to know who carried me cradled in his arms. I had been unconscious for some time, for when I opened my eyes I saw palm fronds overhead. A chicken squawked and flapped. Emerson must have kicked it aside. That was not like him, he usually stepped over them.

"Awake, are you?" he inquired, as I stirred feebly. "Allow me to be the first to congratulate you on behaving in a womanly fashion."

I turned my head and looked up at him. Perspiration had run down his cheeks and dried, leaving tracks through the dust that smeared them. "You may put me down now," I said. "I can walk."

"Oh, don't be an ass, Peabody," was the irritable reply.

"Let me take her," pleaded Cyrus, close at hand as always.

"Not necessary. We are almost there."

"How do you feel, my dear?" Cyrus asked.

"Quite well," I murmured. "Well, but rather odd. My head seems to be disconnected from the rest of me. Make sure it doesn't float away, Cyrus. It is so useful, you know. For putting one's hat onto."

"She is delirious," Cyrus said anxiously.

"She is dead drunk," said Emerson. "Interesting sensation, is it not, Peabody?"

"Yes, indeed. I had no idea."

I was about to go on, explaining some of the effects I was experiencing, when I heard the sound of running feet and a voice cried out, "Emerson! O Father of Curses, wait for me! It is well. The dog was not mad. She is safe, she will not die!"

Emerson's arms squeezed like a vise and then relaxed. He turned, and I saw Abdullah hurrying toward us, waving his arms. He was grinning from ear to ear and every few steps he gave an absurd little hop, like a child skipping.

We had reached the center of the village. The procession that had followed us from the cultivation—men and women, children, chickens and goats—gathered around. Life in these villages is very dull. Any excitement draws a crowd.

"Well?" said Emerson coolly, as his foreman came panting up.

"There had been a stick wedged in its jaws to hold its mouth open," Abdullah gasped. "The fragments pierced deep when the stick finally broke. And this"—

he displayed a filthy, blood-stiffened length of tattered cord—"tied tightly around its—"

"Never mind," said Emerson, glancing at me.

"How horrible!" I exclaimed. "The poor creature! Just let me lay my hands on that villain and I will—oh, dear. Oh, dear, suddenly I don't feel at all well. Wrath, I expect, has weakened my... Emerson, you had better put me down immediately."

Though I felt a great deal better afterward, I found to my distress that I could not stand upright. It was not my foot that prevented this, though it hurt like the devil, but the fact that my knees kept bending at odd angles. I would not have supposed that the anatomy of the knee permitted such flexibility.

"Not such an enjoyable experience as you thought, was it?" said Emerson. "And the worst is yet to come. If you think your head aches now, wait till tomorrow morning."

He looked so handsome, his eyes bright blue with amused malice, his hair waving damply back from his brow and his stalwart frame attired in clean if rumpled garments, I could not even resent the amusement. Someone had replaced the dirty bandage; I presumed it had been Bertha. She had tended me as deftly and gently as a trained nurse, helping me strip off my filthy clothes—for my hands did not seem to function any better than my knees—and attend to the other elements of the toilette. Cyrus had been waiting to carry me to the saloon, where we were now assembled, refreshing the inner man (and woman) as the outer had been refreshed. It was certainly a more presentable group than the crew of weary, work-stained, agitated individuals who had stumbled onto the boat.

Arranging my skirts, I settled back on the divan and allowed Cyrus to lift my foot onto a stool. "You will have your little joke, Emerson," I said. "I feel perfectly fit. I confess it is a relief to know I will not have hydrophobia. When I think of Abdullah's courage in examining that poor wretched dog! He might have contracted the disease himself."

"It is a pity he didn't think of examining the dog earlier," said Cyrus critically. "He might have spared you all that agony, my dear."

"It was my idea to examine the dog," Emerson said. "Locating at short notice an animal in the appropriate stage of rabies is not as easy as you might suppose, and few men, however hardened, would care to risk handling it. However, the idea did not occur to me immediately, and the cauterization could not have been delayed. Every second counts with such injuries. Once the disease enters the bloodstream...Well, there is no need to think of that. The dog was deliberately tortured and shut up in the house to await our arrival. Who knew we would be coming that way?"

"Everyone, I should think," Charlie said. "This is the day of rest; we assumed—"

"Quite right," I said. "That line of investigation won't lead anywhere, Emerson. The villain must have thought it was worth a try. All he stood to lose was one wretched dog. Thank God we came when we did! Its suffering is over now, at any rate."

"It is so like you to think of that," Cyrus murmured, taking my hand.

"Hmph," said Emerson. "You might better be thinking of what would have ensued if Abdullah had not examined the dog."

"We would have endured days, weeks of suspense," Kevin said soberly. "Even cauterization does not ensure—"

"No, no," Emerson said impatiently. "Your sympathetic suffering, O'Connell, would not have interested our attacker. What did he hope to gain by this?"

"The pleasure of picturing you picturing yourself in the ghastly throes of hydrophobia," I suggested. "Violent paroxysms of choking, tetanic convulsions, extreme depression, excitability..."

Emerson gave me a very old-fashioned look. "You are as bad as O'Connell. You were the one the dog attacked, not I."

"But you were the intended victim," I insisted. "You always forge ahead of the rest of us; you would have been the first to hear the poor animal's cries, and anyone who knows your character would realize how you would, inevitably, respond to such—"

"As you did." Emerson's eyes were fixed on my face. "You ran like the very devil, Peabody. How did you know the dog constituted a danger?"

I had hoped he would not wonder about that. "Don't be ridiculous," I said, with a good show of irritability. "I was not concerned about the dog; I feared it might have been employed as a means of luring you into a trap of some kind, that is all. You are always rushing in where angels fear—"

"Unlike you," said Emerson. "I suppose you tripped and fell against me without intending to?"

"Quite," I said, in my most dignified tones.

"Hmph," said Emerson. "Well. It does not matter which of us was the intended victim. What would we have done, had we believed the dog was rabid?"

Cyrus clasped my hand tighter. "I would have ordered a train and taken her straight to Cairo, of course. The Pasteur treatment must be available in the hospitals there."

"Very good, Vandergelt," said Emerson. "And somewhere along the way, I suspect, a group of kindly strangers would have relieved you of your charge. Unless...oh, curse it!" He leapt to his feet, eyes bulging. "What a fool I am!" And without further ado he rushed out of the room, leaving the door swinging on its hinges.

"Oh, curse it!" I echoed with equal vehemence. "Go after him, Cyrus! Confound my skirts and my foot and my knees...Hurry, I say!"

When I speak in that tone I am seldom disobeyed (and when I am, it is always by Ramses). Cyrus gave me a startled glance before following after Emerson. Charles looked at René. René looked at Charles. Charles shrugged. As one man they rose and left the room.

Kevin stood irresolutely in the doorway, one foot in and one foot out. "Where is he going?"

"I have not the least idea. I can only assume that it is somewhere he ought not to be—certainly not alone and unguarded. Come back and sit down, Kevin, you will never catch them up now. If that was your intention."

Kevin looked hurt. Before he could proclaim his courage and zeal, Bertha ran to him and caught his arm. "Do not go! Stay and protect us! This may be a ruse—"

"On Emerson's part?" I inquired ironically. "It is broad daylight and most of the men are still on board. Do sit down, Bertha, and stop wailing."

His male vanity soothed by the appeal of a helpless female, Kevin slipped his arm around the slight, trembling form and led the girl to a sofa. She sat staring at me, her eyes very wide and dark. Then she wrenched the veil from her face, as if it smothered her.

"He was there before you," she said. "How is it that the dog attacked you instead?"

"I got in its way," I said.

"By chance? I do not believe that. I saw how quickly you ran. How you must love him!"

"Anyone would have done the same," I said shortly, for I am not in the habit of discussing my personal feelings with strange young women.

"Not I," said Kevin frankly. "At least not if I had been given time to think before I acted." He sighed deeply and patted Bertha's hand. "Och, but that's the curse of our confounded British moral code. It is drummed into us from childhood and is part of our nature. I've done me best to conquer it, but there have been times when even I have instinctively behaved like a gentleman instead of thinking first of my own precious skin."

"Not many," I said.

Bertha was trembling violently. Kevin seated himself beside her and began to croon reassurances in a particularly vile brogue. I paid them no further heed. My eyes were fixed on the wide windows of the saloon, through which I had beheld Emerson rushing full-tilt up the bank toward the village, hatless and coatless, his hair blowing wildly in the breeze. The others had followed him; but I paid them no heed either, even in my thoughts.

Long before I had dared hope they returned. I could have cried out with relief. Cyrus must have stopped him and persuaded him to listen to reason—or, more likely, Emerson had had second thoughts. He was not, as a rule, susceptible to persuasion, however reasonable.

He and Cyrus walked side by side, with the two young men trailing them at a respectful distance. It was pleasant to see such amity between them; they appeared to be engaged in serious conversation, and I would have given a great deal to overhear what they were saying. Never mind, I thought; I will get it out of Cyrus at a later time.

CHAPTER 14

"Men always have some high-sounding excuse for indulging themselves."

The snake, the crocodile and the dog—we had met and overcome them all! The last of the three fates had been the subtlest and most dangerous; if Emerson had not thought to examine the body of the dog, I might even now be in the clutches of our archenemy. I did not blame him for failing to think of it earlier. The idea—irrefutably logical though it was—had not occurred to me either. I had been somewhat distracted at the time. Only those who have faced it can fully comprehend the sick horror that fills the soul at the mere possibility of that ghastly infection. Cauterization is the most effective treatment, but it is not a certain cure.

Emerson had been a trifle distracted himself. I remembered his set, white face as he bent over me, the tightening of his lips as he prepared to lay the red-hot steel against my flesh. But there had been no tremor of those firm hands, no moisture in those keen blue eyes.

Naturally one expects such fortitude in a man of

Emerson's character. However, I would not have held it against him if he had wiped away a few manly tears.

The eyes that looked at me now were not brilliant sapphire but steely gray—my own, reflected in the mirror over my dressing table. We had dispersed to our rooms after luncheon. The others were napping; I was supposed to be doing the same. Cyrus had placed me on my bed and bade me rest; Emerson, passing by the door, had called out, "Try sleeping it off, MISS Peabody; that usually works for me."

How could I sleep? My brain teemed with confusion. I had managed to hobble to the dressing table, not because the contemplation of my own features gave me any pleasure, but because I cogitate more efficiently when in an upright position.

As Cyrus carried me to my room I had taken the opportunity of questioning him about the conversation I had overheard—or, to be more precise, overseen. "I was just trying to talk some sense into him, my dear," was the reply. "He was heading back to the desert when we caught up with him; wanted to have another look at the body of the dog, he said. Don't worry, he's thought better of it."

Would it were so! But I had my doubts. I had never been able to talk sense into Emerson so easily.

Additional food for thought had been provided by the letters I found waiting. Cyrus's messenger, hearing of our imminent return from the wadi, had delivered them to my room. I postponed the pleasure of reading Ramses's latest epistle until after I had read the others, for I had no reason to suppose it would ease my mind.

A brief note from Howard Carter in Luxor informed

me that the town was swarming with journalists who pursued him and our other friends demanding interviews. "I was in the Hypostyle Hall at Karnak yesterday," he wrote, "when a head popped out from behind one of the columns and a voice shouted, 'Is it true, Mr. Carter, that Mrs. Emerson broke two of her umbrellas during the rescue of her husband?' I shouted back a denial, of course, but prepare yourself, Mrs. E., for the worst excesses of journalistic fiction. I expect, however, you are accustomed to that."

Messages from friends in Cairo reported equally infuriating assaults and even more insulting rumors. The letter from Sir Evelyn Baring's secretary—to which he had added a solicitous (and obviously bewildered) note in his own hand—held more comfort. It had been impossible to locate in such a short time all the individuals on the list I had sent, but investigations were proceeding, and as I studied the annotations that had been made I began to wonder if my theory might not be in error after all. Those former enemies of ours who had been incarcerated were still in their cells. Ahmet the Louse had turned up in the Thames some months earlier. I was not surprised; a user of and dealer in opium does not have a long life expectancy. That left... I counted... six. There was no guarantee that all six of them were not on our trail, but the reduction of the numbers gave me an illogical sense of encouragement.

It could not be put off any longer. With a sigh, I opened Ramses's letter.

Dearest Mama and Papa, I have come to the conclusion that my talents lie in the intellectual rather than the physical sphere, for the present at least. It is some consolation to realize that my physical inadequacies will improve to some extent through the natural process of time—or to put it in more colloquial terms, when I grow up. I dare not hope I will ever attain the degree of strength and ferocity that distinguishes Papa; however, what natural talents I possess can be increased by constant exercise and the practice of particular skills. I have already begun this regimen and intend to continue it.

An icy chill seized my limbs. I was unable to cherish any delusions concerning the kind of skills Ramses had in mind. Most of them involved the propulsion of sharp or explosive missiles. It was probably just as well that there was no whiskey in the room and that my foot was too sore to enable me to go as far as the saloon. Like Cyrus, I was beginning to understand how an individual can be driven to drink.

I forced myself to go on reading, wondering when, if ever, Ramses would get to the point.

I must confess, since honesty is a virtue Mama has always attempted to instill in me (though there are times when I suspect it does more harm than good), that I was not the sole originator of the scheme which will, I hope, offer a solution to our present difficulties. The inspiration came from an unexpected source. I have encountered several unexpected sources in the past weeks and I hope I have been cured of my preconceptions along that line, though, as I have said, I look forward to discussing this absorbing subject with you at a future date.

But allow me to describe the event in proper order, as Mama would approve.

Thanks to Aunt Evelyn's gentle intervention on my behalf, I was only restricted to my room for twenty-four hours. Once released, I found myself rather at loose ends. The boys, as you know, are at school. Nefret was reading Pride and Prejudice and was quite absorbed in what has always struck me as a rather silly story. The ladies with whom I am acquainted are not at all like the ones in the book. Little Amelia very kindly offered to play Parcheesi with me, but I was not in the mood for juvenile companionship. (Do not fear, Mama, I was very polite. I would not hurt the dear child's feelings for the world.)

Ordinarily I would have gone to the library to pursue my researches into Egyptian grammar, but it seemed the better part of wisdom to stay out of Uncle Walter's way for a while. I therefore proceeded to Aunt Evelyn's sitting room, with the intention of making further inquiries (in the most tactful manner, I need not say) as to why she possessed a large black parasol.

She was not there, but Rose was tidying the room. I offered to help her with the dusting but she declined quite decidedly. She had no objection to engaging in conversation, however.

The exciting events of the last night but one were of course foremost in both our minds. I had already told Rose all about it but she asked to hear it again, so I willingly obliged. (She did not know why Aunt Evelyn had the parasol either, and refused to speculate.) The subject to which she kept returning was the reprehensible behavior of Ellis. She does not get on with Ellis, as I believe I told you. Ellis is quite a lot younger than Rose. She is thinner than Rose too, and has bright-yellow hair. I do not know what, if anything, these facts have to do with Rose not getting on with Ellis. I make note of them only as a matter of information.

"No better than she should be," said Rose with a sniff. "I told Miss Evelyn she wouldn't do. I know her kind."

"What kind is that?" I inquired.

Before she could answer, supposing she had intended to, Aunt Evelyn entered. She beckoned me to join her on the sofa—which I was happy to do—and took out her embroidery. It gave me a strange feeling to see her sitting there, as neat and quiet as a lady in a painting, when I remembered the fierce warrior maiden of the other night.

"Don't let me interrupt your conversation," she said in her soft voice. "I know you two enjoy talking together; pray go on as if I were not here."

"We were talking about Ellis," I said. "Rose knows her kind. I was endeavoring to discover what kind she meant."

Rose turned very red and began polishing the tea table vigorously.

"Rose, Rose," said Aunt Evelyn gently. "You must not be so uncharitable."

I do not know what it was that emboldened Rose to speak. Usually she just mumbles, "Yes, madam," and shoves the furniture around. I can only attribute her candor on this occasion to one of those premonitions Mama and I, and apparently others, occasionally have.

She was still very red in the face but she spoke up stoutly. "Excuse me, Miss Evelyn, but I think you ought to know. She's always sneaking and prying. I caught her coming out of Master Ramses's room one day. She's no business there, as you know, madam. Master Ramses's room is my job. And what was she doing out of the house at that hour of the night, if I may ask?"

It was quite uncanny, Mama and Papa, how it struck all of us at the same moment. We gazed on one another with a wild surmise. Only it was not really wild at all. Aunt Evelyn was the first to speak.

"Master Ramses's room, you said, Rose? What could she have wanted there?"

I struck myself on the brow. (I have read in books of people doing that, but I doubt they really do. Not more than once, at any rate.) "We can hazard a guess, can we not?" I cried. "How long ago did Ellis come to you, Aunt Evelyn?"

The ensuing discussion was most animated, and the conclusions we reached were unanimous. My chagrin at having overlooked such an obvious culprit was great; but it was I, dear Mama and Papa, who proposed the scheme.

"Let her find what she wants," I exclaimed. "Let her leave us, taking it with her, and without the slightest suspicion that we know her purpose."

Aunt Evelyn and Rose acclaimed this idea with such flattering praise that I was overcome with embarrassment. Even more flattering was their assumption that I would be able to produce a reasonable facsimile of the document in question; for, as you know, dear Mama and Papa, the original is in Papa's... [the last two words had been crossed out] *...is elsewhere.*

I got to work at once. (Forgery is a fascinating hobby. I have added it to my list of useful skills to be honed with practice.) Feeling that verisimilitude was vital in this case, I used a sheet from one of Papa's notebooks. (The one on the Dahshoor excavation, which I had brought along in order to study his reconstruction of the pyramid temple. There are several points I would like to raise with him at a future time.) But to resume: I had to age the paper properly, of course; this required some experimentation before I arrived at the solution of baking the paper in the oven after fraying the edges and sprinkling it with water. I then traced a copy of the map, whose outlines I had good cause to remember, on another sheet from the notebook, and repeated the process. The result was most satisfactory. I need not tell you, dear parents, that the compass readings I wrote were not the ones on the original. I made a few other alterations as well.

The next question was: Where to conceal the document? The library seemed the most likely place, but we agreed it would be expedient to direct Ellis's attention to the precise spot.

Without Rose's enthusiastic cooperation and remarkable thespian talents the scheme would never have succeeded. The library is, it appears, another of those regions into which Ellis has no reason to go. (I expect you were aware of this, Mama; I was not, and I found the definitions of comparative duties and relative social status dependent thereon quite interesting.) Mary Ann, Aunt Evelyn's parlormaid, is responsible for that room. It was necessary, therefore, to remove Mary Ann, for she has not the sort of temperament that lends itself to deception, and also we felt the fewer people who knew of our intentions, the better.

I had time, before I turned the page, to hope poor Mary Ann had not been removed too forcibly. She was a gentle gray-haired woman who had never done any harm.

The incident of the lion had reduced to shreds, as Mary Ann put it, nerves already frazzled by other events, so it was not difficult to persuade her to take a few days' holiday. (It is not difficult to persuade Mary Ann to do anything.) As soon as she left for the station, Rose fell down the back stairs and sprained her ankle. (She really did not sprain it, Mama and Papa, but the performance she put on was remarkably convincing.) That meant that Ellis had to be pressed into service to carry out some of the duties properly belonging to Mary Ann and Rose.

The amiability with which she agreed to take on the task of tidying the library was the final proof of her villainy. According to Rose and Aunt Evelyn, a proper lady's maid would have given notice rather than accept a demeaning task. (Fascinating, is it not? I had no idea such undemocratic attitudes permeate the servants' hall.)

Two more details were necessary: to get Uncle Walter out of the library while Ellis was searching it, and to give her a broad hint as to where to look. Aunt Evelyn assured us she could manage the first difficulty. (They were gone the whole afternoon. I do not know what they were doing.) I took it upon myself to arrange the second matter. I daresay my performance would not have convinced Mama, but Ellis is not very intelligent. I allowed her to catch me in the act of reading the papers Uncle Walter keeps in a locked drawer in his desk. The guilty start with which I pretended to notice her, and the haste with which I returned the papers to the drawer, added verisimilitude to my performance. In my hurry to leave the room, I of course forgot to lock the drawer.

I take great pleasure in informing you, Mama and Papa, that our stratagem has succeeded. Ellis has gone, bag and baggage; and the false document has gone too.

Now, dear Mama and Papa, for the best part of the scheme. (Modesty prevents me from mentioning whose idea it was.) As soon as our plans had been worked out, we made use of that convenient apparatus, the telephone, to reach Inspector Cuff and explain the situation to him. He pretended not to be surprised. In fact he claimed he had been suspicious of Ellis all along, and that one of the reasons why

*he had gone to London was to investigate her ante-
cedents. He assured us that Ellis would be followed
from the moment she left the house.*

*We do not expect a report from the inspector for
several days, but I am dispatching this at once so
it will reach you as soon as possible; for I feel certain that with the document in their possession the
unknown individuals who have behaved so unpleas-
antly will cease to trouble us with their attentions.
Your devoted son, Ramses.*

*P.S. I am still of the opinion that my place is
at your side, for you do seem, dearest parents, to
attract dangerous persons. I have now seven pounds
seven shillings.*

It took me some time to recover from the full effect
of this remarkable document. I attribute the confusion that seized me in part to my enfeebled condition,
though the contents of the letter were enough to throw
anyone into a state of bewildered agitation. What Emerson would say when he discovered his precious excavation notes had been vandalized for purposes of forgery
I dared not imagine. Where Ramses had learned to
pick locks—another "useful skill," I suppose he would
claim—I shuddered to contemplate. (Gargery? Inspector Cuff? Rose??) As for poor Walter, his nerves were
probably as frazzled as those of the much-tried Mary
Ann, though it was gratifying to learn that Evelyn and
he were on such excellent terms.

I put these matters aside in order to concentrate on
Ramses's major piece of news. The picture of Rose,
Evelyn, and Ramses conspiring to deceive a treacherous

lady's maid was so delicious I could almost forgive my wretched child for all his sins, except his ponderous literary style. However, a sobering thought soon intruded. The letter was dated ten days ago. Sethos must have learned of his confederate's success before this; she would have telegraphed immediately, or at least so I supposed. Yet the attacks on us had not ceased. One, possibly two, had occurred after the news could have reached him.

The snake, the crocodile and the dog... There were no other fates mentioned in the little story. Was he going to start all over again?

Perhaps it was the very absurdity of the notion that cleared my mind. Perhaps it was the hope that Ramses's stratagem would be effective—that the news had not yet reached the Master Criminal. At any rate, I found myself wondering if the parallels with the Egyptian fairy tale were not something more than coincidence or supernatural influence. Could the imitation be deliberate? Had the mind that had conceived the complex plot been influenced by "The Tale of the Doomed Prince"?

A number of people had known I was studying that tale. Mr. Neville's was the first name to come to mind, but he had mentioned it at the dinner table that evening in Cairo. Many of our friends had been present.

Had Sethos been among them?

The idea had a kind of insane attraction. That sinister master of disguise might well have been challenged by the prospect of playing the role of an individual as well known and distinctive in appearance as the Reverend Sayce, for example. I did not believe it, however. No one had greater respect for Sethos's abilities than I, but there would be no need for him to take such a risk. He had secret allies and employees throughout the world of archaeology. One of our guests might have mentioned my interest in the little fairy tale to such an individual. Regretfully I was forced to admit that this line of inquiry was no more fruitful than others I had considered. It led back to the same group I had always suspected of supplying information to the Master Criminal: archaeologists. Some of them might have done so in all innocence.

Every clue snapped in my hand when I attempted to grasp it. Noting the skill with which the bearded villain had inserted the hypodermic needle into Emerson's vein, I had thought he might have had formal medical training. That suspicion availed me naught, now that I knew Sethos was the man in question. He had shown himself, on several occasions, to be well acquainted with the use and application of various drugs. In fact, I reminded myself, most excavators are familiar with simple medical techniques, since they are often obliged to deal with injuries incurred in the field.

Another line of inquiry that I had hoped at first might limit the field of suspects did nothing of the kind. The officers of the Sudan Expeditionary Force were not, all of them, in the Sudan. After the fall of Khartoum many had been given leave. I had myself seen one familiar face in the lobby of Shepheard's. I had forgotten his name, but I remembered now where I had met him—at the house of General Rundle at Sanam Abu Dom. Sethos need not have been in the Sudan to acquire information from the officers who had known of our expedition.

In a burst of frustration I brought my fist down on

the table. Bottles and jars shook violently; a little vial of cologne toppled over.

The thud of the falling bottle was echoed by a knock at the door. There was only one individual I yearned to see at that moment, and I knew it was not he; Emerson did not tap softly on doors. "Come in," I said unenthusiastically.

It was Bertha. The change in her appearance was so astonishing, I forgot my painful musings for a moment. Head and face were bare; she had put off her mournful black for a blue-and-white-striped robe. It was a man's galabeeyah; married women always wore black, and since girls were hustled into matrimony at indecently young ages, no female garment would have fit Bertha's mature figure. Though somewhat large for her, the robe displayed that figure to advantage, for the fabric was fine and I suspected she was wearing nothing under it. Her braided hair hung over her shoulder in a shining rope, big around as my wrist. Her face was clear and unmarked; her complexion was as fair as my own.

Before I could remark on this she said, "I came to see if you wanted anything. The burn must pain you a great deal."

It throbbed like fury, in fact, but I do not believe discomfort is relieved by dwelling upon it. "Only time can improve it. We are somewhat deficient in ice here."

"Something to help you sleep, then."

"I cannot afford to dull my senses with drugs, Bertha. We are too vulnerable as it is."

"Won't you lie down, then?"

"I may as well, I suppose. No, I don't need to lean on you. Just hand me that parasol, will you?"

It was not the one I had carried that morning. I doubt I could have touched it again. Fortunately I always have several spares.

Bertha helped me arrange my garments and handed me a glass of water. I felt a trifle feverish, so when she dampened a handkerchief and began wiping my face I did not object. Her hands were very deft and gentle. That gave me an idea, and when she finished I said, "I am glad you came, Bertha. I have been wanting to talk to you. Have you ever thought of training as a nurse?"

The question seemed to surprise her a good deal. I am accustomed to having people react that way to my remarks, however. Those whose minds do not function with the agility of my own often fail to follow my train of thought.

"We must think of something for you to do," I explained. "The nursing profession is open to women, and although I would prefer to see females battering their way into occupations hitherto dominated by men, you do not appear to me to have the force of character necessary for social reform. Nursing might suit you, if you can overcome your squeamishness."

"Squeamishness," she repeated thoughtfully. "I think I might do that."

"It is only a suggestion. You ought to give the matter some thought, however. I will be sending you back to England as soon as this situation is settled. I would do it now—for candidly it would be a relief to have the responsibility for you off my hands—if I thought you would consent to go."

"I would not consent. Not until the...situation is settled." Hands folded in her lap, face composed, she studied me with considerable attention for a time and then said, "You would do that for me? Why should you?"

My eyes shifted under her steady gaze. The change in her was quite remarkable, but my reluctance to answer was due to quite another cause—one which did me no credit. I overcame that reluctance, as I hope I always overcome weaknesses of character. "I saw what you did, Bertha, that night I came for Emerson. If you had not flung yourself at the door and tried to hold it against the man who meant to murder him I might not have got my pistol out in time. It was the act of a true, courageous woman."

A faint smile touched the corners of her lips. "Perhaps it was as O'Connell said—I did not have time to think before I acted."

"All the more credit to you, then. Your instincts are sounder than your conscious acts. Oh, I confess I have had some doubts about you. You will laugh," I said, laughing, "when I tell you that at one time I suspected you might be a man."

Instead of laughing she raised her eyebrows and ran her hands slowly over her body. The tightened fabric clung to it in a way that left no room for doubt. "The man you call Sethos?" she asked. "Even veiled and robed, only a very clever man could carry off such a masquerade."

"He is a very clever man. You ought to know."

"I don't think it was he."

"It must have been. Though I would not have believed he could use a woman as he did you...Ah, well, it only goes to show that even so astute a judge of character as I can sometimes be deceived. He chose a proper pseudonym in this case—the sly, creeping serpent, the deceiver of Eve."

Bertha leaned forward. "What does he look like?"

"Ah, but you see, that is the difficulty. His eyes are an indeterminate shade; they can appear gray or blue or brown, or even black. His other features are equally susceptible to alteration. He explained to me some of the devices he uses to disguise them."

"So you have spoken with him—been in his presence."

"Er—yes," I said.

"But surely," Bertha said, watching me, "no man can disguise himself entirely from the eyes of a woman who...who is as keen an observer as you. Was he young?"

"It is easier to counterfeit old age than youth," I admitted. "And in his attempt to...In his consummate vanity he did display certain characteristics that are probably his own. He is almost of Emerson's height—a scant inch shorter, if that—and well-built. There was the elasticity of youth and physical strength in his step, his...I think I have told you all I can. From what I saw of your erstwhile master, those characteristics would fit him."

"Yes." We sat in contemplative silence for a while, each occupied with her own thoughts. Then she rose.

"You should rest. May I ask you one thing before I go?"

"Certainly."

"Does he remember you?"

"He has good cause to...Oh. Emerson, you mean?" I was weary; a sigh escaped my lips. "Not yet."

"He cares for you. I saw his face when he held the knife to your foot."

"No doubt you mean to cheer me, Bertha, and I appreciate the thought, but I fear you do not understand the British character. Emerson would have done the same for any sufferer and he would have felt the same pity for—for Abdullah. Especially Abdullah. Run along now, and do think seriously about the nursing profession."

I wanted to be alone. Her words, kindly though they had been meant, had cut deep. How desperately I yearned to believe Emerson's distress on my behalf was more than that any English gentleman would have betrayed toward any sufferer. Alas, I could not so delude myself. And Emerson was (despite certain eccentricities) unquestionably an English gentleman.

Though I was not feeling quite my energetic self that evening, I insisted upon joining the others. I confess I felt like some heroine of fiction when I entered the saloon, reclining gracefully in the respectful grasp of my friend Cyrus and attired in my most elegant dressing gown. It was the same one I had worn that night in Luxor when Cyrus came to my room with the telegram from Walter, and as I fastened the clasps and tied the bows I was reminded of the extreme mental anguish I had suffered during that endless period. It was a salutary reminder. No matter what dangers yet faced us— no matter how doubtful my success in winning back Emerson's regard—no torment could compare with those terrible hours when I had not known whether he lived, or would ever be restored to me.

The faces of those who rose to greet me were

wreathed in smiles of welcome and (if I may not be considered immodest for mentioning it) admiration. The face I had hoped to see was not among them. He was not there.

"Curse it!" I said involuntarily.

Cyrus paused in the act of lowering me onto a sofa. "Did I hurt you? I am such a clumsy old—"

"No, no, you did not hurt me. Just put me down, Cyrus."

René hastened to me with a glass in his hand. His expression indicated that he at least appreciated yellow silk and Chantilly lace. He was French, of course.

"No, thank you," I said. "I don't care for sherry."

"Here you are, ma'am." Kevin pushed René aside. "Just what the doctor ordered. I took the liberty of making it good and strong. For pain, you know."

The twinkle in his eye as he handed me the glass brought an involuntary answering smile to my lips. I knew he was remembering a certain occasion in London, when he had entertained me in one of those curious establishments known, I believe, as public houses, and had choked on his own drink when I ordered a whiskey and soda. Not Kevin, I thought again—not the young man who had fought at my side against the masked priests, who had stood by us—when he was not writing insulting stories about us—during the Baskerville murder case.

"And may I say," Kevin went on cheerfully, "how well that yellow frock becomes your sun-kissed cheeks and raven locks, Mrs.—er—Miss Peabody."

"Never mind," I said. "He is not here. Where the devil has he got to now?"

There was a brief, uncomfortable silence. Glances were exchanged.

"Not to worry, ma'am," Charles said. "Abdullah has gone with him."

I put my glass carefully down on the table before I spoke. "Gone," I said. "Where?"

All eyes, including mine, were fixed on Charles. He was saved from his difficulty by the advent of Emerson himself. As usual, he left the door open. Glancing at me, he remarked, "A hair of the dog, MISS Peabody?" before heading for the table and pouring a stiff whiskey and soda for himself.

Several replies came to my mind. Dismissing them all as unnecessarily provocative and unproductive of information, I said, "What luck?"

Emerson turned, leaning against the table with his glass in his hand. His expression roused the direst of suspicions. I knew that look well—the brilliance of those sapphire-blue eyes, the tilt of his brows, the little quirk at the corner of his mouth. "Smug" is perhaps the wrong word. It always suggests, at least to me, a certain primness which could never under any circumstances apply to Emerson. "Self-satisfied" is closer the mark.

"Luck?" he repeated. "I suppose you would call it that; I prefer to think of it as the result of experience and training. I have found another boundary stela. I thought there must be another one along the northern perimeter. It is in sad condition, so it behooves us to copy the inscription as soon as possible."

Charles choked on his sherry. "I beg your pardon," he gasped, pressing a serviette to his lips.

"Quite all right," said Emerson genially. "Contain

your delight, Charles; I promise you will be the first to have a go at it."

"Thank you, sir," said Charles.

"I cannot imagine what is wrong with me," I exclaimed, pressing my hands to my throbbing head. "Ordinarily I can follow Emerson's train of thought, even when it is incomprehensible to normal people, but I am at a loss to understand him now. He is up to something—but what?"

I was not talking to myself, but to Cyrus. He had insisted on taking me back to my room immediately after dinner. Since there were no other volunteers I accepted his offer, for I was not feeling quite up to par.

He did not reply at once, being preoccupied with the difficulty of opening the door while both hands were supporting me.

"Allow me," I said, reaching for the knob.

Cyrus's efficient steward had tidied the room and left a lamp burning. It was not until Cyrus was about to lower me onto the bed that I saw something that brought a cry to my lips. "Curse it! Someone has been going through my papers!"

Cyrus gazed around the room. Being a man, he saw nothing out of place. "The steward..." he began.

"He would have no excuse for opening the box in which I keep letters and personal documents. See, there is a corner of paper protruding; I hope you do not believe I would be so untidy! Hand me the box, will you please?"

It was a metal container of the sort solicitors employ; I had not locked it, since the only papers it presently contained were the letters I had received and my notes on "The Tale of the Doomed Prince." The rubbings I had made in the royal tomb and my excavation notes were in another portfolio.

Quickly I sifted through the pile of papers. "There is no doubt about it," I said grimly. "He did not even bother to replace them in the same order. Either he is criminally inexperienced, or he did not care whether I detected his efforts."

"Is anything missing?" Cyrus asked.

"Not from here. Er—Cyrus, would you mind turning your back for a moment?"

He gave me a hurt, quizzical look, but at once complied. The rustling of the bedclothes must have driven him wild with curiosity; his shoulders kept twitching. Like the gentleman he was, he remained motionless until I bade him turn around.

"Even more curious," I said, frowning. "Nothing *at all* is missing. One would have supposed..."

"That a trained thief would look first under the mattress?" Cyrus inquired, eyebrows raised. "I won't ask what you've got there, Amelia, but you sure could find a better hiding place. Never mind; doesn't the fact that your treasure, whatever it is, has not been taken suggest that it was only a curious servant who searched your papers?"

"It suggests to me that the searcher's motive is even more sinister than I could suppose, since I am unable to determine what it is."

"Oh," said Cyrus. He scratched his chin.

His lean frame and rough-hewn features, the epitome of masculinity, looked quite incongruous in the pretty, luxurious room. I invited him to sit down, and he perched uncomfortably on the edge of a fragile chair.

"It's no wonder you're feeling poorly, my dear," he said. "Most men would be flat-out after such an experience. I wish you would take it easy."

I ignored this ridiculous suggestion. "Since idle speculation as to the motives of the searcher is a waste of time, let me return to the subject of Emerson. He is extremely pleased with himself, Cyrus. That is a bad sign. It can only mean that he has discovered a clue to the identity or the whereabouts of our enemy—some fact already known to him, or it would not have prompted his cry of 'What a fool I am!' What can it be? If Emerson can think of it, I ought to be able to. He was talking about taking me to Cairo—strangers on the train...medical attention...Of course! What a fool I am!"

The dainty chair creaked ominously as Cyrus shifted his weight. I was too excited to note this evidence of discomfort. "Follow my reasoning, Cyrus," I cried. "If we had believed that I—or Emerson, who was the intended victim—had been infected, we would have set out for Cairo. Our enemy would have intercepted us. But why would he delay until we were on the train? He would have a better opportunity of ambushing our party between here and Derut—on the felucca that carried us across the river, or along the road to the railroad station. He was here, Cyrus—here in the village, staying with the 'Omdeh in all probability, for that is where tourists find accommodations—and that is where Emerson was going, to the house of the 'Omdeh! If you had not—"

The chair gave off a series of alarming squeaks. Cyrus leaned back, eyes fixed on the ceiling.

"Cyrus," I said very gently. "You knew this. You lied to me, Cyrus. I asked you where Emerson had gone, and you said—"

"It was for your own good," Cyrus protested. "Doggone it, Amelia, you scare the dickens out of me sometimes, the way you figure things out. You sure you don't practice witchcraft on the sly?"

"I wish I did. I would like to be able to put curses on certain people. Speak up, Cyrus. Tell me all."

I had been absolutely correct, of course. A party of tourists had arrived that morning, on horseback. They had requested the hospitality of the 'Omdeh but had changed their minds and departed, somewhat abruptly, shortly after we returned.

"They—or someone who reported to them—must have overheard Abdullah announce the dog was not rabid," I mused.

"The whole darned countryside heard Abdullah," Cyrus grunted.

"It was not his fault. It was no one's fault. So that is why Emerson was wandering around the northern cliffs this afternoon! He believes the 'tourists' are still in the neighborhood. It may well be so; our enemy is not likely to give up now. And Emerson means to deal with the fellow himself, of course. I cannot permit that. Where is Abdullah? I must—"

I started to swing my feet off the bed. Cyrus sprang to my side; gently but firmly he forced me to lie back. "Amelia, if you don't stop this I will hold your nose and pour a dose of laudanum down your throat. You will only aggravate your injury if you don't give it a chance to heal."

"You are right, of course, Cyrus," I said. "It is so

cursed inconvenient! I cannot even pace to relieve my pent-up feelings."

How quickly he had overcome his embarrassment at being alone with me in my room! He was now actually sitting on the bed, and his hands still rested on my shoulders. He looked deeply into my eyes.

"Amelia—"

"Would you be good enough to get me a glass of water, Cyrus?"

"In a minute. You have to hear me out, Amelia. I can't stand this any longer."

Out of respect for feelings that were—I am convinced—genuine and profound, I will not record the words in which he poured them out. They were simple and manly, like Cyrus himself. When he paused I could only shake my head and say, "I am sorry, Cyrus."

"Then—there is no hope?"

"You forget yourself, my friend."

"I'm not the one that's forgotten," said Cyrus harshly. "He doesn't deserve you, Amelia. Give it up!"

"Never," I said. "Never, if it takes a lifetime."

It was a dramatic moment. I believe my voice and my look carried conviction. I certainly meant them to.

Cyrus took his hands from my shoulders and turned away. I said gently, "You mistake friendship for deeper feelings, Cyrus. One day you will find a woman worthy of your affection." Still he sat in silence, his shoulders bowed. I always think a little touch of humor relieves difficult situations; I added cheerfully, "And just think— it is most unlikely she will have a son like Ramses!"

Cyrus squared his broad shoulders. "No one else could have a son like Ramses. If you mean that as consolation, however...Well, I will say no more. Shall I fetch Abdullah to you now? I guess if I don't you'll hoist yourself out of bed and go stumping off after him."

He had taken it like a man. I had expected no less of him.

Abdullah looked even more out of place in my room than Cyrus had. He studied the frills and furbelows with a scowl of deep suspicion, and refused the chair I offered. It did not take me long to force him to confess that he too had deceived me.

"But, Sitt, you did not ask me," was his feeble excuse.

"You ought not have waited till you were asked. Why did you not come to me at once? Oh, never mind," I said impatiently, as Abdullah rolled his eyes and tried to think of another lie. "Tell me now. Precisely what did you learn this afternoon?"

Before long Abdullah was squatting comfortably on the floor next to the bed, and we were deep in friendly consultation. Accompanied by Abdullah, Daoud and Ali (he had at least had sense enough to take them with him), Emerson had attempted to learn where the mysterious tourists had gone. No boatman admitted to having taken them across the river, and it was unlikely the former would have lied—for, as Abdullah innocently expressed it, "the threats of the Father of Curses are stronger than any bribe." That meant that the men we sought were still on the east bank. An itinerant camel driver had confirmed this assumption; he had seen a group of horsemen heading for the northern end of the plain, where the cliffs swung close to the river.

"We lost them then," Abdullah said. "But they must

have a camp somewhere in the hills or on the high desert, Sitt. We did not look farther; it was growing late, and Emerson said we would turn back. He was looking very pleased."

"Of course he is, curse him," I muttered, clenching my fists. "That explains his sudden interest in boundary stelae; it is only an excuse to search that area and, with any luck—as Emerson would probably put it—be violently attacked again. Furthermore, he believes I am out of commission and cannot interfere with his idiotic scheme. Well! Just wait till he sees—"

An almost imperceptible twitch of Abdullah's beard made me break off. His is a particularly impassive countenance, or so he fondly believes. Since he also believes that I have occult powers, he finds it difficult to conceal his thoughts from me.

"Abdullah," I said. "My father. My honored friend. If Emerson tries to leave the boat tonight, stop him by any means necessary, including violence. And if you tell him of our conversation . . ."

I paused for effect, having found that unuttered threats are the most terrifying. Besides, I could not really think of one I was capable of carrying out.

"I hear and will obey." Abdullah rose in a graceful flutter of skirts. The formal words of submission would have impressed me more if he had not been trying to repress a smile. He added, "It is very difficult, Sitt, to walk the knife's edge between your commands and those of Emerson. He said the same thing to me not an hour ago."

CHAPTER 15

"I always say there is nothing more comfortable or commodious than a tomb."

I was up and dressed at dawn, belt of tools strapped at my waist, parasol in my hand. My martial appearance was only a trifle marred by the pale-blue woolly slipper on my left foot. Leaning heavily on the parasol, I made my way to the dining saloon. (The stairs presented something of a difficulty until I thought of ascending them in a sitting position.)

There was less fuss and complaint than I had expected. Kevin greeted me with a knowing grin, and Cyrus's feeble, "Amelia, I really don't think you ought…" was never completed. Emerson looked at the pale-blue woolly slipper, raised his eyebrows, opened his mouth, closed it, and reached for another piece of bread.

After we had finished eating, Cyrus went off to make sure the donkeys were ready. Bertha, followed by the three young men like ganders after a comely lady goose, had offered to collect my gear, an offer I was glad to accept.

"Just a moment, Emerson," I said, as he pushed his chair away from the table. "I want to speak to you for a moment about Charles."

He had not expected that. Pausing with his hand on the back of the chair, he studied me suspiciously, his head tilted. "What about him?"

"He has not told you of his fear of heights? Oh, dear, I feared he would not. Men are so—"

"He did tell me," Emerson interrupted. His brows drew together in a scowl. "How he ever expects to qualify as an archaeologist I cannot imagine. What with tombs in the cliffs, and pyramids, and—"

"That is all right, then," I said, recognizing the start of one of Emerson's notorious lectures. "It was cruel of you to tease him about it yesterday."

"Don't push me too far, Peabody," said Emerson between clenched teeth. "I am holding on to my temper with both hands as it is. How dare you turn up this morning in that preposterous slipper wearing that expression of maddening self-confidence? I ought to lock you in your room and tie you to the bed! By heaven, I will!"

Though my parasol was fastened to my wrist by its little strap I made no attempt to prevent him from sweeping me up into his arms. I am a strong-minded woman, but even the best of us is not always able to resist temptation. When he started toward the stairs, I said firmly, "Just carry me directly to a donkey, if you please. You may as well spare yourself time and trouble, Emerson, for no method you employ will suffice to keep me in that room if I choose to leave it."

Emerson deposited me on the donkey and stormed

off, shouting at Abdullah, since he knew there was no use in shouting at me. Abdullah glanced at me. If he had been English he would have winked.

We were soon on our way. Bertha and I rode donkeys. After considering its options with an uncanny air of deliberation, the cat chose to ride with me. The others walked, including Kevin, over his piteous objections. Our path led us almost due north along the bare desert track that passes through the mountain defile at one end of the Amarna plain and runs parallel to the river before rising again over the hills to the south. Nothing marked it except the prints of men and donkeys; on either side the waterless waste lay empty under the sun. Yet once this had been the royal road of a great city, lined with fine houses and painted temples. From the Window of Appearance of the king's palace he had thrown collars of gold to favored courtiers. Now only low mounds and sunken hollows remained; time and the ever-encroaching sand had destroyed the evidences of man's ephemeral presence, as they would one day destroy all traces of our own.

The distance from Haggi Qandil to the northern boundary is a little over three miles. Already the sun was hot. Kevin puffed and groaned and mopped his streaming brow. I offered him my parasol, but he refused it; some silly notion of appearing unmanly, I suppose. I only hoped he would not inconvenience me by collapsing with heat prostration. Unlike the others he was unused to the climate, and Emerson moderated his pace for no man—or woman.

To the right, several miles distant, were the northern tombs and the boundary stela we had seen on the first day. Emerson did not turn aside. As we went on, the cliffs curved more sharply toward the river, until only a narrow space a few hundred yards wide separated them from the bank. The shade they offered was welcome, but I began to feel the same sense of oppression that had overshadowed me while we were camping in the royal wadi. The rock face was even more broken here (or so it seemed to my anxious eyes), not only by crevices and innumerable small wadis but by the remains of ancient quarries.

At last Emerson came to a stop and looked up. Anubis jumped down from my lap and went to stand by him.

High above on the stony wall I saw fragmentary reliefs and rows of hieroglyphic signs. So there was a stela. I would not have been surprised to find that Emerson had invented one. This was a new one—new to archaeologists, I mean, for it was certainly very old and worn—and far north of any of the others. A brief tremor of archaeological fever ran through me, but it quickly passed. I felt sure Emerson had not come here to add a few more hieroglyphs to the texts of the boundary stelae.

Cyrus managed not to swear aloud, though he choked on the unuttered word. "Holy—er—Jimminy. All this way—for that!"

"The text is probably identical with the others," I replied. "But you know how battered they all are; we may find a portion here that has not survived elsewhere, and fill in some of the missing sections."

"Well, *you* sure aren't going to find anything," Cyrus declared. "Only a lizard could slither up that cliff. Come and sit down here in the shade, my dear—what there is of it."

He lifted me off the donkey and placed me on the rug Bertha had spread out. The men were already unloading the supply donkeys. René and Charles, goaded by Emerson's caustic comments, pitched in with a will. Kevin flung himself down at my feet with a martyred sigh and begged for water.

I poured a cup for the afflicted journalist and reminded him that it was his own fault he was enduring thirst and heat. "Curiosity killed the cat, you know, Kevin. I hope yours may not be the death of you."

"Speaking of cats," Kevin said, "tell me about that diabolical-looking creature that follows the professor around. I thought when I first saw it that it was the one you adopted after l'affaire Baskerville, but this one appears to be much more savage and less domesticated."

"We are taking care of it temporarily for a friend," I replied. "There is no news story in that, Kevin. Will you excuse me? I want to see what they are doing."

"Should you be walking on that ankle?" Kevin asked, as I levered myself to my feet with the aid of my trusty parasol.

"It is not broken or sprained, only a trifle sore. Stay here, Kevin, I don't need you."

Under Emerson's direction the men were fitting together a rough scaffold, binding the strips of wood together with rope. It was a horribly ramshackle affair, but I knew that it was a good deal sturdier than it looked. I had often seen our men scampering up and down such structures with the insouciance of tightrope walkers, apparently oblivious to the way the boards creaked and swayed. This time, I knew it would have to bear a heavier weight.

Cyrus was so intent on the work that he did not see me until I stood next to him. I brushed aside his protests and his attempt to pick me up. He followed me, still protesting, as I hobbled on.

Beyond the shoulder of rock a ravine cut at a sharp angle into the cliff. The usual litter of broken stone and flood-deposited pebbles covered its floor, and the sides were laced with black shadows where crevices of all sizes and shapes broke the rocky walls.

I looked up and my heart gave a great leap as I saw the figure of a man silhouetted against the sky. Then I recognized Ali. Leaning precariously over the edge, he helped another of the men to climb up beside him. Turning, they looked down, not at me but at those just around the corner of the cliff.

"What are they doing?" Cyrus asked curiously.

"Ali and Daoud are lowering ropes. The men below will fasten them to the top of the scaffold. There is no other way of anchoring the structure, since even steel spikes, which we do not have, would be difficult to drive into solid rock. Emerson will tie another rope around his waist as a safety measure. At least I hope he will."

"If he does not, you will remind him," Cyrus said with a smile.

"Certainly. I had better go and make sure."

Before we went on, I turned for another look at the desolate valley behind us and at the cliff that bounded its northern side. The rickety scaffold and those on it were fully exposed to anyone who might be lying in hiding behind the tumbled rocks on the top.

"You and your men are still armed, I observe," I said.

"And will be," Cyrus said grimly. Shading his eyes with his hand, he looked up. "Yep, that would be a good spot for a lookout. I'll send one of the boys, if you'll go back and sit down."

He gave me no opportunity to argue, picking me up and walking with long strides back to the rug. Emerson was already on the scaffold and René was climbing up to join him. Both, I was relieved to observe, wore safety ropes.

The sun rose higher and the shade shrank. Cyrus's foresight had provided even for that; his men rigged a little shelter, with piled-up rocks and canvas stretched over it. By the time the men stopped for food and rest, the temperature was well into the nineties. Of them all, René appeared most exhausted, which was no wonder, since he had been on the scaffold in the boiling sun for several hours.

As the long afternoon wore on without incident, the uneasiness with which I had faced the day ought to have lessened. Instead it mounted, hour by slow hour, until every inch of my skin felt raw and exposed. I was surprised and relieved when Emerson announced that we would stop for the day. It lacked several hours till sunset: I had expected he would go on, as he always did, until the last possible moment.

The announcement was greeted with a universal sigh of thankfulness. Hands on his hips, fresh as ever, Emerson swept scornful eyes over his sweating subordinates and scowled at Kevin, who was reclining gracefully at Bertha's feet.

"Tomorrow you can employ your detectival talents elsewhere," he announced. "You are a nuisance, Mr. O'Connell; listening to you groan and complain distracts me, and unless I miss my guess, you are on the verge of heat prostration. The rest of you aren't much better. We may as well go back."

Ordinarily the dry baking heat of my beloved Egypt is much more to my taste than the climate of my native health. I may have had a little temperature that afternoon. However, I am more inclined to believe that it was nervousness—for Emerson, not myself—that made me feel so warm and miserable. That sensation lessened as we started on the homeward path. I had for once been in error; the danger I expected had not materialized. I reminded myself that it was perfectly in character for Emerson to be distracted from threats to life and limb by an archaeological discovery, but I felt sure he had not abandoned, only postponed, whatever underhanded scheme he had in mind. I would have to watch him closely that night.

Musing thus, endeavoring to anticipate Emerson's next move, lethargic from heat, lulled by the ambling pace of the donkey, I fell into a kind of waking doze. I was not asleep. The donkey must have stumbled, or I would not have come close to pitching head-foremost off its back.

A hand at once steadied me; blinking, I saw Cyrus's face beside me. "Hang on a little longer, my dear," he said. "We are halfway home."

I looked around. To my right the village of El Til huddled among the palm trees. A faint breeze from the river carried the scent of the cooking fires. The swollen molten orb of the sun hung low over the western cliffs; Akhenaton's god, the living Aton, was about to leave the world to darkness and a sleep like death. But he would rise again as he had risen thousands upon thousands of times, to fill every land with his love and waken every living creature to praise his coming.

I am often given to poetic fancies. I could have wished they had not come upon me at that particular time, however. They cost me several precious seconds.

Bertha rode beside me, silent as a statue. The donkeys had drawn ahead of the weary men. I saw them coming along behind us in a ragged procession. Kevin was among the last stragglers; his fiery hair blazed in the rays of the declining sun. Charlie walked beside him, slowing his steps to those of his limping friend. René...

I snatched the reins from Cyrus and brought the poor donkey to a sudden halt. "Where is he?" I cried. "Where is Emerson?"

"He is coming," Cyrus answered. "Just behind. He and Abdullah stopped to—"

"Abdullah. I don't see him either. Or your two guards. Or the cat!" The truth, the terrible truth, struck like a bolt of electricity. "Curse you, Cyrus," I cried. "How dare you? I will never forgive you for this!"

I much regretted having to knock him down, but I would never have got away from him otherwise. He was trying to pull the reins from my hand when my parasol struck his arm away. In avoiding a second blow he tripped over his feet and fell. I dug my heels into the donkey's side.

I think it was my scream of pain that inspired the donkey to rapid motion; I had forgotten I was wearing only a slipper on the injured foot. Since no one but the donkey could hear me I allowed myself to use a few expressions I had learned from Emerson. They helped to relieve my feelings, but not a great deal.

They had all conspired against me—Cyrus, Abdullah, and of course Emerson. It was small consolation to know that it had taken all three to get the better of me. How long had they been planning this? Since the previous night, at least; the expedition today had been designed only to put me off the track and wear me out so that by the end of that long tiring day my vigilance would relax. I ground my teeth. What a dastardly, unsportsmanlike trick!

I have never struck an animal and I did not do so on this occasion. The sound of my voice crying "*Yalla! Yalla!*" was spur enough. Ears back, the little donkey thundered on at a speed it had probably never attained before. Like all the donkeys on all my expeditions, it had been given good care since it came into my hands, and now kindness had borne useful fruit, as the Scripture assures us it must.

As I rode I strained my eyes in the hope of seeing a moving form among the foothills. I saw nothing; the uneven terrain offered ample opportunity for concealment, and his dusty clothing would blend with the pale shade of the rocks. He had gone that way, I felt certain, following the curve of the bow while the rest of the group headed straight south along the royal road. I could only guess at his ultimate destination, but I knew his purpose as clearly as if I had heard him proclaim it. Somehow, by some means that eluded me, he had arranged for an encounter with our deadly enemy.

I hoped to head him off before he got to wherever he was going. The donkeys had walked slowly; Emerson's pace could equal theirs, even over rough ground. By cutting across the plain at an angle, I intended my path to intersect his, not at the point where I judged he must be at this moment, but at some point ahead of where he would be when I arrived. He could not be far from his intended destination now; even Emerson would not be fool enough to tackle such a dangerous foe in darkness. At least Abdullah was with him, and two armed men. Perhaps the situation was not so desperate as I had feared. Nevertheless, I did not regret my action. Emerson's impulsive nature requires the restraint of a cooler individual.

I expected there would be pursuit, but I did not look back. My eyes were fixed on the cliffs, which were rapidly drawing nearer, and as I realized where I was headed a hand seemed to grip my heart and squeeze it. To the left a row of dark rectangles broke the glowing pink of the sunset-brightened cliffs. They were the entrances to the northern tombs, the final resting places of the nobles of Akhenaton's court. To the right, not far distant, was the entrance to the royal wadi. Was it that ill-omened place Emerson had selected for the setting of the last act of the drama?

No, it was not. The entrance was some distance away when I saw him. For once he was wearing his pith helmet, so even the distinctive black hair was concealed. It was a cloud of smoke that betrayed his presence. Perched comfortably on a rock, he was smoking his pipe and watching my approach. Perched comfortably on a nearby rock was the cat Anubis, watching Emerson. On the ground at Emerson's feet was a rifle.

Rising, he brought the donkey to a stop by tearing the reins out of my hand. "'Ubiquitous' is certainly one word for you," he said. "'Inopportune' is another that comes to mind."

I was not deceived by the calm of his voice, for it had the low purring note that indicates Emerson's really serious rages, as opposed to his little fits of temper. His eyes moved from my face to that of the rider who was bearing down upon us. Cyrus must have taken Bertha's donkey. I hoped he had not whipped the poor thing, to come so fast.

"Can't I trust you to carry out the simplest assignment, Vandergelt?" Emerson inquired.

Cyrus dismounted. "I will tie her to the donkey. Hold her hands while——"

I brandished my parasol. "The first man who lays a hand on me or the donkey——"

"It is too late," Emerson said. "He, or one of his men, is behind that ridge just north of us. There is another one to the south. It is a safe assumption that they are armed, and you would be a tempting target on the open plain. He let you approach unharmed so that he could gather us all into his little trap before he pulled the strings tight."

He rose to his feet, stretching. "Get down," I exclaimed.

"Neither of them can get us in their line of fire without exposing themselves to Abdullah or one of Vandergelt's men," Emerson said. "That was one reason I selected this spot. Another reason..." He turned. "Behind that little spur of rock there is the entrance to a cave. When I first discovered it some years ago I thought it might be a tomb, but it was never—"

The sharp crack of a rifle interrupted his lecture and cast some doubt on the accuracy of his assessment of our present situation. Stone chips spattered down from the cliff. Some must have struck the poor donkey; with a terrified bray he bolted, tearing the reins from my hand. The other donkey followed. Pausing only long enough to snatch up the rifle, Emerson ran, pushing me ahead of him.

Behind the spur of rock he had indicated there gaped not one but a dozen cracks and fissures, at least three of which were wide enough to admit a human form. Through one of these, which appeared no different from the others, Emerson propelled me. Cyrus was close behind.

The space within was roughly circular and approximately ten feet in diameter. It narrowed toward the back like a funnel and went on into darkness; how far, I could not see.

Emerson whirled to face Cyrus. "Abdullah was supposed to be covering that fellow," he said in an ominous growl. "Where are your men, Vandergelt?"

A series of shots struck the cliff face nearby. There was no answering fire.

Emerson drew a long breath. "Well, well. I suppose this weapon you kindly lent me . . . ? Yes, I see. One bullet in the chamber. A poetic touch, that. I ought to use it on you."

Cyrus stepped forward till the muzzle of the gun touched his breast. The light was almost gone; I could see only their outlines as they faced one another.

"That is not important now," Cyrus said coolly. "What matters—" He gestured at me.

"Hmmm, yes." Emerson leaned the rifle against the wall and flexed his hands. "There is another way out of here."

"What?" Cyrus cried eagerly.

"Oh, come, man, you don't suppose I would be stupid enough to lead us into a dead end? I had this in mind as a bolt-hole in case my plans went awry. Which," Emerson said caustically, "they certainly have done. The trouble is, the exit tunnel is very narrow. I barely made it through last time. We can only hope it has not been blocked further since."

"What are we waiting for, then?" I demanded. I had not spoken before because my brain was reeling under the impact of the dreadful implications Emerson's speech had contained. Why had not Abdullah and Cyrus's two men returned the fire of our attackers? The rifles all belonged to Cyrus; had the one he had given Abdullah also been rendered ineffective? The suggestion of treachery, from the man I had considered a dear and trusted friend, was almost too much to bear. That treachery had not been directed against me, for Cyrus had not anticipated I would be present. I knew only too well what motive he might have for wishing to betray Emerson.

But this was not the time for retribution. We were all in peril now; escape was the most important consideration. How glad I was that I had rushed to Emerson's side! "What are we waiting for?" I repeated.

"Only this," said Emerson. He took me gently by the shoulder and struck me on the chin with his clenched fist.

When Emerson hits people, he hits as hard as he can, which is quite hard indeed. I presume that being unaccustomed to judging the amount of force necessary in a situation such as this, he underestimated it. I do not suppose I was unconscious for more than a few seconds. He had gathered me up as I fell; when my senses returned I realized that my head lay against his breast, and that he was speaking.

"...if they have not already, that we are unarmed. Someone must hold them off for a while. If you are stuck like a cork in that bloody tunnel when they break in..."

"Yes, I understand."

"You should be able to squeeze through, your shoulders are a trifle narrower than mine. If you cannot, try to block the tunnel from the other side. And take that damned parasol away from her or she will batter her way back out."

Cyrus said quietly, "If I cannot get through, I will return and fight with you."

"The more fool you, then," said Emerson rudely. "Take her, man, and go."

Needless to say, I had no intention of permitting such a scheme. I knew I must bide my time, however; if I indicated my intention to Emerson he would hit me again, perhaps harder. I preferred to take my chances with Cyrus. My parasol hung from my wrist, held by its little strap. I lay limp and unmoving as Emerson transferred me to Cyrus's arms. I had thought he might give me a last, lingering embrace before doing so, but he did not, possibly because another bullet striking nearer the entrance sprayed the interior of the cave with stone pellets.

Emerson had not been engaging in empty melodrama (though, like all men, he is prone to grandiloquent gestures). He was perfectly confident he could hold off any number of armed men single-handed. And he had the effrontery to lecture *me* about overconfidence! If we could survive long enough, there was a good chance of rescue. Whatever Cyrus's intention (and I could not believe Emerson's accusation was true; there must be some mistake!) he was now in danger too, and his men would not abandon him. Not if they wanted to be paid, at any rate. René and Charles had seen him follow me; our loyal men would hasten to my aid even before they heard the ominous echo of gunfire. Yes, they would come. And we—all three of us—could defend the narrow entrance to the cave until they did.

Stygian darkness wrapped round us as soon as Cyrus passed into the tunnel. It was narrow, but the ceiling was high enough to permit him to walk upright, at least at the beginning. I knew when it grew lower because Cyrus reeled back with a cry when his head hit it.

This seemed an opportune moment. I did not want to wait until we got into some space too confined to permit easy movement. Taking a firm grip on my parasol I stiffened, straightened my lower limbs, and slipped neatly out of his grasp. Between the bump on the head and the suddenness of my movement he was caught off guard; I was able to slide past him and proceed quickly on my way. I was vaguely aware that my foot hurt like blazes, but it did not slow my pace. Being by now accustomed to the vagaries of pockets and pistols, I was able to extract the latter from the former without difficulty.

I had not gone far when I heard voices, and the calm, measured tones, the absence of any sound of altercation, surprised me so that I slowed my impetuous pace. Was it rescue, so soon? I must make certain before I fired my pistol that I did not injure a friend. Pausing at the end of the tunnel, I peered cautiously out into the cave.

He carried a lantern in one hand, and in the other, the right hand, he held an object that explained the need for light. It is difficult to be sure of hitting a rapidly moving target in total darkness, particularly when the target is intent on hitting you. The object was not a rifle; it was a hand weapon of some sort. I am no authority on pistols. All I could see was that it was a great deal larger than mine.

Vincey's golden locks were a trifle windblown; otherwise he was as neat and composed as he had been on that fateful night in Cairo when I first met him. The ugly angle of his jaw softened as he smiled.

"Don't try to reach your weapon," he said pleasantly.

Emerson glanced at the rifle, which lay on the floor a few feet away. "It is empty."

"I surmised as much from the fact that you did not return our fire. It might have taken me a while to find your hiding place if Anubis had not kindly led me to it. You were wise to propose a truce, though I must warn you not to expect that anything to your advantage will arise from it."

"Ah, well, one never knows," said Emerson. His eyes went to the cat, which stood midway between the two men, its eyes moving from one to the other and its tail bristling. "I thought you would be unable to resist my invitation, Vincey. I observed the childish pleasure you derive from gloating over people."

Vincey's smile broadened. "I hope you aren't going

to claim you did not accept my carefully prepared alibi. Hindsight, my dear Emerson, surely."

His back against the rough wall to my right, Emerson watched the other man intently. "You must take me for a fool," he said with a curl of his lip. "I saw a great deal of you during those days when I was your guest. How many pleasant hours of conversation did we enjoy, you lounging in that tasteless overstuffed chair and me in—a less comfortable position? I could hardly be mistaken as to your identity. How did you manage to involve von Bork in this dirty business?"

"That sickly little wife of his is in need of medical attention," was the reply. "Sentimentality is weakness; a clever man knows how to use it to his advantage."

A hand grasped my arm. I shook it off. There was nothing Cyrus could do now. He knew if he tried to seize me I would struggle, and that would betray our presence to the smiling blackguard with the very large gun.

Emerson shook his head. "You have played your hand well in the past, I admit, but you have already lost this latest move. My friends are on their way. You cannot hope to carry me away from here before they—"

"I fear you do not understand. The rules of the game have changed. I am no longer in need of the information I hoped to get from you. When I leave this place you won't be coming with me."

"Hmmm." Emerson rubbed his chin. "I always thought of you as a practical sort of fellow, Vincey. If you have what you want, why risk your neck chasing after me?"

Vincey's smile widened till it stretched the muscles of his face into a ghastly grimace. "Because you would continue to risk yours to prevent me from carrying out my plan. I can't have you breathing down my neck for the rest of my life. I admit I will derive a certain personal pleasure—call it sentimentality if you like—from killing you. You defied me, you defeated my deadliest schemes— and worst of all, you had the audacity to patronize me when I was down and out!" His voice rose in pitch. "I am going to do this slowly. The first bullet in the leg, I think. Then an arm—or perhaps the other leg—"

I had only delayed because I was curious about what he had to say. Aiming with care, I pulled the trigger.

Emerson prudently dropped to the floor. The bullet hit Vincey in the left arm. He let the lantern fall, but the wound must have been slight, for with a violent oath he swung around and pointed the gun in my direction. I pointed mine in his direction, but something spoiled my aim; it must have been Cyrus, plucking at me, or the fact that a bullet hit the wall beside me, causing me to start. My next two shots, fired in rapid succession, went wild. One of them, I was distressed to observe, struck the floor quite close to Emerson's outstretched hand, causing him to swear loudly and pull his hand back. I fired again—and heard the hammer fall on an empty chamber. I had forgotten to refill the pistol after Emerson used it to summon help.

There was nothing for it but direct attack. I burst out of the mouth of the tunnel, straight at Vincey. Unfortunately the same idea had occurred to Emerson. We collided heavily; as we toppled, he twined his arms around me and tried to turn me so he would be on top. Again, our minds worked as one. My efforts succeeded; I landed on top of *him*, and strove to shield his body with mine.

It was a little difficult to keep track of what was happening, for I was busily occupied in trying to protect Emerson, who kept squirming. Vincey had been somewhat confused, I believe, by the rapidity and apparent randomness of our actions. He hesitated for a perceptible moment before taking careful aim.

I closed my eyes and clung to Emerson. We would die in one another's arms, as he had once proposed. The idea did not appeal to me any more now than it had on that occasion.

The echoes of the shot deafened me. It took me some time to realize I was still breathing—unhurt, unwounded—and that there had been two shots, so close together the reports had blended into one. I opened my eyes.

Directly in front of me was Emerson's arm. His elbow was braced against the floor; in his hand was the rifle, which pointed up at an oblique angle; on the trigger was his finger.

Now I understood why Emerson had lured his foe into the cave and left the weapon lying on the floor, as if useless to him. There had been only one bullet. He had certainly employed it in the most effective manner possible.

Pushing me away, he rose to his feet. I rolled over and sat up, my ears still ringing from the noise, my head in a whirl. When one has resigned oneself to death, it takes a while to get used to being alive.

Vincey lay crumpled on the floor, in a spreading pool of gore. Another man lay close by. He lay on his back; Vincey's bullet—the one meant for us—had struck him square in the breast and flung him backward. The lantern light lay gently on his still face and quiet, outflung, empty hands.

CHAPTER 16

"The combination of physical strength and moral sensibility, combined with tenderness of heart, is exactly what is wanted in a husband."

Too late!" I cried, wringing my hands. "He gave his life for us! Oh, Charlie, if you had only come five minutes sooner!"

It was not so long as that, in fact, before our rescuers arrived. Charlie had been the first to enter; now he knelt, head bowed, by the body of his kindly patron. His grief was so genuine I much regretted having suspected him.

"I doubt it would have mattered," Emerson said. "At the first sound of your approach, Vincey would have acted, and the result would probably have been the same."

"You are right," I said. "Forgive me, Charlie. I was so fond of him; and you see, he gave his life for—What did you say, Emerson?"

"Nothing," said Emerson.

Charlie rose slowly to his feet. His face was drawn

with pain and sorrow. I reiterated my apology. He tried to smile. "I will always feel the same regret, ma'am. You can leave him to us, now—to me and René. You look in pretty sad shape yourself. Go along, why don't you, and console Abdullah; he was trying to fight two fellows with rifles the last time I saw him."

We removed Abdullah from his victims; they had only been trying to defend themselves, and they fled as soon as they were able. "Explanations will be forthcoming in due time, Abdullah," I said soothingly. "It was all a mistake."

"So long as you came to no harm," Abdullah muttered. Since it was too dark to see clearly, he so forgot himself as to run anxious hands over Emerson's frame, and would have done the same to me, I daresay, had not propriety prevailed.

Our loyal men fought for the privilege of carrying me, so I allowed them to do it in turn. Emerson did not offer; the cat in his arms, he stamped along in such a brown study that he did not even seem to hear Abdullah's persistent questions. Finally I said, "We will tell you the whole story later, Abdullah, after we have rested. Be content now with knowing that it is over. Er—it is over, isn't it, Emerson? Emerson!"

"What? Oh. Yes, I think so. There were others involved, only too many of them; but most were Vincey's dupes or hired thugs. He was the mainspring. Now that he is gone, I believe we have nothing more to fear."

"Did you kill him, O Father of Curses?" Abdullah asked eagerly.

"Yes," said Emerson.

"It is good," said Abdullah.

Not until we reached the *Nefertiti* did Emerson lower Anubis to the ground and take me from the arms of Daoud, whose turn it was. "Rest and eat, my friends," he said. "We will come to you later."

Anubis preceded us up the gangplank. As I watched him trot briskly along, quite ready, as it appeared, to abandon his dead master without the slightest show of regret or remorse, I could almost share Abdullah's superstitious fear of the creature. "Vincey had trained him to respond to a whistle," I said softly. "That is how he was able to abduct you. And tonight—"

"Tonight he responded as *I* had trained him," Emerson said. "I did not set out to kill Vincey, though I was prepared to do so if there was no other choice. He had begun to annoy me. I would rather have taken him alive, however, and I expected he would follow the cat when it followed me."

"Trained him?" I exclaimed. "How?"

"Chicken," said Emerson. Stopping in front of my door, he extended one hand and turned the knob. "And, of course, the effect of my charismatic personality."

The steward had lit the lamps. As the door opened I let out a cry; for facing me was a pair of dim but dreadful forms, their garments in tatters, their red-rimmed eyes staring wildly, their haggard faces gray with dust.

It was our reflection in the tall pier glass. Emerson nudged the cat aside, kicked the door shut, deposited me on the bed, and collapsed beside me with a heartfelt groan. "Are we getting old, Peabody? I feel somewhat fatigued."

"Oh, no, my dear," I replied absently. "Anyone would be weary after such a day."

Emerson sat up. "Your protestations do not convince me. Let me put it to the test." And, seizing me in a firm grip, he crushed me to him and brought his mouth down on mine.

He went on kissing me for quite a long time, adding other demonstrations that almost distracted me from the astonishing realization that had burst explosively into my dazed brain. Finally I succeeded in freeing my lips long enough to gasp, "Emerson! Do you realize that I am—"

"My wife?" Emerson removed himself a short distance. "I certainly hope so, Peabody, because if you are not, what I am about to do is possibly illegal, certainly immoral, and probably not becoming an English gentleman. Damn these damned buttonholes, they are always too—"

The blouse was ruined in any case.

Sometime later (quite some time later, in fact) I murmured, "When was it that you remembered, Emerson?"

His arm encircled me and my head rested on his breast, and I felt that Heaven could hold no greater bliss. (Though I would only admit to such an unorthodox opinion in the pages of this private journal.) We were in perfect amity and would always remain so; for how could discord mar such understanding?

"It was a memorable moment," Emerson replied. "Seeing you come tearing along, waving that absurd little pistol, without the slightest regard for your own safety...And then you spoke the words that broke the spell: 'Another shirt ruined!'"

"Oh, Emerson, how unromantic! I would have

thought—" I flung his arm away and sat up. He reached
for me; I scrambled back on hands and knees. "Curse
you, Emerson!" I exclaimed passionately. "That was
days and days and days ago! Do you mean you kept me
dangling in limbo, suffering agonies of doubt, fearing
the worst, for days and days and days and—"

"Now, Peabody, calm yourself." Emerson pulled
himself to a sitting position and leaned back against the
pillows. "It was not so simple as that. Come here and I
will explain."

"No explanation can possibly suffice," I cried. "You
are the most—"

"Come here, Peabody," said Emerson.

I went.

After an interval Emerson began his explanation.
"That moment of revelation literally staggered me; it
was as stunning as an electric shock, and as brief. For
the next few days fragments of forgotten memories
kept coming back, but it required several days to put
all the pieces together and fix them in place. To say I
was in a state of confusion is to understate the case. You
will admit, I believe, that the situation was somewhat
complex."

"Well..."

"The same could be said, of course, of all the situations you have managed to get us into," Emerson went
on. I could not see his face from the position I occupied
at that time, but I could tell from his voice that he was
smiling. "In this case it seemed wiser to keep my own
counsel until I had got things straight in my mind. I
often had trouble doing that even when I did not have
amnesia to contend with."

"Your sense of humor, my dear, is one of your most attractive characteristics. At the present time, however—"

"Quite right, my dear Peabody. This delightful interlude cannot be prolonged; there are a number of loose ends to be tied up. Let me be brief. The loyalty of at least one of our companions was in serious doubt. The only people I felt certain I could trust were you and Abdullah—and our other men, of course. To confide in either of you would have been to endanger you and confuse the situation even further—were that possible."

He stopped speaking and—did something else. Greatly as I enjoyed the sensation, I recognized one of Emerson's old tricks of distraction. His explanation had been glib and quite unconvincing.

However, his reminder of the stern duties yet to be faced had a sobering effect; firmly though reluctantly I withdrew from his embrace.

"How selfish is joy," I said sadly. "I had almost forgotten poor, noble Cyrus. I must help Charlie and René make the necessary arrangements. Then there are our dear ones in England to be reassured, and Kevin O'Connell to be threatened into silence, and...so many things. You must write to Ramses at once, Emerson. Er—you remember Ramses, I trust?"

"Ramses," said Emerson, with a chuckle, "was the most difficult of all my memories to assimilate. On the face of it, my dear, our son is fairly unbelievable. Don't be concerned; I have already written to him."

"What? When? How did you...Curse it, Emerson, was it you who searched my room? I ought to have known; no one else would make such a mess."

"I had to know what was happening to our family,

Amelia. I was suspicious enough earlier to take the precaution of warning Walter, but as my memory returned I became deeply concerned about them. Ramses's letters touched me a great deal; I could not leave the poor lad fretting about my fate."

"You left me fretting," I snapped. "Just tell me one thing before we rise and fight again, so to speak. When you kissed me in the tomb—"

"It wasn't the first time I kissed you in a tomb," said Emerson, grinning. "Perhaps it was the ambience that snapped my self-control. I was a trifle put out with you, Peabody. You frightened me half to death."

"I was well aware of that. And *you* were well aware of our relationship, don't try to tell me you were not. Yet you—you...You never kissed me like *that* before!"

"Ah," said Emerson, "but you enjoyed it, didn't you?"

"Well...Emerson, I am seriously annoyed with you. You enjoyed it too, didn't you? Bullying me, taunting me, insulting me—"

"It had a certain titillation," Emerson admitted. "Like the days of our youth, eh, Peabody? And I confess I did enjoy being wooed again. Not that your methods of winning a man's heart are exactly...Peabody, stop that! You really are the most—"

Between laughter, fury, and another emotion that need not be described, I had quite lost control of myself. How matters would have developed I do not know, for a knock on the door interrupted them just as they were becoming interesting. Swearing, Emerson went into concealment in the bathroom; I assumed the first garment that came to hand and went to the door.

The sight of René's sad face sobered me. He was

attempting to control his grief with manly fortitude, but it was clear to sensitive eyes like mine.

"Forgive me for disturbing you," he said. "But I felt you would want to know. We are taking him to Luxor, Mrs. Emerson. He had expressed his desire to be buried there, near the Valley of the Kings, where he had spent the happiest years of his life. We must leave at once if we are to catch the train from Cairo. You understand the need to avoid delay..."

I did understand, and appreciated the delicacy with which he had expressed this unpalatable fact. I wiped away a tear. "I must say good-bye to him, René. He gave his life—"

"Yes, dear madam, but I fear there is no time. It is better this way. He would want you to remember him as—as he was." René's lips trembled. He turned away to hide his face.

"We will follow, then, as soon as we are able," I said, patting his shoulder. "His friends must be notified; they will wish to attend the memorial service. I will speak a few words, on that beautiful and appropriate theme: 'Greater love hath no man than this, that a man lay down his life for his friends.'"

René faced me. "Leave everything to us, madam. You will stay at the Castle, I presume, when you are in Luxor? I feel certain Mr. Vandergelt would want that."

"Very well." I gave him my hand. With a graceful Gallic gesture he raised it to his lips.

"Mes hommages, chère madame. Adieu, et bonne chance."

*   *   *

I knew our little group would be sadly reduced in number that evening, but I did not expect to find the saloon deserted except for Kevin. He was scribbling in his beastly notebook, of course. When he saw me he made a feeble attempt to rise.

"Sit down," I said, doing so myself. "And don't pretend to be overcome with exhaustion or grief."

"I am grieved about poor old Vandergelt," Kevin said. "But if a man has to go—and all men do—that was how he would have wished it to be. 'Greater love hath no man—'"

"You will no doubt quote that in your story," I said severely. "We must discuss that, Kevin. But where is everyone?"

"René and Charlie have left for Derut, with—"

"Yes, I know. What about Bertha?"

"In her room, I suppose. I asked for the pleasure of a conversation with her, but she put me off. As for your—er—the professor—"

"He is here," I said, as Emerson entered.

To my fond eyes he had never appeared handsomer. His damp hair lay in shining waves; only the ugly half-healed scar marred the perfection of his chiseled features. With a smile at me and a scowl at Kevin he went to the sideboard. "The usual, Peabody?" he inquired.

"If you please, my dear. We might drink a toast, to absent friends and love passing the love of—"

"Watch your tongue, Peabody. That cursed journalist is writing down every word."

He handed me my glass and then confronted Kevin, whose jaw had dropped and whose eyes were popping. "I want to see your story before you send it off, O'Connell. If it contains anything libelous I will break both your arms."

Kevin swallowed. "You—you have just destroyed my lead, Professor. You have regained your memory!"

"Is that the absurd tale that is making the rounds? How interesting. I wonder how much the courts will award me in damages when I sue the lot of you."

"But I never—believe me, sir—" Kevin stammered, trying to cover the paper with his elbows.

"Good," said Emerson, baring his teeth. "Now, Mr. O'Connell, I am going to give you your next dispatch. You may take notes," he added graciously.

It was, I confess, as neat a lie as I might have composed. Emerson omitted all references to the Forth affair, describing Vincey as "another of those old enemies who keep cropping up." His vivid descriptions of our various thrilling encounters with Vincey kept Kevin scribbling furiously. "So," Emerson concluded, "having tired of his attentions, I lay in wait for him this evening, with the assistance of Abdullah and two of Mr. Vandergelt's guards, whom he kindly lent me. Vandergelt was supposed to keep Mrs. Emerson out of the way. That did not succeed, thanks to her inveterate habit of—"

"'Love gave her insight into her adored spouse's intention,'" Kevin muttered, his pen driving across the page. "'And devotion lent wings to her steed as she rushed headlong....'"

"If you dare print that, Kevin," I said, "*I* will break both your arms."

"Hrmph," said Emerson loudly. "Let me finish. Owing to an unavoidable—er—misapprehension on the part of my assistants, Vincey was able to get past them and enter the cave where we had taken refuge. A slight altercation ensued, in the course of which Vincey shot Vandergelt. I was—er—unable to reach my own weapon in time to prevent it, but my bullet reached its target a moment later."

"A bit terse and flat," Kevin muttered. "Never mind; I can fill in the details. So what was the fellow's motive, Professor?"

"Revenge," said Emerson, folding his arms. "For an old, fancied injury."

"'Years of brooding over an old, fancied injury had driven him mad...' You wouldn't care to be more explicit? No," Kevin muttered. "I see you would not. And the attacks on Mrs. E.?"

"Revenge," Emerson repeated firmly.

"Yes, of course. 'Knowing that no dart could strike deeper into that devoted heart than danger to his...' Yes, that's the stuff. I can reel that off by the page."

"You are incorrigible, Mr. O'Connell," said Emerson, unable to repress a smile. "Remember I insist on seeing it before you send it off. Come along, Peabody, I promised Abdullah we would talk to him."

The story Emerson told our men was quite different. It was like coming home again, to perch on a packing case on the deck with the men gathered around, smoking and listening, with occasional "Wahs!" and murmurs of amazement interrupting the tale. The stars shone brightly overhead; the soft breeze stirred Emerson's hair.

Some of what Emerson said was new to me as well. He had had an advantage over me, of course, having "enjoyed" Vincey's hospitality so long, as he put it. And when I thought of that despicable villain, lounging at ease in his comfortable chair and gloating over his suffering prisoner, I only regretted that Emerson had despatched him so quickly. I had observed the incongruity of that article of furniture in the foul kennel where Emerson had been imprisoned; but not until I heard the note in Emerson's voice when he referred to it did I fully comprehend how so harmless an object as a red plush armchair could become a symbol of subtle and insidious cruelty. I would never be able to sit in one that color again.

Vincey's alibi had been wholly convincing to me. The written evidences of his residence in Syria had been forged, of course, but even if I had questioned them I would not have got around to checking their validity until it was too late. Nor had I Emerson's reason for doubting poor Karl von Bork (I reminded myself I must inquire after Mary and see how I could be of assistance to her), especially when Bertha confirmed . . .

"What?" I cried, when Emerson reached this part of his narrative. "Bertha was Vincey's spy all along?"

"One up for me," Emerson remarked with a self-satisfied smile and a vulgar gesture.

"But her bruises—her courageous gesture in throwing herself at the door of your cell to prevent the guard from entering—"

"She was only trying to get out," Emerson said. "She wanted no part of murder and she was frantic to escape. Seeing you come popping down out of the ceiling like a demon in a pantomime was enough to throw anyone into a panic. I myself was—"

"Please, Emerson," I said with as much dignity as I could command. It was not much; the horrid little creature had fooled me completely. I wanted to squirm when I remembered telling her she should overcome her squeamishness. Squeamishness! It must have been she, then, who drove the knife into Mohammed.

"Yes," Emerson said, when I expressed this opinion. "She was as deadly and sly as a snake. Small wonder, when you think of the life she has led."

"I suppose her sad story of being thrown into poverty by the death of her father was a lie, too," I said, clenching my teeth.

"Oh, is that what she told you? I fear her—er—career began much earlier, Peabody; she had been Vincey's companion for several years. One of his companions...As for her bruises, they were all paint and padding. Weren't your suspicions aroused when she refused your medical attention and kept her face hidden until the supposed injuries could heal?"

"Oh, curse it," I said. Abdullah had concealed his face behind his sleeve and several of the younger men were snickering audibly. "Was that why you went to... Never mind."

"I had set out to win her over early on," Emerson said. His voice was quite serious. "By appealing, not to her better nature, but to her self-interest. She is a brilliantly clever young woman, with no more morals than a cat. Vincey was only the latest of her—er—associates. Affection had nothing to do with those relationships; she has changed allegiance as often as expediency dictated, seeking, I rather imagine, a man whose amoral intelligence was the equal of her own. Women are sadly handicapped in criminal activities, as in all others; society makes it difficult for them to employ their natural talents without the assistance of a male partner. I fear, Peabody, that your honorable and forthright character limits you when it comes to dealing with such persons. You always try to bring out the hidden virtues in people. Bertha had none."

I let him enjoy his triumph, though of course he was mistaken. I remembered the expression on the girl's face when she said, "How you must love him." It had not been one of contempt or sneering amusement. She had been touched; I knew it. And I did not doubt that Emerson's splendid attributes—of character, I mean—had softened her as they had affected so many other women.

"She carried your message to Vincey, then," I said. "When you informed him you would be at the rendezvous tonight."

"Rendezvous," Emerson repeated throughtfully. "It certainly was, wasn't it? You are correct, Peabody. She had never lost touch with him. Several of the villagers were in his employ; all she had to do was slip a note to Hassan or Yusuf when we passed through the village. While we were in the royal wadi she communicated with him by leaving messages in a selected spot not far from our camp. One of the villagers served as post-boy; those rascals know every inch of the cliffs and can creep in and out and up and down unobserved.

"I did not succeed in convincing her that she would be better off with us than with Vincey until after we returned to the dahabeeyah yesterday. She...What are you smirking about, Peabody?"

"Nothing, my dear. Do go on."

"Hmmph," said Emerson. "I laid the whole case before her and promised her immunity if she joined us, and imprisonment if she did not. The message she passed on this morning did not incriminate her; it was only a notification to Vincey that I would be along the northern cliffs this evening."

"But," said Abdullah, who was not especially interested in the evil machinations of women, much less their reformation, "why did the men who were supposed to defend you take me prisoner instead? Were they also in the evil man's pay? For surely Vandergelt Effendi would not—"

"That is right, Abdullah," I said. "Emerson, I believe we had better go now. You have not eaten, and you must be very tired."

Emerson took my hint. It was not a subject I cared to discuss. With the memory of Cyrus's sacrifice so fresh in my mind I would not, could not, think of how close he had brought us to disaster. I knew the motive that had prompted him to commit the one ignoble gesture of his noble life, and I blamed myself for failing to realize the depth of his feelings for me. It must have been my rejection that had driven him to madness. Temporary insanity was the kindest and most likely explanation for his betrayal of Emerson—which he had redeemed with his life.

Bertha did not come to dinner. When we went to look for her, we found her room empty and her few possessions missing. Inquiry produced the information that a woman of her description—which would, I admit, have fit most of the women in the village—had hired a boat to take her across the river several hours earlier.

To my surprise Emerson was not—or at least he put up a good pretense of not being—surprised. If I must be candid, which I always endeavor to be (at least in the pages of this private journal), it was a relief to have her off my hands. How much of an obligation we owed her was questionable; if one balanced the evil against the good, I doubted the debt would have been in her favor. She was a woman and she had been much tried; but really, as I pointed out to Emerson, it would have been hard to find a suitable career for such a person.

"Hmmm," said Emerson, fingering the cleft in his chin. "I rather suspect, Peabody, that she has found a suitable career by herself."

He refused to elaborate on this enigmatic remark, so I did not pursue it for fear of provoking sentiments that might mar the activities I had planned for the remainder of the evening.

Thanks to the assiduous assistance of Cyrus's steward, we were able to catch the afternoon train the following day. He salaamed profoundly when we thanked him and bade him farewell, and I assured him that if he required a recommendation I would be happy to render him the praise his excellent service deserved. It was sad to say farewell to the *Nefertiti*. I doubted I would see her like again, for as I have said, such elegant sailing vessels were fading from the scene.

Emerson slept a good deal of the way, with Anubis curled up on the seat beside him. We appeared to have acquired another cat. The creature followed Emerson as devotedly as Bastet did Ramses, and I knew my husband's sentimental nature well enough to be certain he would not abandon the animal—especially when it showed him such flattering attention. Anubis's change of allegiance was not a sign of cold-blooded self-interest; it demonstrated an intelligent appreciation of Emerson's superior character. I wondered what Bastet would make of the newcomer. The possibilities were somewhat alarming.

But there was little room in my heart that day for dark forebodings. I had brought a book from Cyrus's excellent library, but I read very little; it was pleasure enough watching the rise and fall of my husband's breast, listening to his deep sonorous breathing, and occasionally yielding to the temptation to stroke the lines of weariness that yet marked his face. Whenever I did, Emerson would mutter "Cursed flies!" and swat at my hand. At such moments the happiness that filled me was well-nigh unendurable. Soon our loved ones at home would know the same happiness; we had dispatched telegrams early that morning with messages of undying affection and assurances that all was well.

Night had spread her sable wings over the ancient city when we arrived. We hired a carriage to take us directly to the Castle. As it rattled away I looked back and saw, or thought I saw, a familiar form dart into the shadows. But no, I told myself, it could not have been. Kevin had left several hours before us, to catch the up-train to Cairo.

The carriage lamps shone dimly through the dark. The slow plodding of the horse's hooves formed a fitting accompaniment to my melancholy thoughts. It was difficult to imagine the Castle, in which Cyrus had taken such pride, without him. Every room, every passageway, would be haunted by a tall, kindly ghost. I fancied Emerson must feel the same; in respect for my feelings he remained thoughtfully silent, holding my hand in his.

I assumed René had notified the servants of our imminent arrival, and indeed we were greeted by the majordomo as welcome and expected guests. Bowing, he led the way; but when I realized where he was taking us, I stopped.

"I cannot face it, Emerson. Not the library—not tonight. We spent so many hours together in that room, his favorite..."

But Anubis had preceded us along the hall, and the servant threw the door open. The scent of smoke—the smoke of a fine cigar—reached my nostrils. From a deep leather chair near the long table, with its scattering of books and periodicals, a man rose. Cheroot, goatee, beautifully tailored linen suit... It was the ghost of Cyrus Vandergelt, exactly as he had appeared in life.

I did not swoon. Emerson claims I did, but he is always trying to find evidence in me of what he calls "proper ladylike" behavior. It is true—and who can blame me?—that my knees gave way and a gray mist swirled before my eyes. When it cleared, I realized that I was seated on the sofa with Emerson slapping my hands and Cyrus bending over me, his goatee quivering with kindly concern.

"Oh, good Gad," I cried...But the Reader can well

imagine the agitated iterations that escaped my lips in the course of the succeeding minutes. The warm clasp of Cyrus's hand assured me it was he, and not his apparition; the application of a mild stimulant restored my customary calm; and before long we were busily satisfying our mutual curiosity.

Cyrus was thunderstruck to discover he was supposed to be deceased. "I only got here an hour ago," he exclaimed. "The servants told me you were expected, which was sure good news, but they didn't tell me I was dead. You'd think one of 'em would have mentioned it. How did I pass on?"

"First we had better hear your story," said Emerson, with an odd glance at me. "Where have you been for the past weeks?"

As I listened, a queer creeping feeling came over me. It was not the first time I had listened to such a tale.

"They snatched me right after I got off the consarned train in Cairo," said Cyrus. "I felt a little jab in my arm—reckoned a mosquito bit me. Then everything went fuzzy. I remember a couple of fellows stuffing me in a carriage, and that was it, till I woke up in what looked like a luxury hotel—bedroom, bathroom, a fancy sitting room with overstuffed chairs and bookshelves. Only difference was, there weren't any handles on the doors."

He had been treated with perfect courtesy, he assured us. The food had been prepared by an excellent chef and served by servants who did everything for him except answer his questions.

"I was beginning to wonder if I'd spend the rest of my life there," Cyrus admitted. "I went to bed as usual last night—I guess it was last night—and if you can believe it, I woke up this morning in a first-class compartment on the Cairo-to-Luxor express. I raised a commotion, as you might expect; the conductor grinned and leered at me and informed me I'd been a little under the weather when my friends put me on the train. They'd handed him my ticket, straight through to Luxor, so that was all right. Folks, I was in something of a daze, I tell you, but I decided I might as well come on here and then try to figure out what was going on. I have a feeling you can tell me."

"I have a feeling we can," said Emerson, glancing at me.

I was bereft of speech. Visibly pleased at being the chosen narrator, Emerson launched into his tale. Not a word, scarcely a breath, was heard until he finished.

"Aw, shucks!" Cyrus gasped. "I tell you flat out, Emerson, I wouldn't believe a yarn like that if anybody else had told it. I don't think I believe it anyhow. How could anybody fool you into thinking he was me? You've known me for years."

I had been studying Cyrus's lean, lined face. The years had not been as kind to my old friend as I had believed. I ought to have known that trim, tall (but not so tall by several inches) body and that remarkably well-preserved face were not his. The goatee had not been his either! How relieved Sethos must have been to dispense with it.

Naturally I put the matter more tactfully. "We had not seen you for several of those years, Cyrus. His imitation of your speech and mannerisms was perfect; he is a natural mimic, and he had several days to study you, from hiding, before he left Cairo. His most useful weapon, however, was psychological. People see what they expect to see—what they have been told they are seeing. And once they have convinced themselves of that belief, no evidence to the contrary can persuade them they are wrong."

"Never mind the psychological mumbo-jumbo, Amelia," Emerson growled. "I suppose, Vandergelt, you do not have individuals named René D'Arcy and Charles H. Holly on your staff?"

"Staff? I don't have one. Hoffman left me last year to work for the Egypt Exploration Fund. I was going to look for an assistant in Cairo. There is a young fellow named Weigall—"

"No, no, he won't do," Emerson exclaimed. "He is not without ability, but his propensity for—"

"Emerson, please don't wander off the subject," I said. "Like Cyrus, I am finding this difficult to credit. Both those pleasant young men were lieutenants of...of..."

Emerson tried very hard to get the words out, but could not manage it. "...of the...of the Master... Er—yes. We ought to have known they were not archaeologists. Holly's fear of heights was suspicious, and neither of them displayed the degree of knowledge they ought to have had; but there are few excavators who are worth a damn these days. I don't know what the field is coming to, what with one thing and...Yes, Peabody, I know; I am wandering from the subject. They were—er—*his* men, as I began to suspect when they hustled him away so precipitately. The crewmen of the dahabeeyah were hired, like the guards."

"Oh, dear," I murmured helplessly. "Cyrus—

Emerson—I do hope you will forgive me, but I am quite beyond sensible thought at this moment. Perhaps we should all have a good night's sleep and discuss this further in the morning."

Cyrus was too much of a gentleman (in his rough-hewn American way) to resist such an appeal. Assuring me that the servants had our rooms prepared, he escorted me to the door. "It has been a busy day for all of us, and no mistake," he said. "Mrs. Amelia, my dear—I hope you believe that I would have been as anxious to serve you as that goldurned rascal appears to have been. Which reminds me—"

"That was what made his masquerade so convincing, Cyrus," I said. "That he acted as you would have done. My dear old friend, this day has brought one happy result. I am so glad, so very glad, that the reports of your death were greatly exaggerated."

As I had hoped, my little joke distracted him, and left him chuckling.

"Good work, Peabody," said Emerson, as we mounted the stairs arm in arm. "But you only postponed the inevitable. Between now and tomorrow morning we had better come up with a good explanation for Sethos's energetic activities for and against us."

"I am not certain I fully comprehend his motives myself," I admitted.

"Then you are either stupid, which I do not believe, or disingenuous, which is equally unlikely," said Emerson coldly. "Would you care to have me explain them?"

"Emerson, if you are going to pretend you knew all along that man was not Cyrus Vandergelt, I may...I may be forced to..."

I did not complete the sentence. Emerson had shut the door of our room behind us. Taking me into his arms, he held me close. It was a sacred moment—a silent but fervent reaffirmation of the vows we had made to one another on that blissful day when we two had become one.

One of the supreme moments in a woman's life must be when she hears from the lips of the man she loves, without prompting or even little hints, the precise words she secretly yearns to hear. (It is also, I believe, a rare occurrence.)

"I loved you from the first, Peabody," Emerson said, his voice muffled against my hair. "Even before I remembered you. From the moment you dropped down from the ceiling brandishing that pistol I knew you were the only woman for me—for even in trousers, my dear, your gender is unmistakable. All those days I was like a man wandering in a mist, seeking something desperately desired..."

"But you did not know what it was," I murmured tenderly.

Emerson held me off at arm's length and scowled at me. "What do you take me for, a moonstruck schoolboy? Of course I knew what it was. Only there seemed no easy or honorable way to get it. For all I knew then, I did have a boring conventional wife and a dozen boring conventional children somewhere in the background. And you certainly did not behave like a conventional wife. Why the devil didn't you pound the truth into my head? Such restraint is not like you, Peabody."

"That was Herr Doktor Schadenfreude," I said. "He insisted..."

After I had explained, Emerson nodded. "Yes, I see.

That fills in the last portion of the puzzle, I think. Shall I tell you how I reconstruct the story?

"To answer the question you asked some time ago—no, I did not know who the devil Vandergelt was. I didn't know who the devil anyone was! As my memories returned I did not even question the fact that he seemed to have grown younger instead of older since I last saw him. I accepted him because you and the others did.

"I did not suspect him then; but long before that, while we were still in Cairo, I had begun to wonder if we had not been assigned a personal guardian angel. Didn't it strike you as curious that we managed to escape so many unpleasant encounters because of the apparently fortuitous appearance of rescuers? The first time, when you were carried off at the masked ball, I managed by sheer good luck...Well, if you insist, my dear Peabody, a certain amount of physical and mental agility on my part brought me back in time to retrieve you from your abductor. That was Vincey, of course. I presume you had informed all our archaeological acquaintances that we were attending the affair? It would not be difficult to search the sûks and find the merchant from whom the famous Sitt Hakim had purchased articles of male attire.

"Our ensuing adventures began to assume quite a different complexion. The police official who led his men into a part of Cairo where the police never go, in time to drive off the hired thugs who had us cornered; the bumbling young German archaeology student who fired a warning shot just when a workman—who could not be found afterward—tried to lure you away with promises of a tomb—which also failed to materialize; the fellow in the sûk, who collapsed and was carried off by his 'friends'—you didn't notice that, did you? I did, and it confirmed my feeling that we ought to get out of Cairo as soon as possible.

"Abdullah told me of the party of drunken young Americans who miraculously appeared on the scene in time to prevent you from being carried off the night Vincey snared me. It became apparent to me that there were two different parties interested in us. One was bent on taking one or both of us captive; he did not seem to care which. The other sought to ward off the attacker, but the fine timing of the incident in which I was taken prisoner indicated it was you alone the guardian angel cared about.

"We will never know the truth, but I feel certain my reconstruction of Sethos's activities is fairly accurate. He had got wind of the Forth affair early on; as we both realized, he was the most likely person to have done so. He—curse it, I hate to give the fellow credit, but I must—he held his hand. He had promised you he would not interfere with you again, and he kept his promise (damn him!) until the moment when he realized that others were after Forth's treasure and that you might be in danger from them. That gave him the excuse he wanted to break his sworn word.

"As soon as news of the attempted abduction at the ball reached him he was on the scene, organizing his men. In one guise or another he must have been watching you day and night. Mind you, he felt no obligation to protect ME. From his point of view the most desirable result of the business would be your survival and my demise; but he was (curse the swine!) honorable enough to refrain from direct action against me. All the attacks on us were instigated by Vincey. Sethos only intervened to protect you from harm. In order to do that he was forced to assist me as well, but he must have prayed to whatever gods he favors that Vincey would succeed in doing away with me.

"At last he got his wish. I was gone, and you, he hoped, were or soon would be a grieving widow. Cyrus Vandergelt, an old and trusted friend, appeared on the scene, overflowing with tender sympathy and very little else. It was due to the efforts of you, my dearest Peabody, and our devoted friend Abdullah, that I survived. I could almost feel sorry for Vandergelt-Sethos; what a blow it must have been to him when you dragged me back into the land of the living!

"He was quick to recover—damn his eyes—and with characteristic ingenuity found a means, as he hoped, to rid himself of me while remaining within the letter if not the spirit of his vow. I must admit Schadenfreude was a brilliant inspiration. There is such a man, I suppose? Yes, but surely it ought to have struck you as a strange coincidence that he happened to be, at that moment, in Luxor? Well, well, I understand; I would have been in the same state of perturbation had our positions been reversed.

"The Schadenfreude who visited me was another of Sethos's confederates, well primed in his role. What an absurd concoction of lunatic theories he presented! The aim, of course, was to keep us apart and antagonistic to one another. Peabody, you adorable idiot, if you had had the sense to—er—force your attentions upon me, as you would probably express it...But I believe I understand the mixture of modesty and quixotic romanticism that prevented you from doing so. Though how you could ever have doubted..."

(A brief interlude interrupted the even course of the narrative.)

"So there we were at Amarna, with Vincey still on our heels and Vandergelt-Sethos wooing you with every device of luxury and devoted attention he could find. It was a pretty contrast to my behavior, I confess! Any sensible woman, my dear, would have given me up as a bad job and accepted the devoted attentions of a youngish, adoring American millionaire. He hoped his wiles would prevail, and he hoped even more that Vincey would succeed in doing away with me. But you remained steadfast. Not only did you repel his advances...at least I hope you did, Peabody, because if I thought you had considered yielding, for even a split second...I will accept your assurances, my dear. Not only did you repel him, you followed me like a devoted hound and risked your life over and over to keep me from the nasty consequences of my reckless behavior. You must have driven Sethos wild.

"At the end he could bear it no longer. You ought to have realized that I had not the slightest suspicion of Vandergelt, or I would not have conspired with him to set up an ambush for Vincey. Even then—confound him!—he refrained from taking direct action against me. However, he did as much as he could to ensure my death without firing the actual shot. The two men he sent with me had been ordered not to interfere with Vincey; they also prevented Abdullah from coming to my assistance. Nor could I have defended myself. As you observed, the rifle he lent me had only one bullet. The significance of that little touch still eludes me. Perhaps I was meant to use it on myself rather than face capture! Or perhaps he expected me to test the weapon; if I had found it was unloaded I might have retreated from a position that was clearly untenable.

"I rather imagine that once Vincey had killed me, the two guards would have dispatched Vincey. A happy ending from Sethos's point of view; with your enemy and your inconvenient husband dead, you would eventually find consolation in the arms of your devoted friend. Sooner or later—if I read his character aright—he would have confessed his true identity and restored Vandergelt to his own place. He could not have continued the masquerade indefinitely, nor would it have suited him to do so. He would have sworn to abandon his criminal activities—told you, as he did once before, that you and you alone could turn him from evil to good...Damn the fellow's vanity!

"Thanks to your inveterate habit of meddling, my dearest Peabody, things did not work out quite as Sethos had planned. I had an inkling of the truth in that moment when we confronted one another, with the evidence of his betrayal of me unmistakable, and his devotion to you equally plain. He did not speak to me as Vandergelt in those last moments. I hope you don't believe, Peabody, that I was making a noble gesture when I handed you over to him. I fully intended to get out of that ambush with a whole skin and beat Vandergelt—or whoever he was—to a pulp.

"At the end...I cannot assess his character fairly. Yet

he attacked, barehanded, an assassin with a rifle, and took the bullet meant for us—for you. Nothing in his life became him like the leaving it.

"In fact," Emerson concluded, "nothing else in his life became him in the slightest. I only hope, my dear Peabody, that you are not in danger of succumbing to that sloppy sentimentality I sometimes observe in you. If I find you have set up a little shrine with fresh flowers and candles, I will smash it to bits."

"As if I would do anything so absurd! Yet he did have a code of honor, Emerson. And surely his last act must atone in some measure—"

Emerson put an end to the discussion in a particularly forceful manner.

Sometime later I lay watching the slow drift of moonlight across the floor and enjoying the most exquisite of sensations. I knew I risked breaking that heavenly mood if I spoke, and yet I felt I must say one more thing. "You must admit that Sethos was capable of inspiring considerable devotion in his subordinates, and that they carried out his last wishes as he would have done—freeing Cyrus and sending him to us in order that our grief might be assuaged at the earliest possible moment. I wonder where they took—"

Emerson's shoulder was by now as rigid as a rock. "You might set up a cenotaph," he suggested with ineffable sarcasm. "A coiled snake, I think, would make an appropriate adornment."

"It is odd you should mention that, Emerson. You remember the little fairy tale I have been translating—'The Tale of the Doomed Prince'?"

"What about it?" Emerson's tone was slightly more

affable, but I had had time to reconsider what I had started to say. He would taunt me for the rest of my life if I admitted to the superstitious fancies I had entertained about that harmless story.

"I think I know how it ended."

"Oh?" Emerson replaced the arm he had withdrawn when I began speaking.

"The princess saved him, of course. Defeating the crocodile and the dog as she had done the snake."

"That is quite an un-Egyptian ending, Peabody." He drew me close. "There are some interesting, if coincidental, parallels in the two cases, though, aren't there? The prince was as reckless and obtuse as a certain other individual I could name, and I have no doubt the brave princess saved his worthless neck as persistently and cleverly as you did mine, my darling. Even the dog... We encountered no crocodiles or snakes, however. Unless Sethos could be considered—"

"My dear." Though every nerve in my body thrilled with rapture at his eloquent and generous tribute, I felt obliged to remonstrate. "We have spoken enough about Sethos. 'De mortuis nil nisi bonum,' you know."

"I don't know, though," Emerson muttered. "I wish I did."

"I don't understand, Emerson."

"Good," said Emerson.

Before I could inquire further he proceeded to institute certain activities that required my complete attention and ended the discussion. Emerson's powers in that particular area have always been extraordinary, and, as he had occasion to point out in the course of the proceedings, we had a lot of lost time to make up for.

*   *   *

STOP PRESS. From our special correspondent in Luxor. ASTONISHING RESURRECTION OF AMERICAN MILLIONAIRE ARCHAEOLOGIST. Mrs. Amelia P. Emerson: "Divine Providence Answered My Prayers." Professor Emerson: "Mrs. Emerson's Brilliant Medical Talents Have Wrought a Miracle."

"The earlier dispatch from this correspondent reporting the tragic death of American millionaire archaeologist Cyrus Vandergelt turns out to have been somewhat inaccurate. Mr. Vandergelt's injuries, received in the course of the exciting events described in yesterday's *Yell*, were not as severe as was presumed. The news was received in archaeological quarters with…"

Dearest Mama and Papa:

It is with rapture unalloyed that I anticipate the joy you will experience when I tell you that within a few days of your receipt of this letter you will be able to clasp me in your arms. You will be able to clasp Gargery too, if you should be so inclined, though I think such demonstrations would embarrass him a good deal. You owe him forty-one pounds six shillings.

GLOSSARY OF ARABIC WORDS AND PHRASES

afreet: evil demon
Allah yimessîkum bil-kheir: God give you a good evening
Amerikâni: American
Alemâni: German
baksheesh: tip, present
burko: face veil
dahabeeyah: houseboat
effendi: sir
essalâmu áleikum: peace be with you
fahddle: gossip
fellah (pl. fellahin): peasant
Feransâwi: French, Frenchman
galabeeyah: loose man's robe
habib: friend
hakim: doctor

harîm: women's quarters
hezaam: sash
Inglizi: English
jinni (pl. jinn): demon
jubba: vest
khafiya: Bedouin headcloth
marhaba: welcome
mashrabiyya: carved screen
narghila: water pipe
'Omdeh: local magistrate
reis: captain, foreman
sabil: water fountain
safragi: waiter
sitt: lady
sûk: bazaar, market
Touareg: a desert tribe
ukaf!: stop!
wadi: canyon
yalla!: go on! hurry!
zemr: kind of oboe